RIDE WITH ME

A QUAKING HEART NOVEL – BOOK ONE

An Inspirational Romance Story

Edited by
Mick Silva
Dr. Holly Smit

Cover design by P and N Graphics
Cover cowboy art by Joyce Geleynse

This book is a work of fiction. Any similarity to actual persons or events is purely coincidental.

Janith Hooper

Ride With Me

A QUAKING HEART NOVEL – BOOK ONE

An Inspirational Romance Story

6th Street Design and Publishing

DEDICATION

To Bob Hooper (Hoop), my wonderful husband of forty years and counting. In spite of the years it took to publish this first book, you have always believed in me. Thank you for your spiritual leadership and your support in my writing process. It is because you are my rock that my mind and spirit are free to write. I do it for you and I do it for God.

CHAPTER 1

Montana. Wild country. Still untamed, so she'd heard. Mostly from fellow Californians. She didn't believe it, of course. This was 1959, after all, not the 1800's before law and order took shape. Cowboy territory. That thought made her smile.

Jessica settled back in the rigid train seat and tried to imagine life on Uncle Roy's cattle ranch. She hoped her decision to come here had been a good one, even if only to escape her mother's badgering about husbands for a while. Since the day Mom had approached her with her uncle's request, from that point until now Jessica's heart nearly raced out of her chest at even the thought of Montana. Yet, as nerve-wracking as this bold feat was for her, something momentous seemed to lure her here.

She gazed out the window to blurred Idaho flatlands. Sun seeped through the glass, warming her face. The train rocked with a steady rhythm, and the clacking of the wheels against the tracks lulled her into a welcomed numbness.

Out of the corner of her eye, a shape appeared on the plains. She sprang upright. Laying her palms against the cold pane, she squinted out the window. A black horse and rider raced a few yards off, parallel with the train. They rode fast to keep pace, yet the man's powerful body, hunching over the animal's withers, seemed to roll effortlessly with the motion. He turned his head toward her, tapped his hat in a two-fingered salute, and flashed a brilliant smile.

She glanced behind her to the aisle. No one there. She peered back at him with brows raised and pointed at herself. *Me?* she mouthed.

He gave a nod, spurred his horse in the flank, and shot forward. The long-sleeved white shirt stretched tight across his shoulders and flapped at his back. Fascinated, Jessica strained to watch, but soon he was out of sight.

A high pitched squeal of brakes disrupted her admiration. *Why are we stopping?* The train lurched, heaving Jessica forward, then back as the train came to a halt. A silhouette filled the doorway of the day coach. *The* man.

His gaze roamed over the travelers until it landed on her with a swell of intensity that made her heart skip. He strode forward, eyes locked to hers. He seemed to double in size as he approached. Dusty boots, worn blue jeans, dark stubble beneath his battered Stetson, and oozing inborn masculinity.

Her heart thundered when he stopped at her row. With two long fingers he pushed up his hat brim.

Her breath hitched.

Disarming green eyes sparkled with amusement. He stretched out a hand. "Ride with me," his deep voice rumbled.

She looked at his hand, then back to his face and fluttered a blink. Somehow her hand found his, and he guided her upright. With one lithe move he encircled her waist, curled her against his chest, and dipped his head. Her pulse sped as her gaze abandoned his eyes for his descending mouth.

She hiccuped.

He drew back, a corner of his mouth tipping up. "Do you need a pillow, ma'am?" he asked.

Jessica's eyes snapped open, her right eyelashes catching for a moment against unyielding glass. She tried to focus. Arid prairie still slipped by. *A pillow?*

"We won't arrive in West Yellowstone for another hour. You look mighty uncomfortable."

Yellowstone? She jerked back and stiffened. Drool slid down the window. Wiping first her mouth, then the window, she turned toward a gray-haired man wearing a conductor's hat. He looked amused. Instant heat infused her face.

"Ma'am?" he repeated, holding out a pillow.

She eyed the man. Old, with a paunch lapping over his belt. Nothing like the brawny cowboy who'd nearly locked his lips to hers. She shook her head to clear it and took the pillow with a shaky hand. "Thank you."

He smiled and walked on.

A dream? Hallucination? So real. She stared at the empty aisle beside her. A hollow ache rose from deep inside, making her nearly swoon. She slumped back and for a few minutes counted her breaths to calm the odd thumping in her chest.

Her gaze caught on a carving on the seatback in front of her. Bending forward she saw a small heart notched into the wood, encompassing two sets of letters. She traced it with a fingertip, and a new heaviness pressed in on her chest. She'd never before had her initials joined with a boy's.

Jessica sighed and sank back in the seat. She was far too old for such youthful foolishness. Or for daydreams of sturdy cowboys. Rubbing her stiff neck, she spotted several people stealing glances at her. Did she still have drool on her chin? She swiped a hand across it. Dry. Exhaling a big breath, she tried to reclaim a degree of poise.

Why exactly had she agreed to come here—to serve food to hungry cowhands as Mabel's new assistant? She thought of what Mom had said. All those men and no competition, maybe her old maid daughter would finally snag a husband. Of course, she hadn't actually said the words *old maid*.

But Mom wasn't the reason she was here, she had to remind herself. Uncle Roy needed her. Desperate for someone reliable since six helpers had quit in less than two months. She'd be expected to handle a task that many had bungled before her. Her stomach spun another revolution at the thought.

She rubbed a hand against her heart, remembering the embrace of the handsome hero in her dream. Maybe things would be different in cowboy country—

A whistle blew, startling her out of her thoughts. Wheels scraped against the tracks, and the train pitched. The jumpy little man across the aisle squeezed the paper cup he held. Helpless to stop it, she watched as liquid arced in her direction and landed square on her chest. She sucked in a quick breath and looked down. Heavily creamed coffee inched across her white blouse.

"Sorry, missy! Didn't mean fer that ta happen."

Jessica grimaced. A sticky mess. Figures this old timer would dump a bowl of sugar in the brew. He leaned toward her, glanced at her chest and smiled sheepishly. Half his teeth were missing and the other half were blackened by chewing tobacco he had tucked under his lower lip.

"It's okay." She snatched her purse from the floor and scavenged for tissues. As she dabbed at the stain, hysterical laughter welled up inside her. This just figured. Her life seemed to take these unprecedented turns—likely why she'd built so much *character* thus far.

The train's whistle sounded again, announcing their arrival. She gave up the useless task of making herself more presentable, stuffing the sodden tissues back in her purse.

The little man eyed the stain on her blouse, and shrugged another apology.

Jessica offered a reassuring smile, then quickly made her way down the aisle to the small steps, and out onto the platform. After retrieving her suitcases, she stood with one in each hand as she looked around uneasily for the uncle she hadn't seen in over twelve years. Would he look the same? Jessica watched as families embraced one another. Several businessmen, briefcases in hand, shuffled through the crowded mass and into the train station. She noted most of the women wore pants and boots, and some even cowboy-type hats. So unlike the women back in Sacramento who wore dresses with pearls at their necks. She glanced down at her wranglers, and breathed a sigh of relief for her foresight.

Jessica checked the group again. Where was Uncle Roy? A stab of dread pierced her. Not allowing herself to dwell on the negative, she followed the last of the group into the depot. She perused the bustling station. No towering men with wide shoulders. Feeling forgotten and still a little soggy, she struggled out the front doors. Only strangers occupied the bench seat that fastened to the wall under a sign: *Union Pacific Railroad of West Yellowstone*. She scanned the lawn, the parked cars, and the street. No familiar faces.

Moving to the bench she plunked down her heavy bags, collapsed onto the seat, and waited. She crossed her legs, scratched a fingernail on her thigh, uncrossed her legs, and read an abandoned newspaper. The sun drifted across the sky a few degrees while disillusionment closed in, merging with apprehension—like the sweat mingling with the coffee on her blouse. This always happened to her. Ever-faithful, amenable Jessica Harper, waiting for people who desperately needed her help.

If it was so all-fired urgent, why aren't they here?

This absurd idea had been too good to be true. She'd give them an hour, maybe two. Then if they still weren't here, she'd buy a ticket and head back home.

But, to what? she found herself wondering. She loved her family, she truly did. But sometimes—actually, most times—she felt used and unappreciated as the housekeeper and sole caregiver for five younger brothers and sisters, while her mom flitted about doing community ventures, and her dad worked more hours than any man should.

Okay, so she wouldn't go back. At least she could escape her demanding life for the summer. Besides, she would never knowingly disappoint anyone. Least of all an uncle she hadn't seen for over a decade.

Leaning forward, she rubbed her lower back, never taking her eyes off the corner where Yellowstone Avenue intersected Canyon Street. *A watched pot . . .*

A shiny blue and white Edsel motored around the corner. It passed in front of her, smiling faces of a family of four inside. Happy, right where they belonged, probably off to vacation in the park. A sharp yearning nearly overpowered her. She inhaled deeply, feeling bone tired. Her round-the-clock bus then train trip from California had been draining. The longer she waited the louder her heart beat in her ears, clicking off minutes audibly, rubbing her nerves raw. She pressed fingertips to her temples to ease the throbbing.

Down at the intersection, the unmistakable clopping of hooves against pavement reached her. A wagon pulled by a huge chestnut horse with a single rider rounded the corner. *A horse-drawn wagon?* The slight man with bent shoulders and a cowboy hat too large for his build was perched atop the wagon's bench seat.

Right away she noticed the little man's attention was locked to the front of the hotel across the street. Jessica swung her gaze there and saw a man dressed like a lumberjack—big as one too—who'd stomped out of the hotel and was in hot pursuit of a fleeing woman in a skimpy dress and high heels. He reached her in a few long strides, grabbed her arm, and swung her around to face him, nearly throwing her off her feet. His face was beet red, and he was swaying like a drunk and shouting, though Jessica couldn't hear his exact words. The woman looked terrified. When she tried to escape, he grabbed a wad of her hair and yanked her back. Jessica jerked in reaction and her mouth dropped in open horror.

There was little doubt the lumberjack was enraged with the . . . strumpet?—*could the hotel include a brothel? What kind of place was this Montana?*

The scene was one out of an old western movie, only without the hero. Jessica glanced around at the dazed people standing in small groups. They were stilted, frozen to the sidewalk and lawn, mouths agape. No one stirred.

Well, for pity's sake. What are people made of here?

A memory of saving her little brother from a young bully flashed in her mind, giving her courage. No thought for her suitcases, she bolted to her feet, ran down the pathway to slip between two cars, and dashed across the street.

By now, the lumberjack had a solid hold, and Jessica was surprised the victim wasn't screaming at the top of her lungs. She would be. And kicking and squirming too. She figured the strumpet's insides had frozen into a lump of panic.

Afraid to get too close yet unwilling to let this go on, Jessica yelled from a few yards away. "Hey, mister! Let her go!"

No such luck today. This bully didn't even look at her.

In an instant, Jessica was back in sixth grade taking on Billy Renshaw, the school tormentor, who'd chosen her little brother as his next target. She tried to take Billy on, but had only managed to get in the way of his elbow and wear a black eye for days. Still, her intervention had been enough to make Billy stop.

Jessica brushed a finger under her right eye. Was she willing to get another elbow in the face if it saved the woman? But this man was no elementary school bully, and something far worse than a black eye would be Jessica's reward this time around.

Frantic, she examined the by-standers. There were too many men just watching. Disgusted at their lack of involvement, she raced up to a solid-looking man she thought could do the job. "Can't you do something? Has someone gone for the Sheriff?"

Just then the rickety hitch wagon she'd seen at the corner pulled up even with the brute. In one fluid motion, the driver set the brake, threw off his hat, and leapt onto the ruffian's back. He rode the guy like a bucking bronco. Only, the newcomer was no John Wayne, but a scrawny old man.

The lumberjack roared. He dropped his hands from the woman and thrashed behind him, trying to land a solid punch. But, the little champion nimbly evaded each attempt.

In the next moment Jessica glimpsed the little man's face. Is that . . .? *Walt!* Walt had been Uncle Roy's most loyal ranch hand for as long as Jessica could remember. Had to be in his seventies by now. What was he thinking, attacking a man a third his age and twice his size?

The beast backed hard into a support post. Jessica jumped as if she'd taken the blow herself. Walt grunted but kept his arms locked. The lumberjack's face flushed crimson, his movements slogged. He stumbled, once, twice, and then collapsed to his knees. Walt's boots hit the boardwalk. He released the brawny neck and caught the man's shoulders to keep him from slamming face first into the planks. Done.

Walt extended a hand to the petrified woman who'd been standing wide eyed and stone still. Her small hand lay on her chest as if her very breath had stopped, and Jessica could see her trembling. Walt touched her elbow. She flinched then smiled weakly at him.

"Why don't we go find someone ta fetch the Sheriff?" Walt carefully took hold of her elbow to escort her inside.

When he returned, he scrubbed his palms down his

pants, bent to retrieve his hat to settle it on his head, and then squinted in the direction of the train depot.

"Walt," Jessica said from behind him.

He twisted to look over a bony shoulder.

"Walt?" She waved a hesitant hand.

Turning fully, he studied her face. "Jess-girl? That you?"

Somehow words eluded her as she stared at him. Other than more gray hair, deeper lines in his leathery face, and a little more bowed, he looked the same as when she was twelve. Half a lifetime ago.

Finally, she forced out, "How'd you do that?"

"What?" He hiked a thumb toward the vacated fight scene. "That?"

Still in a daze, she nodded.

Walt swatted a hand through the air. "Twernt nothin'. Growin' up ya either fought back or got yerself locked in the outhouse." He threw his head back and guffawed. "I fought."

Jessica tried to keep from grinning, but didn't quite succeed. "You do this kind of thing often?"

He rubbed his hands together. "Ah . . . well, sorry 'bout that. Probably aren't much used to that kind of thing in California, eh?"

She shrugged and shook her head.

He seemed to remember himself then and ambled to her, grasping her by the shoulders. "Well tarnation, girl, let's have a look at ya. You look differnt. All growed up and purty as yer momma with those big green eyes." He pulled her into an embrace. "Don't they feed ya, though?"

She smiled. This was the Walt she remembered. Though she wondered why Uncle Roy hadn't come for her, for the first time since she left California she unwound a little in Walt's care.

"We need to git. Mabel's needin' ya back at the ranch ta help put on the grub, and if we're late we may's well camp out fer a spell—like fer life, if ya know what I mean." He wheezed and slapped his knee.

A sudden sapping of strength made Jessica's knees wobble. Walt grasped her elbow and held for a beat, then helped her up to the wagon seat. "You must be plumb tuckered, girl. What ya need is a relaxin' wagon ride. Let's get movin'."

Jessica gripped the wooden bench as the wagon lurched forward. Walt took a wide turn on the street, jumped down to gather the suitcases Jessica had abandoned at the depot, and then proceeded to the center of town.

Jessica looked over at Walt. "You still use wagons here."

His mouth crinkled into a grin as he handed her a canteen. "Yer in Montana now. Bessie 'n me's been around a long time together, ain't that right, girl?" The old horse seemed to toss her head in reply. The wagon rattled along. Walt turned them onto Canyon Street and headed out the northern end of town.

"Sure glad you'll be helping 'ole Mabel in the kitchen. She's been goin' through one helper after 'nother. She says it's cuz they get taken in by our good-lookin' foreman. I don't know about any of that, but she's definitely been meaner'n usual." He glanced at Jessica out of the corner of his eye and elbowed her lightly. "Kinda hopin' she's not spittin' in the soup."

Jessica glanced away; sure that her smile looked more like a grimace. *Our good-lookin' foreman*, Walt had said, reminding her of her mom's clear-cut goal for her: 'Find a handsome cowboy and catch him any way you can.' But, Jessica had agreed to come here to help Uncle Roy and Mabel—and yes, to get away from Mom and the family for a time. Certainly not to glom on to the first man she saw.

"Jess-girl, tell me 'bout yerself. Is Jesus your Lord?"

Stunned by the blunt question she chuckled, until she noticed him waiting for her answer. "Why yes, Walt. Yes, He is. How about you?"

"Yes ma'am, fer most of my life." Walt's shoulders sagged a bit. "Been tryin to share with the cowpokes here for years. But ain't dun no good."

His sadness touched her heart. Jessica found herself wanting to hug the little man. In spite of the rising desire to help Walt in his endeavors, her stomach churned. Would anyone understand her apprehension in joining the crew at Harper ranch? She was a Californian, after all. She already knew how unwelcome her lot was in Montana. Maybe she should tell Walt about her concerns. He'd likely understand. She shook her head. No. She wouldn't burden him with her petty fears.

She twisted in her seat to catch a final glimpse of receding West Yellowstone and her last chance at easy escape. Just past Walt's shoulder she caught sight of a big body of water off in the distance. Keeping his eyes on the road, Walt answered her unasked question. "That's Lake Hebgen. It's a beaute, ain't it?"

"Shore is," she teased, trying to slough off her anxiety.

A new smile brightened his kind face.

"I'm sure you've made a big difference with the men, Walt. God's Word never returns void." Tough crowd, cowboys.

"Me and Roy are the only ones on the ranch who love Jesus. After all this time." He seemed deep in thought.

"Still it's my ole heart's desire the rest find God. Hopin' jest livin' right will rub off on 'em, if ya know what I mean. Not as young as I used ta be though, so don't have much time left on this here green earth to make a diff'rence."

Jessica pondered his comment, recognizing Walt as a kindred spirit. She often shared the *good news* with others and knew its unparalleled joy, but also the disappointments.

The chestnut mare snorted, bobbing her head with every step, and pulled harder to make it up a small incline. Since the wagon's pace was slow, Jessica took in everything; the ruts in the road, a ground squirrel dashing through the prairie grasses, puffy white clouds overhead, the absence of telephone poles. *No telephone poles.* That's right. Mom had mentioned they didn't have telephones or TV's on the ranch. How did they keep up with the world? Would they know, or even care, that Alaska and Hawaii had just become the 49th and 50th states?

Life would certainly be different here.

The entrance to Harper ranch came into view. Framed by three large timbers, the Big 'H' symbol hung centered at the top of the structure like the gateway to a more serene way of life. Though, thinking about what Walt had to say about a sourpuss Mabel, when the wagon passed through it, she was anything but serene.

CHAPTER 2

The thunder of hooves thrummed in Clint's ears. That alone was enough to get his blood surging to the tips of his toes, making him feel alive. But today was about more than a man and his horse. Today was about justice.

The elusive beast darted ahead of him through the trees. He gave the gelding his head and chased at the heels of the mountain cat. Clint spotted a branch in time to dip his weight into his right stirrup, stretching beside his horse's neck to duck under it. He broke through the brush and into the clearing beyond.

The other five horsemen crashed through one by one behind him and divided. They circled an array of boulders to close in on their target. The golden flash they'd been tracking for the better part of an hour bolted up a huge stone and disappeared.

Clint's horse reared, striking back to the ground with an irritated snort. He scanned the area for the sure cause and his gaze caught on the peak of the nearest boulder. There stood the cougar looking like a monument of strength, with taut muscles poised and ready. Carefully,

Clint stripped his rifle from its scabbard. The lithe cat crouched, preparing to spring toward him. With little time to react, Clint raised his rifle.

The cat lunged.

He fired.

* * *

Clint felt a jolt, like a touch to an electric fence. Warmth from the sun was on his face, his belly—*why am I lying flat?* He tried to rise but a spike of pain rammed through the back of his head. He stopped cold, ears ringing. Trying to pry his eyes open he struggled to sit up.

Someone put a hand to his shoulder. He wrenched his eyes open. Focus. He saw a face—hazy—couldn't quite get a fix on it. The mouth was moving but Clint couldn't make out a word.

Finally, he caught a sound. ". . . all right, son?" A man's voice.

Clint blinked and squinted, not sure who spoke.

"Clint . . . it's Roy. Can you hear me?"

"Roy," he rasped. "Help me up."

"Dang it all. Don't go movin' till we know what's busted. Anything hurtin'?"

"What happened?"

"Don't you remember the cat? Knocked you clean off your horse. You got a piece of its ear, looked like. Left a small trail of blood."

"Get me up, Roy."

"Hold your horses." Roy plied strong fingers to Clint's neck, forcing more pain into his temples with each probe. "Does this hurt at all?"

"No," Clint lied.

The pain was there all right, but it wouldn't kill him. This whole trip had given him grief. All he'd wanted was to find and eliminate that killer cat. And all Roy had done was needle him about marriage until he about burst. He welcomed the humiliation over the cat besting him in front of his men, since maybe that'd stop Roy.

Roy took hold of one of Clint's arms, shoved a hand to his back, and hauled him to a sitting position.

Clint gripped his thighs, white-knuckled, until the stabbing pain faded. His gaze shifted to Roy. "Is my horse all right?"

"He's fine, son."

He motioned toward the up-side-down Stetson. "Grab my hat, will you?"

One of his men chuckled and said to the others, "Ah, he's all right. Back to barkin' orders."

Roy offered his hand. Clint grabbed his forearm, and Roy tugged him to his feet. A wave of dizziness swept over him.

Roy stayed close. "Better?"

"Yeah . . . sure."

Clint reached up and touched the back of his head where the ache seemed to center. A knot had formed. Sucking in a deep breath, he ambled to his gelding, took hold of the reins, grabbed his hat—held out to him by one of the men—and mounted with ease in spite of his aching head.

Turning his horse, he faced his men. "The cat's long gone. We're heading home . . . for now."

Carefully settling his hat back on his head, ignoring the pinch of pain there, he reined around to the path that led home. Without a word, the rest followed.

Clint tried to quiet his mind. Thoughts of the event

that had brought them here resurfaced. That beast had killed one of his favorite geldings. His gut crawled at how his horse had suffered before they found him and had to put him down. The cat had run them around in circles for three days, but he determined to find it and make sure it never touched another living thing on Harper Ranch. Just not today.

If only the cougar was my sole problem.

"Heads up!" Roy hollered, just before a low branch of a knotty pine smacked Clint in the face. Roy rode up next to him. "Your mind must be a hundred miles away."

Clint growled low in his throat.

"You actin' mute now? What's up with you anyways?"

Clint darted a glance at Roy, then pulled his gaze back to the path. "Nothing time won't heal, if that's what you're after."

Roy cocked his head. "We've been together, what? Sixteen, seventeen years now? Too long for you to fool me." Roy seemed to study his face. "You still sore for what that cat did to your horse? We'll get him, son, sooner or later."

Clint bit the inside of his cheek, knowing that once Roy started jabbering he'd dig into that *other* subject any minute now.

"Veronica supposed to be waiting for you?" Roy ventured.

And, there it was. "Dang it, Roy." Clint doubled his fists. If the old coot didn't back off with the woman stuff, he couldn't be responsible, even if it was Roy.

"Just figuring—"

"No," Clint snarled. "And I won't be asking her to marry me anytime soon"—though, he knew he should—"in case you're just figuring that as well."

Clint tugged on the reins to slow up. He didn't want this conversation . . . again. Remorse already plagued him everyday concerning Veronica. He'd hoped this trip would have given him a respite.

He watched the older man pull a kerchief up from his neck and run it over his glistening face. Roy slowed his horse. "I understand. But a fine looking lady like that can make a man pretty happy. Why wait?"

"You want her?" Clint fired back. Shame, like a fiery torch, burned away at his conscience. Veronica *was* beautiful. And he owed her. He mustn't forget that. She'd gotten him to put a halt to the fifteen year pattern of self-destruction he'd carved out for himself since the moment he'd hit puberty. He met her just over three years ago, and it had taken a year for her to drag him into a more normal life.

And then, he'd done a terrible thing. He'd torn out of the relationship and left her behind, adding yet another notch on his *despicable behavior* belt. All for a new path that had been just as destructive.

He'd kept her near, though. Out of obligation. Or just plain guilt.

He knew he should marry her. He owed her that. He wasn't worried about his heart. It had been dead and buried a long time ago. Didn't plan on love either. But, he couldn't quite wrap his mind around marriage. Not to anyone.

Roy smirked. "The trail can get pretty lonely. Promise you'll think on it."

Clint kept his eyes straight ahead. "Like I've told you before, Roy, I promise nothing. Only that if she's made of glass, she might break."

CHAPTER 3

When they came over the final rise, Jessica gasped at the beauty of a land that stretched into an immense valley. She inhaled through her nose, as if the clean air might somehow smell different out here. The breeze felt cool against her damp skin. Closing her eyes, she let it calm her.

When she blinked her eyes open, the sturdy country home loomed before her, like a respected matriarch, strong and proud. It had been built in the late 1800's, and she'd heard they'd added on to it every decade since. Even from a distance it looked a lot bigger than she remembered.

The center of the house had the original two stories, but the roof now slanted downward to a one story addition on the south side only—the expansion of the kitchen and dining area, Uncle Roy had said. The barn was its usual burnished red, whereas the house and outbuildings were now white with green trim. That was new, reminding her how things would be different this go around. She wouldn't be a visitor, enjoying the comforts of her uncle's home on this grand setting. This time she would be expected to perform. And not just for Mabel, but for all those men. She shuddered, feeling a sudden inclination to run back the way she came.

"Beautiful, ain't she?" Walt said, giving Jessica a start. "Whene'er I come up an' over that last hill I'm reminded of why I love this here place."

His words eased her sudden desire to escape. She drew in a deep breath and gazed over the land again, experiencing the beauty of it through Walt's eyes. The swollen stream—with diamond-like sparkles on each swell—coursed by four cottages nestled in a copse of trees; the barn situated across the road from the front of the house had a corral extending from it, and a passel of cowboys cheered a bronc buster from the railing.

Almost at once, all heads turned to the east, drawing her attention there as well. The men at the rail waved their hats to greet the half dozen men riding toward them. The lead horseman sat straight-backed in the saddle, poised and sure of himself. He was a big man, yet he rocked in agile unity with his steed. The other five men followed a ways behind, riding as if bone weary with shoulders slumped and heads inclined.

Jessica brought her focus back to the first man. Though a fair distance away, she observed the way a gloved hand held the reins loosely at his thigh, and his black hat was pulled low over his eyes to avoid the sun's assault. The sight of him was especially masculine, and somehow so . . . familiar.

Then it came to her. The magazine at the Five and Dime. The cover had a silhouette of a man astride his horse. The caption had read: *America's most sought after male—the cowboy*. Without a second thought, Jessica had whisked the magazine out of the rack and into her cart, taking it home to read every glorious detail in private.

A whisper of a breeze coursed across the low grasses, rippling her blouse, tousling her hair. Her body buzzed all over—but somehow she knew it had nothing to do with the breeze. A flash of heat filled her cheeks. She hadn't even arrived and just like that was ogling one of the cowboys. She grunted in disgust at herself. She would *not* follow her mother's scheme. Tugging her attention away from the man, she looked over at Walt.

Walt was studying her. "Seems ta me God brought ya here for a purpose, Jess-girl. Last few girls Mabel had workin' fer her were city slickers—beauties, all of 'em. Had grand notions of finding themselves a cowboy ta marry up with." He cocked his head toward the man she'd been admiring. "That one in partic'lar. When he'd lose interest they'd up and quit." He paused. "But I can see yer differnt."

"In what way?" Jessica asked, realizing she needed to be more discreet about where her eyes roamed.

"He's a good man." He tipped his head toward the lead cowboy again. "But I can see yer smart enough not ta let yerself be used like that."

Used by him? She hadn't seen him up close yet, but she'd bet she wasn't pretty enough for that to happen. Not with this particular man.

Still, there it was. Her goal for the summer. Steering clear of the cowboys—this one especially—and succeeding with Mabel where the others had failed. She could do it. She had to, for so many reasons. Most of all, to prove to herself that she existed as her own woman now and not some empty-headed young girl.

That settled, some of the tension seemed to drain

away, leaving her muscles more relaxed. Yet the ever present apprehension spiraled about in her stomach.

She hiccuped.

Walt gawked at her.

She shrugged. "Sorry. Nerves."

His sparse gray brows furrowed.

"Stomach churning," she tried again.

Walt still looked confused.

"Gives me hiccups. Always has."

He shrugged, then looked away. "Be there in jest a handful a minutes."

The wagon creaked, protesting the descent down the hill. When they drew nearer she told herself it was only the altitude steadily squeezing the air out of her lungs.

The wagon halted. Two cowboys bounded out through the squeaky screen door, and onto the back porch. They both froze when they saw her.

"Whoa," the shorter man said. "We didn't know one of the supplies you'd be bringing back would be of the female persuasion, Walt. Who's this?"

"Now, you jest mind yer manners, boy. This here's Jessica Harper, Roy's niece. Behave yerself 'round her, ya hear?" Walt glared at the stocky cowboy. "Jessica, this here's Pete Johnson." Bending close in a mock-whisper, he said, "You be sure ta watch out fer that one. He's a bit on the crazy side, if ya know what I mean."

Pete made to object, but Walt raised his voice. "The other's Johnnie Williams. He's a bit shier and more man-nered-like. Don't hafta worry so much 'bout him, but stick close to me just the same."

She looked over the taller cowboy. He had black hair, thick under his sweat-rimmed hat. A hint of white teeth peeked through a neatly trimmed goatee. *Shore do make 'em good-looking 'round here*, she thought, smiling back.

Johnnie's steely gaze penetrated hers. "Howdy, ma'am." He bowed his head to pull at his hat.

His eyes fastened back to hers with a look so intense it should have unsettled her, but she found it remarkably soothing. "Pleased to meet you both," Jessica said.

The attention from these men made her head spin. Men rarely noticed Jessica since her younger sister was the beauty in the family, and always seemed to be near.

Pete moved forward and extended both hands to help her down from the wagon. Jessica waved him off. He backed up a step and glanced down at her chest. "Get in a tangle with a cup a coffee?"

Walt cleared his throat. "Like I was sayin'."

Jessica stepped onto the edge of the wagon and jumped down on her own. Once on the ground she dusted her hands together, then glanced from one man to the other. They looked stunned. Had they never seen a woman manage such a thing on her own? Amused and feeling a little more confident, she made her way to the back door. When she reached for it she hesitated, wondering if she shouldn't wait for her uncle to re-introduce her to his cook. "Will Uncle Roy be in here?"

"Not yet," Pete said while unloading the wagon. "Just go in and holler for Mabel."

"Okay." Her heart sank. "Thanks." Though she spoke to Pete she looked toward the eye-catching Johnnie. Something didn't compute with this man. She'd always been good at reading people. Though he looked the part of a cowboy—sturdy and long-limbed—there seemed much more to him than mere outward appearance allowed.

Jessica stepped into the house with a squeak from the

screen door. It slapped shut behind her. She let her eyes adjust then glanced around. The dining area looked to seat about thirty people on large picnic tables with benches and chairs angled around them. Beyond the dining area was the kitchen itself, with two large stoves, two sinks, and a commercial sized refrigerator. A median counter took up much of the floor space. Amazed for a moment that she didn't remember any of this, she immediately sloughed it off. Tomboy that she was, she wouldn't have been much interested in the interior of a ranch house back then.

The short, hefty cook hacked at a pile of chickens at the far counter. Jessica paused several feet behind her to gather courage and study the familiar woman—the white hair bound in a bun at her nape, her seersucker apron tied ever so neatly around her plump waistline with a perfect crisp bow. Jessica took in a calming breath. "Mabel?"

Mabel whirled around and gasped. A pudgy hand flattened against her chest with a thwack. "Land sake, child. You scared the wits outta me. Everyone 'round here knows better than to sneak up while I'm fixin' grub." She panted a beat.

Jessica gulped. "I-I'm sorry, Mabel. I didn't mean to frighten you. I'm Jessica Harper, Roy's niece." She edged closer. "Weren't you expecting me today?"

Mabel stiffened. "Course I know who you are." She started to look Jessica over, stopping on her stained chest.

Jessica flushed, and said, "Coffee. On the train."

Half a head taller than Mabel, Jessica stared down into her face. She had noticeably aged. Wrinkles creased the pale skin around her mouth and eyes. *Laugh-lines? Or maybe frown-lines.*

"Do you remember me from about twelve years ago when my family and I visited Uncle Roy? We weren't here long. I was pretty young. I'm sure I look a lot different than I did back then—" *Stop rambling.* "Anyway, it's good to see you again, Mabel."

"You look the same, just a mite older." Her gaze slid up and down. "Don't they feed ya in California?"

Jessica stifled a grin. "I'm here to help, so put me to work. What can I do? Or maybe I should bring my suitcases in first? Which room will I be staying in?"

"Whoa, girl." Mabel finally set down the knife and faced her, wiping her hands on her apron. "First things first. Your room is at the top of the stairs, first door to the right. Get one of those fellers to see to your suitcases. Then I'll see what I can find for you to do." She turned back to continue her preparations, motioning at the big clock on the wall. "Need to get the grub on by six sharp or we'll have to hog-tie some angry cow pokes." She swished a hand at her. "Move it."

Jessica whirled around, whacked her knee on the counter but ignored the jab of pain, and hustled outside to recruit helpers.

CHAPTER 4

When Jessica stepped outside, Pete and Johnnie must have heard the screen door slap behind her since both ceased what they were doing and straightened.

"We found your suitcases," Pete said. "Ready for us to take them up for you, lovely lady?"

She jerked her gaze to Pete, face burning with embarrassment. She'd never once been called that before. Not even by her Dad.

Pete winked at her and bent to retrieve two of the cases. Johnnie lifted the other one and the three of them made their way into the house and toward the stairs. When they crossed the great room, Jessica glanced about the western style furniture and then to the huge fireplace and smiled; the six-point deer head was still mounted there after all these years. Everything here was as she remembered. It gave her a warm feeling in the pit of her stomach. As though she'd come home, which in itself seemed odd to her. The last thing she should be feeling is *at home* in this uncommon place, with a dead deer head on the wall.

When she reached the two waiting men, she turned the knob to the bedroom door and pushed it open. The room instantly delighted her senses. It was large and fully furnished with a feminine flare. On the four-poster bed lay a colorful hand-made quilt with matching throw rugs on the floor. Curtains of white lace wafted in the breeze at the large window. And, there was fresh air. Lots of fresh air. Jessica crossed to the sill, tipped her head back and breathed in deeply. She gazed out at the surroundings: open spaces, wildflower-dotted meadows with Herefords scattered throughout, a clear mountain stream, two sleepy hound dogs, and cowboys milling in and out of the barn. Beauty and silence.

Maybe the serenity *had* actually begun to seep in.

Jessica took a last big breath and turned. "Thank you, fellas. I guess I should change and go help Mabel."

Pete looked shaken, like he'd stayed on the dance floor long after the music had stopped. "Yes, ma'am." He turned and dashed out of the room.

Johnnie lounged against the doorjamb. His one-sided grin had grown a bit more. This man was sure easy on the eyes. Jessica had to put her brain back in gear. "Well. . . thank you . . . Johnnie is it?"

"Yes, ma'am. Happy to help. Anything else, let Mabel know." He straightened, tugged on the brim of his hat and left.

She sighed. Maybe she'd be okay here.

In short order Jessica changed to cooler shorts and a clean cotton blouse. The outfit's green color made her hazel eyes bright with similar color, boosting her confidence. Ready as she'd ever be, she headed downstairs.

Heat from the day had accumulated in the kitchen,

and her jangled nerves had invited friends. Nonetheless, she was ready to work. Anxious, in fact, to get her life here started, and move past the newness.

Mabel took one look at her, rolled her eyes, and didn't hold back her comments. "Well, if you insist on wearing almost nothin', don't blame me if those cowboys don't keep their tongues from waggin' and their eyes from gawkin'."

Jessica's own eyes widened as she stared at Mabel. She gulped, feeling like she'd swallowed something without chewing. When she found her voice, she strained to force out the words. "Is this inappropriate, Mabel? Everyone wears bermuda shorts in the summer where I come from."

"Well o' course they do. You live in California. Everyone knows you Californians are a little short on good sense when it comes to dressin' . . . and other things, I hear."

Jessica flushed at the implication. But she didn't want to stir up trouble right off the bat. "I'm sorry. I didn't realize. I'll run up and change."

"Oh no you won't, little miss! Too late now. The men'll be wantin' their meal, and we're behind. Come over here and shuck some of this corn. You do know how to shuck corn, don't you?" Mabel held out an apron for her.

Worried and wondering what would happen now at supper, she stepped forward to let Mabel tie the apron at her back. With so much left to do and so little time, Mabel and Jessica worked on the last of the meal preparations in silence, to Jessica's immense relief. Before she knew it, the screen door flew open and cowboys poured in and plunked down at the tables. Jessica forced herself not to turn around. She concentrated on yanking off green husks and silk from the corn and plopping each cob into the boiling water of the huge Dutch ovens atop the stove.

Mabel took a few steps toward the men to get their attention, her arms akimbo. Frowning, she said, "Haven't I told you boys time and again that I'd ring the triangle for you ta come in for supper? What're ya all doin' here?"

We're all hungrier than a mountain lion on the hunt, Mabel," a man said. "You know we'll sit here like decent folk 'til you're ready. Right boys?"

A quick glance told Jessica the lanky spokesman had his back to the kitchen, oblivious of her.

No one answered.

"Right boys?"

When the man still didn't get an answer, from anyone, Jessica heard him spin around to hunt for what seemed to hold them all captive. She felt his stare on her back.

The quiet lengthened until Jessica couldn't stand it anymore. She slowly turned to face the men. Pushing her palms down her apron, she scrunched a bunch of fabric in each hand, painfully aware of the many sets of eyes inspecting her bare legs from ankle to knee. It was her clothes, of course, since she'd never drawn this kind of attention in her entire uninteresting life.

Heat rose up her neck and burst into her cheeks.

She whipped back to the counter, crossed her legs at the ankles to lessen the view, and ripped into the corn with a vengeance.

Mabel broke the silence, pointing a stubby finger at each of the men as if she were counting strays. "Okay, quit oglin'. Not like you haven't seen a girl before. This is Roy's niece. He'll be here shortly to introduce you, official like. Until then, you can stay only if you promise to sit there like gents."

In the next few minutes, more of the cowhands entered

the kitchen and went through the same scenario. At first Jessica was flustered, then flattered, until she remembered that in the past few months these men had seen many *pretty* girls come and go through Mabel's kitchen.

Deciding her best course of action would be to ignore their inspection, she went about serving drinks. Before long the front door opened to a burly man she instantly recognized—Uncle Roy. She breathed a sigh of relief.

Should she run to him? Wait until he came over to her?

As soon as he spotted her he strolled across the room and captured her in a mammoth hug. "Jessica. You made it!" He plunked her down and stepped back. "Let's have a look at you. You're a woman now, and a mighty handsome one at that. Look like your mom."

Mom's looks? She'd always thought of her mom as beautiful. He was just being kind.

"Hey everyone…" He scanned the room and then nodded as if concluding that most of the cowboys were here. "This is Jessica, my niece. She's here to help Mabel feed your greedy bodies. Make her feel welcome, but I expect ya to treat her with respect."

He grinned then and reached around her to snatch an apple slice off one of the platters on the counter. Mabel slapped his hand. "What're ya tryin to do, create bad habits 'round here? They all do what they see you do."

"Sorry Mabel, I'm starvin'. Serve 'em up. Clint's right behind me."

With a well-rounded hip Mabel crowded Jessica into the corner of the counter, startling her. Though Jessica was taller, that fact apparently didn't faze the little cook.

"Listen up, girl." Mabel's hot breath blasted Jessica's

neck. "You're to stay away from Clint. Keep your mind on your work and we'll get along just fine."

Jessica caught her breath, stunned by Mabel's boldness. She looked down into the older woman's snapping brown eyes. Jessica had been pushed around her whole life. One of the draw-backs of a compliant nature. This time something inside triggered. She wanted to fight back, be her own boss and make her own decisions, now that she was out on her own. She blinked at the belligerence inside her. Another unwelcome surprise from overwrought nerves.

Mabel waited. Ultimately, she nodded and Mabel wandered off.

Jessica whipped back to the corn, picked up too many cobs at once, and plopped them into the water, grimacing when the hot splash nipped at her hand.

Within minutes the front door opened. Jessica turned to see a man standing outside. He had his head bent as he clomped his feet. Spurs jangled with each stamp against the porch planks, and ranch dust peppered in all directions. When he stepped through the doorway, late afternoon light shone at his back, setting him in shadow. She stared at that silhouette, lost in a recollection she couldn't quite gather. She shook off the allusion.

This had to be Clint. The same man who'd led the group into camp earlier that day. There was no mistaking those broad shoulders and exceptional height. His blue chambray shirt, rolled at the sleeves to show corded forearms, added to an overall appeal. He lifted his Stetson from his head, and winced. He thumped the hat once against his thigh before hanging it on the hook beside the door. Dust particles seemed to hang on the air.

Entranced by the man, she braced her back against the counter to keep from swaying. The rest of the group had gone back to laughing and talking, but her attention remained riveted on the vision before her. Bringing a gloved hand to his mouth, he bit down on two fingertips with straight white teeth, and tugged. He retrieved the glove from his mouth, did the same with the other, then dropped both gloves on the small table by the door. Once his hands were free, he reached one hand up to rake his fingers through hair the color of rich mahogany, kissed by the sun. In spite of the effort, his hair seemed untamable. And, as if making a statement to that effect, one unruly curl flung itself stubbornly onto his tanned forehead.

Jessica's senses hummed, as if awakened for the first time. She took a deep breath—had her lungs shrunk?—and tried to settle her thunderous heart.

Casually, the imposing man bent at the waist and reached around the backs of his solid thighs to untie his chaps. Once released, he plopped them onto the battered chair by the door, pinched at the faded blue jeans sticking to his thighs, and swung the door closed.

Jessica couldn't move. In fact, she wondered if her body had forgotten the simple task of taking in air. No wonder Mabel had warned her away from him. She had never in her life been so impacted by just watching a man, especially one she hadn't met. She imagined Mabel's past helpers having the same reaction, and understood their failure for the first time.

Mabel skirted around her, busy with the supper. She glowered at Jessica each time she passed by. Though Jessica peripherally noticed Mabel's exasperation, she couldn't seem to peel her gaze from Clint. *Great way to start my first day.*

Clint turned toward the kitchen, running both hands through his hair this time, and caught a glimpse of Jessica. When their gazes met, his hands stilled in his hair, biceps bulging against his shirt sleeves from the stilted action. Her heart thumped hard against the wall of her chest.

Dropping his hands to his sides, he strode toward her, spurs clinking with every loose-hipped step. The smell of leather, the great outdoors, and hard-working-man—surprisingly pleasant—teased her nose as he drew near. A thatch of dark hair peeked out the V at his open collar. She couldn't quite look into his eyes, so she fixed her gaze at that V.

He towered over her and came so close she could feel heat rolling off his body. She stood stupidly in place while her heart thundered. If she didn't calm down soon she'd begin to pant, since her lungs couldn't seem to keep up. Finally, she forced her head back to look up at him, instinctively knowing it would give him an advantage of some sort not to.

She felt paralyzed. By something. He reminded her of . . .she didn't know. Or, couldn't seem to remember.

Funny. He seemed bewildered, as well. Neither of them looked away. Jessica studied every detail of his face—appealing and rugged with the day's dark stubble shadowing his skin, and beyond good-looking.

He scrubbed his right palm down his hip and extended it to her. "Hello, ma'am, I'm Clint Wilkins." His voice was deep, rich. "And you are?"

She took his hand, watching as his swallowed up her cold trembling one. She jerked with the electricity that seemed to arc between them. When she peered back up, his perplexed expression had changed to a knowing smile.

Only by sheer force of will, and embarrassment at his ability to read her so well, she straightened. This man would not make her fumble around like a smitten school girl. She was a woman, for goodness sake. She needed to act like one. Problem was, her pulse raced. She couldn't think. Definitely couldn't breathe right. But the real crisis was if she didn't keep her head she would immediately fail, sooner than all the others before her. Walt's words came back . . . *they get taken in by our good-lookin' foreman.*

At last he released her hand and moved back a step. She gasped as if the space had let in much needed oxygen.

His grin broadened. *Arrogance?* But as she stared, she wondered, forcing her emotions to take second chair to her mind. There lingered something about him, other than his enormous good looks. Something . . . else. Something . . . greater. As she worked at determining what that was, his grin vanished and his brows began to furrow.

Oh. Goodness. What was it he asked me?

Uncle Roy jumped in. "Clint, this is my niece, Jessica. Jessica, Clint is like a son to me, and as you may recall, my foreman."

"N-nice to meet you." She sounded so . . . young. She lowered her eyes to break the hold he had on her and turned to offer help to Mabel. She tripped over Uncle Roy in her haste and almost groaned out loud.

"Just remember what I said," Mabel whispered in warning.

Twice Jessica tripped on outstretched boots, almost losing the platter of fried chicken in someone's lap. More than once she spilled the cider on the table and on the men. She felt the stares boring into her back and knew she must look like a bumbling idiot. All because of the amazing man she'd just met.

Though she couldn't get her mind off him, he seemed content to sit with his men and chow down, not once looking at her.

A huge desire swelled up in her to interest him. But then, that remained out of the question. No one like him would ever be interested in someone unremarkable. It was a pipe dream, and one she had long since stopped dreaming. That being the case, her only recourse was to ask the Lord to keep her from making a fool of herself, help her to stay detached and levelheaded around him. To act her age.

CHAPTER 5

Jessica opened sleep-deprived eyes and blinked at the new morning. When her mind cleared away the morning fogginess, she oriented herself to her surroundings. Threads of light barely illuminated the pleasant room. She tossed back the covers, dressed quickly, and after making her bed, went straight to the kitchen.

No Mabel. No Roy. No one. The place seemed cold without the activity of warm bodies and mindless chatter. Not yet knowing the routine for breakfast, she decided to step out the front door to watch the sunrise.

Jessica leaned against a porch post, arms crossed in front of her, enjoying the pine scent and crisp morning air. Caught up in the beauty of the break of dawn she didn't immediately notice Clint until he was halfway between the barn and the house. Her heart tripped when she spotted him, and she watched in awe at his show of confidence in just the way he walked with hat pulled low and a hand busily rolling up a sleeve to his taupe-colored work shirt.

When he drew up he tapped the front rim of his hat and said, in that deep voice, "Mornin'."

"Good Morning, Clint," she croaked with a voice she hadn't used yet.

"You're up mighty early. Mabel doesn't usually get to the kitchen until six. The boys feed the barnyard animals before coming in for breakfast about seven-thirty. What brings you outside this early?"

"I didn't sleep well last night." Not sure why she'd told him that, and hoping he wouldn't ask her why, she hurried on. "So, I thought I'd get up and enjoy the beauty of the morning. Mainly, I wanted to see how God would paint the sunrise today. Look at that." She nodded toward it.

He scoffed as he glanced at it. "Looks like a shower later."

"What makes you say that?" They were at eye level now since he lingered two steps below her. A woman could get lost in those eyes and never want to be saved. Not just green, but variegated with mostly emerald slashes and spots of lime, surrounded by a thin dark ring of forest pine. Unusual, arresting.

"Red skies at night, cowboy's delight. Red skies in the morning, cowboys take warning."

"You mean sailors . . ."

His blank stare made her wonder if he really knew the old saying. She decided not to push it. "What's that have to do with showers?"

"Watching for what to expect from Mother Nature."

"You mean from God—" She bit off the rest and cringed. She hadn't meant to go there.

He paused, looking grim. "Whatever you say." He tapped his hat brim with a finger and stepped up and around her to the porch. Glancing back he said, "See you inside for breakfast."

Jessica pressed a hand to her hot cheek and groaned. Her first real conversation with this man and what does she do? She flattens him with a sermon. *Lord, You've always been such an important part of my life that I can't keep from sharing about You. Help me to learn to draw people to You, not make them run the other way.*

The gray bronc—from yesterday—caught her attention as it restlessly circled the corral. She understood the animal's plight, feeling trapped and anxious about what was to come. Thankfully, the mixture of fresh air and scents of the ranch helped to settle her nerves.

Finally, ready to face the day, she turned to go inside.

The minute she stepped across the threshold she heard the sound of percolators gurgling. The scent of freshly brewed coffee teased her nostrils. Clint lounged at one of the tables with his back to the kitchen, holding a large mug of the robust brew.

How could she work here, seeing him for three meals a day, and cope. Well, somehow she would. That was all there was to it.

"Deep in thought again, I see," Mabel said as she nudged Jessica in the ribs.

She flinched. "What's for breakfast, Mabel?"

"The usual. Mush. Bacon, eggs, biscuits and gravy. Roy always likes whatever fruit's in season. Right now I got huckleberries to serve up. You need to get busy."

"What do you want me to do?"

"Mabel would have you do it all—" a deep voice cut in, "—if she could get away with it. Wouldn't you Mabel?" Clint swung around, coffee cup in hand.

"Now, you jest hush up. Yer just mad at me cuz your

latest love interest ran outta here all bent outta shape, couple weeks ago."

Clint narrowed his eyes at her. "As I recall, Miss Mabel, *you're* the one who chased out that last girl."

"Humph! I've had six helpers in the last two months that haven't worked out, and you, Mr. Wilkins, seem to be the only common thread." Her stubby little arms flailed about as she made her point. "And once you take up with them, they stop workin'."

Clint laughed, surprising Jessica. He must be the only person on this ranch who didn't fear Mabel. Jessica found she instantly loved the sound of his laughter, as rich as his voice and rolling out from his depths.

"You're so blasted mean to them, Mabel. You'd better watch out with this one, though. She's Roy's kin, remember. Try a little kindness."

"You promise me you'll leave this one alone, and we'll do jest fine." Mabel turned her back to stir the mush.

Clint laughed and pivoted back to the table.

Jessica's stomach plunged to her toes. Funny how a conversation starring her could make her feel so nonexistent.

Her heart seemed to have chosen its mate, and the fact that it was the same choice as dozens of others stung like a prickly thistle. Bad enough to have been in the room for the conversation, but Clint's amusement over Mabel's worry wounded her deeply. She didn't even know the man. And he didn't know her. Still, her mutinous body had promptly flooded her face with intense heat. She was thankful no one else had been present to hear *their* banter, and see *her* fierce blush.

Lord, why am I always so out of place?

Nonetheless, she made a pledge to herself and God right then: not to fail Mabel or lose herself to Clint. She would work twice as hard as the others and ignore this beguiling, gorgeous cowboy.

* * *

Days sped by while Jessica managed busyness to the point of distraction. If Clint was near, she immersed herself in her chores. If it was possible to avoid him, she did. A sort of peace had emerged since she'd been fairly successful stuffing away feelings into deep emotionless crevices. Something she was especially practiced at since her school wallflower days. She managed by force of will to keep her mind on what pleased Mabel and off of Clint.

She remained steadfast, until one Wednesday morning. The men had eaten a quick breakfast, and had long since dispersed. Jessica stepped out to the front porch. She hummed happily while shaking out the little kitchen rug. Hearing in the distance a pounding against the dirt, she leaned over the porch railing for a better view. Clint, on his sleek black horse, raced to the barn like hellhounds were on his heels. He yanked back on the reins. The gelding's front legs straightened and its hooves plowed into the ground. Clint vaulted into the dust cloud and disappeared into the barn.

He emerged with a large satchel in hand, scanned the camp, and spied her. Her eyes went wide at his inspection, and wider still when he set off at a jog toward her.

No! No more girlish fancies. She willed herself to turn away and mindlessly gave the throw rug another whip.

Dust and caked mud shot out from it. She blinked and choked and refused to look his way.

Jessica heard rather than saw Clint draw near. He leapt up all three porch steps and clamped a large hand to her shoulder so fast it made her jump. Or was it from the heat of his hand? He whipped her around. "I need your help. Ride with me?"

Her mouth went dry. Those words . . .

"Um . . ." Somehow she had to formulate a response, but couldn't seem to. She glanced at the house for any sign of Mabel. Her common sense screamed *No!* Instead, she nodded.

"Good. Let's go." He took a tight grip on her hand, backed down the steps as she followed after, then twisted to sprint toward his horse with Jessica in tow. She tossed the little rug over one shoulder and forced rubbery legs into action, straining to keep up with his long-legged strides.

He took hold of the gelding's bridle and positioned him . . . for him to mount? "We've no time to saddle you a horse."

Her heart dropped a beat then slammed into break neck speed. He meant for *them* to mount. Suddenly, she had to struggle for her next breath.

"You'll need to get up first." He whisked her around to face the horse and stuffed her boot in the stirrup. Heat shot through her, mixing up her thoughts. She must not have hustled enough since she felt a push at her hip to guide her up and over the saddle. He tugged her foot free, shoved his own boot in the stirrup, and swung up behind her.

Strong arms encircled her waist, derailing her thoughts, propelling her pulse. His gloved hand gathered the reins in front of her. She stared down at that hand as

Clint guided the horse around and heeled him in the flank. Within seconds they sped into a full-on gallop. All Jessica could do was hold on to the saddle horn, pull her knees in tight, and remember to breathe.

In the history of spine-tingling rides, this one took first place. Clint's focus was obviously on the emergency at hand, but Jessica could only think about the feel of him behind her. His right hand had spread at her midriff to keep her secure, and he was leaning into the forward motion, pushing her body with him. His breath was stirring her hair, his hard chest at her back.

Just when I thought I could handle being around him and now this. Lord help me.

They rode over several small rises and soon left the cooler air off the stream to make their way into a pasture filled with dozens of grazing Herefords.

Clint straightened the angle of his back and slowed his steed to a steady trot. The jarring tempo made Jessica wonder how Clint kept from smacking his chin on the top of her head, until she felt his puffs of breath above her left ear. Sudden goose bumps prickled down her side.

They threaded their way through the herd. Soon, she saw a cow lying on its side. When they drew near she heard its bellow. It was plump with calf and in obvious distress.

Clint released Jessica and jumped off so quickly, she toppled off right behind him. She let out a huge gasp. He circled back and caught her easily, as if she were a small child. He held her to his chest for endless seconds, his arms like steel bands around her as if terrified he'd almost lost her. That was ridiculous, of course.

Her mind was playing games, dangerous games.

Finally loosening his grip, he let her slide down his

body. Since the day she'd met this man he hadn't noticed her one wit. Not one look. Barely hellos. Nothing to speak of, *and now this?* Once her feet touched the ground, he held her away from him and searched her eyes. To assess what? If she was all right from the ride, from the dismount, his closeness? He looked confused. But, then, so was she.

In the next moment he stepped back dropping his arms, did an about face, and advanced to the cow as if nothing had happened between them. *Had it?* The whole episode had probably only taken a fraction of a minute. She stood frozen to the spot where he'd left her, feeling silly.

"Help me, Jessie. She's losing strength."

His voice snapped her out of her juvenile thoughts. She ran to his side. Tears scalded her eyes as she confronted the animal and its agony. She didn't know what to do, but a compelling instinct took over and she squatted to stroke the cow's neck with slow, soothing movements, cooing as only a woman could do.

She glanced up at Clint. He had paused, his eyes skimming down her cheeks at the path her silent tears had made.

She squeezed her brows together. "Can we help her?"

He moved then, swinging the bag to the front of him and ripping it open. He removed what appeared to be a piece of machinery. Jessica flew to her feet and stared at the contraption. He couldn't be thinking to use that on a live animal.

"Come on over here," he said. "You hold the block against her pelvis once I attach the chain."

"Attach the chain?" she whispered, half to herself.

The apparatus—a big wooden block with metal links attached and a bar across what appeared to be a large screw—looked threatening. How would this thing deliver a calf?

Clint rolled up his sleeves and grabbed the length of chain. Planting his knees into the dirt behind the cow he shoved an arm up the poor animal's birth canal.

Jessica recoiled.

He unleashed a hardy curse. "I was afraid of that. Help me roll her over." He slipped his arm free, dropped the fetter on the block, and sprang to his feet. Darting around her, he squatted at the cow's distended abdomen.

Jessica stared blurry-eyed at the crown of Clint's hat, only too aware of her flagging knees. The cow's eyes bulged with fear or pain or both as she huffed. Clint placed both palms beneath the swollen belly. He signaled with a nod for her to do the same. Jessica copied his pose, pressing her hands against the hide.

"On the count of three we're going to lift, push, and hope the calf shifts. You ready?"

All she could do was give a quick nod.

"Okay, one, two, three . . ." They lifted and, with all they had, shoved. Clint used the strength of a shoulder while his hands pushed hard against the back legs. The cow bawled as it teetered for only a moment before it rolled to the other side.

Jessica lost her balance, about to tumble over the cow when a strong arm encircled her waist and tugged backward. The momentum thrust them both to the ground, hard. Jessica's head bounced once on Clint's chest and a loud *whoosh* escaped him.

She couldn't seem to move. And he *didn't move*. Humiliation overpowered her until concern for him took over and she could think again. She must have knocked the wind out of him. Finally, he stirred beneath her. Flexing his stomach, he brought them both to a sitting position. On a pant he said, next to her ear, "Cozy as this is, we still have critters to save."

She tensed. He had been waiting for her to move off of him! Embarrassed beyond reason now, she wriggled from his hold and pushed off his knees to her feet. Out of the corner of her eye, she saw Clint smile and bit back a groan. He shoved off the ground, rolling to his feet with ease, then hustled to the cow's rump and their task at hand.

Again he squatted, grabbed the chain, and shoved it back up the birth canal. "The legs. Good."

Minutes clicked on as Clint grunted, and sweat trickled past the dark stubble of his jawline. He must have succeeded in securing the manacle to the calf's front legs since he beckoned Jessica over his shoulder. "Hold the block against her pelvis while I work the winch."

His eyes drilled into hers until she nodded. Slowly, he pulled his arm free. His skin and the rolled part of his sleeve glistened in the sun, dripping gobs of blood and orange fluid. Jessica stared at it, light-headed. Clint waited for the next contraction and then began a vigorous twisting. Jessica marveled at his pace. His muscles strained, yet they didn't give out, while she wedged the block against the pelvis. The cow bellowed again—an agonizing sound. Jessica's stomach balled into a knot at that cry of pure pain.

Jessica scrabbled and pushed and prayed in charged silence beside Clint. Finally, she saw the small hooves coming through the opening with the chain wrapped securely around them.

"Jessie, pull back on the block."

She did, and as she backed up with the block in her

arms, Clint grabbed the calf's hooves. He stuffed his heels into the mushy ground and strained backward.

"Grab the oxygen tank, irrigation syringe, and coffee can out of the bag," he grunted. The entire calf slipped out and lay lifeless on the ground. Jessica had the next objects ready for him. Clint began the task of resuscitating the motionless creature. He cleared the membranes off the head and suctioned fluid from each nostril. Then he opened its mouth and repeated the process. He started up the small, hand-held oxygen tank, putting the tube inside the empty coffee can.

"Hold his head up."

She scooted over, slid her knee out, and propped the calf upright against her. Clint glanced at her in surprise before he pushed the calf's muzzle into the can where the oxygen ran. They waited as he stroked its body from ear to tail, trying to stimulate it. Stopping momentarily, he removed the chain from around the front hooves, touched them tenderly to make sure he hadn't marred them, and resumed massaging the calf.

Jessica waited, unmoving. She tore her gaze from the lifeless animal and examined Clint's profile. His expression broke her heart. The unmistakable concern etched in his strong features drew her to him like the winch had done with the calf. He cared. He really cared about this helpless little creature.

The calf's nostrils flared. A leg twitched. And then the little guy lifted his head and kicked Clint in the knee. Clint looked over at Jessica and grinned so huge and glorious that it filled her with an inexpressible joy. She couldn't help but return his bright smile. She felt exuberant, like it had been the birthing of her own child. A true miracle.

"You saved their lives. You're a hero," she said in a breathy voice.

He heard her and stared straight into her eyes, a frown crinkling his brow. If she didn't know better, she'd think he'd never been praised before.

A small smile flickered across his lips, "You were pretty amazing yourself, little one."

Her heart skittered. *Little one.* She stared back at him, looking for a reason for that particular intimacy. Nothing showed on his face.

He rose to his feet to go check on the mother, leaving her to cradle the calf's head. Jessica stroked the rust and white newborn, wiping its perfect little face clean, all the while talking in quiet tones.

"Okay, Jessie, it's time to let him go so his mother can come clean him up." He removed the oxygen tank and coffee can. Jessica scooted out from under the calf, carefully settling the head on the ground. The mother came near to sniff her newborn and began licking in earnest.

"He'll be fine now," Clint said. "He should be up on his feet within the hour. We'll make sure that goes well, then we can head back."

Jessica took in a slow, pleased breath and smiled.

Clint looked down at her sitting there in the dirt, messy and rumpled, and presented her with the most endearing crooked grin she'd ever seen him give, melting her to the grass and dirt and goo.

He repacked the equipment, then dropped down next to her, wiping slimy palms against his jeans and his forehead with a sleeve. Lifting his Stetson from his dampened head he dropped it on a patch of grass next to him.

He looked tired but pleased as he draped his forearms across raised knees, and offered her a grateful smile.

She regarded that smile and the man. Somehow he seemed most at home out here with the elements and the animals. So different from the Clint his reputation painted. This had to be the true man. The one he wanted to be. *So, why did he act so differently with others*—bigger than life, daunting yet charming? A charm almost expected of him.

She smiled back. "I loved being a part of this, Clint."

His eyebrows shot up. "No kidding? I don't know any woman who would have done what you just did. At least, not happily."

With a fingertip she etched circles in the dirt. "Maybe it's because I was raised on a ranch. We have animals." She looked back at him. "But I've never helped with a birthing before. It was amazing, exhilarating, it felt . . . important."

A slow grin stretched across his exquisite face, lighting his eyes. "You didn't say a word about my grabbing you off the porch to ride double with me, racing to who knew where? Didn't complain. Not once. And there you sit with blood and slime all over your lap smiling and telling me you loved being a part of it?" His hearty laugh rang out into the summer breeze. When his laughter died off, he shook his head but kept his eyes on hers. "You're an unusual"—his smile dropped away—"but amazing lady, Jessie."

She swallowed—hard. He kept calling her Jessie. No one had called her that since junior high and she'd been thankful, never liking how it sounded. Now, the name seemed to roll off his tongue and into her soul.

"I . . . I guess I am a little strange." *I'm a little strange?* She squeezed her eyes closed, pressed her lips together, turned her face away so he wouldn't see her blush. Why did she always open her mouth before thinking first? Silence hung thickly between them.

When she looked back, wondering why he hadn't said anything more, there was a twinkle in his eyes. *What's he thinking now?* While she looked him over, from his ring of dampened hair down to his blood-spattered boots, a great need gripped her. A need to keep Clint here forever, talk to him, study him, get to know the real man. She turned to face him, crisscrossed her legs, and hunched over them. "It's a big responsibility, being the foreman of this huge cattle ranch. How'd you come to be that?" Then excitedly, she added, "But wait. Start from the beginning. When and why did you first come here?"

Clint's face clouded over. She found herself frowning with him.

He remained mute for several beats, staring straight through her. Jessica couldn't stand the pain she saw on his face. The deep lines around his usually sensuous mouth, so breathtaking when he smiled, had gone slack. His green eyes, only minutes ago the color of early spring grass, had dimmed, grown cold and distant.

Her stomach knotted. What had she asked of him? "Clint? Are you okay?"

He cleared his throat, dropped his hands off of his knees, and sat up straighter. "I . . . um . . . came to live with your Uncle Roy when I was fourteen."

"Oh." She pulled her knees up and encircled them. "What brought you here?" She wanted to ask more, like where was his mother, did he have siblings, what about a father? But she could see she'd already asked too much.

He averted his gaze. His Adam's apple sank below his shirt collar before it rose again to his throat. "That's a story for another time, I think." His voice sounded strained.

She bit her tongue hard to keep from blurting out questions she so desperately wanted to know about this man. She wanted to help. But her cautious side decided a change of subject would be the wiser course.

"How did you become Uncle Roy's foreman at such a young age?"

He gave a stiff laugh. "I'm not all that young, Jessie." He raised a forearm and swiped at the sweat trying to fall in his eyes. "At first Roy put me in charge of caring for the horses, then breaking horses. I still tease him today about how he started me out on the toughest horses I've ever had to train—two really spirited geldings." "You break horses?"

He shifted his gaze to her.

She smiled in admiration. "That's amazing, Clint. What don't you do?" The minute the words were out heat flew into her cheeks.

Clint smiled with understanding, embarrassing her all the more.

She gazed down at her shins, running her hands up and down them. "Um. What ever happened to those horses?"

He nodded toward his horse. "You're looking at one of them." She saw a muscle knot in his jaw. He exhaled a tight breath. "The other was killed by a cougar."

Her stomach lurched. "How horrible!" The vision of such a beautiful creature being unmercifully torn to shreds by a cougar made her whole body quiver. She forced her attention to the nearby gelding. His head hung leisurely with the reins piled in a clump next to him while he munched on tufts of grass. "Look at this guy, all peaceful-like, without a care in the world. He's not even tied to anything and yet he stays. You did that, didn't you?"

A soft chuckle accompanied his reply, "It's not that big a deal, little one. He's a great horse by nature."

"Maybe so, but you're the one who had to tame him, and teach him to obey you."

After getting her fill of watching his horse graze, she looked back at Clint and found him studying *her*. She was taken aback by that. His gaze was warm, tender, as it scanned her face. Not used to looks like this, she wiggled uncomfortably.

He shifted, stretching out his long body. He leaned back on one elbow and crossed his legs at the ankles. When he plopped his Stetson back on his head and a lazy grin spread across his face, she took a moment to admire him. *If he were on the front cover of 'An American Cowboy', I bet every last copy would sell.*

She licked her dry lips. "What do you like most about Montana?"

With a long finger he shoved the rim of his hat up enough to see her clearly. He broke off a piece of grass, and rolled it between his fingers. "Everything, I guess. The quiet when it's me, my horse, and the cattle. The beauty of the land, the changes of weather. Even the snow—though it challenges us every year—the work . . ."

He stopped and met her curious gaze. His eyes captivated Jessica. Penetrating, and warm at the same time. The sunlight glittered across them, now reminding her of green gems, and such a contrast to the tanned face and new growth of dusky beard. Just looking at him made her tongue stick to the roof of her mouth.

"What about you, Jessie?" His low, resonant voice barely broke through.

"Huh? Oh yeah, I love you, too," she replied dreamily.

Clint pressed a knuckle to his lips. Coughed. Though he had his mouth covered, his eyes danced.

She blinked in confusion. Was he trying not to laugh? "What did I say?"

"I'm sure you meant you love *Montana*, too."

Horror pulsed through her veins as awareness hit. She pushed loose hair back to her ponytail with shaky hands, fumbled with the rubber band.

"What brought *you* to Montana?"

She exhaled in a gush, hesitating only long enough to regain her poise, then look back at him. "I, um, came to help Mabel."

"Oh yeah, that's right. Dear Mabel. Running girls off faster than she can bring them in."

"She says it's your fault."

He laughed. "I know. It's an ongoing battle she and I have. This is one area we disagree. Most we don't."

"Tell me about Mabel."

"I can tell you this. Mabel may be tough, but she's big-hearted. You do fine with her."

"I don't know." Jessica shook her head in disbelief. "You think so?"

"You have a good heart, too."

She blinked. "How would you know that?"

He gave her another lopsided smile. One that made her shiver a little, in spite of the heat. "I observe. You're a good person, Jessie."

He noticed me? She wanted to know more but didn't know how to ask. Before she could figure out how to go about it, he looked away. Quick as lightning, he snatched a creature off the ground. Whatever it was, it was small. It froze in terror within his fingertips while he studied its face. He smirked like he had a secret, sat up, and leaned over to hand it to her.

She opened her hands trustingly. "Ohhh . . . cute . . . a lizard. I've never seen one like this before. What kind is it?" She captured it between her palms and looked at its little face.

Clint grinned as he watched her. Settling back to his side he said, "It's an alligator lizard—just a baby."

She studied its little head. "Huh. It looks like an alligator. Do they get as big as one?"

"No. They can grow up to a foot." Mirth entwined with his words. "But I wouldn't be handing you an adult. They can be pretty vicious."

She rested her gaze back on the reptile. "Hello, cute little lizard. It's okay, I won't hurt you." Soon its tiny eyes drooped and shut. She lifted the top hand and stroked its back as it lay motionless in her palm.

"You have a way with little creatures. Looks to me like its sleeping, not just scared spitless."

Jessica looked up at him with an amused smile. "Scared *spitless*?"

Clint broke into a wide grin. "Well, you wouldn't like the alternative."

They laughed together. It felt good, right. Soon their laughter faded and they fell silent as Jessica held his gaze, braving his deep probe right to her core. What was he thinking right at this moment? She couldn't tell. Only that it was something significant.

She began to feel dizzy from lack of breath.

As if he sensed she needed it, he came to her rescue. "So, no more questions?"

She needed to engage her brain. "Hmm . . . Where do

all the cowboys on this ranch come from? I mean, they're all different age groups, but none of them seem to have families."

"Well . . ." He lifted his hat up, raked a hand through his hair, stuffed it back on. "Most come to escape their old life, I reckon. Some to be part of something—a family. But, there's kind of an unwritten code around here—the past gets to stay in the past."

"And your past?" she asked without thinking, as always.

He turned his face from hers and grew quiet. From the side she noticed the crisp line of his strong jaw as muscles bunched. Guilt tightened her throat. The joy had vanished. For long moments, his eyes seemed to rest on the pine trees clustered at the stream. An impulsive desire to comfort him in the form of a hug came over her.

Before she could move, he spoke. "Like I said, Jessie, the past gets to stay in the past." He shifted his eyes to her. She could see his apology, but didn't miss the sadness there.

Angry at herself, she decided not to ask that question of him again. While she pondered how to bring his joy back, a particular question niggled her mind. "Why is it you've never married?" *Did I actually ask that question out loud?* She wanted to grab the words and stuff them back down her traitorous throat.

Shock registered on Clint's face. His eyebrows rose, then fell into a scowl, then shifted again into another expression entirely. Pain? Regret? She couldn't tell. She remained still, breathing shallowly, not knowing what to do but wait. Surprisingly, now she didn't want to hear his response. She searched for a way out of the awkwardness.

He swung a cool gaze back to her, his eyes pricking hers. "I'm not the marrying type, Jessica. It's that simple."

His cool answer stabbed her heart, deflating it like a punctured rubber ball. The silence between them grew deafening. Sweat trickled down her spine from the hot sun.

Right then the calf stood up on wobbling legs, and Jessica whooshed out a pent up breath. She caught the same relief in Clint's expression yet somehow that saddened her.

"There he goes." Clint swept to his feet in one motion. After giving the calf a few minutes to steady himself, he gave the head a little shove under the mother to help him find milk. Turning back to Jessica he smiled. She was drawn to the creases that had deepened around his mouth. Staggering how a simple smile could improve already extraordinary looks. But she saw tension in that smile and wished she hadn't broached the subject of marriage. Still, she wondered why it affected him so much.

"They'll be fine. Let's go back."

He gathered up the satchel, hung it on his shoulder, and headed for his horse.

Jessica released the little lizard back into the wild, and followed. She swung into the saddle with only a small push from Clint. When he hefted himself up behind her, her blood raced. He closed in, swallowing her up in his massive embrace.

Hot breath stirred on her cheek. "We'll be taking it a little slower this time. Lean against me. Easier on your back." A hand settled on her abdomen and gently tugged her against him. She sucked in a breath and stiffened, closed her eyes to fight off the longing his closeness brought her.

His lips tickled her temple. "Relax, little one." His intimate, yet curt, instructions caressed her ear, making her shiver, but, though she was tucked into his solid frame, an intangible wall had arisen. Silence hung between them as together their bodies rocked with the motion of the steed.

When they arrived at the main camp, Clint steered his gelding into the barn and reined in at the far stall. He loosened, but didn't immediately release his hold on her. As the horse remained still and she stayed comfortably pressed into his chest, the hard beat of his heart resonated straight into her back, firing her senses. She wondered why he didn't move, but was glad for every second of contact he was willing to give.

A breath huffed into her hair, and he shifted in the saddle. Instant recollection of her not moving off him earlier hit her like a charging bull, and with it a flood of heat throbbed in her cheeks. She flung her frame forward, nearly toppling over the horse's head.

Clint caught her shoulders and dragged her back. "Whoa, now. What're you doing?" he barked. The agitated horse bounced to the side and tossed his head, nearly slamming her in the nose. She was so embarrassed, all she wanted to do was get down and disappear into the house.

The saddle creaked as he moved to dismount. Once he stepped down, and before she could open her mouth to protest, he reached up to clasp her waist. He was so tall she only had to tilt her head down a bit to stare into his eyes. His pupils were large and he looked at her with some kind of unnamed emotion. Angry she hadn't moved? Agitated she'd upset the horse? But, it didn't look like either of those things. It looked more like—

He tugged, startling her. She had to grab his shoulders to keep from falling. His eyes remained fixed to hers, and like there was an invisible tether, she couldn't look away. He pulled her out of the saddle and into his arms, then lowered her so slowly she wondered at the strength it took to hold her like that. Finally her feet touched the hay-sprinkled ground. Jessica counted five heartbeats before he dropped his hands.

A look of puzzlement crossed his eyes briefly. Then, without a word he tapped the rim of his hat in thanks, or good-bye.

Jessica could only nod.

He backed up a couple of paces to give her space and somehow she put feet to motion. With head held high, and with strength her rubbery legs didn't have, she sauntered past him toward the house before her heart could burst from its strange brew of elation and uncertainty.

CHAPTER 6

Friday night was upon them and with it the biggest square dance of the year. Jessica planned to attend. Mostly, to watch the men she fed every day interact someplace other than in the dining hall. Yet, a dark pall had blanketed her since early this morning.

Seeing Clint daily had made him a part of *her* personal orbit. To see him around other women—a perfectly natural occurrence considering his reputation—brought a lung-squeezing dread. In the weeks she'd spent in his general vicinity, she'd hoped to glimpse a flaw—a mistreatment of his men, a kick of an animal, mouthing-off to Roy, anything—to loosen his grip on her heart. But it wasn't to be so. If anything, her respect for Clint had risen exorbitantly and thoughts of him occupied her mind more every single day.

But, tonight, deep in her heart she knew she would be witness to his one serious flaw. His womanizing. But, dang it all. She'd earned this time tonight. This dance was a way for her to get out and have some fun. So, it was time to give her mind a rest, to let go, let loose. Even if that meant risking pain from the man who'd be unaware he was causing it.

Jessica found her way to the pick-up truck, stretched to climb up into it, and scooted to the middle, careful to keep her full-skirted sundress from riding up. She'd chosen the broad-strapped dress in green to bring out that same color in her eyes, and hoped the style wasn't so different from Montanan get-ups that she'd stand out. She'd considered her usual ponytail, but ruled that out for loose waves tucked behind her ears and down her back.

Johnnie slid behind the wheel and brought the old truck to life. To her relief, Pete—a regular motor mouth—bounded into the passenger seat. He prattled on about the weather, the season, mundane things, and Jessica nestled into the comfort of not having to listen too hard.

". . . and Clint told us about your helping him with the cow and calf, Jess."

Jessica reared her head toward Pete. "*What?*"

Pete hadn't heard her. He wasn't looking at her. He just kept right on blabbing. "Clint never talks 'bout his women, so the cowhands probed 'til he finally said you were a natural, helpin' and carin' about those critters."

Silence.

The truck bumped hard into a pothole. As they bounced, Pete took a deep breath and jumped in again. "We was surprised. Clint's never asked another gal ta do that before. Ever." He turned a rakish grin on her then. "Said you rode together on his horse and that he—"

"Whoa boy," Johnnie cut in. "Clint said nothing about that ride." Johnnie leaned in to briefly catch Pete's eye.

Warmth rushed up Jessica's neck and into her cheeks.

Pete looked flustered all of a sudden. "Aw, rats. I should shut-up when I'm talkin'."

Johnnie grunted. "Yeah, you should."

Jessica's thoughts were still on Pete's revelation when Johnnie parked in the field within a sea of vehicles. Pete leapt out of the truck and left the door wide open to head for the crowd. She glanced past him at the activity in the barn. Even from a distance she could see she was completely out of her element. Most of the time, since arriving in Montana, she felt inadequate—like a Shetland pony amongst thoroughbreds. Tonight that sentiment was escalating.

Johnnie came around to her side, and bent in. His hat brim rapped against the roof, bringing her gaze to his. He looked at her with a question in those startling blue eyes. With hand extended, he waited without so much as a word. She ripped her attention away from the look of tenderness he was giving her, and placed her palm in his outstretched hand. Once on the ground she gave his hand a small squeeze of thanks before pulling hers away.

The sun slid below the horizon, streaking shades of pink across the darkening sky. It was glorious as always, but didn't do a thing to remove her apprehension. Try as she might to prepare herself for this evening, she felt ill-equipped. They moved toward the entrance, and her mouth grew drier. When they stepped through the entryway, a flood light from above flashed across them, heightening her nervousness.

A square dance was in full swing. One man shouted out commands, ". . . swing your lady, dosado . . ." Whirling partners breezed by. She tried to make out faces she might know, but everyone was jouncing and twirling so much, and the music and whooping was dizzying, and she had to lean back against the post. She glanced up to escape the whirling crowd and steady herself.

The interior of the barn was huge. On the outside it

had looked like a normal burnished-red ranch barn. Inside, mammoth beams supported the entire structure from corner to corner. Dropping her gaze she noticed bales of hay scattered about the perimeter where many sat and visited or held hands. The band on a platform at the back wall consisted of four men garbed in western motif. Two played guitars, the third a banjo, each singing behind a silver microphone that seemed to swallow their faces.

She perused the mass of people. The cowboys tended to wear some form of white shirt tucked into their jeans with a black string tie, while the gals wore full western-style skirts with lots of petticoats, ruffled blouses, and cowboy boots. Different from poodle skirts, bobby sox, and oxford shoes, back home. At least Uncle Roy had talked her into wearing boots.

Jessica shook off the inkling of unease and allowed herself to be nudged along into the throng of people. Always protective, Johnnie, stayed at her side.

Smiling up at him, she said, "I'm going to mosey around a bit. Enjoy yourself. Don't worry about me." She thought she saw a flash of disappointment in his eyes, but he nodded his agreement. Before she could move off, a sudden outpouring of giggles at the main entrance caught her attention. Jessica looked past the gaggle of women to a cowboy at their center, sauntering into the building—a head taller than the rest, all brawn and easy confidence. Only one man could pull off that walk, and Jessica's chest tightened at the sight of him.

Clint was breath-stopping. He wore what the rest of the men did, yet was worlds apart from any of them; Samson to mere man. More attractive, if that were even possible, than he had been each day since the moment she'd laid eyes on him. His new black Stetson sat low on his brows, so she couldn't see his eyes well, but he was grinning, flashing white teeth at the host of pretty ladies. Jealousy burned through her, making her legs feel hollow.

Without a word to Johnnie she slipped away. She needed to escape the view, to sit. There didn't seem to be a single spot open so she headed for the dark end of the barn. She ambled about like a lost little lamb when a hand roughly clamped her elbow and propelled her toward a hay bale. She jerked her head up to find a familiar face leering back at her. Though she knew him to be Brad Turner, one of the cowhands at the Big 'H', they had never been formally introduced.

He shoved her down next to Darrell, his ranch buddy. Always quiet during meals, he seemed to radiate dark intensity, but never as strongly as tonight. Brad was tall and lanky, and if the hard angles of his face were ever to soften, he might be considered nice looking. Darrell, greasy with deeply pocked skin, had yet to say anything, though he had turned to give her a carnal stare with cold black eyes.

She scooted to the edge of the bale.

Brad sat on her free side, wedging her against his buddy. "Well now, pretty lady." His gaze slid down the length of her body. "What brings you to our side of the barn?"

Their side? With a sinking feeling, she shifted to stand. Brad restrained her hand—a subtle entreaty. She took a quick breath, then leaned forward again. This time he pressed her palm firmly to the bale until she bore the prick of the hay against her skin. She didn't frighten easily, but his hint had crossed over to a demand, speeding her pulse.

He leaned closer. "You're not going anywhere. I haven't had a dance with you yet."

His dark eyes bore into hers. Jessica shuddered all over. *Calm down. There are people near. All you have to do is scream.*

"I need a drink," Jessica said, and tried to wrench free.

Brad pressed harder. "Nah, I don't think so. You can sit a spell before we dance."

Jessica saw a tall figure with a black Stetson, making his way through the bordering crowd. Her heart accelerated, knowing that shape and swaggering walk anywhere.

Clint marched straight up to them, all towering strength. His eyes darkened and his jaw ticked as he pinned first one man then the next with an open glare. It seemed a full minute had passed when he stuck out a hand. "Dance, Jessie?"

Jessica's eyes were pegged on Clint when she became aware of Brad's clammy hand slipping off the back of hers. "Yes."

Her palm connected to Clint's, and a frisson of sensation spiraled up her arm. She floated next to him through the crowd to the hub of the dance area. Making a slow turn, he gently placed her hand to his shoulder. His muscles flexed as he pulled her close, and bowed his head to fasten his eyes to hers. The tip of his hat tapped her head. Shadowed now—under that brim—the world fell away, and left only them on that dance floor.

When his fingertips at her waist caressed the back of her right arm, she lifted it to him. His hand caught hers and engulfed it in warmth. They finally moved, to the slow song, *Love is a Many Splendored Thing*.

Jessica could barely hear the music through the whooshing of blood in her ears. Already on adrenaline overload, her heart hammered against her chest and right into his. Would he know the real reason?

They'd only taken a few steps when Clint abandoned her hand to tuck a finger under her chin, lifting it so she would look him in the eye. Her breath caught in her throat. "Jessie, you need to stay away from him. This is not the first time I've had to intervene before Brad Turner could mistreat a woman." His low voice rumbled up from his chest right into her bones. "Shy away from them both. If I wasn't short-handed for the round-up, or if they weren't so good on cutting horses, I'd cut 'em loose. I may still. They're no good."

Eyes so compelling they seemed to demand her strict attention held hers in tow. Her fingers bit into his shoulder. She recognized he had saved her as Uncle Roy's niece, or possibly just any damsel in need. Nothing more. Still sheltered under the rim of his hat, she watched his eyebrows furrow. He seemed to be waiting for a response.

She swallowed through a dust-dry throat. "It was so dark at that end . . . I knew I'd made a mistake the minute he grabbed me."

An understanding smile squeezed into the corners of his mouth, and he nodded. He re-gathered her hand and curled her into his body to finish the dance in silence. She trembled against him. He'd think it was from the incident with Brad. That was good.

She enjoyed holding this man, knowing a repeat of it would be as likely as a lunar eclipse. She needed him, too—this savior from the evil that had invaded her tonight. Her body slowly calmed in his embrace. She soaked up his warmth, breathed in his pleasing scent—spice and soap and man. He shifted his snug hold and nuzzled her hair. She closed her eyes and reveled in the sheer intimacy of that move. Hope spiraled up like the smoke curl from a homey fireplace.

Please, Lord, let this song last.

Her mind began to play tricks on her, like Clint's hand opening across the curve of her spine, pressing her closer. She had to stop these little imaginings—the so-called tender looks, the imaginary lingering touches—like the possessive hold it only *seemed* he had on her right now.

But then there was the swaying of their bodies to the music, to a rhythm all their own . . . and it was heaven.

Clint suddenly tensed and stopped their swaying.

Jessica reluctantly leaned back from the wall of his chest to look up. He was staring over her head at something or someone. Lips pressed together, and jaw set, he looked . . . annoyed. Or was it guilty?

The music droned on, but Jessica inched back, feeling a jolt of loss. A light tap came to her shoulder. She swung away from Clint's body and saw a petite woman with long blonde hair and icy blue eyes. The blonde drew up on Clint and tilted her perfect-skinned face to grant him a wide smile. With a jeweled hand she stroked his upper arm. "You saved her. You're always so gallant." She twisted enough to give Jessica a frosty stare and, with an acidic voice for her ears only, said, "Next time, be smarter."

With smile back in place, she turned back to Clint. "The group has missed you."

For a cherished moment, Clint dueled with Jessica's stare, and she saw tangled emotions in his eyes. But then he took a step back, gave a slight pull on his hat brim, and said, "Jessie," then allowed himself to be led away and into the fray of faceless women awaiting him. He never once looked back.

Jessica felt something die inside her. She watched him walk away, hand-in-hand with her rival. *Her* rival?—how laughable. He'd rescued Jessica. A valiant knight, like the woman had said. When it was over, Jessica had been dismissed. His duty was done.

The rush to her system left her drained and her limbs leaden. When she heard the music stop, she forced her rigid legs out of the dance area.

Johnnie sauntered toward her. His long strides brought him near her quickly. "Jess? Can I get you anything?"

"I'm . . ." Dazed, she finally looked up at Johnnie and said, "Yes, I could use some water, if you don't mind."

Johnnie examined her for a few seconds then turned toward the refreshment table. While he was gone, she scanned the barn for a safe place to deposit her emotionally weary body. The only reasonable spot was on a hay bale behind that pack of Clint-ogling cowgirls. She rolled her eyes. But she had no choice. She needed to sit and didn't dare go to the wrong side of the barn again. She would have to do her best to *not* watch, was all.

The beauties cajoled, flirted, and rubbed up against him, all while Clint looked decidedly uncomfortable. Finally, with a grim look on his face, Clint grasped Miss Perfect's hand, spun her around, and steered her to the dance floor. She brooked a smile so big, Jessica wondered if she would break her beautiful, blue-eyed face. Jessica watched as he gathered her into his arms to dance to Patsy Cline's *I Will Follow Him*. Clint's large hand fixed her to him. He didn't talk, didn't smile, just danced. Once or twice Jessica saw him loosen the embrace to study her face as she talked. What was that look he gave her? Capitulation? Lust? Love?

Jessica squeezed her eyes shut and grasped a lock of hair, twirling it around her index finger. A lump formed in her throat, constricting the bit of breath left in her lungs.

Johnnie startled her with a squeeze to her shoulder. She looked up at him. He tenderly grasped the tendril she was annihilating, unwound it from her finger and held up a paper cup of water before dropping down next to her. "You all right?"

No. Not all right. She wanted to run screaming out the door, get on a train back to California and hide in her old life, never to return. But that wasn't an option.

Johnnie glanced at her, then followed her gaze to the dance floor. "Ah. I see. Amazing, isn't he?"

"What do you mean?" Jessica choked out.

"You know. How he can talk to any of the ladies and how they all seem to want him."

The statement pushed her misery to the background as aggravation came forth. She shifted her whole body to face him, though he didn't look at her. "I don't get it, Johnnie. You're a handsome, caring man. Why are they not clamoring over you?"

Johnnie didn't move, making her uneasy and wishing she hadn't asked the intrusive question. He finally wrung his gaze from the dirt floor and then up to her. A sad smile curved his mouth. Jessica's heart dropped. Why was her tongue always engaged before her brain? Still, she wondered about Johnnie—attentive, capable, protective Johnnie. And fine-looking. Don't forget fine-looking.

"Never mind," he said. "Let's dance." He took her glass and twisted it into the dirt. With his hand under her elbow, he led her gracefully to the dance area.

Johnnie pulled her into his embrace and rocked with the music. His hold was warm, strong. Yet when he pulled her close, her heart beat normally. So unlike her dance with Clint.

When the music stopped they made their way back to the hay bale. She tried not to, but in the end she found herself perusing the barn for signs of Clint. She located him all right, in time to see him with a hand to the small of Miss Perfect's back, scooting her toward the large barn door. Grief stabbed her at the thought of them together . . . somewhere else.

It was near midnight when Johnnie settled her in the passenger seat of the truck to drive her back to the ranch house. Crazy Pete had caught a ride in the bed of someone else's pick-up truck. She grinned at how he'd hooted and hollered into the night as they'd spun around and driven off toward town.

Johnnie was his usual quiet self. She was thankful for that, since her eyes drifted shut when thoughts of Clint invaded: Clint's hand as he'd tugged her away from Brad and guided her to the dance floor, the sway of their bodies to the melody. If she closed her eyes real tight she could almost relive the heat of his embrace. But, as in the way of all memories, the bad encroached—the *woman* interrupting the perfect cadence of the dance, and the moonbeams shining down on Clint's tall form as he'd escorted her out into the night.

A squeak of hinges startled her. Johnnie was standing at the open truck door, the ranch house at his back. A gust of night air hit her bare arms, and she shivered. He offered a hand to help her down. She smiled at him—forever the gentleman—as she put her hand in his. He had removed his Stetson and a dash of moonlight swept across his face adding a silvery brilliance to the cobalt hue of his eyes.

He helped her out of the old truck, led her to the front door, and turned her slowly to face him. Lifting a hand he brushed at her temple, trailed his fingertips down her cheek, and stopped at her jawline. He inched closer.

"Thanks, Johnnie," she said and stepped back.

He dropped his hand to his side. "My pleasure."

Before he could say another thing, she let herself into the house and didn't stop moving until she'd slipped between cool sheets. But now all she could think was of Johnnie's disappointed eyes and the slow scuff of boots as he'd plodded back to the bunkhouse.

Hours passed before she heard the muffled sound of horse's hooves outside. She rose and went to the window. In the moonlight, where only shadows took shape, she spied the ethereal form of a large cowboy astride his gelding—hat pulled low, jacket collar turned up against the cold. The stiffness of her body reminded her she'd been subconsciously waiting for Clint's return.

She glanced at the clock—2:30 a.m. Turning away from the window she dashed back to her bed and threw herself onto it. Clenching the pillow across her head, she breathed into the cotton sheets until she ran out of air, then twisted to her back and threw the pillow off. It hit the wall with a satisfying thud. But moments later, despair crept in. She crossed her arms over her face and felt the wetness there. Sleep would not be her companion this night.

CHAPTER 7

Jessica entered the kitchen to the smell of hot flapjacks and the sight of Mabel fussing over the stove. Maybe the old woman would leave her alone this morning. One could only hope. Ever the killjoy, Mabel glanced over her shoulder. "Stayed up a bit late last night, eh girl?"

"Got home about 12:30 or so, I guess." Jessica paced to the cupboard and started pulling out plates.

Jessica sensed Mabel's stare on her profile, but didn't stop in the gathering of dishware. A tremor of uneasiness sliced through her. She guessed she'd be reprimanded for tuckering herself out before her work day even started.

Mabel stuffed one hand on her rounded hip, the other flapped the spatula at Jessica as she spoke. "Now, don't you go gettin' yerself all worked up over the big guy. I already told ya he's a lady's man. He's not for you, so stop thinkin' about him."

Jessica plunked the plates on the counter with a clatter. "I wasn't thinking about Clint."

"See, what'd I tell ya. You knew exactly who I was talkin' about."

Caught in her own trap, she wanted to groan, but

instead she went back to the cupboard for mugs. It took so much stamina to face Mabel each day. Without sleep she felt the fight desert her. "Maybe I *was* thinking about him," she mumbled. She should stop here, but her mouth didn't listen. She turned to face Mabel. "What makes you say he's not for me?" The moment the question escaped her lips she regretted it.

"Pfff. You're not his type, girly. He likes 'em blonde and beautiful." She moved the pan off the burner, and scrunched her face in contemplation. "And dumb as a rock."

A strangled giggle escaped Jessica's lips. She bit her bottom lip to keep it in, but to no avail. With a loud whoosh of air she burst into unrestrained laughter.

Mabel joined her and they both laughed until tears streamed down their faces. Sadness at the reality of it all tried to engulf Jessica, but she laughed all the harder. Tension from weeks of trying to please Mabel ebbed from Jessica with every bout of laughter they shared.

For the first time since working with the ranch cook, Jessica realized Mabel just spoke the plain truth, whether people liked it or not. She couldn't help but admire that.

"But I don't get it," Jessica said. "He's a smart man. Foreman of a huge cattle ranch. At thirty-one." She shook her head, and moved to the stove to toss the sausage in the hot skillet. "Why ever would he be interested in *dumb* girls? That seems so . . . so beneath him somehow."

The cook quieted a moment. Jessica could sense Mabel choosing her words carefully. "Well, Jess, he's been hurt a great deal in his young life, something most people don't know anything about. But because of that hurt I think he finds it easier to court girls he can stay distant from, ya know? Wants to have fun, not get too close." Her face grew somber. "But Roy's tired of it. Been pushing him to marry."

Jessica choked as she tried to swallow, then coughed. "Marry?" she squeaked out. "Is there someone he wants to marry?"

"Oh, no you don't, girlie. That's for Clint to know and for you not to."

"Mabel! You can't mean that!" She was at risk of Mabel's harsh words, but she didn't care. "You have to tell me more. Is Clint getting married?"

"I'll not be a party to gossipin', so turn yourself right around here and let's get this breakfast done before the boys hit that back door."

Jessica stared at her, mind buzzing until a splatter of sausage grease burned her wrist. The pain was almost welcome.

* * *

June passed into July, and Clint remained officially single. The waiting and wondering were sheer torture.

The fourth of July celebration at the neighbor's ranch had come and gone. Like always, Clint had been overrun by the local unattached women. One in particular—the petite blonde. Still, no announcement.

Then came the pre-round-up ranch frenzy, and Jessica welcomed the frantic workload. Anything to steer her thoughts in a more positive direction. The cowboys wolfed their dinners,

listened to Uncle Roy's pep talk, and turned in early. All except Johnnie and three others who waited for Clint and any last minute changes he would make to their plans.

Jessica tried to keep the clinking of washed dishes to a minimum, but her hands shook so.

Darn nerves. She prayed hiccups wouldn't ensue. It had been days since she'd seen Clint, busy as he was bringing stragglers in from the high country. She slung a damp dishtowel over her shoulder and decided to stack silverware in the drawer. At least she wouldn't break anything if her fingers fumbled any worse.

The screen door squeaked open and slammed closed. Jessica froze, staring at the spoon in her hand. Heavy boots clunked over the hardwood floor. She forced her gaze up. Her heart leapt as if in call to him. Clint stood near, with feet shoulder-width apart, like he was ready to single-handedly take on the world. But no, that was all wrong. He was grimy from head to toe, his head hung heavy, and he swayed a little in the kitchen's entryway. Dead on his feet before round-up even began.

Jessica ached inside. What she would give to take his head in her lap and stroke his hair until he closed his eyes and slept a dreamless sleep . . .

His eyes met hers. "Jessie."

She blinked, vaguely aware she was stroking something in her hand. She glanced down.

Spoon. She was caressing a stupid spoon. She dropped it in the drawer and planted a smile on her face. She tried to appear unflustered. "Clint. You're tired. Can I get you some coffee?"

"Sure." He stared for several more heartbeats, then shuffled away to join the men at the table.

While the others listened to Clint's plans, Jessica kept their coffee mugs filled. As she'd done with the others, she braced a hand to Clint's sturdy shoulder and leaned in to fill his cup. He turned his head toward her, slid his eyelids closed. His nostrils flared with a quiet intake of breath. The men were busy talking so they hadn't noticed. But she had. When his eyes re-opened, a softness was there. Then it was gone. Leashed.

"Would—" She moistened her lips. "Would you like some food? I could heat up something, or bring you a piece of apple pie? The others have eaten."

One side of his mouth tilted up. "Some of *your* apple pie?"

"Yes."

"Then, yeah, I'll have that. Thanks." He rubbed his forehead and refocused. "Johnnie, the butanes will need to go with you in the morning. . ."

Clint's voice droned on, but Jessica didn't catch a word as she returned to the kitchen to prepare Clint's dessert.

An hour passed before anyone rose, and one by one bid her goodnight. She watched Clint grab his hat, snug it to his brow, and disappear from view.

Johnnie was the last to head to the door. But before he went out, he rocked back and

caught Jessica's eye. "Jess, would you like to come to a round-up? I'm in charge of the one closest to the ranch house. You're welcome to watch if you'd like."

A burst of joy shot through her, but immediately drifted away. Why hadn't Clint mentioned her going? Would she see him there? "I would love to."

He grinned. "Knew you would. I'll be going out at sunrise. You can come later. It's the corral to the east. I'll saddle the little mare and leave her for you."

"Thanks."

He pulled at the tip of his hat. "Night, Jess. See you tomorrow." He let himself out the back door.

Lord, what do you want me to do about that sweet man? My heart bends hard toward Clint, but if you've sent me here for Johnnie . . .

CHAPTER 8

Jessica tiptoed down the stairs to the kitchen, rubbing a palm over her fluttering stomach. She slipped open the small drawer next to the sink, rummaged around for pen and paper—with half an ear listening to old house creaks—and jotted her upcoming whereabouts for Mabel. Resting the note against the bowl of fruit on the counter, she spun to the door.

A wall of formidable cook met her. Jessica yelped and jumped back. "Mabel! You startled me. "

The cook's arms barely reached across her stout chest. "And where're you off to, girlie?"

"I left you a note." Jessica nodded her head toward the fruit bowl. She planted a shaky smile on her face.

Mabel crossed to the note and raised her brows as she read. "And who're you goin' out there to see?" A sudden resentment struck Jessica. She narrowed her eyes at Mabel. Who did she think she was, her mother? "I was invited to go watch a round-up and that's exactly what I'm going to do." She waited for Mabel's expression to change, but it didn't. Jessica's arms dropped to her sides as her confidence slipped a notch. "It's all right, isn't it?"

"I ain't your ma. Watch yourself."

Mabel's comment confused her. Watch herself? Before Mabel could change her mind, Jessica hustled to the barn. Standing contentedly near a stall, saddled, with the reins wrapped loosely around a post, Jessica found the gray mare Johnnie had promised her. Delighted to be on her way, she mounted and trotted east.

As she reined in at the corral, unsuspecting calves lingered near their grazing mothers. *The calm before the storm?* Johnnie and a couple of others were inside the corral arranging some sort of portable apparatus. Johnnie raised his head. He flashed her a dazzling smile and bounded over the fence. "Good morning, early bird."

"Cock-a-doodle-doo." She chuckled and looked past him. "Can I help?"

Admiration with a touch of amusement crossed his face. "You want to help?"

"I'm not afraid of hard work, Johnnie. Yes. I want to help."

"You're very different from Mabel's usual helpers. You know that don't you?" He laughed. "Okay, come on in here and I'll put you to work." He perused her from hat to boots. "Looks like you're dressed for it too, I see."

His comment pleased her. She'd done her best to look the part with wranglers, sleeveless top tucked in, plain leather belt and boots—no frills. She'd tied her long hair in a low ponytail and had her straw cowboy hat pulled down on her forehead. Nothing girlie about her outfit today, though Johnnie's tender inspection made her feel wholly feminine.

She walked through the gate Johnnie held open for her. "How does this whole round-up thing work?"

He pointed. "See that portable squeeze we built? We drag the calves there, and vaccinate, de-horn, and castrate them."

Jessica grimaced. "Wow, a lot for the little critters to endure all at once."

"That's not all. That barrel—" He nodded toward the rusted fifty-five gallon drum. "—holds the branding irons. You can guess what for." He pushed his hat brim up an inch, and the sun glinted off sapphire eyes. "Have you ever been to a rodeo, Jess?"

"Sure. Love 'em."

"Well that's what we do here, except we don't let the calves go. They get the real deal here—the works."

"What happens to them afterwards?"

"The cows stop their bellowing and find their calf, comfort it."

Fascinating. "How?"

Johnnie smiled at her concern. "You know, lick them, be there for them."

"It may be a grueling day for the cowboys, but I can see it'll be much worse for the calves. Poor things."

Jessica trailed after Johnnie. An hour later, after Jessica's fingers burned from twisting screws and securing pipes together, the cowboys started spilling into the corral. Jessica watched, nodded to a few, and noticed a dust cloud coming up the path. Her heart quickened when she recognized who led the group. Just then, a small whirlwind of dust whipped at Clint's hat and shirt, and the gelding's tail. Seemingly unaffected, he tucked his head into the onslaught and galloped along, the elements no match for this hardy man. The gelding slowed to a trot, and the rider changed his rhythm to match. Even as his hips rocked, his broad shoulders barely moved—*poetry in motion.*

He drew up. His distinct scowl broke her spell as he dismounted. "I don't think I've met our new cowhand." Clint's gaze never left hers as he strode to the corral fence.

Jessica hustled over to where Clint stood, not wanting him to reprimand Johnnie. She gave him what she hoped was a confident smile.

"I hope you don't think you'll be in the corral during the round-up."

Jessica inspected his face for a moment and saw no sign of teasing. His stern comment irritated her. He was always so charming to everyone else. "Good morning to you, too."

He gave one quick nod and cocked a brow.

Her irritation raised a notch. She scowled at him.

Clint slung his arms over the top rail. He clasped his hands together right in front of her nose, his eyes hard as granite. "What are you doing out here?"

"Helping them set up. For *fun*."

At first he looked dubious, searching her for the truth. A wry smile shifted his lips, and softened his features. "For fun."

"Maiming poor, helpless calves is fun, right?"

He broke into one of his hardy laughs. But, as quickly as it began it stopped. He tilted his head down and raised both brows. "Fun or not, you *will* be leaving the corral."

Jessica's stomach seemed to ball into a fist. She was a capable woman. Had lived her entire life without any help from him—from any man. Maybe she *hadn't* planned on being in the corral when they started.

But now . . .

She jutted her chin and waited in silence, unwilling to move, surprised at her own stubbornness.

"Jes-sie," he drawled. Leaning a little farther over the fence he gave her an I-call-the-shots stare. His gaze left her eyes and landed on her lips. Her heart tripped. But no. He was only noticing the determined curl of them.

She had to consciously loosen her pucker before she said, "I could help, you know."

He raised his eyes to hers again. "No. You won't be helping. You can watch."

Her brows plowed into a deep furrow. She wanted to say something more but thought better of it. "As you wish."

"Good girl."

She blinked in disbelief.

"Okay, wrong thing to say." The corners of his mouth twitched. And his eyes gave him away as well—twinkling in amusement. He wanted to laugh at her. And that changed everything. It took a lot to push her, but once pushed—

She crossed her arms at her chest. "On second thought . . ."

Gone was the smile. His face hardened. "You'll do as I say, or you'll go back to the ranch house," he said, a little too loudly.

The exchange drew the attention of other cowboys. Johnnie's head whipped up. He started toward them. Clint held up a hand to Johnnie without taking his eyes off Jessica.

Egotistical jerk. Jessica glanced over her shoulder at Johnnie halted in immediate obedience, but his fists were clenched and his mouth was set. Clint waited for her response.

She clamped down on her back teeth; something she did when one of her brothers thought they could bully her. She worked at slackening her jaw enough to speak. "What is it, Clint? Are you thinking women are too delicate to help?" She winced at how angry her words sounded, when she'd just planned to calmly ask, 'Why don't you want me to help?'

Clint backed up a step. He clasped the top of the fence with both hands. His knuckles turned white under the pressure, obviously furious. But why?

He stepped forward again and leaned well over. The bill of his Stetson came within inches of her forehead. "Jessie." Though stern, his voice had dropped an entire octave and was hushed, like he intended the conversation to only be heard by the two of them. "I want you to leave the corral. Now."

What was it with this man? As the foreman he had been used to ordering people around. But she wasn't one of his hired hands. She was Uncle Roy's niece for crying out loud. She had clout! How could she back down? She looked over his rugged features, trying to determine what was behind his need to boss her around. The longer she refused to obey, the more his eyes flashed with some inexplicable emotion. Something inside her shifted, and realization hit even before he spoke.

"Please," he ground out so quietly she barely heard him.

Of course. He had to save face with his men. How would it look if he backed off and kowtowed to the boss's niece? She had brothers. She knew firsthand about men's egos. Her intention hadn't been to make him look bad.

Now, she couldn't react fast enough. "Yes. Certainly."

"Thank you, Jessie, for your cooperation." He looked relieved, yet a little shook up. She probably needed to leave the corral before he'd relax. He turned, took two steps, and then stopped. Over his shoulder he said, "I've invited someone out here. Veronica. Maybe you can explain to her how a round-up works, since you've been here for the set-up." He crammed his hat farther down on his head and continued his walk toward the other men.

Her jaw dropped open as awareness dawned, with claws. If she'd looked down and seen her heart ripped from her chest, she wouldn't have been surprised. He had invited another woman out here. And he wanted her to *entertain* the hussy.

She whipped around to where she had tied her horse. *Escape!* Ah, but she couldn't. And now the day that had promised to be her best would be added to her long list of worst.

* * *

Johnnie watched Jessica twist around on her boot heels, all indignant-like, and glare at Clint's retreating back. Good for her not to let Clint with his intimidating man-in-charge attitude stampede over her. She stopped and looked over at her little mare. Why would she do that? But then Jess reached back, grabbed part of her ponytail, and a rock landed in Johnnie's stomach. Sure enough. She pulled the lock of hair over her shoulder and wrapped it around that index finger of hers. She remained still and twisted that lock round and round her finger before finally turning to head for the chute. As he figured, sheer despair showed on her face.

What has Clint said to her this time?

During the past few weeks as Johnnie's fondness for Jess grew, his respect for Clint had plummeted, since the man seemed oblivious to Jess's affections. Johnnie liked to stay near, to be on hand when the need arose for soothing Jess's Clint-bruised feelings.

Like he wanted to do now.

"I need to leave the corral, Johnnie," she said in a small voice. "I'll be over by the mare." When she pivoted to leave, he caught her arm and eased her back around to face him.

"What did he say to you, Jess?"

She kept her head turned away, doubling his admiration for her. She always wanted to be strong. It seemed to him, for her to lose composure and show weakness meant someone would have to give of themselves to comfort her. She was too selfless for that.

"Nothing," she said, impressively steady. "He doesn't want me to be in here when you bring in the calves. That's all."

"Jess, look at me." Still holding her upper arm, he gave it a little shake.

She waited a long moment. He knew her. She was busy pushing raw emotions down, steeling herself against his scrutiny. Finally she met his gaze.

"It was more than that. What was it?" He gave her a look he hoped sent the message that he wouldn't let it go.

"He asked me to explain things to Veronica when she gets here, that's all."

"Awww, no! He didn't invite her here!" He released Jessica's arm and threw both his hands in the air. These beauties of Clint's were shallow and snobbish. He would never understand that man. The women he chose were opposites of him in every way but good looks.

Jessica didn't say anything more, but her questioning

gaze pierced him. He didn't know what to say to her that wouldn't cause more hurt. She finally asked, "Why, what about her?"

"She doesn't belong at a round-up." He started to turn away, but the need to forewarn Jess stopped him. Veronica was a devious one. Clint could handle her, but Jess was not in that league. "She'll be a pain to have around. Watch your step."

* * *

Jessica was left standing there, her mind busily assessing Johnnie. A guardedness swept over her, but not from Johnnie's warning. Not entirely, anyway. She squinted through the dust swirled up by his boots. He walked with the same lanky strides as always, straight-backed, chin tucked in that purposeful pose she'd come to associate with him. But he was not the same. He had sounded different. Articulate and absent the usual drawl. That alone gave her pause, made her wonder if he was who he seemed to be. But she didn't want to think about that right now. She was floored by rage and too busy to spend another moment on mysteries with no answers.

And trying to make sense of the bomb Clint had just laid on her.

Jessica settled into a good location, and the round-up began. It was a grandly orchestrated show of muscle power: calves fighting against ropes; horses flexing in tight turns; cowboys' hard bodies pulling, tugging, holding; mother cows bellowing; dirt flying; dogs biting at the heels of the calves to direct them—a dazzling show.

She counted seven cowboys at this round-up, including Clint. Two were on horseback, taking up the majority of the arena. They roped the calf, branded it, then released the legs to pull it by the rope at its neck to the portable squeeze. There, other wranglers de-horned, vaccinated, and castrated the males. A bucket nearby harbored the calf bits and pieces. Two cowboys handled that while two brought in one calf after the other from outside the corral. After de-horning, Clint used pliers to remove the nerve in each hornless, bloody crater before plastering it with salve.

Once each grueling experience concluded, the bewildered calf was released to its mother. Relief flowed through Jessica each time a mother found her poor tortured calf and the bawling ceased. She knew this was a necessary part of cattle ranching—to discourage rustling and keep the calves healthy—yet, it was a bit barbaric to watch.

Still, Jessica had gotten so involved that she found herself standing on the side of the fence leaning in to get a better view. Johnnie and Clint had both taken note of her enthusiasm, each giving a gratifying grin when they happened to catch her eye. She was flattered by the approval of both men.

Then everything changed.

No more than an hour had passed when Jessica heard a truck pull up beside her. She twisted around in time to see someone get out of the passenger's side, flick a hand of dismissal to the driver, and close the door. The truck spewed grit as it made a big loop to head back to the ranch. Jessica had been so caught up in the round-up, she'd forgotten all about the *other* woman who'd be joining them. Her exasperation rushed out of her on one long breath.

As Jessica examined the beautiful, petite blonde, her mouth went dry. The same woman who'd interrupted the dance between her and Clint. The one he had left with.

Today she flaunted a fancy cowgirl outfit—a short jeans skirt with silver beads imbedded in swirls and a white ruffled blouse, boasting her curves. Matching cowgirl boots revealed shapely legs. From under her hat, glorious straight hair flew about her face in the breeze. Her skin was tanned, her make-up and nails perfect. She looked every bit the 'Miss Montana' that she was. What a stunning couple she and Clint made. Jessica grimaced at the traitorous thought.

She stared as Veronica made her way to the fence a couple feet away. She walked right past Jessica as if she were a simple spectator watching her glide down a model's runway. She had eyes for her Clint only as she carefully stepped up on the bottom slat of the corral fence and waved a debutante's gesture, trying to catch his attention.

Though she had stood there for less than a minute, Veronica's face abruptly contorted and she wrinkled her nose. "What is that awful smell?" She gagged slightly but regained control.

Right then Clint's head rose up to offer Jessica another heart-stopping smile. But when he caught sight of Veronica, his smile gaped wide with pure delight. Veronica's grimace shifted to a spectacular, perfect-toothed grin back at him.

Jessica's heart all but wrenched to a stop. Almost in slow motion she watched the exhibition unfold before her. Clint circled an arm above his head. The rest of the cowboys responded with amazing swiftness as the whole operation ceased. He stepped away from the squeeze and hollered, "Take a break," then strolled to the fence to greet Veronica.

Didn't Mabel say Clint might marry? The connection to Mabel's words stopped Jessica's breath. This had to be the one. She thought of closing her eyes against the pain, but like a person watching an execution she couldn't tear her gaze away.

He gave Veronica a quick kiss on the mouth. Instant tears sprang into Jessica's eyes and she turned her face to hide a sniff. Veronica offered a syrupy greeting to Clint. Harder to take were the charming words he gave right back.

While a mixture of disgust and defeat vied for first place in her emotions, Jessica felt a touch to her arm. She blinked back insistent tears, hoping for a graceful recovery before rotating back to Clint. Her gaze lingered on the hand he'd laid on her arm before meeting his eyes. A puzzled furrow twitched at his brow. Jessica blinked away the last of the moisture clouding her vision while Clint studied her. Would he see the pain there? If she lowered her eyes, he would guess. Instead she lifted her chin and forced a smile.

"Jessie, this is Ronnie." Catching Veronica's stern look, he corrected. "Rather, this is *Veronica*. Veronica, this is Jessie."

His words were for Veronica, but his gaze remained fastened to Jessica. "Jessie's been watching a while, plus she helped Johnnie set up, so she can answer any questions for you. Right, Jessie?" He looked confident that she would agree. That irked her a little, since he was right.

"Sure." She gave Veronica a compliant expression with a half-hearted smile.

Before turning back to the squeeze, he patted each girl on a cheek. Jessica reveled in the warmth of his skin on hers, while Veronica, the minute Clint's back was turned, grimaced, and spat out, "Ugh, he stinks. Like this place does. I don't know why he insisted I come to such a vile spectacle. I guess some women fit in." She looked Jessica up and down. "Though it's beyond me the interest true femininity would have out here."

Jessica cringed.

A wave of odors from the arena wafted on a gust of wind, biting her in the nostrils. Jessica breathed through her mouth, waiting for it to pass. Veronica gagged and bent at the waist, gulping in deep drafts of air.

Veronica's comment about true femininity still sizzled in Jessica's brain. Her good sense left her and the need for retaliation took its place. She signaled one of the men and pointed to Johnnie. The man tapped Johnnie on the shoulder and nodded in her direction. The second he looked at her she pointed to one of the buckets and motioned to have him bring it to Veronica.

Johnnie looked confused as he checked out the bent-over Veronica, then studied Jessica. Jessica bit hard on her bottom lip to keep from smiling. Smart man, he immediately picked up on Jessica's intentions and didn't disappoint. Grabbing a partially filled bucket, Johnnie jogged over to the fence, stepped up two rungs swung the bucket over and deposited it under Veronica's bowed head. She took one look in the bucket, lurched upright, and screamed. The ear-piercing sound reverberated throughout the arena.

"What are you trying to do?" she screeched as she scowled at him, then gagged, then hollered in exasperation, then gagged again. She glowered at Johnnie in between her bouts of near retching.

Johnnie ignored her convulsing throat and gave her a riveting blue-eyed look with his most captivating smile. "Just trying to help, beautiful. Looked like you needed to heave."

Smooth . . . very smooth. Jessica fought to keep her lips pressed together.

His task done, Johnnie pivoted to leave, a wry smile twisting his lips.

The episode was so comical Jessica would have whooped with glee if she hadn't worried about disappointing Clint. *The little snit is getting everything she deserves.* But as Veronica looked like she would heave, for real, guilt swelled in Jessica's conscience. She sighed and grabbed a fairly clean towel from the post nearby, dipped it into the drinking water bucket, and hurried back to the beauty's side.

"Let me help," Jessica said. She nudged Veronica in the opposite direction of the smells and mayhem of the corral, walking her out to catch the fresh breeze off the meadow. She plastered the cool, wet cloth on Veronica's forehead. Veronica flinched away, but looked so puny Jessica figured she didn't have the strength to fight back. Jessica wiped at her cheeks and her throat and slid the cloth around the back of her neck.

When the dazed woman took two full breaths of clean mountain air, and seemed to get her bearings, she pierced Jessica with a venomous glare. "You stupid . . ." She yanked the rag from her neck. "You stupid—ridiculous—*tomboy*!"

It wasn't even that great an insult, but coming from Clint's love interest, the comment stung. Jessica wanted nothing more than to dish out more humiliation of her own, but a passage from the Bible, out of Matthew, came to mind. 'Love your neighbor as yourself'." She bit back a retort.

Clint jogged up, as if he were at Veronica's beck and call. The jealousy inside Jessica swirled again, but she pounded it down. Clint's mouth was drawn and his eyes were cold. He took one look at the moisture on Veronica's face, pulled his handkerchief out of his pocket, and handed it over without a word. He strode back to the corral, shaking his head as he went.

Veronica looked shocked, and Jessica flushed. Veronica must have planned on Clint coming to her rescue. She probably even expected him to leave the round-up to take her away from the *vile display* he had demanded she see. It was obvious she didn't expect what he did do. Veronica turned west and stomped off.

Jessica looked skyward, seized again on the verse from Matthew, and sighed. She jogged after Veronica. "Wait. Take my horse."

Veronica swung around like a wildcat. Jessica expected all ten bright pink nails to slash out at her. Instead, she went still in a perfect Miss Montana pose. "Fine, I'll ride," she finally said, as if she'd never heard of a greater imposition in her life.

They walked back to the little mare. Jessica untied the horse and held the reins while she waited for Veronica to awkwardly climb up two rungs of the fence. Once there, rather than turn back to the horse, Veronica looked toward Clint. She waited for him to raise his head, not minding in the least Jessica had to wait and watch as well. When he eventually glanced up he tipped his hat in good-bye, gave Jessica an impassive look, then casually went back to work on the calf in front of him.

Veronica's reaction came in stages. First she stiffened, then her fingers turned white where they gripped the fence. She growled loudly and swiveled toward the horse. Her face was now blood red. Jessica didn't say a word, just held the horse steady as Veronica gave an unsteady jump and almost missed the saddle. The horse sidestepped, startled by the sudden motion, and nearly lost its rider. Veronica clung to the saddle horn so hard, she looked more like a stooped hag rather than a pageant beauty. Finally settled, she ripped the reins out of Jessica's hands and took off like a shot. Bad idea, since the mare would speed up even more when the barn was in sight. Jessica smiled. Oh, to be the fly on the wall for that bone-jarring ride. Still, she prayed the debutante would make it back in one piece. Though, with any luck, she'd be enjoyably disheveled.

During the remainder of the calf marking, Jessica mulled over Clint's reaction to Veronica. He had acted as if he hadn't cared one whit about her. Why would he have invited her if he didn't care if she stayed? Had this been a test? Did he hope she shared his love of the ranch? Maybe he had planned to ask her to marry him out here. Okay, maybe that was a stretch. Still, the blood in Jessica's head seemed to pool in her feet. She didn't understand any of it.

At the end of the round-up exhausted cowboys began to disperse, each heading back to camp. Johnnie came to the fence where Jessica had been attentively watching the whole event, dangled his wrists over the top slat, and gave her a sparkling smile. "It looked like you enjoyed yourself today, young lady."

"Oh, I did." She leaned in conspiratorially and wagged a finger at him. "Loved the part you played with the princess. Didn't know you had it in you."

He grinned. His white teeth flashed through the grime on his face and goatee. "Yeah. Love teasing those self-absorbed types." He lifted a shoulder to wipe the sweat from his face. "You and Mabel'll be busy making Rocky Mountain Oysters tonight. Yum."

"Rocky Mountain *whats*?"

His eyes twinkled with mirth. "You'll find out. Check

in with Mabel when you get back." He glanced to where Jessica had originally tied her horse. "I see you had to let your horse go. Wait and I'll give you a ride back to the ranch."

Clint came up from behind and put a hand to Johnnie's shoulder. "Not necessary. It's my fault she had to give up the gray. I'll take her back. You finish up here."

CHAPTER 9

Jessica's nerves crackled at the thought of riding again with Clint. But when she looked at Johnnie, all she could see were taut features and a bent-knee stance. Like Johnnie had just taken a blow.

She turned back. "Look, Clint—"

Johnnie waved her off. "It's okay, Jess. Go with Clint." He whipped about and strode off. Jessica stared at his retreating back.

"Let's get you back," Clint said curtly. "You'll need time to clean up before you're pressed into duty for the big feast."

With one hand he gripped the top slat and vaulted over the fence with practiced grace. *How does he do that after such a long day?* He took her by an elbow and led her to his horse. "Ready?"

She tried to speak but could only nod.

She planted a boot in the stirrup and hesitated, wondering if her rapidly flagging knees would have the strength. Before she could glance over a shoulder at Clint, his hands were on her rear. He gave her a swift but forceful shove, and nearly sent her over the saddle. He caught and righted her. Once she was seated, he lifted his big body up behind her. His arms encircled her to capture the reins and turn them toward home.

Now alone on the trail, Clint slipped an arm around her waist and tugged her snug against him, as if they made this ride together every day. He lifted her hat and plopped it onto the saddle horn, freeing wisps of hair to fly about in the warm afternoon breeze. She pushed them back from her damp forehead. He leaned in, his chest pressed into her back. His warm breath delighted her ear, sending a shudder down her spine. "How do you manage to smell so good after being out here all day? Forgive how I must smell."

His smell of working male, dirt, and leather was familiar, pleasing, even though he'd been in the relentless heat like everyone else. Curious, since he'd also been the only cowboy who hadn't shed his shirt at some time during the round-up.

Their progress toward camp seemed uncommonly slow. Jessica was thankful for that. She whiffed the pines and heard the stream's melody at a distance. She enjoyed every breathtaking minute with the man she'd come to admire in so many ways. A man who'd wrapped her heart up in a tidy little package to do with as he pleased. And therein lay the problem. What he decided to do with it would affect the rest of her life.

"It seemed you were enjoying yourself today, Jessie. Were you?" Clint asked, jolting her out of her reverie.

Jessica turned her face slightly so he'd be able to hear her. Strands of her hair brushed against his chin, tangling up in his stubble. He didn't remove it. Instead she heard him inhale and felt him tighten his hold at her waist. In that instant she couldn't draw a full breath, and not from his hold. She waited a beat trying to gather the breath needed to speak. "I loved it. I want to help next time."

He remained quiet. She wondered if he didn't like her request or hadn't heard her. Finally she had to ask, "Are you still back there?"

"Oh yeah." His voice rumbled low. "I'm here." He spread his fingers open on her flat stomach and . . . *moved them*? Heat crept up her neck and throat. Soon a rush of blood infused her ears and set them tingling. Her heart began to pound in earnest.

He lifted his Stetson and held it atop his thigh. An instant later hot breath touched the nape of her neck, then the scratch of stubble. She stiffened in surprise.

"Easy now," he murmured against her neck.

It's okay, it's okay. He wasn't actually kissing her skin, as such. He was just rubbing his cheek—and breath— along it. Smelling what was left of her fragrance was all. But then that theory was obliterated when the wet warmth of his mouth slid along where his breath had been, and her mind almost couldn't register the shock of it. All on its own, her head dropped to the side. What was she doing? Giving him better access? A moan of delight escaped her before she could stop it. He groaned in answer.

Why is he doing this? With me? When had she become one of his *women*? And why, since he could choose anyone he wanted?

Yet, she didn't want it to stop. He'd managed to snatch away the reins of her good sense and now had full control. So much so that she feared, were they somewhere other than on a horse, she would be sorely tempted to give away her long guarded virtue. The gelding sidestepped just then, startling her. She sat up straighter and tried to steady her breathing. The touch of his lips started again, at the crook where her neck met her shoulder. *Why? To put another notch in his belt?*

The ranch house appeared as a shimmering black shadow in the distance, a visible period marking the end of her tangled traverse through emotion. They rode in silence to the corral. Clint reined the horse to a stop and pulled back from her. A breeze stirred between them, cooling her overheated body. She couldn't speak, didn't dare move. They remained this way for a long while.

Finally, Clint whispered near her temple, "Okay, little one, we should go."

So affectionate, like they'd been together for years instead of emotional strangers. She didn't know what to think.

Putting his hat back in place, he swung his leg across the horse's backside and dropped down. Reaching up from behind, he grasped her by the middle, and waited for her to swing her leg around as well. He held her against the solid barrier of his chest as her back slipped down his torso. When her feet touched the ground, he tenderly rotated her to face him. Thankfully, his hands held tight to her upper arms since her legs didn't seem to have bones. Their gazes fastened together. That self-controlled, almost cool gaze he usually wore had completely deserted him. His eyes seemed to drink her in, leaving him raw, exposed, and unprotected in a way she'd never seen before. She felt joined to him somehow. *No wonder women love the attention of this man. He's looking at me like I'm* the one.

"Well now, isn't this a fascinating sight," came a harsh feminine voice.

Clint stiffened and dropped his hands from her. He

slowly turned to find Veronica. "How long have you been standing there?"

She folded her arms across her ample chest and her normally beautiful face seemed to distort. "Long enough to see you two sitting on top of each other on that horse!"

Clint's jaw seemed to cramp. He splayed long fingers at his narrow hips and tilted his head toward her. "If you hadn't thrown that childish fit and left the round-up on Jessie's mare, we wouldn't have been on the same horse, now would we?"

He turned back to Jessica, and with a quiet voice said, "You'd better go on in. Mabel will be looking for your help."

Jessica's throat tightened to the point of strangling words she might have said right out of her. Dismissed? So easily? She jerked her chin down, part nod, part recoil, and wobbled toward the main house. At the porch, she glanced over a shoulder. Clint's gaze locked onto hers, stony and desperate at the same time, just like the set of his jaw. Then his focus shifted back to Veronica.

Jessica took the next step more slowly, watching to see what he would do.

Clint confronted Veronica, speaking in a steady voice, emphasizing each word. "If you want to stay, you'll need to be more agreeable. Take that frown off your face, for one. Go to the house and offer your help, for another. If you're there, I'll see you—if you're not, I won't."

He lifted his hat in mock salute, then crammed it back down on his head and struck out for the barn, towing his gelding behind him.

Jessica couldn't believe her ears. He had actually repri-manded Veronica. With Jessica he'd been tender, even intimate. But the minute hope floated up from somewhere deep inside her, she recognized it for what it was—an illusion. *He's the ultimate virile –and don't forget, philandering—man. Of course he would react to a woman pressed so close to him on a horse.*

Away from his touch now, she could think more clearly. Even though he was undoubtedly irritated with Veronica, it was laughable to think Clint had any true interest in an ordinary woman such as herself. She knew better than that.

She squared her shoulders and entered the house in search of Mabel, finding her in the kitchen bent over a bucket of calf parts. "I'm going to clean up," Jessica said, her voice straining. "I'll be back to help you." For once Mabel didn't have a snide remark and nodded her agreement.

As Jessica was fixing to climb the stairs, the front door flung open, and Veronica strutted in, her mouth in a pout. She sped straight to the bottom of the stairs, effectively blocking Jessica's assent.

Jessica bounced back a step and gaped at the brash woman.

"Clint says I need to help, so what can I do?"

Jessica stared into flaring blue eyes that had locked boldly to hers. Anxious to be alone with her thoughts, Jessica pointed toward the kitchen. "Go see Mabel. She's right in there."

Veronica pushed past her and sashayed off to the kitchen.

Alone in her room, Jessica paced back and forth in front of her dresser mirror. She paused once to stare at her reflection. "What does Clint see in that woman?" she whispered to her image. She took a good long look at herself. If desolation had a look, it was there in her eyes. Disgusted at her own feebleness, she paced again.

She couldn't in good conscience claim a reason why it should bother her that Veronica had her hooks in Clint. Except the obvious. She, Jessica Elaine Harper, wanted him. Wanted him soul-deep.

She groaned and scrubbed her hands up her face, sliding fingers into her hairline. She'd been happy today. Clint had noticed. She'd proved to him that this was the life she loved. Grabbing the base of her ponytail she tore off the rubber band, thrust her fingers through her hair, and madly attacked the wind-blown snarls.

Clint would never belong to her. He didn't seem to belong to anyone. She could yearn for him all she wanted and it wouldn't matter. She'd never be in the same league as Veronica. But then, by golly, Veronica wasn't in the same league as her either.

Her fingers snagged in a ball of tangles, and she tugged, trying to loosen them while pain shot into her scalp. If her mom were here, she'd be pushing Jessica to go after the man, offering anything . . . everything. If for no other reason than to show Veronica up. No! She refused to succumb to that pathetic state. She would find a way to manage the evening's celebration, and somehow show Clint that he deserved more. Someone who wasn't just a beautiful shell.

She threw off her soiled clothes and used her new-found determination to fuel her plan. She would dazzle Clint. Not out of spite. Not to somehow show Veronica up. As Jessica. Nothing more. Nothing less.

She bathed, washed and dried her hair, and brushed it until her natural curls shone like liquid amber. She donned a full skirted, light green dress with little cap sleeves, cinched tight to emphasize her small waist. The neckline was scooped, but not too revealing, and the skirt length was discreetly at her calves. She applied her lilac fragrance and only light make-up since her skin already glowed from the day in the sunshine. Though her outfit bespoke the refined femininity of California, she wore cowboy boots—and with them her love of an untamed Montana. This time when she took a quick look in the mirror, she smiled. Yes. Now, at least her self-respect was showing.

She traipsed into the hallway with renewed confidence and bravado, and rounded the corner to head down the stairs. The front door swung open. Clint took one step in, glanced up to where she had paused on the landing, and stopped dead in his tracks. She heard his breath hitch. After that he stood perfectly still.

He was devastating in his white shirt with thin blue stripes tucked into snug jeans. His emerald eyes flashed against his deepened tan. Catching her bottom lip between her teeth, Jessica studied his expression. It was the same one he'd shown her before Veronica's interruption at the barn. When it sank in that this was awe in his eyes—for her—a thrill of pure victory burst through her. His reverent gaze raked over her, from her hair to her booted feet and back up to her eyes. Jessica drank in that gaze as if it was a gentle caress.

She hoped he'd speak first or move, since she seemed incapable. Five heartbeats later—or was it seven—he gave a deep pull on the brim of his Stetson, and in a low voice for her ears only, he said, "Evenin' Jessie. You're prettier than a picture. I'll bet you smell good, too." The last sentence he'd expelled on a breath, as if he had only planned to think it.

Heat rushed into her cheeks as her bluster rushed out. "Hello." She slowly inhaled. "We'll have the meal ready before you know it." She gave him a sweet smile. He was only here early to see about Veronica, she knew that. But it didn't matter. He got a good glimpse of her best, and that pleased her. For now.

* * *

Clint meant to say more. *Speechless.* That never happened to him. Not ever. For some reason all he could do was watch Jessie descend the stairs with her soft skirts woven about her legs and her shiny hair bouncing at her shoulders and chest. How could a woman, able to keep up with day-to-day demands of ranch life, look so incredibly feminine? When she had come down those stairs, and shyly scooted past him, he was astounded at her appeal and his own reaction to it. Her sweet scent still filled his nostrils. He twisted to watch her until she disappeared into the kitchen with his heart hammering up his throat. When was the last time that had happened?

He blinked at the far wall, his mind a wheel spinning in mud. He'd come here for . . . something. The lilac fragrance trapped his mind in neutral. He could float here forever—

The raucous sizzle of pan grease sounded from the kitchen and with it the sharp reminder

that he was famished. There was cooking to be done. And . . .

The gears in his head finally engaged, caught traction, and propelled him back to reality.

Veronica.

His gaze swung toward the living room and caught on the person in the overstuffed chair near the fireplace. His galloping heart slowed to a crawl. Veronica glared at him, her face dead white. She steepled her fingers, calmly, with such exquisite control, in fact, that he could be sure of only one thing. She was livid.

Clint stuffed his hands in his front pockets, his own fury rising like Yellowstone's Old Faithful. Veronica had witnessed the private moment between him and Jessie, and that alone made him want to wrap his fingers around her wrist and drag her to the Packard to take her home.

The princess rose to her feet, a dazzling smile changing her face. Obviously, she'd decided on charm rather than the anger Clint knew resided just under that smile. She strolled up to him and leaned in, blinking twice before she spoke. "Well, now, don't you look grand, cowboy, all cleaned up and smelling so good?"

He peered down into her upturned face and gave her a half-hearted smile. "You seem happier. That's good. Shall we go see if we can help with supper?"

Her countenance fell. When she frowned, she could look downright vile. He'd never noticed that before.

"Do we have to? Why can't you and I just spend some time together?"

He leaned down near her ear so no one else could hear. "We'll be helping in the kitchen, Ronnie. Like I told you earlier."

"Why?" Her voice sounded in a squeal, carrying to the other room. "So you can spend more time with that homely little girl in there?" She flung a hand toward the kitchen.

Heat rushed through Clint's face and seemed to settle like red-hot branding irons on his ear lobes. He reached out, gripped Veronica by the elbow, and shoved her toward the front door. She stumbled once, but he hardly noticed. Flinging the door open, he practically lifted her over the threshold, slamming the door behind him. Once outside, he pushed her around the corner of the house and freed her to face him.

"If you can't watch what you say, I'll take you home right now."

A hard light shone in her eye. She wrapped slender arms around his waist and wriggled her body into him. "Good idea. I can take care of you right away, then."

He hadn't planned on that. He closed his eyes to the feel of her body, momentarily losing all thought. He fought the response she'd known this action would cause. He silently cursed his own weakness. Finally, he took her by the shoulders and pushed her back at arm's length. "You know the big feed's tonight. You staying or not?"

He studied her, watching whole hosts of emotions dance across her face; anger, disbelief . . . finally acceptance. She'd played all of her cards and lost. He awaited her decision.

She straightened, pulling her arms free of him. "Fine, let's go in."

He held her gaze a moment longer. "You're going to watch what you say around Jessie. Are we clear?"

A fire engine red flush shot into her cheeks. "Why do you care so much about her, anyways? Is she taking care of you too, huh big fellow?" As soon as the words were out, her eyes widened and her mouth gaped. She scrambled forward, trying to take hold of him again.

But that one had lit his fuse. He cupped a palm to her cheek and chin to hold her away from him. "You don't know the first thing about her. She's not like that. She's still pure and she'll stay that way until the proper time!"

The words stunned Clint. His own words. He jerked his hand away from Veronica and went still. Why on God's green earth had he said that? Why was he so protective of Jessie? When had he ever felt even remotely possessive of a woman? That sentiment had always seemed foreign to him, until this very moment.

"Listen, Clint." Veronica sighed. "Let's not—"

But the blood had begun to rush so fast past his ears, he didn't hear the rest. He watched

Veronica's lips move—no, flap—without purpose. Like a wall of glass separated him and her. He pushed a hand through that wall and set his fingers on her waist. Her mouth snapped shut. He

guided her numbly back through the front door.

Mabel bustled through the kitchen doorway and lit up at the sight of them. "Oh, there you are. Jessica said you wanted to help."

Veronica glided away from his hand. Her cold glance lashed back at him, but he hardly

felt it. No, his gaze had already settled on Jessie in the far corner, with her crisp white apron,

fetching party dress, and such an expression of concentration as she peeled calf testicles that he

wanted to laugh for the sheer joy of the contradiction she was.

The joy transformed into something harder. "Ronnie, come on over here. We'll get you an apron and you can help Jessie separate the testes."

He watched for her reaction and got what he expected. Immediate disgust clouded her face. "You want *me* to take them out of their wrappers like she's doing?" Her face paled under the film of makeup and ranch dust. "You've got to be kidding!"

A clear description of Veronica came to mind right then—phony. He knew something had been amiss with her, but until now he couldn't quite put his finger on it. He never could abide a woman who faked emotions. Never knew how they really felt about him. Like some big screen actress, making a name for herself. It didn't work with him, and was the main reason he never stayed with them for long. He bit the inside of his cheek, hard, to keep from saying something unkind. When he could trust himself, he said, "I wouldn't kid you. It's got to be done. We'll be frying 'em up for the *big feed*. What did you think it was?"

She glanced into the bucket and went white as a Montana snowstorm. Clint had a bad feeling about this. She started to gag in earnest, so hard he could see her stomach convulse. This, at least, she wasn't faking. Clint ushered her out the back door at a run. Over the back porch railing she let fly. Though he sympathized with her predicament, he knew it was time to cut her loose from his life. Permanently, this time. It wouldn't be easy. He'd have to do it before the guilt slid in and took an irreversible hold. But he'd finally had enough.

CHAPTER 10

Jessica kept the fried oysters coming while the cowboys and Mabel loafed at the dining tables. Mabel seemed to enjoy every minute of laughing over the funny stories of the day. Jessica was pleased since this gave the hard-working cook the time to interact with the men instead of constantly slaving for them.

Funny how a small thread of affection for Mabel had weaved its way into her heart.

Jessica flipped over the current batch of little round morsels then glanced in Veronica's direction. She was still asleep on the couch, where she hadn't moved since her bout of heaving. Jessica's gaze wandered over to Clint. Her heartbeat skipped when she caught him looking at her. A sight to behold, he lounged backwards on a bench seat, his broad back against the table, elbows resting lazily on its surface. His shirtsleeves were folded up to his elbows, and his long legs, locked at the ankles, were stretched out in front of him. A lazy smile lifted one corner of his mouth, softening the angles of his face. His look was . . . endearing.

Tearing her eyes from Clint, she caught Johnnie glancing back and forth between Clint and her, a deep frown evident between his dark brows. A little stab of guilt twisted her stomach. She looked away, toward Mabel. Oh! Mabel had a death-threatening glower on her face. Jessica whipped back to the task at hand, determined not to bring the cook's full ire in her direction.

Before long, Johnnie came to Jessica's side. "Thanks for the great oysters, Jess."

She peered up into his vivid blue eyes, and when she did she caught a glimpse of Clint over Johnnie's shoulder, a patent scowl covering his face. Throwing off her curiosity about that, she gazed back at Johnnie.

"Best ones I've ever wrapped my lips around. I'm heading out. Wanted to say good night."

Jessica wanted to ask if he was all right, but figured he was just tired. She smiled. "You're welcome, Johnnie. Anytime."

Johnnie turned to leave.

"And Johnnie?"

He stopped and glanced over his shoulder. "Thanks for inviting me today. I had fun."

Johnnie stuffed his hat over his dark hair, gave her a short nod, and strode out the back door.

Turning to her task, Jessica scooped out the batch of cooked oysters with her slotted spoon and arranged them on a platter. She started another batch to fry then hurried to serve the cowboys who remained. Stretching between Clint and Pete she set the plate on the table using Clint's shoulder for balance. When she stepped back to go, Clint clamped his hand over hers, trapping her against him. Her breath caught. She looked down at the large, sinewy hand that held hers captive—a dusting of hair on work-roughened knuckles, protruding veins on the back that trailed up his strong, tanned forearm.

He didn't say a word, just waited as his heat penetrated her hand. It seemed like eons later when he looked up at her. The minute those welcoming green eyes beheld her, she was transported to a world all their own.

Mabel disturbed that world when she nudged Clint in the ribs. "Let her go. She's got work to do."

* * *

Clint never took his eyes off Jessie as he loosened his grip and let her hand slide out from under his fingers, his every callous scraping against her soft skin. She stumbled back a step, then twisted away to dash back to the stove.

A heated flush of anger rose up Clint's neck as he crooked his head toward Mabel and tried to keep his voice down. "She *has* been working all evening, Mabel, if you haven't noticed."

"You decided to give up one gal for another, have you? Again?"

"What the heck are you talking about?"

"Seems to me you got one on the couch and are flirtin' with yet another one of my helpers."

Clint dropped his voice to a low rumble near Mabel's ear. "Don't. Worry. About it."

Clint didn't give her a chance to comment more before he was on his feet striding into the kitchen. He wondered why his legs had brought him here. For a moment he stood behind Jessica, examining her, unnoticed. She looked entirely too feminine with her ruffled apron and her skirts hanging loosely at those shapely calves, barely visible between short boots and skirt. So different from the other side of her—the tomboy type she normally portrayed, and which he'd come to know well.

Her shiny hair hung in smooth waves at her upper-back. He edged closer, compelled to weave his fingers through it, when her scent hit his nostrils and he sniffed in the intoxicating bouquet.

She spun around at the sound. "Oh!" Her gaze hit his. "Are you okay?"

"Sure," he answered, not surprised her concern was of him.

Clint hadn't been prepared for what clawed at his heart at the sight of Jessie working at the stove. She looked like a sweet little ranch wife cooking for her man. He found himself wondering what she'd look like dressed in only the apron. He shook his head, baffled by why he would ever go there. He couldn't seem to come to grips with why she affected him like this. He decided to test this growing need. A little more time around her and he was sure to cure himself of the problem.

"Didn't—" His voice caught. He cleared his throat and started again. "Didn't take you long to learn how to cook these things. Yours are far better than Mabel's ever have been." He tried to casually look over her shoulder into the pan. "So, what's your secret?"

She turned her face up to smile at him and something lurched in his stomach. "Do you need to know, when you have me to cook them for you?" As soon as the words were out she stiffened and her smile vanished. Dropping her gaze to the pan she began flipping them with a vengeance.

He smiled and tilted his head so he could watch her sweet face fill with color. She always did spit out every thought on her mind.

Waving a hand in front of her face, she said, "Whew. Warm in here." She glanced at him, his face inches from hers, laughed nervously, then turned back to her task. "You see . . . it's that I don't let them burn." She spoke into the pan. "Mabel doesn't stand here to watch them, is all."

"Well, whatever it is you do, they're great. What can I do to help?"

Her cute little brow quirked. "You would help?"

He nodded.

She smiled, and her eyes twinkled. "Okay. Grab the paper bag."

He looked around, saw a tiny paper bag on the counter and lifted it with his thumb and forefinger. "This little thing?" he said, grinning.

"Yes."

"Okay. Now what?"

"There's already flour, salt and pepper in it, so grab a handful of oysters and drop them in. Close the top. Shake. You'll soon find how simple this is, and then your praise for me will be moot."

When she looked up at him again her face shown with such natural enthusiasm; so joyful, so pure of heart—that he couldn't quite take his eyes off her. Jessica made the first move. Her eyes dropped to the little bag his huge hand dwarfed.

Unsure of himself for the first time in recent history, he advanced to the counter and fumbled with the bag. Trying to hold it open with one hand, he awkwardly scooped up a handful of oysters and dropped them in.

She started to giggle as she watched him wrestle with the task.

"Why are you laughing?" he asked as he frowned in concentration. But soon her contagious laughter brought his own chuckle to the surface.

"It's just something to see woman's work being done by the beautiful foreman—"

"Beautiful?" he interrupted, barking out a laugh. Though called a lot of things pertaining to good looks, he'd never been called that before.

Her head snapped up to look at him. Her eyes were twice their size and her mouth formed an 'O'. "Did I just say what I think I did?"

He couldn't hold back. The expression on her face was so delightful, and so surprised that he exploded into laughter. She flushed all the way to the tips of her ears. Still laughing he gave her a playful bump with his hips—harder than he'd intended. It displaced her. She would have crashed into the counter if he hadn't swung an arm around her waist and hitched her to him.

Time stood still with her secured tightly to his hip. She sucked in a breath, so delicate it sounded more like dove wings than shock. But the shock was all his, because a prickle had begun in his fingertips and flamed all the way to his toes, leaving his bones vibrating to a tune he couldn't hear. Jessica Harper, armed with nothing more than a greasy spatula in one hand and a breaded oyster in the other, had just blown a hole through his armor. He ought to step away. Needed to. But he found himself drawn closer in.

Damp wisps of hair had curled tightly along her temples from the heat of the stove. He followed those little wisps back to her dainty ears. Dropping the little bag on the counter he reached up to lift one damp lock and hook it behind her ear.

He shouldn't have touched. Yet, the need to touch more called to him. He heeded that call and ran his knuckles down the soft skin of her cheek. "So incredibly soft . . ." he said with throaty quietness.

"That's the sweetest thing you've ever said to me," she whispered.

He'd barely heard. "Beautiful, and now sweet?" he whispered back.

The desire to tease her left him as he stroked the pad of his thumb over her full lower lip. She gasped, and his control slipped. If they were alone he'd kiss her. Instead he labored to bring his gaze upward. Her eyes had grown larger and were searching the depths of his. An emotion drove forth. One he'd never had for a woman and refused to name. And that made fury start to take hold.

Don't look at me like that, he tried to convey with his eyes. *I'll regain my sanity when I let loose of you*. Her lips parted again as if to speak, and his sanity sprouted wings. The need to kiss her rose beyond his ability to resist. He caught her face in his palms. Focused on her soft mouth. Lowered his head.

Footsteps. Crossing the great room. Before their lips had brushed, he stopped. Jerked his head up to listen.

Jessica sprang out of his arms and rotated to the stove.

Clint glared at Jessie's back—at the shiny hair curling at her spine, the big apron bow at her middle, her hem tapping at soft legs. He felt empty . . . and hungry . . . and madder than hops she had turned away from him. He wanted to grab her back, complete their mating of lips, find out what that made him feel, then strip those feelings down to bare bone, and take a good hard look. Figure out what was happening to him.

His unwanted visitor stepped into the kitchen, and he turned to greet her.

"I'd like to go now," Veronica said in a firm voice.

Clint's heart sank at that announcement. She was

right. He needed to take her home. First, he needed to say goodbye to Jessie.

When Clint revolved back to Jessie, he found her staring up at him, wide-eyes shimmering. Her lips had flattened. She was confused, and hurting, and if he read her right, a bit exasperated. He felt like a heel, but there was nothing to be done about it.

Forcing the words past his grim mouth, he said, "Thanks for the great meal, Jessie."

* * *

Clint's palms slipped against the Packard's steering wheel as he struggled to make the turn down Veronica's street. He tried to remember the last time, if any, he'd felt like this. His body, weak with exhaustion from the round-up but more so from unwanted emotions, had broken out in an abnormal sweat. He wound the window down, letting the fresh air cool him. The evening breeze hit his face, drying the moisture and bringing back a degree of normalcy.

Though his body relaxed a little, his mind chugged through every occurrence that had happened this day with the two women currently complicating his life. One had elicited guilt while the other had broken through barriers to stroke his heart with something like tender fingers. The incident in the kitchen had shaken him. No doubt about it. Why Jessie? She definitely wasn't his type, so what was the draw? Why in the world did he want to spend time at the stove helping her, watching her cook, laughing with her, teasing her . . . touching her?

A set of headlights blinded him for a moment, rousing

him from his thoughts. Once the car passed, the secluded street only bared light from his own steady beams. They pierced the darkness and bounced off the pavement and tall grasses growing at its edges. He glanced over at Veronica. The full moon sliced a shaft of light through the window and onto her lap. He grimaced when he noticed she twisted a handkerchief around and around her jeweled fingers, her agitation clear. In fact, he figured by her gestures that she had passed angry and had reached seething. Clint remained silent, working on what he would say to her at her door when he dropped her off.

"Penny for your thoughts," she said sweetly, disrupting the quiet and surprising him with her even tone.

He mulled that over. What thoughts would she even want to hear?

Not waiting for an answer, she continued, "We'll be alone, soon. I'm looking forward to . . . you know . . . the touch of your hot breath on my neck." She reached out a slender finger to caress his temple then slid it slowly down to trace the hollows of his ear.

He jerked a bit at her touch. "Yeah. Maybe."

"Maybe?" she squeaked. "Isn't that what we've been waiting for all day?" Disappointment had overrun her voice, making it sound pinched.

He stole another glance. Rolling his eyes he thought about how predictable and sad this game was she played. She'd been exciting once. But whenever she was unhappy—which was more often than not these days—her face contorted into a harsh pout, leaving him to wonder why he ever thought her beautiful.

She scooted close and pressed into his arm.

This is why I don't trust her, he thought with a sigh. What he witnessed in her body language always played out differently when she switched to bold action. She forced her soft body against his arm. A burst of warmth careened through him, but he doused it with a force of will. She caressed his thigh with one hand, and with the other, trailed her fingertip around the back of his ear and down the pulse in his neck as she'd done plenty of times in the past. He usually leaned into that classic maneuver of hers. Tonight he stayed rock steady, eyes pegged to the road, back stiff as a two by four.

They fell into another silence, though she remained relentless with her touch. How had she coaxed him into intimacy so many times before? For the first time he felt compelled to analyze how she'd done that. Sure, he'd been attracted to her beauty and her body, but lately that wasn't what sent him over the edge. What did?

"Whatcha thinking, big guy?" she said with sweet finesse. "Tired?" She palmed the nape of his neck and rubbed. "How's a bath sound? All that smelly hard work you did with those cows. That would ruin a lesser man. But, you . . . well, nothing lessens you."

Clint's stomach knotted. Blatant seduction in its perfect form. That was how she'd reached him, kept him, and almost gotten him to marry her. Besides the guilt that held him to her, she practiced sweetness. Pure and simple sweetness.

Feigned sweetness. This time he could see the act as clearly as if he were watching the local high school drama team. He took a quick look into her eyes. She hated having to do this. It was going against her grain to be sweet to him. Yet here she was, willing to endure what was necessary to gain his undivided attention. He wanted to laugh out loud. How could he have missed this for so long? Then it struck him. He hadn't been looking. If he had married her, it would have been to appease Roy, and fulfill his own debt.

And, no wonder she stayed so jealous of Jessica. Jessie's sweetness bubbled out of her, as natural and appealing as a hot mountain spring.

Clint pulled the Packard up to the front of her small cabin, and trudged around to open her door. Night air cooled the sweat off his brow, relaxing his protesting body a little. When he opened her door, before he could offer her a hand she launched herself into him, stretching her arms around his middle and squeezing. He took a step back under her momentum and stiffened. She only snuggled against his body with more vigor, and stretched to nibble on his throat.

"Come on, handsome. Let's go inside and I'll change into something—ah—more comfy while you make us a drink."

He took his eyes off her to stare into the blackness of the night, hoping to rid himself of the twisting emotions inside; lust, disgust, emptiness. A small gust of wind lifted Veronica's loose hair into his face. Irritated, he heaved a sigh, pulled the blonde wisps off his stubble and looked down at her. "Ronnie, I'm sorry—"

"Listen, Clint, I know I don't look my best right now."

He had to agree. Her mascara had run, her makeup was amuck from the bout of heaving she'd done, and her hair was stringy. Still, before now, if she'd been a little disheveled, it wouldn't have mattered to him. "But I'll go in and clean up. Come on, we can—"

"Ronnie," he broke in, capturing her shoulders and stepping back to force her from him. He hoped his eyes showed compassion, and not exasperation. "I don't see any reason to keep up this façade." He kept his voice smooth. "We were never meant to—"

"It's her, isn't it? That homely little intruder—"

"That's enough, Veronica!" Fury filled his ears with a low roar. He worked his jaw muscles, trying to regain control. "We talked about this. You and I were never meant to be long term. Had some fun for a time, and you knew that going in. It has *nothing* to do with Jessie."

Tears streamed down her face. Was this anger? Regret? "I saw how you looked at her." She wiped at her cheeks with an open palm. "How you almost kissed her. Don't deny it!"

The air evaporated in his lungs, as surely as if he'd just taken a fist to the gut. He stared into her face, guilt taking first seat, confusion a close second. He felt himself laboring for air around a constricting throat. He *had* almost kissed Jessie. And he didn't know why.

He stared upward, focused on the tips of the pine trees swaying in the breeze. Silvery against the moonlit sky. He concentrated on pulling the air in and out of his lungs.

"Come to think of it"—Veronica leveled her gaze at him. —"You haven't been *with* me, really with me, since she showed up!" She searched his face. "Are you even listening to me?"

When he didn't answer her, he was only slightly aware when she sighed audibly. "Come in, Clint," she said, with that sweet voice again.

Clint broke out of his spell, grasped her by the elbow and marched her up the path toward her front door. The small porch light exposed her jumbled blonde mane as she rummaged around in her purse for her keys. He remembered a time when he'd been drawn to the beauty of her hair and the appeal of her well-endowed body. He found himself comparing Veronica to Jessie and shook his head. No *real* comparison. Jessie had substance. All Veronica had to offer was what one could see, and there had been no denying her unequaled attractiveness. Suddenly he felt small and shallow at his obvious knack for bad choices. Yet there remained a reason he chose women like Veronica— arm candy with no entanglements. No risk to the heart.

He camped on that for a split second and wondered if he shouldn't spend one last night with her.

Before the thought had a chance to settle securely in his mind he berated himself. No, he couldn't do it. It wouldn't be right—not for her. And, it would put another fatal gouge in his heart as well. Mostly, these interludes he entered into were purely for physical satisfaction. Never mind that they always left him emotionally distressed. But if he were to indulge tonight the usual distress would be doing a tango with a whole host of other emotions as well. He took a deep breath and let it out as he drove a hand through his hair.

All he felt now was uneasiness and a desperate need to close this chapter of his life.

Veronica unlocked the door and looked up at him. He leaned down and kissed her platonically on the forehead, guiltiness tying him in a knot. "Good-bye, Ronnie. Take care of yourself."

Before he turned toward his car, he saw her face alter. Ignoring what might come next, with long-legged strides he headed for the car.

Behind him he heard the smack of her boot heels bustle after him. "Wait, Clint. Wait!"

He winced at the pleading in her voice, furious at

himself for hurting her. He hated this part. The loving 'em was fine. Leaving 'em was pure torture, for both of them.

He stopped short, and she plowed into the back of him. "Oof! Man. Like I've always said, you're a solid one. Built like an oak." She laughed nervously.

He kept quiet, but turned to face her.

"Now, Clint. You don't really mean this. We've meant too much to each other." She read his face. "I've given you *all* of me. *Everything!* And, what about what I've done for you? You *can't* leave me now. You won't!" She straightened to full height and schooled her features, like he'd seen her do dozens of times before. Leaning in, she snarled, "You owe me." He fisted his hands and closed his eyes a moment, pausing to think. If he were a prayerful man, now would be a good time for it. Clinging females—this one in particular—always made him quick-tempered since they prodded his conscience, and his honor.

"Veronica—"

"Don't you dare say it, Clint."

If evil had a face, he was looking straight into the very depths of it. All the beauty Veronica possessed had fled, and in its place had settled a sort of red haze. For the first time, he noticed how her nose resembled a pig's as it wrinkled up in a vicious sneer. The corners of her mouth had drawn down, creating a jowl-like effect to her cheeks.

"We are *not* through! You'll see." She raised her chin, twisted around and wiggled for all she was worth back to her front door. The door slammed behind her.

Sickened, Clint trudged to his car and dove for cover inside it. Except, he smacked his head against the door frame, cracked his elbow against the steering wheel and caught his foot in the door as he yanked it closed. *Some foxhole this bucket is.* "What's happening to me?" he roared into the empty car, gripping the steering wheel with white-knuckled force.

Jessie.

He barked out a mirthless laugh and shook his head. If anyone could see him now they'd think he'd lost his mind. Maybe he had at that. Consummate lady's man, Clint Wilkins, was now fighting a battle with his heart over a woman who shouldn't even be in the running. Ha! The joke was truly on him.

He finally got a grip on his thoughts and headed for the local bar—whatever it took to drown these new feelings and dodge the lasso that kept trying to ensnare his heart.

* * *

Clint's vision blurred. He blinked several times, but the massive wood sign ahead continued to waver and furl like a flag in the breeze. He squinted. Yep, the bar-H brand was there, front and center, fired into the wood plank years ago by his own hands. The Harper Ranch sign. What a day that had been, when he'd displayed it in all its glory to a proud and grateful Roy Harper. He'd been twenty-one then, and eager to please.

Funny. If someone had told him back then that in ten years he would be foreman of this large spread and nothing else to show for his life, he would have called them a liar. He'd had goals and dreams once upon a time. Now look at him. "You've really come a long way, Wilkins. A real fete, driving home drunk after breaking it off with the dream girl of every cowpoke in Montana. Heck, probably in the surrounding states as well."

He snorted, then laughed, losing control of the Packard for a moment as it fishtailed on the dirt road. "Whoa, Besss . . . ie."

Alert enough not to wake the whole camp at two in the morning, Clint drove past the ranch house at five miles per hour. He managed to park the great old car, tumble out, and click the door shut as softly as possible. He swayed a bit before he let loose of the door handle. Dang, he couldn't remember the last time he'd gotten drunk. Oh he drank, partied, caroused, but get drunk? No. It was hard on the body and usually got a person into trouble. He'd done that plenty of times in his youth. Not now. That was something he had curbed a long time ago. So what was his excuse now?

He glanced up at Jessie's room on the second story and froze. She stood by the open window in her white nightgown with hands clasped to the sill. Her long hair fanned out in the gentle breeze. The moon had cast an angelic halo about her, making his breath catch in his throat. He placed a hand against the cold metal of the car, trying to still his dizziness—from the booze or from her appearance, he'd never know for sure.

He stared at her image a long time, not able to move. *She's really something*. The second the words entered his conscious mind, he halted all thought. She was something all right. Ever since she took that first step onto this ranch, his well-ordered life had plowed its hooves into the ground and halted. And like a horse fidgeting against the bit, his life waited for him to let loose of the reins and get back to normal. So, why *hadn't* he done that?

Before he could get his fill of the sight of her, she disappeared from view, leaving him bereft and more confused than ever. A reaction this powerful could only be explained one way. A way that would take him down a path he had vowed never to take. He dropped his head before the spinning overwhelmed him.

It was the drink, that's all. Just the drink.

CHAPTER 11

Clint was bone-deep bushed, and hung over. He ambled over to the horse trough, threw his hat off, and plunged his head in, shoulder deep. He never did that. In fact, he usually got after the cowhands if he caught them doing such a thing when a barrel of rain water sat just three yards away. Today it felt right—matched his grungy mood. He straightened and shook his head, the water sluicing down his face and onto his shirt. He glanced up. The too-bright sunshine blinded him for a split second, intensifying his headache. Growling, he raked his fingers through his soaked hair and grabbed his hat off the ground, not bothering to dust it off before sticking it to his wet head. He sauntered to the house, hoping he was late enough to have missed Jessie. The innocent daily prods she delivered to his rusty heart had to stop, before he did something he'd regret.

He banged through the back door. His jeans were dirt-streaked from the day's toil. The work shirt was wet to his shoulders. Dirty water dribbled down his neck. He knew he looked like something the bull drug through a mud hole, but he didn't care.

Taking a step inside, he tried to stand on rigid legs but swayed a bit. Man, he was plain worn down. He tried to will himself not to look toward the kitchen, but failed. His heart skipped. There she was—*Jessie*—leaning against the kitchen counter, dishtowel in hand, her gaze bouncing from one cowboy to the next as she laughed over something one of them had said. A real need to snap every one of those toying men in half reared up. And Jessie—he wanted to shake her free of that darned relaxed attitude, as if nothing was amiss.

He kept his gaze away from her as he ambled across the wood floor toward the stove. The men eyed him with concern. Some glanced at his wet shoulders, others the hat he never wore indoors. Let them wonder.

"Here," Mabel said, eying him warily, knowing better than to take him on right now. She shoved an empty bowl in his hand and gestured to the big pot on the stove. He silently lifted the lid and ladled out stew. Without preamble he took a seat and dug into the hot meal.

"Hey, Wilkins," one of the men shouted from the farthest table. "You been kinda moody lately. Need to get your antlers trimmed? You must be long overdue."

The room exploded into a cacophony of laughter. Clint ignored them, kept his head down, and continued shoveling in the food.

"Yeah," the voice of Brad Turner. "The way you ogle the boss's niece, why don't ya just—"

Clint launched out of his seat, so fast his chair smashed into another and both went sailing into a wall. In two swift strides Clint stood toe-to-toe with Turner, fastened a hand to the cowpoke's neck, and slammed him to the floor with one effortless heave.

Two cowboys jumped in and peeled Clint's hands off, wrestling him to his feet. Determined to rearrange Turner's face, Clint strained forward again. He labored against the men, dwarfing them in size—a wild beast against human constraints.

He darted a furtive glance at Jessie. Her eyes were moon-sized, and registered awe. But it was the panic he saw there as well that sapped the fury right out of him. He yanked his arms out of their bonds, let them hang to his sides.

Turner coughed, his hands reaching up to his throat. "Are you *crazy*?" he rasped. "What's she to you anyway?"

Clint didn't know the answer to that. No time to think, he lurched forward. "She's nothing to me! Just none of *your* stinkin' business." Clint loomed over the man. The rest of the crowd quieted like crickets to an intruder. "I've had enough of you! You're fired!" he roared. He thrust a finger toward the door. "Get your gear and get off the ranch!"

"What the—" Turner staggered to his feet, retrieved his upended hat from the floor, and probed each man with a fierce gaze. "Fine. I wouldn't stay if ya paid me double. Your *almighty* foreman is nuts! And so are all of you if you stay on here!" He slapped his hat across his leg and stuffed it on his head.

"Randy, Darrell," Brad yelled. Two of the cowboys escorted the man out the back door. His two cohorts followed meekly behind.

Clint stood in place, vibrating with surplus rage. He'd never been this out of control, no matter what the circumstances. It had to be the hunger or the fatigue. He shook his head, trying to loosen his good sense. He didn't understand himself anymore.

Pete stepped up to him and brushed at his shirt as if that would calm him. "Why don't you go see Veronica?"

Clint shot a brutal glower at him.

Pete looked chided but confused. "No Veronica?"

"Not anymore." With that Clint stomped to the back door, and lit out into the night.

* * *

Clint slipped quietly through the back door, conscious of the late hour. Roy sat at one of the rough-hewn tables with his back to the door, staring down at playing cards laid out in front of him. It looked like he was playing solitaire. That surprised Clint. Roy had lectured many a time that Poker was the only card game worth wasting time on.

Roy rubbed a knuckle to his forehead and heaved a breath. He glanced up at the clock, half past ten, then started to shuffle. Apparently, he hadn't heard Clint come in. Clint rocked back on his heels. "You needed me?"

Roy whirled in his seat. "Yeah. Come in, son. Grab some coffee and sit down."

Clint closed the door, hung his hat, and made his way to the cupboard. It had been a long, unproductive day, and he still bore the effects of the hangover. He searched for his usual chipped mug, filled it, and took a seat at the table across from Roy.

Clint poured sugar in the cup and stirred. "What's up? Is this about Turner?"

"Thought you didn't use sugar."

"Sometimes."

"Nope. It was time for Brad Turner to find a new home. You should have fired him long ago. And his cronies."

"What then?"

"We'll wait for Jessica."

Clint popped his head up, his pulse speeding. What in the world was Roy up to now? He narrowed his eyes. "What's this all about, Roy?"

The blood seemed to drain from Roy's face.

The door opened just then, saving Roy from having to answer. Jessica entered, glanced at Clint, then shot Roy a perplexed look. She turned to close the door. It clicked closed, but she didn't move—looked to have stuck in place. Ah, so, Jessie was suspicious of this late night chat as well. She straightened her shoulders and turned with a smile in place. Didn't look like much of one. Clint knew how she felt.

She took a couple of steps in. "You wanted to see me?"

"Where were you?" Roy asked.

"Taking a walk by the stream."

"It's dangerous there at night," Clint snapped, keeping his eyes pinned to his cup.

"Grab some coffee and come sit with us," Roy said.

Jessie looked like she wanted to do anything but. In the end, she meandered to the table, cup in hand, and sat at the end of Clint's bench. Her cheeks were pleasingly pink from the night air, matching the color of the sweatshirt she'd pulled low over her jeans.

"I want you two to go up to Mary's in the morning."

Clint ground his back teeth.

Jessica shifted, looking uncomfortable. "Who's Mary?"

Roy looked at Clint. He glared back. He wasn't going to help Roy explain Mary. He wanted to know the reason for this sudden need to send him and Jessica on a trip together.

"I've known Mary for years. When she got married I let her and her husband live in one of my cabins." He nodded his head to the east. "'Bout half day's ride up the mountain. After her husband died, I encouraged her to stay on. Wanted her to move in closer, but she wouldn't have it. The cabin's located in a thick area of forest and there's no phone. No communication of any kind. So we take her supplies and check on her every other week."

"You'll be taking her supplies, and Clint, you'll do your fix-its like usual. Plan on being gone three days."

Jessie's brows rose slightly.

"Mary can teach you how to quilt," Roy went on. "She made the quilt on your bed." Roy looked a little sheepish. He cleared his throat. "You'd best get packed tonight. I'll make sure the wagon's ready by the time you're done with breakfast."

Clint was ready to explode. Roy eyed him gingerly then looked to Jessie. "Jess. It can be warm during the day but it gets cold up there at night, so take a warm jacket." He heaved a sigh. "Any questions?"

Clint could hear his own pulse thud.

"Anything you want us to tell Mary, for you?" Jessie finally asked.

"No. Make sure she's okay is all."

Roy ran his finger around the deck of cards. "Clint?"

"What!"

The older man grimaced. He met Clint's stare. "It's time Jess met Mary."

"Roy—"

"Jess," Roy said, cutting Clint off but not taking his eyes off him. "Go get packed and get to bed, honey. Tomorrow'll be a long day."

She looked from Roy to Clint and back again. "Sure." She rose, kissed Roy on the cheek, and scooted up the stairs. Clint watched until she was out of sight. Then he looked down into his mug for a long while as if the liquid would calm his rising fury.

When he raised his chin and caught Roy's gaze, Roy looked unmistakably uneasy, yet formidable all the same.

Clint stared straight through him. Roy swallowed. Running a hand down his face, Clint huffed a sigh. "Why are you doing this, Roy?" He tried to rein in this inexplicable rage that seemed to be building. "I know you were upset with my breaking it off with Veronica. This your idea of *fixing me up?*"

Roy looked legitimately shocked. "No. I—shoot, Jess's not for you. She's not even your type."

Clint couldn't control the frown that statement created. Vexing protectiveness crowded in with his anger and left him scowling outright.

Roy studied him for five heartbeats. "Well, I'll be . . ."

"What the hell is that supposed to mean?" Clint barked, rising to his feet.

"Nothin'. Nothin' at all."

"You're right. She's not for me. You just try and remember that, old man." Clint glared down into Roy's eyes. "I'm turning in. Anything else you need before I do?"

Roy hesitated. "Nope. See ya in the morning, son. Sleep well."

Clint ripped his hat off the hook, nearly yanking it out of the wall, and slammed out the back door.

CHAPTER 12

Tuesday morning began in genuine harmony. The breakfast had gone well. The cowboys had acted cordially. The summer sky was wide and blue, the sun shining. The wagon was loaded and ready for Clint and Jessica's trip. The only sign of unrest was in Jessica's stomach. The breakfast—what little she ate of it—had not set well. Now, her nervous tension was at an all-time high. She prayed away any impending hiccups.

Jessica stepped out the front door to make her way to the wagon. She spotted Clint coming from the bunkhouse, toting a large knapsack on his back. His long strides ate up the width of the road, and he was at the wagon in a few seconds flat. He was a sight to behold. Dressed in an all green shirt—the same shade as his eyes—worn blue-jeans and the familiar black Stetson pulled low over his forehead, he looked cowboy-perfect. So different from her own ordinary looks and attire of tawny colored wranglers and a flamingo-pink blouse.

He threw the sack in behind the wooden seat and in one swift move was up and onto it. He took up the majority of the bench. She stared up at him, and her legs flagged. How in the world was she supposed to fit up there, too?

"Morning, Jessie. Ready?" Clint said in his rich, vibrant voice, sounding immensely more relaxed than he'd seemed to be in the last few days.

She nodded. Walt came out of nowhere and wrapped a bony hand around her elbow. He helped her step up and didn't release her arm until she was settled on the seat. "You kids have a safe trip, ya hear. Clint, you take good care 'o this here girl," Walt said, pointing a gnarled finger in Clint's direction. "She's a special one, dear boy, if ya know what I mean."

Clint chuckled. "Don't you worry, Walt. She'll be safe with me."

Already in second gear, her heart leapt into third. *Does that mean he'll keep me safe, or won't ravish me?* She almost laughed out loud over her own bad joke. Silencing her mind of foolish thoughts, she sifted through ideas for something simple to talk about.

Clint loosened the reins from the brake handle and, with gloved hands, adeptly wove them through his fingers. He flicked his wrists. The horses lunged forward until the reins snapped taut, and the wagon leaped. Jessica was glued to the far edge, as far from Clint as possible, when he whipped the reins again to speed up the horses. Forcing herself to breathe deeply, Jessica finally began to feel somewhat normal.

When at last they began their ascent up the narrow road, Clint slanted a glance at her. He leaned forward slightly to peer at her bowed face. She knew she looked ridiculous with her rear-end pressed into the corner of the wooden seat and her death grip on its rim.

"Do you want to ride *outside* the wagon, Miss Harper?"

She turned her head toward him. He grinned, the first one she'd seen on him in a long while. The vision melted her clear down to her bones.

"Very funny, *Mr. Wilkins.*"

What could she tell him? No. I'm just trying not to touch you and faint away from a racing heart? "I-I was hanging on in case we hit a bump or something. I wouldn't want to fall off so you would have to save me, now would I?"

His smile dissolved, and the same underlying hostility he'd carried for days shown through. "Seriously, Jessie. Move over."

She was not capable of even trying, her muscles had arrested. With a huff, he stretched over, wrapped long fingers about her middle and tugged her close.

A furnace-blast of heat swept through her. *I'm never going to survive this trip.* "Why did you do that?" she asked in a small voice.

"Because I *don't* want to have to save you. One good bump and you'll fly right off this thing. Believe me. I've seen it happen, more than once."

"Oh." A pause. "Okay." Of course that's what he'd think. He was here to keep her safe, by Uncle Roy's request. That was all.

The wagon seemed to shift and vibrate over every little rut in the road, and why on earth did they secure these stupid seats up so high and with no real hand holds, anyway? She looked around frantically trying to find something, *anything*, to hang on to. "What is there to hold onto when we hit bumps?" she said with no real thought.

In the next instant the wagon dipped into a rut. With a quivering creak, it lurched back onto the graded road and nearly tossed Jessica out of the seat. She clung to the first thing her hand hit: Clint's knee. It was hard, like pure bone. So wide, her fingers almost couldn't grasp it.

"I think you've found it. You've got quite a grip there for such a little thing." His laugh rumbled low. "And you can leave your hand right there. I can't keep you from falling off if you're not close enough." She couldn't have released her fingers if she'd tried. They seemed to have stuck there.

Though she kept her eyes on the road, she sensed his scrutiny. All at once feeling like a city slicker instead of a born and raised farm girl, she flushed and shot him a glance. He looked as if he were trying to decipher the blush. "You okay now, little one?" he asked.

She closed her eyes, steadied her thoughts and then her voice. "How about we talk about you for a change?" Warming to the idea she gulped in some air and plunged in. "Where did you grow up?"

Jessica watched his grin vanish. After too long a lapse he said, "I was born in Cheyenne, Wyoming." A very long pause, then, "Now, it's your turn. Tell me about California."

"Oh, no you don't," she teased. "That's hardly fair. You need to tell me more about *your* upbringing first . . . your mom and dad. Do you have siblings?"

Jessica was suddenly intrigued, thinking she might find out more about the mysteries of this man. And maybe more about the life he had left behind. Though on the surface Clint seemed quite able to handle anything life threw at him, there were rare times—like this—when she glimpsed his pain, in the sadness of his eyes, in the slump of his shoulders. She knew the Lord could help him with anything that plagued his soul. She wanted to help.

"No, I don't," he said gruffly, his dark brows dropping into a scowl.

Jessica could see distress on his face. His strong jaw was clenched, his lips pressed tight. "You don't have siblings?"

"No, I mean I don't have to tell you more."

The pain seemed to hang on his countenance like a shield of armor—heavy with the weight of his wounds, and impenetrable. Her heart went out to him. "What is it, Clint?" She kept her voice soft. Remembering her hand still rested on his knee, she gave it a delicate squeeze. "What happened in your childhood to hurt you so?"

He looked shocked, then contemplative, but through it all his gaze never once left the road. When she thought he didn't plan to answer, he finally said, "That was a long time ago. Like I told you before, it's better left in the past."

No. In this he was wrong. What Jessica saw on his face put her in mind of an injured man, his lifeblood draining out. Would she leave him to try to survive on his own? Absolutely not. She was compelled to help.

"Is what happened in your past what has made you so angry with God?" Why was finding out about his past such a pressing need for her? Did she think it would help her to understand the man? To justify his philandering nature somehow?

His head snapped over to look at her. "Who told you I was mad at God?"

She saw the instant rage in his eyes. Over her knowing he was mad at God, or her exposing his anger, she didn't know. "Well . . ." She was never any good at lying, so she didn't. "Walt told me—now, don't do that. Don't be mad at him. I noticed the way you reacted to a comment I made to you about God painting the sunrise, so I asked Walt about it. That's all."

The muscles in his cheek twitched again and she suspected he was trying hard to hold his temper. "So, if Walt's so smart—" His tone was clipped, harsh. "What did he tell you?"

"He said you had a pretty tough life." Had she cornered him? By the look on his face, she had. "You know, Clint, rather than being angry with God, He can help you."

His scowl deepened. Okay. So, she had crossed the line.

Clint fumed in silence for a long while. Jessica didn't attempt to say any more. The last thing she wanted to do was push him away from God entirely.

Truth was, her own attraction to Clint was getting in her way. That made her no different from Mabel's past helpers. They'd all had their own agendas concerning Clint. Now, she was clearly one of them. *Please help me to be a better advocate for You, Lord.*

Time clicked on with Clint still mute as they rose in altitude up the mountain pass.

She breathed in the fresh, cool air and began taking note of the scenery. She could see now why a car couldn't be taken up this road, as it narrowed with ever deeper ruts. The strain on the wagon and horses grew with each passing mile. But the beauty was indescribable. Fragrant pine trees crowded in on either side, as thick as if God had personally plunged handfuls of them into the ground. And every now and then they gave way to glorious meadows dappled with wildflowers. Scenic and serene.

As they came around a bend in the road the horses spooked sideways, and shook their bulky heads. Jessica shot a frightened glance at Clint—saw the concern on his face.

"Slide over and hang on to me, Jessie. We've got trouble." Clint worked to control the steeds. "They smell something."

Jessica slid into Clint and stretched her arms around his torso, barely able to clasp her hands on the other side. His abdomen tensed in anticipation of what was to come, though his tone was surprisingly even. "Bessie. Bonnie. Settle down now, girls."

The chestnut cocked an ear back to catch his voice, but instead of calming, she reared as high as the harness allowed. Bonnie—the more stable of the two—hopped, her ears pinned back and tail swishing. Jessica's throat went dry. Each bump and tug on the harness rocked the entire wagon—and riled the horses more. Bonnie finally caught the edginess, and off they ran.

Jessica clung to Clint. She tried to stay out of the way of his arms while he tugged back on the reins. He continued his call to the horses, but they were having none of it. They just kept pulling harder uphill. Clint jammed his feet against the floorboards to lock himself—and Jessica—into the seat.

The wagon slammed into a pothole. Jessica lost her grip on Clint. She scrambled to clasp her hands back together. "Lord, help us." Even with the horses bolting straight up the hill, Clint managed to keep them on the road.

Under the tremendous strain the wagon gave way with an ear splitting crack and pitched to one side. Jessica's hands tore away from Clint and she squealed his name. She bounced at the seat's edge. Clint caught her by the waist and dragged her back to his side. She clawed at his chest to get another stronghold. But, she needn't have worried. Clint's grip on her was rock hard.

The wagon dragged along the ground on its axle, the right front wheel missing. Clint looped his left arm twice about the reins, his right foot skidded along the wooden floorboards until his boot wedged into a crevice at the sideboard. Leaning to the left with all his weight, his straight leg held them in place. His fingers were digging into her side to keep hold.

The horses snorted and huffed. They were tiring, thank goodness. "Whoa, girls. Whoa. Come on Bessie, Bonnie, slow down, girls," Clint chanted.

Finally, after what seemed an endless time, the animals slowed and came to a halt. They tossed agitated glances over their shoulders, eyes flashing, nostrils flaring. Their harnesses jingled with the pitch of their heads.

"Gotta get you out," Clint barked. He unwound his arm, stepped across Jessica, and jumped off. He turned back to extend his arms to her. She fell into him, trembling and sick from fear. He scanned the area and pointed to a nearby log. Using the last of her strength she staggered over and dropped hard on the unyielding wood, wincing in pain.

Clint went to the horses. He ran an open hand down their necks and lathered sides—checked where the reins had dug into their hides and grimaced. Jessica observed every tender touch he gave the animals, heard every soothing word. It was a marvel to her, because Clint's own arm was a mass of torn shirt fabric and dripping blood. No wonder Uncle Roy had trusted him and him alone for this journey. Who else could have assured her safety when his own life had been threatened?

Clint assessed the damage to the wagon, then un-harnessed the horses. He grabbed a gunny sack, water jug, and bucket from behind the seat and walked the animals into the woods. He must have rubbed them down since it was a while before he returned.

Jessica breathed a sigh of relief when he came into view. "It's going to take me some time to repair this wagon," he said. "We'll have to hole up here for the night while I do repairs."

He looked exhausted, pale and drawn. He glanced around as if to evaluate their predicament. "The thing that concerns me is the wildlife that will smell the food in here." He patted the side. Jessica wasn't sure if he was actually talking to her or making plans aloud. "We'll be back off the road ourselves, but we'll have to build a big fire and I'll stand guard through the night."

Clint glanced up and Jessica followed his gaze. The puffy white clouds that hung in the sky all morning had turned dark gray at their centers and seemed to be piling up on each other.

Jessica stiffened. What was worrying him, the weather, or worse? "What scared the horses, Clint?"

Grim, he caught and held her gaze. She wondered by his expression if he thought he'd said too much already. He glanced away. "They smelled something. A predator of some kind. They're still agitated even though the run wore them out pretty good. Should settle down soon, though."

She waited for him to explain. When he finally looked back, he studied her for a beat, seeing the question in her eyes. He blew out a long breath and turned back to the wagon to shuffle through things. "Probably a grizzly or mountain cat."

How could he be so calm? Was he doing that for her sake? "Which one, do you think?" She hated that her voice wobbled. He didn't look at her. If he had, he would have seen the sheer terror in her eyes.

"I have my saddle rifle and plenty of ammunition," he said, ignoring her question. He rummaged until he could trap the rifle and a box of cartridges under his bad arm.

"Have you shot a grizzly before?" She sounded wimpy, even to her own ears, but she didn't care. "I thought I'd read where they're the kind of bear that will actually seek out humans to do them harm. Is that true?" She was talking too fast. Adrenaline still raced through her veins and now seemed to be log jamming inside her.

The whole time she babbled, he gathered supplies. He stopped, peered down at her from under his hat. "I thought your Bible tells you not to borrow trouble, Jessie. I heard you praying. Don't you believe your God will protect you?"

The rebuke caught her off guard. At first anger surged through her. Then a flush of embarrassment. An unbeliever shouldn't have to remind a believer that God was her protector. This was a perfect example of how she fell so short of God's expectations, on a regular basis. Clint didn't know how she struggled with her own faith and she was glad for that, anyway. Otherwise, what good would she be to him?

What had he asked? "You're right. He will protect me." She was thinking clearer now. "But, He's not just my God, Clint. He'll protect you too. In fact, I believe He protected us just now."

"Is that right?" Frosty emerald eyes stared at her. "I thought that was me."

"Well, true. You *were* pretty amazing," she said, then blushed at actually saying those words . . . again. His coolness seemed to thaw as a hint of a smile formed. Moving closer, he handed her a couple of items. "Here, take these to the camp." He nodded his head. "Through there. I'll bring this pile. Then I've got to go find the wagon wheel."

They walked toward the horses in silence. It was still a few hours before dark, but Clint detailed what Jessica could do to set up camp and get ready for the dangers of night.

Clint shed bedrolls, a canteen, food, and cooking equipment, but kept the rifle. He turned to go after the wheel, but Jessica stopped him, touching a hand lightly to his injured arm. "We have bandages and alcohol in the wagon. We need to take care of this arm. Hold on. Let me look."

Clint let her peek through the opening in his sleeve. "In all the excitement I forgot about it," he said. "Well, what d'ya think, Doc? Will I live?"

Was he trying to lessen the worry with his teasing words? Jessica tried not to let their situation trouble her. She took hold of the torn sleeve and ripped it farther up his arm. The reins had yanked a portion of his skin wide open. He had a long gash, below the elbow, and it was bleeding pretty steadily. Jessica tried to be delicate in her ministrations, though she knew it must be throbbing with pain by now. Carefully, she parted the wound and found a small piece of leather stuck in the muscle. With slow movements, she carefully picked the piece out of the seepage. When the object had been purged, blood gushed even harder.

"Oh, Clint! You're losing a lot of blood. I wish we could stitch it, but we'll need to at least wrap it." Without thought, she reached up to his neck and began untying the knot of his handkerchief. He jerked in surprise, but then went still while she accomplished the task and slid it from his neck. She pulled the wound together, tied the cloth around his arm and knotted it.

Jessica looked up into Clint's eyes, concerned. "We need to clean this out and bandage it better. We should do that before you try to fix the wheel. Come on. Let's go find the first aid kit."

His wound was pretty bad, and Jessica was concerned about his loss of blood. As they walked back to the wagon, she tried to think of a way to convince Clint to let her help him with the wheel. "Listen, Clint. I don't have a weapon, and, well, not to be a fraidy-cat or anything, but shouldn't I go with you to get the wheel after you're all patched up?"

The smile that never failed to weaken her knees did a slow spread across his face. She stumbled. He caught her elbow for a couple of steps as if it was an everyday occurrence to catch enamored females. "A fraidy-cat you say?"

She returned his smile. "Haven't you ever heard that saying before?"

"Can't say as I have. Where'd it come from?"

Jessica thought for a moment. "Maybe it came from a cat's inability to stand up to a dog twice its size. Now, I'm thinking about having to stand up to a grizzly *many* times my size." Peering up at him out of the corner of her eye, she scrunched up her face in a sorry-to-be-so-silly look and shrugged.

He laughed outright.

There was that laugh she loved, and when he smiled it accented the creases in his cheeks and glorious white teeth. She gazed up to admire the smile that was such a rarity these days.

"You can come with me. Maybe I'll need your help."

When they reached the wagon, Jessica went to where the medical supplies were packed, but Clint veered away and took off toward the lost wheel.

"Wait. What are you—Clint!" she hollered after him. "We need to fix your arm . . ." Jessica let the sentence drop, since he and those long strides were already progressing down the road at a pretty good clip. She hustled after him, doing her level best to catch up.

Clint glanced up at the gathering clouds again, but just kept walking.

"Stop! You need to let me treat your—oh, phooey." Clint ignored her appeal, like she wasn't even talking. *Aggravating man!* Fine, since she wasn't dissuading him, she would change the subject to the *other* problem at hand.

She caught up to him, yet still had to skip a step here and there to keep up. "You never did answer me about whether you've shot a grizzly before."

He inhaled a big breath and blew it out through puffed cheeks. "Don't like to, but they get after the cattle, and sometimes the horses, so it's necessary."

His gaze rotated between the road ahead and occasional glances at the sky. Did he think it would rain, make the roads muddy, leave them to have to sleep in a downpour? Worried about lightning? *What?*

"Recently, a rogue grizzly's gotten a vile taste for blood."

A glance at him told Jessica *this* was what Clint was worried about. They were silent for a few dozen paces.

He crooked his head in her direction, must have seen her unease. "Don't worry, little one. I'll keep you safe."

Her heart skipped at the nickname. And the thought hit her. Grizzly or no grizzly, she would love to keep this man up here all to herself—for life. And, since Veronica was no longer in the picture, hope sprouted.

Coming around a bend in the road, they spotted the wagon wheel, thankfully still in one piece. Clint headed toward it.

"Wait. You're going to need help."

Once again Clint ignored her, but shoved the rifle in her arms. He bent, lifted the wheel with a grunt, and began rolling it back up the road. Shrugging, she resettled the weapon under one arm, cradled in her elbow, and let the barrel tilt toward the ground.

He glanced at her. "You've carried a rifle a time or two."

"And I've shot them a time or two," she copied with a grin. "Yours looks to be a Winchester lever action 30/30."

Clint's eyebrows shot up. "Well, now, I'm impressed. How'd you know that?"

She smiled. "My dad has one like it, so I'm cheating a little."

The grunts from his efforts with the wheel filled the silence between them.

"So, do you shoot?" he asked in a gust of a pant.

"Sure. I have a little Remington .22 rifle, and shot-guns too."

He shot her a look of admiration. "Tell me. What do *you* use a shotgun for?"

Guns were one of her favorite subjects. True pleasure filled her at this topic. Before she could answer, a short, breathless chuckle escaped his mouth at her sudden joy.

"Mostly on our jack rabbit hunts," she started. "We begin at one end of the ranch, all spread out to either side, then walk the length of it, staying even with each other as we cross. Whenever a jack rabbit jumps out, and starts running, whoever's closest shoots it. It takes a few hours, but we love it."

"No kidding. Don't know *any* women who would do that."

"I know." She grimaced. "Pretty *manly* of me, huh?"

He pushed for several strides without a word, then said in a serious tone, "That's the last thing I'd think of you."

She sucked in a quick breath, thrilled he had said that, until she remembered he was a charmer by nature. It would behoove her to remember that.

Clint gave a few more hefty pushes on the wheel. "Do you ride much, other than double—with a man?" He was smiling when she looked over at him. A rivulet of sweat dripped from his forehead to his jaw and off onto his shirt.

She smiled, thinking of those two occasions with him. "I love to ride. I have a little pinto pony at home."

"Yeah? We'll have to go riding sometime." He grunted. "On two separate horses." Totally out of breath now, Clint rolled the wheel up and leaned it against the wagon. He tugged off his hat, wiped the sweat from his face and leaned back against the frame. "Whew, what a work out," he panted. "I'll take a breather . . . then get to work fixing it."

"Where's the water jug, Clint? I'll get some for you."

"Under the seat."

Jessica found the container and thrust it at him. He didn't take it. Instead his eyes joined hers and dimmed to a smoky jade. Her arm holding the jug began to quiver from the extra weight. *What is he up to now? Why doesn't he take it?* She tried to swallow, and thought about taking a drink herself. *Breathe Jessica.* She nudged him in the stomach with the jug.

He finally broke their eye contact, and took the vessel, slowly twisting off the cap. He slung his head back to gulp the water, and while he was busy drinking, she studied him. It was no wonder every female from miles around seemed to be drawn to this man. Just look at him. The muscular cords in his neck stood out under his tanned skin. Even with a sticky hat ring in his hair, his arrant maleness dominated him. Faded jeans, old beat up boots, and a bloodied shirt, yet he exuded a quiet, unobtrusive power. Maybe it was the way he held himself. Or maybe it was his height, or how he filled out his work shirt. But one thing was for sure. He was all cowboy, all man, and one day she would melt clean away just being near him.

The bright red on his arm caught her notice. She grimaced as she went to him and inspected it. It was bad. Blood had soaked the makeshift bandage and it was dripping at a pretty steady rate. "You must've broken it open. I shouldn't have let you bring up that wheel before fixing this," she mumbled. "You need to sit somewhere . . ." She twisted about to check the area. "Come on. That log where you sat me earlier." She seized his right hand and started for the log.

His fingers squeezed hers and gave a sharp tug. With a yelp she whipped back to him like a practiced tango partner, and smacked into his chest. His good arm encircled her waist to steady her. Then ever so slowly, he pulled her in tighter, her face only inches from his. His overheated body radiated a sort of urgency that made her heart pound alongside his.

"I'm fine right here, Jessie," he whispered, his heated breath stirring against her cheek.

Yep. Now was the time—she'd soon be a puddle at his feet. But, she didn't understand him. Since the night of the oyster feed, he'd avoided her. Avoided this. *Why now?*

As if coming to his senses, he freed her so abruptly she stumbled back a few steps.

Standing a few feet from him now, she gaped, speechless, amazed at what he'd done. What was worse, he had the audacity to look appalled, like she'd somehow trapped him into that embrace. That stung.

"All right. But when I dump the alcohol on your wound, don't you pass out on me."

"Pass out?" He glared at her. "I've never passed out in my life. Don't plan to start now." He stole the alcohol out of her hand, untwisted the top and shoved it back at her. "We need food and it's going to be a long night, so let's get this over with."

Jessica advanced to his side. Hurt and frustrated by his constant change of behavior, she took hold of the sleeve and ripped it all the way up. Next, she un-wrapped the handkerchief. When she saw the gruesomeness of the gash, her wounded pride abated. She sighed. "This is really going to hurt, Clint, but I think it's vital we sterilize it as best we can. Do you want to bite down on something?"

His look let her know he was done with the pampering.

She shrugged. "Okay. Have it your way."

She poured the alcohol into the deep gouge. His loud grunt of pain startled her. Her head whipped up to check his face. He was squeezing his eyes shut tight. His bunched up jaw muscles looked as if they would burst right through his dark stubble. She made a face and started blowing on the gash. "Are you going to be okay?" she said between blows.

She watched as his tanned skin began to take on an obvious pallor, worrying her that his passing out might actually happen.

"Clint, I think you'd better sit." The minute she said this, his body slumped forward. She dropped the alcohol bottle and caught him around his middle. His head drooped over her, and a soft groan vibrated into her shoulder. She could hardly hold him up, he was so heavy. She adjusted her grip and dragged him as best she could toward the log. To some extent he was alert enough to help her with his weight, but she feared he would pass out all the way.

How the two of them managed to get to the log and plant him on it was a miracle. Jessica shoved his head between his legs, knocking his hat off in the process. To her relief, after a brief time, and several deep breaths, his color began to return. He raised his head enough to eye her—his agitation and embarrassment palpable.

Jessica ignored his daggers and offered him water. He took a couple of sips while he scowled at her from behind the canteen.

"Are you okay now? Do you still feel faint?"

Below his narrowed eyes, his splendid mouth moved, "Don't ever say the word *faint* about me again."

She gave him a knowing smile. "Don't worry. Mum's the word," she said, trying to lighten the mood.

It wasn't to be lightened, however. One look at him and she knew that. She ignored his glum look and went to retrieve the rest of the first aid supplies. Dropping to her knees before him, she laid supplies on the log. After a more gentle cleaning, she tore open some bandages and began butterflying the wound.

She stole a glance upward and found Clint's eyes roaming over her. His gaze slid up her throat to her chin. When he reached her lips, her heart pounded so hard she thought he'd feel the shudders. Nervously, she licked her lips. His nostrils flared with a huge intake of breath, and his gaze jerked up to hers. She wished she were as good at reading men as he was women, but she had no idea what that look in his eyes meant.

The breeze was playing havoc with her hair. Clint stared at the wayward lock that had escaped her ponytail and now tangled up in her lashes. Before she had the chance to brush it away, he tenderly freed the strand and slipped his fingertips down the length before tucking it behind her ear.

"Thanks," she said, so softly he couldn't possibly have heard.

But he had, and nodded.

His eyes penetrated hers. She couldn't look away, like he had trapped her to him. When his gaze fell to her lips he bent forward.

CHAPTER 13

Clint leaned in, nearing Jessie's mouth.

"Oh!" She jumped. "Oh no, don't pass out Clint." She patted both cheeks in concern.

He felt heat rise under those hands. "Jess—"

"Put your head between your legs." She tried to push his head over.

He resisted. "I'm not—"

Her eyes widened with worry, and she pushed at the back of his head again.

He gave in. Holding back a smile over her misguided concern for him, he braced his forearms against his knees, and hung his head between them. And then, like the springing cougar had done, truth smacked him dead center. A near blunder, for the second time. He'd almost kissed her. And, she'd innocently misunderstood. A heavy, dark gratitude seeped in as he contemplated how he would have ever explained away a kiss.

It was absurd, but he still wanted that kiss. Craved it, in fact.

"I'm okay," he said into the dirt. He raised his head enough to risk a quick glance into those eyes again. He'd been fine, minding his own thoughts, harmlessly looking over her curvy body, flawless skin, and shiny hair as she'd fixed his arm. That was all. Then those eyes, like chameleons, had taken on the color of the surrounding pines; wide with wonder and sheer purity. But the final draw had been those lips. And then he was lost.

So, was he happy she misunderstood, or not?

"I need to get that wheel on now," he said. "A little help up and I can manage it."

She frowned. "I'm not a delicate little flower, Clint. I can help."

Jessie placed her feet under her in a squat. She swung his good arm around her shoulders and heaved upward. Clint strained to his feet, surprised he needed to lean so hard against her. He swayed from the effects of his light headedness, yet at the same time was acutely aware of the warmth of her supple body pressed against his side. He liked the scent of her—lilac, woman, and fresh air. But she was all business now—seriously trying to help him back to the wagon. Worried he would *faint*. He growled under his breath over that.

When he'd stood without swaying for long enough to satisfy her, she let go. Bereft of the feel of her, but thankful, remembering his resolve to stay away from her, he ambled off to the wagon to evaluate what was needed.

"You can help place the wheel once we get the wagon lifted, okay?"

She nodded. "How're we going to lift it?"

"I have a screw jack in the back." He stretched his good arm down the back of the wagon and retrieved it. He squatted, positioned it under the wagon and began the slow process of twisting, experiencing a stab of pain in his arm even while trying to protect it. They watched the wagon rise inch by inch. Moving the wheel to the spot it would need to go, he looked over at her. "Now, Jessie, ready?"

Again she nodded.

They lifted and placed the wheel. Clint worked at securing the linchpin then pushed to his feet and stretched. He glanced at Jessie. Worry etched her face. He must look pretty haggard by now, and she probably noticed how he'd begun to favor the injured arm. He walked over to lift his hat from the ground, to prove he was right as rain, but he had to fight not to show how

dizzy he got standing upright again. He slapped the hat twice against his thigh, lifted a shoulder to wipe the sweat from his jaw, then stuffed it on his head.

"Okay, little one, let's get back to camp and get some grub going." Wanting to distract her from her worry, he mustered up a grin. "I'd be enjoying one of your great meals about now if we were back at the ranch." One more enticement this woman offered. She was a good cook. Beat Mabel hands down.

Jessie blushed at his compliment. "Are you okay? Do you need to lean on me to get back to the camp?"

Clint tilted his head down at her. This time he growled for effect, making her giggle. He liked the sound of that— like tinkling bells—*and* the smile accompanying it.

"It's not a sign of unmanliness for you to ask for help, you know. The truth is they don't come any manlier than you." A scarlet flush flew into her cheeks, and her eyes went wide. She turned brusquely and marched off toward the campsite.

Clint couldn't hold back a chuckle, thinking of how she always seemed to blanket people with words before she thought them through. More often than not she caused trouble for herself with this habit. Still, it was so refreshing, so innocent. It was one of her most endearing qualities. Most wouldn't call it that. He did.

"Thanks, Jessie—" he hollered after her through a huge grin "—but I think I can manage." Nevertheless, he was glad he hadn't kissed her. It was best for him to keep his distance from this sweet girl. For a while now he'd been noticing the way she looked at him, suspecting she had more than a passing interest. He'd seen unbridled passions, for him, from many women. The only difference now— hers was bridled.

Back at the camp Clint got busy preparing everything for the night, happy to see the dark clouds had passed them by. Jessie did all he asked her to do, and by the time the sun slid to the horizon, they were ready. Clint's strength returned a bit as he munched on beef jerky. He found a can of beans and opened it, gripping the portion of the lid that he'd left on to scoot it into the fire.

They had both been pretty quiet up until now. "I'll have to go out a ways and bury the garbage. Don't want to attract any unwanted guests tonight."

Jessie's face paled. "Grizzly?"

Clint could see the fear in her eyes. He nodded.

"Oh." She seemed to go paler. "I'll be praying it doesn't visit, but, do you think . . .?

"Do I think, what?"

"Can I sleep close to you, in case?"

"Of course." After all, keeping her safe was what he was here for.

"Thank you." She seemed to relax as something caught her attention at the horizon through a small gap in the trees. "Look at the sky God painted for us tonight, Clint. All those amazing colors; light blues, pinks, and reds all swirled together with spatters of tiny clouds. You can almost picture God using a paint brush to make little dabs of color on His own canvas, can't you?" She demonstrated, using her gathered fingertips as if they were a brush. "It looks different every morning and every night. Have you ever noticed that?" She smiled, though she never looked away from the beauty.

The corners of his mouth lifted in spite of his weariness. He watched her intently. How her face practically shone with wonder. Her real appreciation of nature never ceased to amaze him, though he was too tired to fight her about God's part in it. "Love the sunrises and sunsets. My favorite time of day," he finally imparted.

Clint settled back against a rock and tucked the rifle against his side. He watched the fire dancing, listened to it crackle as it sent small bursts of light into the oncoming darkness. It had been a long, strenuous day. He knew the night would be even tougher if that grizzly decided to forage through their wagon. The big creature was out there. He'd seen its tracks nearby.

His arm throbbed in beat with his heart. Every muscle in his body ached from their ordeal. If Roy only knew how close they'd come . . .

He shook off that image, not bearing the thought of what the outcome could've been. Sighing deeply he watched Jessie prepare their coffee and clean up the mess for him to bury. She was so different from other women. He tried to imagine Veronica at this scene. She would never have come. But if she'd found herself in this situation it was laughable how she would've acted—whiny, complaining, hating everything about it, and hating him for getting her into it. What made him continue to choose women like her? He shook his head. How shallow he had become, to never take the time to know a woman like Jessica Harper—someone worth knowing.

When Jessie finished filling the coffee pot and carefully nestling it into the fire to perk, she glanced at Clint. He was studying her with what he knew was an unfamiliar expression on his face, and she had picked up on that. *Smart too.*

"What?" she asked.

He gave her a lazy grin. "I was thinking how at ease you are cooking over an open fire. You've done this before."

Jessie matched his smile. "Well, sure. There've been many times we camped out when we irrigated the ranch at night, or even just for fun. I love camping."

"Interesting that you call the farm a ranch."

"I guess it wouldn't make much sense unless you knew the history. It's 700 acres of mostly farm land—row crops to be exact—except for the front five acres or so. Dad kept cattle there for years, hence the name *ranch*. Eventually he sold off the cattle, but the name stuck. We do still have animals: horses, sheep, dogs, unwanted jack rabbits . . . mosquitoes." She laughed.

Her enthusiasm stirred him. She truly loved the outdoors. He could really get used to a woman like that—someone who liked what he liked. "Why do you love camping? Thought you'd hate sleeping outside with the bugs, the cold, no bathrooms."

Jessie stopped to consider it. "I've always liked the outdoors. In fact, when I was younger I think I spent more days in a tree than on the ground."

He chuckled.

"I love the smells and sounds of God's beautiful creation. You already know that I love sunrises and sunsets. I love eating food cooked over an open fire; in fact, I love cooking over an open fire. I love sleeping under the stars, watching them twinkle." She looked up into the black sky blanketed with blinking white lights. "The stars are so bright up here. And they look bigger. Or, maybe it's just what Montana does to the soul."

She stared into the sky and began to sing, "O Holy night, the stars are brightly shining, it is the night of our dear Saviors birth'. . . "

He grinned. "Isn't that a Christmas song?"

She nodded, but kept singing around a mischievous smile.

Clint arched an eyebrow but closed his eyes and settled in, captivated by her sweet singing voice.

And then it happened. Swarms of feelings coming from all sides, like wasps disturbed from their hive. He tried to stop the unbidden thoughts. Thoughts like: She's a woman fit to make a man like him happy for a lifetime.

In the next instant, his chest seized and he struggled for breath. Where had the restraints to his brain gone? Shocked at his own thoughts, he stiffened and sat up. "I've got to go bury the garbage." He rose stiffly to his feet, groaning in discomfort. "I'll be right back. You'll be fine by the fire."

He grabbed the trowel and the small sack Jessie had so carefully placed their trash in and ambled off into the night. He didn't turn on the flashlight. He needed the solace of the darkness to sort out his feelings, using the light of the half-moon to find his way. In the distance the howl of a lone coyote pierced the night.

I shouldn't have been so short with her. It wasn't her

fault she nudged his heart on a regular basis. He rubbed his chest. His heart actually hurt. It was unlike anything he'd experienced in his thirty-one years on this earth. Painful, yet wonderful; compelling, yet terrifying. He wanted to run and wanted to draw close, all at the same time. His emotions were in a jumbled mess, each doing battle with the other. It was what he'd experienced every day since Jessie arrived.

Clint hurried through his task and trudged back to camp. The campfire crackled its greeting, creating a red haze with flickers that licked the darkness. Jessie sat crossed-legged near the flames and had her hands outstretched, warming her palms. When he stepped in close she looked up at him. The flicker of light from the fire danced across her sweet face and gave a fiery sheen to her dark hair. His heart flipped at the adoring expression and small smile.

He cleared his throat. "You should try and get some sleep. I'll keep the fire going. You can sack out right here." He gestured toward the space next to him. Thankfully, they'd brought a supply of blankets for Mary. He laid one out for her, folded a second for under her head, and held a third to cover her body.

"Thank you." She stretched out on the gray woolen blanket. He carefully covered her, her back to him. "Clint?"

"Uh huh?"

"What happened to you when you were a boy?"

He stiffened in surprise. He couldn't do this. *Not this.*

Jessie turned over slowly to face him. The firelight framed her face. The image softened him, tore at his resolve. For a moment the memories of that long ago time tried to scratch a path to his conscious mind. He quickly stuffed them back into the dark recesses, ignoring the concern he saw in her eyes. Instead, he forced his mind to shift directions, to study the silken beauty of her skin and the fullness of her lips.

She propped herself up on one elbow to wait for him to respond. The blanket slid down to her waist and her shiny hair caught the breeze and whipped over her shoulder into a dark fan across her chest. She lifted a hand to flip her hair back. The movement was innocently provocative. His mouth went dry.

"Maybe it would help if you talked about it," she said, breaking the tense silence.

"Get some sleep, Jessie," he said in a voice he hardly recognized.

She hesitated, studying him. At last she said, "Okay . . . good night, Clint."

He sighed in relief. "Goodnight, little one."

Silence fell between them and soon he could hear Jessie's steady breathing and knew she'd slipped into a comfortable slumber.

Clint sat unmoving, listening to the sounds of the night. Jessie's compassion, like a well-placed shovel, had scooped out a healthy section of the all too painful catacomb of his past. It couldn't be dug up and viewed nonchalantly. He guarded it, barely able to cope when an unwelcome memory nudged him. He couldn't fathom a full-on examination of it. He wondered if there would ever be a time when he'd share his past with someone. If he did, it could only be someone like Jessie.

He angled his weight onto one hip, then shifted to the other, resettled his hat. His body ached from hat to boots. But the fears in his mind were worse. That grizzly attacking, Jessie's prying . . .

Jessie.

Something unrecognizable yet potent was drawing

him to her. Like a calf roper dragged along with muscles locked and heels dug in, yet unable to stop the draw. When he was alone with Jessie, like on this trip, his insides were in constant motion—stirred and questioned and checked. It exhausted him. The women of his past had never gained a stronghold—had never even found the path to his heart. Heck, he hadn't even known before now that his heart was in any kind of working order.

He ran a hand down his face and tried not to let the groan slip out. Forget about her. *She's Roy's niece, that's all that's important.* He pressed his back into the rock and shifted enough to cross his feet the other way, checked his rifle, and rested his arms across his chest. He tried to think of other things—the needs of Mary's cabin, the ranch hands, the cattle . . .

His mind didn't adhere to the plan.

Jessie wasn't outwardly striking, or outgoing— Ah, but she *was* outgoing, in her own way, like none of the others had been. Oh, they had pretended to be, in hopes of convincing him they liked what he liked. But sooner or later their true colors became evident. He knew their natures better than they did, and he would eventually pick out the phonies. And, to his consternation, all his choices had been phonies. But then, was he any different? No. No one could trust their heart to him either. Who *was* he and what had he become?

Clint glanced over at Jessie. The blanket had fallen into the curve of her waist. Jessie—so down-home appealing it made him ache. She was the real deal, and his desire for her was fast becoming an unshakable need.

He remembered the point at which plain awareness of her had grown into that need—at the barn dance. Jessie had gone near the rowdy bunch. His dormant protective nature had erupted like a guard dog against a predator when he saw Brad Turner's hand clamp around Jessie's arm.

The rage had been a blast of furnace heat inside. And the only thing that kept Clint from pummeling Brad then and there was the lost lamb expression on Jess's face. What could he do but pull her into his arms . . . to dance—and change the entire course of his life?

The crucial point-of-access to his heart and soul had been tapped that night. And, since then, she'd been prying it open, inch by frightening inch.

A shrill whinny and snap of leather ripped him out of his thoughts. Then something loud crashed back at the wagon. Clint jumped to his feet, and Jessie rocketed to hers a heartbeat later.

"Is that the bear?" Jessie's voice sounded an octave higher. She staggered a bit, probably from shocking her body out of sleep.

"I'm afraid so." He picked up the rifle in one hand and the flashlight in the other, clicked it on, and turned to Jessie. "You stay here. I don't want you hurt." He turned to leave.

Frantically she leaped forward to grab his arm, turning him back to her. "I don't want you hurt either. Can't you let it take what it wants and go on its way?

Her eyes pleaded more than her words, twisting his gut. "I don't want it to get our supplies. They're too hard to come by, and Mary needs them. I'll be fine. Stay close to the fire."

* * *

Without warning, the tidal wave of longing—building since the moment Jessica had laid eyes on Clint Wilkins—crashed over her, eroding her well-known Harper stability and good sense. With no conscious thought, she came up on tiptoes and clasped her hands behind his neck, tugging him down to her mouth. Her lips pressed into his recklessly, as if she could pour her heart into him through that single point of contact.

He didn't hold her—his hands full with his rifle and flashlight—but he didn't stop her either, kissing her back, letting it deepen and lengthen until both of them were completely unraveled. He pulled away, his expression one of anguish. "Jessie—I . . ."

He looked so stricken, and sad, and confused. He opened his mouth to speak but closed it. Staring into her eyes, his seemed to say that this wasn't right, that it could never be. He never said those words. Maybe he couldn't. Not when he wasn't even sure he would return. Like the encounter had never happened, he twisted around and jogged off into the night.

Helplessness seized Jessica in a grip so tight she struggled for her next breath. Clint was running headlong into danger and she didn't have the power to stop it. Clint had the only gun. She was unarmed, except that she could pray. No matter how Clint felt about God, it didn't change the forces that came into play from the prayers of the faithful. She knelt by the campfire, praying aloud Psalm 23. *"The Lord is my Shepherd, I shall not want . . .*

. . . Yea, though I walk through the valley of the shadow of death, I will fear no evil; for thou art with me; thy rod and thy staff they comfort me . . .

Jessica kept repeating the Psalm until she heard the

report of a rifle. She jerked and sucked in a gasp at the sound. She continued her vigil in her head, asking God for Clint's safety, his sure footing, God's full protection on him. Still on her knees with her head bent toward the ground, fear for him and for herself finally burst out of her as an onslaught of hiccups.

Suddenly, strong arms came out of nowhere and lifted her to her feet. *Clint.* He twirled her around and tucked her under his chin. His arms locked her to him, and hers joined in the desperate embrace with fingers digging into his back and their warmth mingling together.

And then the tears came. She wept against him, shuddering with intense sobs.

His ragged breathing slowed, and her snuffles lessened. Soon only silent tears fell from her eyes. When the terror faded and her tears subsided, her heightened senses shifted to the feel of the man himself. They fit perfectly there in each other's arms—familiar, natural, comfortable. Embedded in his solid chest, his scent came to her, encompassed in masculine heat. It calmed her shattered nerves, leaving her trembling for another reason altogether.

Clint loosened his hold. With long fingers caught in her hair, he gently pulled her head back to give him a clear view of her face. His gaze swept over each feature before looking into her eyes. "Are you all right?"

Warring emotions raged through her. "Am I—all right? How c-can you ask if I'm all right?" Jessica hiccupped. "Are *you*—all right?"

Releasing her, he gripped her hand to bring her to the blanket and gently pushed her down. He sat next to her, resting a forearm on one raised knee. "I'm fine. I told you I would be."

"What happened out there, Clint?"

He gazed off into the darkness as if the scene was replaying there. "The grizzly was scavenging for food in the wagon." He glanced back at her. "I heard you praying all the way to the wagon, Jessie." Jessica saw a distinct look of awe on his amazing face. Hadn't anyone ever prayed aloud for this man before? "Peace washed over me, like I'd never experienced before." His gaze flitted back to the darkness again.

She studied his profile as she waited for him to continue. "He was up on his hind legs and stared straight at me. He held very still, like he was one of those chiseled wooden statues." He sighed heavily. "I raised the rifle, with the flashlight next to the barrel so it shone on his face, and shot. Perfect shot, right through the eye." He looked over at her. "He's the rogue bear, Jessie. I saw the marks we put on him. One's where we missed. I don't understand it. He should have been violent. All I could think was that your God had held him still so that I could put him out of his misery . . . and ours."

He smiled just then. An astounded smile that looked unfamiliar on his face.

Jessica hiccupped in stunned silence. There was no mistaking his excitement or his bewilderment. She'd never heard him talk so much—or so fast. Her mouth gaped open.

He sat up straight, his hands on his thighs. "What's wrong?"

With some difficulty, she found her voice, "How ca-can you grin like that after what you've been through?"

He began to laugh. The hardiest laugh she had ever heard from him. He continued to laugh until he realized she wasn't responding. He stopped and stared at her. An unreasonable fury rose within her. As she sat there, her hiccups rang out into the stillness. "What could y-you possibly be laughing at?" she finally choked out.

"You. You're sitting there all concerned about me, hiccupping your little head off. It's just so . . . you." Then came another round of singular laughter.

Still confused and outraged at being laughed at, she managed to say, "What is wrong with you? How can you t-take this so lightly? You were almost killed out there, and there was n-nothing I could do to help, but pray!" Anger was getting the best of her now. That, and these blasted hiccups!

He seemed to be biting back a grin, forcing seriousness. "I was not almost killed, Jessie. I told you I had done this before. *You* were my only concern. For me it was a necessity. He was dangerous. It had to be done, that's all."

Not knowing what else to say, she lay down on her side facing him. Sitting back up, she grasped the second blanket, flung it over her and stretched out again. "Ma-Men!" she hiccupped. "I'll never understand you."

His expression hardened. "Probably a good thing. There's no real need." He looked weary all of a sudden like the weight of the day's events had finally caught up to him.

"Try to sleep, Jessie. One of your sunrises will be waking us up soon enough."

Flipping another blanket next to hers, Clint spread out his huge frame until not a hint of gray wool showed. Bringing his good arm up, he rested his head on his hand and stared up at the multitude of stars.

She hiccupped.

His low chuckle came from deep in his throat, sending a shiver of pleasure through her.

"Goodnight, little hiccupper. Hope you'll be able to sleep with those."

* * *

Clint inspected Jessie's sweet face as her breathing steadied and became heavier. Small hiccups escaped her parted lips even in sleep, making him grin. The memory of the kiss she gave him earlier slid back into his thoughts. She had shocked him, pulling his head down for that knock-your-socks-off kiss. What he had desperately wanted to do was dump his supplies on the spot, wrap her in his embrace, and take over. The kiss had deepened anyway, awakening him to a side of Jessie he hadn't wanted to explore but now couldn't quite forget.

But it had changed things. Now he would have to figure a way to tell her they couldn't be anything more than friends. *Friends*. An interesting rumination, considering he didn't have female friends. He nearly laughed aloud. The women in his life were always lovers—*never* friends.

It was different with Jessie. If he were honest with himself, he wanted more than a friendship with her. But, life had taught him you didn't always get what you wanted. Besides, what she'd want, he *didn't* want—commitment, marriage.

A log in the campfire burned through and fell with a thump, showering sparks over his boots. Shaking his head, he forced his pondering away from her yet again, and tried to catch a few winks.

Tomorrow was soon enough to set this straight.

CHAPTER 14

Clint warmed his backside on the rekindled campfire, and stared east into the dawn of the new day. Long, narrow clouds—resembling thin ribbons—threaded their way throughout the awakening image. He'd mistakenly figured morning would bring a clearer picture. But like the tangled up clouds, so went his jumbled thoughts.

Clint scrubbed his hands through his hair, noting how it had grown too long. Tending the horses and fixing a small breakfast would take his mind off things. Off Jessie, and what to do about her. He started the coffee and brought out a jar of leftover mush and biscuits. A 'just in case meal' Mabel had insisted they bring. Smart woman, that.

The biscuits hung over a small portion of hot embers from a forked stick and the mush bubbled next to it in the half-buried bean can, when Jessie stirred. She breathed in deeply and stretched under her blanket. "Mmmm. Smells good. What're you cooking?" she asked with a lazy, sweet smile.

Something about that angelic face, flushed from sleep and the rising sun's warm glow, made him want to look his fill. Pleased, but not surprised, by her cheery nature after sleeping on the hard ground for so few hours he was reminded that since the first day he'd met her, she'd displayed a positive outlook and nearly always wore a smile. That is, unless she was blushing over something she'd blurted out without thinking. He smiled at that and at her. "Mush and biscuits. It's the coffee you smell, I'm sure."

Jessie sat up, taking in the sights. "It's beautiful out here; now that I can actually see it. Are you all right? How are the horses? Oh. How's your arm?"

"Whoa, whoa, and whoa, so many questions, so little time," he teased.

"Okay." She stood and stretched again, not the least bit aware of the tantalizing show she gave him.

Clint cleared his throat and turned back to the fire.

"I'll only ask one then. How are *you*?"

The corners of his mouth slanted upward at her concern for him. He lifted the biscuits from their perch. "Fine, Jessie. Come on over here and eat. We need to get back on the road. Still have about two hours before getting to Mary's, especially since we've got to take it a little slower with that wheel."

Sheepishly she asked, "Can I use the . . . um . . . little girl's tree first, please?"

He chuckled. Her absence of sophistication was gratifying. "Sure. Go over there behind the horses." He gestured with a shoulder. "There are some supplies for you to use." He nodded his head toward them. "Be sure to bury everything."

She cringed at discussing such a private need with him.

Clint watched her until she disappeared from view. To

make sure she was safe, he told himself, though he knew that wasn't entirely true. Even in yesterday's wranglers and pink blouse—the color of her blushes—she seemed to shine with the glory of a sunrise. What a marvel she was. And a mystery how she affected him the way she did.

When she returned, he was hunkered down in front of the fire dishing up her meal. A glance caught her inspecting his bunched up thighs. He shoved to his feet to offer her the plate. He had taken off the bloodied shirt, but the new one had yet to be buttoned, revealing his hair-dusted chest. Her large eyes slid down over the exposed skin. He stood frozen in place with her plate in his outstretched arm while her gaze followed the natural flow of the hair that tapered down his belly. Her mouth parted, and he caught his breath. Her eyes stopped on his belt buckle before suddenly widening in horror at what she'd just done. She glanced back up while a deep flush filled her face.

An overwhelming rush of desire gripped him at her thorough inspection, and he knew she was seeing a potent look in his eyes now. One he was trying hard to mask and failing miserably at.

He'd seen that kind of perusal from other women many times in the past, and a few from her. But this time he was shocked at his own reaction. He was troubled at her show of desire. A desire he was sure she was too inno-cent to know she'd shown him. Part of him wanted to act on it. The other part wanted to run for the hills. The part that wanted to act was intensifying with each new incident between them, making it harder to keep her at arm's length.

He coughed and thrust the food at her until she grasped the tin plate. Taking hold with shaky hands and nearly overturning it, she thanked him and backed away.

"Everything's ready to take back to the wagon. We need to eat and head out," he said while hurriedly buttoning up his shirt then shoving it into his pants.

She kept her gaze averted. "I'd like to check your arm first."

"It's fine, Jessie. You can do that at Mary's."

With no more conversation they ate, Clint directed the clean-up, gathered the horses and supplies, and then they headed for the wagon. Jessica sucked in a huge breath at the sight of the dead grizzly bear. "Oh Clint, it's massive. I can't believe you had to face that thing!"

"Yeah, big," he replied while hitching the horses to the wagon, and re-organizing the mess the bear had made. He hated leaving the bear to be foraged by the wildlife, but by its outward signs last night he was fairly sure it wasn't rabid, and the priority at this point was to get Jessie safely to Mary's.

Her eyes were the size of saucers. "Weren't you scared at all? I'm afraid I would have fainted dead away."

"Guess that's the difference between men and the weaker sex, eh?" He enjoyed needling her.

"Weaker sex? Well, when it's time for the babies to come we'll see who the weaker sex is," she said without thinking, he figured, since she stopped short. He cocked his head around in time to watch her cheeks mottle with color, and grinned.

He grasped Jessie by the waist and hoisted her up to the seat. He swung up himself, took the reins in his gloved hands and gave them a snap, coaxing the horses along. "Let's take it easy today, girls."

After about an hour of silent riding, Clint felt his body weight slumping harder into the forearms he had resting on his thighs. The reins were loose in his grip now.

Jessie leaned forward to peer into his face, and frowned. "Clint, are you all right? You haven't said a word in miles and you seem flushed to me."

He felt chilled, and dazed. With the back of her hand she touched his forehead. "You're burning up! We should stop. I need to see that arm."

"No! We can't risk stopping."

"Why not?" She scanned the area. "Isn't it safe here?"

"That's not it. I'm not feeling right and if we stop—leave it be, Jessie." He knew what was happening. He'd lost a lot of blood and now his body was trying to fight back. But getting Jessie out of harm's way and safely into Mary's care took precedence over everything.

She put a hand lightly on his shoulder, "Father God, You already know what we've been through, and only you know the dangers we face. Help Clint get us safely to Mary's, and please, heal him. Thank you, Lord."

"You didn't ask anything for yourself." His voice came out weak. Still, he wanted to know if she ever thought of herself first. If she did, he'd never seen it.

"I don't need anything, Clint. I'm concerned about you. Can I take the reins?"

The desire to tease her was so great, he wondered about it, especially at a time like this. "Yeah . . . just like a woman . . . always wanting to take over." He chuckled faintly.

Jessie didn't speak again until the road opened into a clearing and they could see the little cabin with smoke curling out of its chimney. "Thank you, Lord," she said out loud.

He grimaced.

When they arrived at the cabin Clint barely managed

to stop the horses. With the last of his strength, he twisted on the seat and laid a hand on Jessie's thigh to gain her complete attention. When their eyes connected, he said, "Jessie, the horses . . . " He took a deep breath and tried again. "Jessie—"

"Don't worry. I'll take care of the horses." She was staring into his eyes with a slice of fear in her own. He probably looked like death. He certainly felt like it.

She jumped out of the wagon and turned to look for a place she could grab on his body to help him down. He sat on the edge of the seat, contemplating his exit strategy, when she extended her arms up to him. He wanted to grin at the absurdity of it. One wrong slip and he would crush her. But he'd seen her determination before. He gave her a cautious look. "Okay little one . . . let me step down first."

She nodded.

He inched his way down the edge of the wagon until his boots landed hard on the packed dirt. His legs felt like they would shatter at any moment, and he wondered if they'd hold up. Jessie pulled him up against her.

If only I weren't so weak. He would have laughed over his one track mind if he'd had the strength. He needed to focus. To lift dead weight the size of him off the ground would be an impossible feat for her.

"Come on, Clint."

Each step became increasingly difficult. Jessie watched his feet. Clint watched the cabin door. He stumbled and groaned. Her head popped up. Alarm; he saw it in her eyes. *So lightheaded.* Must take another step. He felt his eyes roll back.

* * *

Panic seized Jessica. "No! Clint! You have to do this. I can't carry you!"

Mary's cabin door flew open. The sound sent a surge of hope through Jessica. She glanced up in time to see a mature woman dressed in an apron and worn boots. "Mary, help me!"

Mary clomped down the steps and hoisted a portion of Clint's weight faster than Jessica expected.

They staggered together under Clint's weight to Mary's guest room, and guided him onto the bed before he passed out. Fighting a wave of terror, Jessica removed Clint's hat and boots, listening all the while to his steady breathing. Together they turned him to his back.

Jessica straightened. Her back twinged from all the exertion, but she felt strange comfort

with Mary by her side. "He's lost a lot of blood," she said. The words came out thick, swollen

with tears she could not let loose. There was still too much to do. She glanced at Mary, whose

face was rosy with the same exertion, and whose eyes were intelligent and warm and creased

with worry.

"Tell me what happened," Mary said, "and we'll fix him right up."

Jessica introduced herself and gave a fast version of the accident with the wagon, telling of Clint's injury.

"I'll get some hot water started, to soak his arm in," Mary said, moving toward the kitchen.

"Do you have golden seal? Or better yet, how about colloidal silver? It's a natural antibiotic."

"How did you know? Are you a nurse?" Mary asked from the kitchen.

"No. I grew up on a farm. Dad taught me about natural remedies."

"I'm glad to finally meet you. Sorry it had to be this way."

Jessica began un-wrapping Clint's arm. He groaned in his sleep as she yanked against the stubborn tape. Once she peeled the bandage back, she was alarmed at the swelling and redness and the horrendous smell—like decaying garbage. Seeing the flush of his skin, she touched his forehead. Just yesterday, he'd been cold and clammy. Today he was hot. She worried about a serious infection that bacteria from horse gear could cause

"Mary." She raised her voice so Mary could hear. "We should give him some silver orally, not just topically, as soon as he wakes up. Do you have enough?"

"Plenty," she called out. "It's what keeps me infection free up here."

"Thank God," Jessica said.

"Amen to that," Mary called back.

CHAPTER 15

Jessica decided Clint's clothing needed to be removed, to cool him down. Mary was in the kitchen, boiling water and retrieving medical supplies, so Jessica hesitated, thinking of propriety. But, she was his acting nurse, right? Agreeing with herself, she plunged right in; unbelted, unbuttoned, and stripped off clothes. She struggled with Clint's dead weight. She'd already guessed him to be nearly six and a half feet tall, but now she wondered about his weight—220, 240? He was sticky with sweat, making it harder to remove his denims.

Finally finished, she left him in his undershorts. Taking a moment to check him over, she was aware when her caregiver inspection shifted gears into womanly thoughts. Guilt shot through her, but still she stood motionless, in awe of him.

Clint had been gifted with a perfect body. She let her eyes slowly scan the remarkable man, from his dark hair—curling damply about his forehead—to wide shoulders, narrow hips, and hard, flat stomach. Even his hands and feet were pleasing in their sturdiness. Each straight, dark-haired leg flaunted substantial thighs—no doubt from years on a horse. Below his well-formed knees, strong calf muscles spread beneath the weight of his leg creating an appealing hollow along his shin bones.

In his clothes he'd looked flawless, but now with the evidence put before her she saw that God had created perfection in this man.

Then, the thought hit her. Was there a difference between admiring and lusting?

Mary came through the door then, startling Jessica. She flipped the sheet over him as she heard Mary say, "Oh my, you should have hollered. I could have helped you. I've brought the water and some towels. Also, bandages and silver. Now, how can I help?"

Jessica could have sworn she glimpsed a brief smirk on Mary's face when she first came in. Ignoring that thought she inhaled a much needed deep breath and blew it out through taut lips.

"I'm concerned about bacteria—tetanus in particular. We'll know soon enough if his muscles harden; the jaw mainly. Pray, Mary. That's the best we can do for now. As soon as I'm done here, we'll do that together."

Jessica soaked his arm in hot water laced with colloidal silver, making mental notes that she would need to do this two or three times a day to help it heal. She soaked a wash cloth in cold water, wrung it out, and placed it on his forehead. Once he was neatly under a sheet, with the cool cloth on his head and the arm re-bandaged, Jessica and Mary got down on their knees.

Mary was silent, so Jessica spoke, "Lord, we put Clint in Your Mighty Hands. Please heal his body. Please guide Mary's hands, and mine, in caring for him. We ask this in the precious name of Jesus."

"Amen," they said in unison.

Jessica got up, and helped Mary to her feet. She touched Clint's head one more time and followed Mary through the kitchen, then beelined it straight out of the door. "Be right back, Mary."

Jessica slogged back into the cabin after unhitching and doing all she knew to do for the comfort of the horses. She slumped into a seat. Mary had put oatmeal cookies on the table.

"Thanks Mary, for your help with Clint," Jessica finally said.

"You don't have to thank me, Jessica. I've known Clint for many years, and am quite fond of him. He's like a son to me." She set a glass of lemonade in front of Jessica, and had a cup of coffee for herself. "You two make a cute pair. How long have you known him?"

"No. We're not a—"

"I must say"—Mary swiped two cookies and laid them on a napkin—"I am pleased he's finally met someone who knows the Lord. You'll be good for him, I believe."

"You don't understand, Mary, we're—"

"You seem like a sweet, caring sort of girl." Mary pushed the napkin of cookies toward Jessica. "So, how long have you been courting?"

"Mary!"

Mary jumped a little.

"Sorry, but Clint and I aren't a couple. I've only known him a few weeks. He brought me up here to meet you. Uncle Roy thought Clint could fix things in the cabin, while you teach me how to quilt."

"Oh, I see. I'd love to teach *you* to quilt." She smiled. It looked very much like a cunning smile. "But, I still think you'll be good for Clint. You are smitten with him."

How did she know? But if Mary was such a straight shooter, Jessica could be, too. "I'm not his type. He's made that abundantly clear." She grabbed a cookie and took a big bite, hoping Mary wouldn't see her disappointment.

Mary feathered her hand across her throat. "Oh my, he hasn't been unkind to you, has he?"

"No. Of course not. In fact—"

"I mean, that wouldn't be like him at all." Mary glanced at the door to Clint's room.

Jessica blew a curl off her forehead. "He's gone out of his way to make sure I've been safe, and not just on this trip. He's kind and compassionate—"

"You must let me know if he mistreats you."

"No. He wouldn't. It's just that . . . that he doesn't want—"

"Clint is usually charming and attentive."

"Yes. He is. It's just that—"

"He's a wonderful, caring man. A little wild sometimes, but—"

Jessica reached across the table and grasped Mary's hand.

Surprised, Mary stopped her prattle.

"Clint has been nothing but wonderful." Jessica sighed. "He doesn't want me the way you mean."

Mary slumped in her chair a little, looking weary. "He needs someone like you, Jessica." Jessica gave Mary a dubious look.

"Listen, I've only known you a few short minutes and yet I know this: you love God. You're caring. You're not self-centered or conceited. You're gracious and well-mannered. That all adds up to one big heart. Just what Clint needs. And deserves."

"Mary . . ."

"I know what you're thinking. How can someone think they know who's meant to be together in so short a time? Trust me. I know."

No wonder everyone loved Mary. She cared. Really cared. But the poor woman was misguided when it came to Clint. Jessica knew one thing about him for sure. He would never settle down with just one woman. Least of all her. It saddened her for him. She was sure something had happened in Clint's young life to bring about his reckless playboy existence when everything else about him screamed commitment, loyalty, and honor.

"By the way, how's Roy?" Mary asked.

Jessica grinned. "He's fine. He thinks of you, you know."

Mary looked pleased. She swung her gaze to the kitchen window. "I think of him often."

"Tell me about you two."

Mary sighed and dropped her gaze. She ran a fingertip around her cup's edge. "It's a long, sad story."

"Well, I'm not going anywhere. You two were in love once."

Her head snapped up. "He told you that?"

Jessica just gave a fleeting smile.

Mary looked ten years older all of the sudden. "We *were* in love once. But circumstances tore us apart for a time, and that's when Bill asked me to marry him. We married and Roy gave us this little cabin to live in. Bill was a logger and was gone a lot of the time. We had a good life. He died while on the job—a tree felled in the wrong direction."

Jessica's chest constricted as tears pooled in Mary's eyes. "That must have been dreadful."

Mary sniffed hard, straightened, and shifted her gaze back to Jessica. "That's life, and God's in control." Her voice was thick with emotion. "He must have wanted Bill home. Who am I to argue with The Almighty?" She smiled, but it didn't reach her eyes. "He was a good man."

"What happened with you and Roy?" There went her mouth again, saying things of its own volition. For goodness sake, she had just met this woman. "I'm sorry. You don't have to tell me anything. It's really none of my business."

Mary's smile grew. This time joy flooded her eyes. "Ah, Roy. What a saint he is. Well, it was kind of a misunderstanding. Roy had ranch business in Georgia and was driving back home across the southern states when he was caught in the great flood of 1927, in Mississippi. Countless lives were lost—Roy was thought to be one of them. I was devastated." She swallowed hard. "But, Bill stayed around to comfort me. He was very persuasive and I was impressionable and lonely, and thought never to see Roy again. So, I married Bill only four months after no news from Roy."

She rose to fill her coffee cup, then raised the pitcher of lemonade. "More?"

Jessica shook her head.

Mary sat back down. "Come to find out, Roy had been trapped in an area where he couldn't get word to anyone that he was alive. He spent months helping others rebuild. When he finally made it home, Bill and I were already married."

Jessica was dumbfounded. She stared at Mary.

"I know . . . young and stupid. Bill had been vying for my attention along with Roy all of our high school years and a multitude of years after. I think he finally wore me down. And when I thought Roy was dead, well you know how it ended. The sad thing is, I don't think Roy ever got over it since he never married. He had been in love with me for a long time. I knew it, but he never did ask me to marry him. He waited too long and then never got the chance."

"You know, it's never too late, Mary. I think he's still in love with you."

Mary blinked. "Well . . ." Regret seemed to be imprinted on her face. Mary patted Jessica's hand. "Take it from me, my girl. Don't settle. I should have waited longer. I loved Bill in my own way, but it should have been Roy I married."

The afternoon passed quickly after that. Jessica unloaded Mary's supplies, and cared for Clint throughout the day. Later that evening, she was dozing in Mary's rocker by the fire while Mary finished up the tasks in the kitchen when she heard a thud on the floor in the bedroom.

Jessica leaped from the rocker. The room spun briefly, but she shook off the dizziness and sleep, and ran to the bedroom. Mary's footsteps padded close behind. Clint had fallen off the bed and was lying face down on the floor.

"Clint!" Jessica raced toward him and dropped to her knees by his side.

In the pale light of the kerosene lamp something shiny on his back caught her attention. Multiple thin scars traversed the expanse from his shoulder blades to his waist. Her head jerked up to Mary. Swallowing past the lump in her throat, Jessica mouthed, "He was beaten?"

Mary's look of concern matched hers. She shrugged and looked unsure.

Tears filled Jessica's eyes. "Oh, Clint," she said on a sniff.

He moaned. She turned him over and laid his head in her lap. His nose was bleeding slightly. A careful check proved it wasn't broken. Mary handed her a tissue, and Jessica wiped it clean.

"I'm so sorry, Clint." And she wasn't talking about his nose.

He cracked his eyes open and peered up at her, then down at his body. When he looked back up his eyes were wide and blazing. "What the heck's going on here?" he demanded. "We need to get you back to bed, and I need to soak your arm again," Jessica said in a heavy voice.

"Why am I naked in front of *you*, Jessie?"

The comment stung—the connotation obvious. "You're *not* naked. Do you remember that your arm was injured when the wagon wheel fell off?"

"Yeah. It's fine. Now help me up, we have things to do. Where's Mary?"

"I'm right here," Mary said with irritation in her voice. "Jessica is taking good care of you, so settle down and listen to her."

Clint calmed. "Why am I on the floor?"

"You fell out of bed. Don't you remember?" Jessica asked.

"No, but I think I know why I was trying to get up. I need to see a man about a horse."

Since Jessica had brothers, she knew exactly what he meant. She sat still for a moment, though, trying to figure out how they were going to manage this little problem.

Mary came to the rescue. "I have the thing you need, and this little old lady will help you." When Mary returned she had a container in her hand.

Jessica had helped Clint to the end of his bed by the time Mary got there. "Okay, Jessica, you can leave now, sweetie. I'll help Clint, give him a little scrub down, and put him back to bed. By then the water on the stove should be warm enough to soak his arm."

Jessica left the room, closing the door quietly behind her.

* * *

"So, you met each other," Clint said after Mary had finished his sponge bath.

Mary smiled. "She's a pretty amazing girl. She spent all day tending to everything around here, including you. She's already got my stamp of approval."

"Hold your horses, Mary," he said groggily. "This one's *not* for me."

Mary snickered, infuriating him. He eyed her suspiciously.

"Settle down. I'm not matchmaking, mind you. You're too smart for those kinds of shenanigans. I can tell she's a keeper type, if ya know what I mean."

"Don't need a *keeper type*, Walt."

"Stop growling. You sound like an animal. If you keep fighting it, you'll find yourself alone and lonely." She tugged Clint's sheet farther up on his chest. "So, why isn't she your type?"

He didn't like this conversation, remembering how she, Walt, and Roy maneuvered him into corners about this same subject all too often. Heat seared the tops of his ears, but he didn't feel as tired anymore. "You know exactly why. She's not . . . well, she's not—Oh, blasted, Mary. You know what type I like, so why're you asking me that?"

"Because I want you to face it. What type *do* you like?"

Her usual hook sunk in and took a good hold. Fine. He'd give her a list. One she wouldn't soon forget. But as his muddled brain tried to think through an accurate list, he couldn't come up with anything worth debating. Thoughts of the type of woman Jessie was kept sliding into the mix.

"I'll tell you what type," Mary finally said. "You want a female version of *you*."

He fell silent as he chewed on that statement.

Mary went on. "But lately, that's not even the type you've been choosing. They've been attractive and shaped right, but they're nothing like you. They've been self-centered more than usual." She wrinkled her nose. "Shallow. So beneath you, Clint, really."

So what if that's the type he'd been leaning toward. It was nobody's business but his. It kept him out of trouble and satisfied. Or, mostly satisfied.

"Well, isn't that true?"

He felt more than his ears heating up. "Maybe. Enough said."

She ignored his warning. His angry voice didn't intimidate her one bit. Another norm for Mary. He loved this woman, but he *hated* these conversations.

"And what exactly has that gotten you, Clint? Tell me seriously, what is missing here?"

"That's how I like them, and Jessie isn't that." Even as he said it he discerned another tug on his wooden heart. *She looked like a sweet little ranch wife cooking for her man.* The internal reminder made him want to throw clothes on, ride off on his gelding, and never come back.

"Now listen, Clint . . ."

What was going on with Mary? She'd been relentless in the past about him settling down. But this was heightened meddling.

"Exactly how is Jessica different from what you want deep down—" Her voice had shifted. Tender, full of love. "—other than she loves God, and you know how I feel about that one. Really think before you speak."

Oh, she was going to regret that statement. He didn't speak. At all.

"So, you're not going to face this, are you?" Mary said with dejection in her eyes. She looked at him long and hard. Guilt settled in when he saw true concern in her kind eyes. She was the only mother he'd had for a very long time.

He softened his manner. "You should know all about the reason I prefer to be alone."

"Why? Because Roy's alone and he raised you to be like him?"

That wasn't what he'd been thinking. But okay. "Roy seems to be happy with his life. Being a confirmed bachelor has worked out fine for him."

"Well, maybe you should ask Roy why he's alone. I agree he's a great man to emulate in all aspects, Clint, but maybe there's more to his not marrying than you know about. I suggest you ask him before you make the same mistake." She patted his cheek and stood. "But right now the important thing is to get you well. I'll send Jessica back in here to take care of that arm of yours. When she's done, try and get some rest."

Clint gazed up at the ceiling. Maybe Mary's and Roy's pushing was making him rebellious—sending him in a different direction than he would otherwise go. After all, he could hardly believe he'd actually considered marrying.

So, what exactly *did* he want?

Right now, some peace and quiet.

CHAPTER 16

Jessica stared at the bedroom door. What was taking Mary so long? After about a forty minute wait, the door creaked open and Mary slipped out.

"Is everything okay?" Jessica asked.

"We were catching up. Sorry to have worried you." Mary smiled with understanding. "Don't you fret. That stallion's a fighter, always has been. And God is good, Jessica, but His ways are not our ways. He loves our Clint, and I believe He'll heal him. And it will be far more than his injured arm. Now, you go on in. He's ready for you."

Jessica didn't know what 'healing' Mary was talking about, but decided she didn't know her well enough yet to ask. Turning the doorknob, she peeked inside. "Knock, knock. May I come in?" Clint was on his back, his arms exposed above the white sheet, the wrapped gauze on his left one showing signs of seepage. He turned his head toward her.

"Listen. Can we hurry this up? I'm pretty tired."

"I promise to be quick."

In silence Jessica un-wrapped Clint's arm, then wedged it in the basin of tepid water. As it soaked, she checked his forehead and frowned at how warm he still was. His probing eyes followed her every move. He licked at the edges of his mouth. She dabbed his dry lips with a cool, damp cloth. His barely visible smile curved against the fabric. She smiled back and his shoulders seemed to ease, relaxing into his pillow.

She laid the washcloth across his forehead. "Almost done." She sighed, relieved the nerves he always set on edge had finally calmed.

There. That looked pretty good. At least the wound had a fighting chance. If only she could bring down that fever. She dragged the washcloth off his head and twirled it. She watched it wrap around her hand. Circling the other way, she whipped it again. *Like my heart.* Whip. *Whipped about.* Whip. *This way and that.* Whip.

"What're you doing?" he said, startling her out of her thoughts. "Mary already gave me a thorough bath." His eyes softened. There was a hint of a smile. "You've lost your mind?"

"It's an old trick my mother uses, to cool off the washcloth. Keeps me from having to go through the process of re-dunking and re-squeezing."

"Does it work?"

"You tell me." She laid it back on his skin.

He flinched. "Yep. Works."

"Good. Get some sleep." She took one last look. The stubble had grown darker on his face. Soon the creases near his mouth would disappear under the coat of whiskers. Such a captivating face. "I'll be right outside the door, so if you need anything, call out." She rose to her feet.

With his good hand he snatched the cloth off and caught her wrist. "Jessie. Thanks." Her pulse slammed into her fingers at the heat against her skin. She turned back and looked down. His eyes latched to hers as firmly as his hand held her wrist.

She fumbled for a strand of hair at her neck and twisted it around her finger until his gaze dropped to their linked hands. She exhaled the breath she'd been holding, and slipped her hand free of his grasp. It was like slipping free of a lasso around her neck, only she wanted to be caught. But it could never be. She made her way to the door on leaden legs.

Jessica tried to fall asleep, but managed only to toss and turn on the narrow canvas cot for hours on end. She turned to her side and stared at Clint's open door. He was in there, so vulnerable. So different from the guarded, complex man she'd come to know.

She could hear his breaths—more labored since his fever had risen. She breathed with him. An intake of breath. A huff. Too many in a row. Now, too few. She turned her head so she could hear with both ears. Clint was struggling. She lurched upright, and listened. He was talking in his sleep with mumblings she didn't recognize. Then, an agonizing yell.

Jessica leapt from the cot, nearly losing her balance, and scurried to his side. He was thrashing about, calling out names and . . . *whimpering?* The lamp was low, but still she saw the flush of his upper torso. She put a hand to his forehead—still burning.

Lord, I thought he'd be better by now. Please help him.

"Can you hear me?" She touched his arm. "Clint, you're dreaming. It's Jessie."

His eyes opened. They were glazed, bloodshot with

fever, and seemed to look right through her. "I need you," he breathed out.

He needs me? Of course. She sighed in resignation and grasped the hand that lay on his abdomen. "I'm right here."

Suddenly, with tremendous fevered strength, he squeezed her hand and hauled her across his chest. His broad hand pushed her hip, molding her body into the cradle of his. She caught her breath at the sensations, the new awareness. Desire exploded, and with it an over-powering hunger to explore the male body she felt so small against.

No! She couldn't. Could she? Before she had the chance to decide, he wrapped his arms about her, entrap-ping her to him. He settled his face in her hair, exhaled a slow, hot breath that caressed her scalp, then drifted back to sleep.

It should have been awkward, but was surprisingly natural. This was home. Her soul recognized its mate. She listened to his steady heartbeat against her ear, felt the heat of his fevered body bringing perspiration to her own. He held her fiercely, even as he slept, and she experienced con-tentment as she never had before.

Reality shoved its way in. *If you don't move off him, you'll want to sample it all. All of him.*

Resigned, she pushed against his chest. He didn't seem to notice. Just a little more and she could slink off of him without disturbing his sleep.

Slowly, she raised her head and eyed him. Her hands were fixed on his chest. She squelched the need to thread her fingers into the soft mat of hair there. Abruptly, he sucked in a deep, choppy breath. His eyes snapped open. He stared, dazedly, into her face, nearly nose to nose with her. Blinking, as if clearing his vision of a hallucination, his sight seemed to focus in recognition.

She cringed, waiting for the inevitable rebuff from him.

His vision seemed to sharpen, but he didn't say anything. She didn't move—like if she remained still his eyes would close again, letting her make her escape. Both his hands came to her back, one above the other and merely held her against him as he looked her in the eye. If she had a wish above all wishes, this would be it—to be held in tender care every night in this man's arms. She imagined him seeing her for the first time; as a woman, as someone he could love.

Half-lidded eyes dropped to her lips, and her heart skipped. One moment they'd been locked in a heated gaze and in the next his lips touched once, then latched onto hers. Unchecked desire ripped through her senses like dry kindling in a roaring blaze.

His palms glided up and down her back and if she'd had extra breath, she would have gasped at his boldness. She fought her body's own agenda as it took commands from somewhere other than her own good sense. She'd never experienced anything like this. No one had ever touched her like this before, or kissed her this way before.

He released her lips to search her eyes. His pupils had practically swallowed up the irises. She clamped her eyes closed, escaping from his intense gaze—to decide what to do. Before a single thought came to her, he rubbed his face in her hair.

"Let me breathe you in." He inhaled an uneven breath and let it out with a satisfied murmur against her ear. "You smell so good."

With gentle fingers he combed through her hair, drawing it back from her face, then brushed his lips along the soft skin of her neck. Chills dashed down her side. She ached for him now. The thought both terrified and excited her.

A tingling wave of regret coiled in her stomach. He needed her, but he hadn't said he loved her or even that he wanted her. She couldn't let him take her cherished virtue. Yet the craving for him tore at her and a lifetime of will-power to stay pure began to crumble.

She needed to move off him. Before she could force her body to comply he stretched upward to close the distance and covered her mouth with his again, slow and satisfying. If he'd been aggressive, there was no doubt what she'd do. But, this was Clint. And he hadn't demanded a thing, just enjoyed her with a fragile sort of deliberateness.

"You feel so right," he whispered against her lips.

She wanted to say something back but was afraid the sound of her own voice would break the magic somehow.

The next kiss was chaste. So sweet, so tender, that a moan slipped from her. He groaned in response and flipped them over. Now, under a mountain of muscle, she should have felt trapped. She felt anything but. He wrapped a leg around both of hers and pulled her closer with his calf and heel. The move shocked her, but set fire to her blood. He tantalized her mouth with such a breath-stealing union that she was sure only a man crazy in love could have delivered it. *Could he be?*

Still, how could she not stop this? She knew he wasn't in his right mind. It would never be right unless he was lucid. *He'll never even remember*, she thought, painfully. Then her own lustful obsession spoke to her. *If he doesn't remember, none of this will matter and you can enjoy him for a time.*

He ended the kiss and looked at her. She tried to read

his thoughts through his eyes. *Does he even know who you are, Jessica? Or have you become yet another convenient female body?* Walt's words came crashing back to her, blistering her conscience. Did she want to become one of Clint's disposable women?

A thread of doubt and fear tangled with her excitement.

His fingertips slid delicately from the soft skin under her ear down her neck. Deft fingers untied the tiny bow at the top of the white lace on her gown. He opened it enough to skillfully trace her collarbone to the hollow of her throat. Warm breath tickled her skin. She gasped and shivered.

"So soft," he whispered.

Jessie. Why didn't he say her name? *So soft, Jessie. He knows it's me. He must. It's me he wants.* But logic had its say. *No, it's a woman he needs.*

She shoved away those thoughts, and let his touch go on.

Lust clogged her mind so hard and so fast that God's voice didn't stand a chance. But, her own conscience began to scream at her. *He will never remember this*, it said. *Do you want a man this way who isn't your husband, who isn't planning to love and cherish you? Do you want him to take your innocence from you then desert you like he has all the others?*

She began to argue with her conscience. But I want him. *I want him to love and cherish me. I want him to be my husband.*

Then she heard Him, almost audibly. But that is not his plan, daughter. He doesn't know Me—you do. You must leave his bed.

She froze. It was her Shepherd. She was one of His sheep. She knew His voice. She needed to obey.

Stilling her body of its passion with as much will as she could rally on her own, she asked God for the rest. *Please, Lord, help me. Forgive me.*

And He did . . . both.

In that instant Clint's body went limp, and he slumped to his side. Jessica pushed him to his back as he succumbed to what looked like a deep, restful sleep. Astounded, Jessica brushed her fingertips down his cheek, then put a hand to his forehead. He was cooler to the touch as he lay there motionless, breathing easier.

Without hesitation, Jessica slid out of his bed and returned to her cot. She sensed a harmony with her Almighty God. Forgiven and protected and loved. She'd nearly fallen into the sin of her own making. Tonight He had rescued her. Had given her a caress to her soul—an invisible hug.

Yet, she lay there waiting for a peace concerning Clint that never came. Here was a man who had drawn her heart to him like the tide to the moon. His care and protection of her, his patience, teasing, compassion, even the scared little boy she had caught flickers of, all of it combined to form the man she had fallen deeply in love with. And now a physical hunger had been added to that unreciprocated love.

It seemed the emotions within her were at odds with each other; peace from God's grace, guilt for her actions, love of a man she couldn't have . . .

But worst of all, she detected a chill of foreboding she couldn't quite identify.

CHAPTER 17

Jessica awoke with a start. The sun shone through the little kitchen window, bringing with it sweet warmth; but Jessica wasn't warmed. She should have perceived a light-heartedness this morning, since God had saved her from herself last night. But, her exhausted body reminded her that she had just fallen asleep. Plus, the extra work from the day before had left her weak and sore.

She blinked into the light, but her mind traveled to the guest bedroom door. She touched the ribbon at the top of her nightgown and cringed inside. Even if Clint didn't remember a thing, she did. How could she face the man who had so easily caught her on fire? But, she had to check on him, and shouldn't put it off. Maybe she should eat something first. Her stomach protested that thought, so she discarded the idea. No. She needed to just get this over with.

She straightened her back, modestly cinched up her robe, and tiptoed through Clint's bedroom door. He was sound asleep on his stomach with his head turned toward her. One leg was bent and partially hanging off the bed. The bedding had fallen to the floor. A pang of desire swamped her at the picture he made lying nearly naked like that. Before her mind wondered off on its own, she picked up the sheet and threw it back across him.

At the touch of the cool fabric he awoke and gazed up at her with heavy lids.

"Good morning, sunshine," she said, sounding overly cheery, even to herself.

"Call this good?" he groused.

With a little less exuberance she tried again. "Well, you made it through the night."

"What happened last night?" he asked. A puzzled frown creased his brows. He shifted to his back with a groan as the sheet tangled around him.

She tensed, expecting the worst.

He closed his eyes, hesitating as if deep in thought. "Something happened last night. A dream maybe. No. Something else . . ."

He hadn't said it involved her, but when he opened his eyes and inspected hers she choked in the next breath. He couldn't have remembered. Could he?

She cleared her throat. "Are you hungry? Would you like some breakfast? " With feigned nonchalance she leaned over him, touching his forehead for fever.

Only inches away now, he seemed to be studying her, his brow scrunched in contemplation.

She raised her brows in question.

"What happened to you? Your chin is raw." Worry etched his face now, and his words quieted. "Did *I* do that?"

Lurching upward, nearly knocking over her chair, she scurried into the next room where a small mirror hung near the front door. "I'll make you a little something to eat," she called to him while staring at her reflection, wide-eyed.

Sure enough, a bright red abrasion marked her chin. *Goodneesss. His stubble!* It horrified her that she hadn't even felt it happen! *Could this get any worse? Yes it could. Mary.* Jessica didn't know her well yet, but she knew beyond any doubt that Mary would notice. Women were far too observant of such things.

As if called by her thoughts, Mary entered the kitchen. "Good morning, Jessica. How'd you sleep?"

When she didn't answer, Mary turned to face her and hesitated. Jessica's heart stopped. "Or did you sleep? You poor thing, you were probably up all night with Clint." Mary turned back to scoop coffee grounds into the percolator. "You should try to get some more rest. Go on into my room and use my bed while I take care of Clint's breakfast."

Grabbing the opportunity, before Mary could examine her further, Jessica fairly ran from the kitchen. "Thank you," she called over her shoulder and closed the door behind her.

* * *

Clint heard a clatter and a muffled oath, coming from the doorway. Oh great, another woman's inspection. Yep. Mary, with a tray of food.

"Good morning, sunshine," she said.

He groaned. "Is that the phrase all women say to a dying man?"

Ignoring his foul mood like she so easily did, Mary crossed the room and laid the serving dish on the small end table. "I brought your breakfast—dry toast & hot tea." He made a face. "How're you feeling this morning? Here, let me check your forehead."

Same words, same actions. "Jessie already did this," he groused. He looked past Mary to the open door. "Where is she anyway? I'm worried about her."

Mary's smile spilled across her mouth. "Oh you are, are you? You're the one who's had us pretty worried." She stopped to examine his skin and with a thumb pulled down a lower eyelid to check the color. He grunted at her ministrations. "I sent Jessica to my bed. I'm sure between you and that horrible cot out there she didn't get much sleep last night. She looked pretty worn out." She tilted her head and looked at him with suspicion. "So tell me, why are you so concerned about her?"

"She looked like she'd been in a fight. Missing half the skin on her chin. What happened to her anyway?"

Mary seemed to be holding down a smirk while her gaze arbitrarily roamed over Clint's face. She sidled up next to him and rubbed an open palm up his jawline. He heard it rasp. "You always did grow heavy stubble." Her eyes twinkled with amusement.

Shock hit him with the impact of a rifle butt to the ribs. He pressed a fist into the mattress and worked to sit up. Dizziness brought on a wave of nausea. Mary took hold of his shoulders to steady him as sweat dribbled down his hairline. He leaned his head back against the cold wall to wait for the world to stop spinning.

"Stay there a minute until your color returns."

"You mean . . . my dream about her actually happened?" he said, mostly to himself. *Nah. Can't be. I wouldn't have.* But memories of the incident spun around his cloudy mind. He thought it'd been a dream since she'd been so remarkable. No, more than remarkable—mind-altering. His fever-racked brain grasped at the recollection, awakening his body all over again. Had it been the fever and his muddled brain, or had it been as incredible as he remembered it?

Then guilt crept in. Clearing his head he tried to remember everything he had done to her. Slowly, recollections slid in, one after another; her ardent kisses, the feel of her soft body, her lilac scent—solely Jessie's—the exquisite passion, her unswerving response to him.

She'd come to him. *Why?*

While trying to sort it out and reliving the flawless pleasure, it came to him that he didn't know how it ended. Dread rose along with bile to his throat.

Confound it—she's Roy's niece, *and* someone he'd vowed not to be involved with. So why did he do it? The fever, of course. But the second that lie bored in, he knew he was fooling himself.

Mary had been watching him. "Are you feeling faint?" she asked in a worried tone.

Mary usually read him unerringly, so how could she be so far off the mark this time? He scowled at her. *Women.* "Men don't faint! I'm fine. It's Jessie you should be worrying about." He slumped at hearing his own words. "What have I done?" He ran a hand down his face to linger over his mouth.

Mary's lips twitched.

Clint caught the small gesture and glared at her. "You think this is funny?"

She looked indignant. "I have no idea what you're talking about."

An unfamiliar sort of disquiet came over him. A sense that he would soon face some unknown consequence. "I'm afraid I did a terrible thing to Jessie last night."

Mary frowned with concern. "What terrible thing did you do?"

He gazed out the small window at the shadows from the thick grove of pine trees, lost in the replay of last night's heat. "I've compromised her," he whispered.

"Clint. Tell me what you're talking about."

He swung his gaze back to Mary. "I can't be treating her like . . . like, you know. Like all the others." He squeezed his eyes shut. "For many reasons."

Mary waited.

He growled low in his throat. She wouldn't budge off the subject he'd carelessly opened until he told her. He sighed heavily, kept his gaze averted. "For one, I'm sure the girl is as pure as white snow, and I can't remember all I did to her—" He stopped, all at once self-conscious of how candid he was being to this mother figure.

Mary looked surprised. "Clint. You know better than that. You wouldn't have taken advantage of her."

But, what if he did? Rage, at himself, worked its way up his spine. He kept his voice in check so Jessica wouldn't hear through the thin walls. "As far as I knew, last night had been a dream. If you hadn't figured out why Jessie's skin was so raw, I might never have remembered!" He dragged a hand through his hair. "Dang it all, Mary. Now what do I do? She acted funny. Rushed out of here like she was barefoot on a hotbed of coals when I asked her about her chin." He paused and closed his eyes to reclaim some composure. "How do I approach her to find out what happened?"

"*You're* asking *me* what to do about a woman?" She barked a laugh, but stopped when she noticed his grim expression. "Well, son, truth has always been my policy. I think when she wakes up you two should have a little chat." Mary winked then, and gave him a motherly pat on his hand. "Now, let's not worry your pretty little head about it." Clint cringed. "Have some breakfast."

Mary really looked too blasted happy about this. Getting way too big a kick out of his discomfort—as if she was hopeful his worry for Jessie meant something more than it did. He had to admit, at least to himself, that this was the first time he was concerned over a woman the *day after*. Though Mary believed him foolish in his thinking, he was careful to choose women who liked his attention with no attachment.

But somehow, this time, *this woman*, was different.

* * *

After a quick nap, Jessica powdered her chin until it looked passably normal, then donned jeans and a long sleeved T-shirt. Once her hair was up in its usual ponytail, she peeked out Mary's bedroom door.

Mary saw her and smiled. "Good morning, sunshine."

Jessica smiled at the familiar phrase. "Mornin'."

"Come on over here and get something to eat. You still look a little peaked. Did Clint keep you up all night?"

The smile she tried so hard to maintain faded.

Sympathy showed on Mary's face. "Come on over and sit down. Clint's doing pretty well this morning. His fever is still there, but he's at least lucid. You'll need to work on his arm after you eat. I've already fed him and he kept it down, which is always a good sign."

Mary's words rattled on, and when the woman paused in expectation, Jessica squeezed out a breathy, "Okay." But all she could think about was having to face Clint again.

Mary seemed to understand Jessica's need for silence. She left her to her breakfast and retreated to her bedroom.

Jessica ate the scrambled eggs and toast with Mary's plum jam as slowly as her conscience would allow. When she took the last bite, she rose, put her plate in the sink, and retrieved the supplies. She crept into his room, relieved to see Clint lying on his back, light snores rumbling up from his chest. *Please, God, let him stay asleep.*

She carried the little chair closer and wedged it between the bed and small stand where the porcelain bowl of boiled water sat cooling. Delicately, she lifted his injured arm into her lap. In his sleep he looked younger, more at peace, even after such a restless night. She took a moment to appreciate the chiseled planes and hollows of his features. His dark stubble had already grown in thick, adding to his rugged good looks, and a lock of sun-streaked hair lay over one eye, tangling with long black lashes any woman would die for. Unable to stop herself, she pushed the errant strand from his eye and back into his hairline.

The movement startled him awake. His eyes opened, found hers and stilled. The air fairly crackled with electricity. Clint stared at her in a way she didn't understand, literally drinking in the sight of her. She felt mesmerized by it, pulled in like a beckoning at the crest of a waterfall.

* * *

Triggered by memories clear to him now, Clint tore his eyes from hers in order to seek out the places he remembered tracing with his lips: the soft skin beneath her earlobes, her supple neck, the hollow at the base of her throat, that tempting mouth . . .

This woman had not only awakened, she'd somehow engaged, long-buried emotions. But then, he'd been out of his mind with fever. He allowed that thought to calm him and remove his guilt a bit. Now he needed to find out how far he'd taken it. "You look tired. You okay?"

"I'm fine," she said, though it was obvious she wasn't. Her face showed the strain. Her skin was pale, and half circles darkened her eyes. She looked crestfallen. Knowing he had caused it, his heart ached in a new way.

"Let's have a look at this arm," she said in a small voice. Slowly she started to unwrap his bandages, grimacing when it stuck to places where blood and pus had dried. She scooted the wash basin over on its small table and put his arm in it. "We'll soak this, bandage and all, so I can remove it without causing you more pain."

Clint heard the sadness in her voice. He grieved over what he'd done, how he'd somehow hurt her. He knew he couldn't avoid it any longer. "Look, Jessie, about last night."

Her head shot up. Her eyes were huge with alarm. "You remember?"

"Yeah . . . well, no. Not at first. I didn't realize it was real. Thought it was a dream until Mary put two and two together about your chin."

Jessica flushed scarlet. She dropped her head and touched her chin.

Aw shoot. Sometimes his words were too straight forward.

Almost instantly her head came back up. "W-what must Mary think?" she stammered.

"She thinks I'm the louse that I am, I guess. Don't

worry about her. She's getting a kick out of this, I'd bet," Clint said, irritated all over again.

"She thinks it's funny?" Jessica groaned. "And why would she think you the louse, when I'm the one who took advantage of you?"

Surprise shot his brows up. "*You* took advantage of *me*?" He worked at not choking out a laugh. Could she be this naïve? Yes, he thought. She could. He chuckled warmly. "That's not possible, little one."

"Why isn't it?" Her expressive hazel eyes went wide with distress. "You were totally delirious, out of your mind with fever." She paused. "Though I didn't know it at the time," she added, almost too quietly to be heard. "But *I* was perfectly in my right mind."

Clint's heart did a funny wavering thing. Her willingness to shoulder the blame tugged at him. "Jessie . . . it's *not* your fault. It wasn't you who hauled me on top of you, now was it? I remember doing that now, although it was like my mind was on fire, and foggy all at the same time." He shook his head, trying to loosen more memories.

She blushed again, probably at his openness this time. Then he watched as she sat up straighter and lifted her chin. "But don't you see? That's exactly what I'm talking about. You weren't in your right mind, or you wouldn't have done it."

Her statement took him aback. Would he have done it? He waited for a gut reaction, something firm and inarguable that could set him back on solid footing. But he was left with only a tepid *no*, one that could be flipped to a *yes* faster than he wanted to admit.

She waited, her eyes boring into his, daring him to disagree. When he said nothing, her shoulders slumped.

Her expression, one of sheer disappointment, broke his heart. He had to remove that fragile, sad look.

Apologize. "Listen, Jessie . . . I . . ." Stumped, he let the sentence drop.

She squeezed her eyes closed at his lousy attempt. Sheer agony colored her sweet face, tearing him up inside. Truth be told, he had been poleaxed by her last night. Now, he needed time to get his mind straight. Problem was, he couldn't formulate any words to make it better for her when he was in such turmoil himself. But somehow he knew his thoughtless efforts to make things right had crushed something precious in her.

His gut twisted, knowing he still had to find out. When her eyes opened, he started again, more painstakingly. "I . . . I don't remember it all. I need to know what happened." That didn't sound quite right. He sincerely hoped she wouldn't think he'd just laid the whole responsibility of it on her.

Her expression shifted from sorrow to dejection, then to a sort of wild look when she finally hit him with a response. "Nothing happened that you don't remember, I'm sure."

"Jessie, really I—"

"No, let me finish," she said, cutting him off and shooting to her feet. A boldness he'd never seen in her before took over. "It was staggering and erotic," she went on, her words biting. Her eyes flashed and her thick ponytail flung about with each emphasized word. "It was delicious and remarkable and I don't regret one minute of it." Her fists were clenched at her sides now. "Though I should, since I'm sure God isn't pleased." She drooped at those words, like she'd withered a little inside. "Then you just . . . went

limp." She swallowed audibly. "Get it? I was so phenom-
enal, I put you to sleep."

She closed her eyes and gulped in an uneven breath,
like she was damming up a great sob. "You were delirious
the whole time!"

She opened her eyes and bounced a glance off him so
fast he wondered if she'd actually done it. He stared hard
at her profile. Mottled red had crept up her neck, and deep
grief lines deepened around her mouth. Lines he never
wanted to be the cause of again in this lifetime.

Her suffering struck him through the heart with the
precision of an iron-tipped arrow. He started to speak but
she held out a hand to stop him then shifted her gaze to
his eyes. Sporadic tears now streaked down her rosy cheeks.
"You're innocent." Her voice had diminished, as if there
wasn't enough energy left to finish. "So, you see, you have
nothing to worry about." She'd choked out her last words.

With that, she turned on her toes and fled from the
room. At the soft, restrained click of the front door, he
flinched, impacted more by that than if she'd slammed it.

Clint cursed, struggling to sit up and get his arm
out of the basin at the same time. All he managed to do
was slosh the water onto the floor. Her blatant confession
rattled him. What had possessed him to do such a thing?
Even delirious, he would have had some sort of restraint,
wouldn't he? The questions and doubts swam through his
mind.

"Mary, are you out there?" he hollered, rattling the
rafters.

Mary hustled into the room with a look of terror.
"What's the matter? Why are you trying to get up?"

He muttered a curse, remembered himself, apologized to Mary and all around felt half out of his mind with powerlessness. "It's Jessie. I got to go find her." He grunted with effort. "Help me up, Mary!"

She hesitated, then brought him her husband's old cane and hefted him to his feet. He wobbled, then planted the cane in front of him and shuffled toward the door.

Mary gripped his forearm. "You're still in your underwear, dear boy. I'll get your pants." He scowled when he saw her almost amused expression.

"I'm glad you find this so amusing, Mary, but I don't! Whether you believe it or not, I would never purposely hurt Jessie. I've got to fix this."

He started for the door again. Mary brought his pants to the front of him. Staring at her, he rolled his eyes and submissively raised one leg then the other. One-handed he buttoned them enough to keep them from falling off while hobbling toward the door. Mary followed.

He glared at her. "Stay here!"

She stopped and nodded her agreement.

Once out the front door and down the porch steps, he staggered toward a small pathway that led to a mountain stream, hoping that was where Jessie had fled. At first he thought the women's predictions that he'd faint would come true, but gradually he gained a little strength, powered by the resolve to find her.

Soon, he heard hiccupping somewhere in the woods. He slowed, cocking his head to guess the direction. Like he'd anticipated, the sounds came from the direction of the stream. He took a short cut, weaving his way through the pines, ignoring the pain the forest floor gave his feet.

He found Jessie on her knees at the edge of the stream, splashing the cool mountain water on her face. Every few seconds a hiccup escaped her.

He trudged toward her but stopped short, not knowing exactly what to do. Planting a shoulder hard against a pole pine, he propped himself upright to keep an eye on her while he tried to figure it out. But all he could think was: delicious, erotic, remarkable. All those charged words coming out of Jessie's mouth may as well have come out of his. *What do I do with this, God?*

What am I doing? Why am I asking God?

Then the answer came as clear as if it had been spoken aloud. Love her with your heart.

Clint blinked. Then blinked again. The fever must have jumbled his mind. But deep down he knew that wasn't it.

A spike of brittle anger rose up. *Now you speak to me, God?* The fury was unreal, a power so overwhelming and ugly that it could only have been fed by Satan himself. Yet it had been dwelling all this time deep in *his own* soul.

But the rage from his past—not gone by any means, only buried—paled in comparison to his present resentment. *How, God, could you have let me hurt Jessie? She loves you! She trusts you!*

* * *

Sensing a presence, Jessica stood and turned and stepped back at the sight of Clint. *How dare he follow—* But the thought cut short at the sight of him. His eyes were closed, his expression frozen in a grimace. One of Clint's bare shoulders gained support from a tree, while his white knuckled fist gripped a cane. A gray pallor had returned under his heavy stubble, and there was a sheen of perspiration on every bit of bare skin. His injured arm hung by his side as water and blood dripped off the ends of his fingers.

A sickening dread came over her. She approached him, not sure what to do. But when his knees buckled and he started to slip down the tree, she ran to hold him upright. Instead, she slid with him all the way to the ground, enduring the bark that bit into the backs of her hands, knowing it did the same to Clint's back.

"Clint! Why did you follow me? You shouldn't be out here!" They slumped against the tree's base with her arms still linked tightly around him.

His eyes opened, and she gulped at how glassy they'd become. "I had . . . to find you," he said on small puffs of breath.

"Why?" Tears pooled in her eyes. "What can we say that wouldn't hurt even more?"

He stared at her with a pained expression, and she knew he agreed. He brought his good hand up to her cheek and weakly brushed a knuckle down it.

The action and the pity she saw in his eyes threatened to break her dam of tears. She steeled herself against the flow and looked down at the sweat glistening on his chest. He hadn't even taken the time to dress. She shook her head. This man . . .

"Do you think you can stand?"

She saw his Adams apple bob as he swallowed hard, then nodded. She draped his good arm across her shoulders, drew in a hefty breath, and pushed upward. He braced himself against the trunk with the other shoulder, scooting up the tree foot by foot. When they were finally standing, she wrapped an arm around his torso. He gripped her shoulder and leaned into her. Together they made their slow walk back to the cabin.

By the time they reached it, barely making it up the steps, Mary flew out the door. She looked stricken. "Oh, my goodness! I shouldn't have let him go." She grasped his free arm and ducked under it to stabilize him. "Not that I could have stopped him."

His skin was pasty. Watery rivulets skidded down his cheeks and cascaded off his jaw. His dark hair curled in wet clumps.

By the time they got him settled he was comatose. "It's my fault, Mary!" Jessica wrung her hands as she paced, feeling like a snared animal in the small room. Mary's gaze stayed affixed to her. "If I hadn't run off like I did, he would be improving instead of so much worse."

Mary blocked her path and caught her by the shoulders. "Jessica, you couldn't have known he'd follow you. And I shouldn't have let him go. Enough remorse from both of us. We're wasting time."

Mary was right . . . of course she was. Jessica rubbed both hands over her face and huffed a huge breath. She went straight to work with a damp washcloth, cleaning off the sweat and cooling down Clint's face. Next she bandaged the infected arm and dressed his scraped back. When she finished Mary did away with his jeans and tucked a sheet around him. With one last look, they left him to sleep.

Jessica sank down at the kitchen table, weary to the marrow. She sipped from the lemonade Mary had prepared for her. "It wasn't his fault, you know." Jessica sighed. "He's probably just embarrassed it was me last night."

Mary's eyes were kind. "Listen, Jessica, I guarantee it's you he's worried about."

Jessica groaned over that painful bit of information.

"I've never seen him so concerned over a woman

before. He's not inclined to follow God's ways, so he partakes in physical pleasures and usually thinks nothing of it. It's why he never gets involved with someone like you. Why he finds himself in painfully uncharted territory right now."

Hadn't Mabel said something like that in the ranch kitchen a few weeks ago? "Exactly what do you mean he would never get involved with *someone like me?*" She braced herself, not at all sure she wanted to hear Mary's answer.

"He . . . he believes you to be a maiden—untouched."

"He said that?" Blood rushed to Jessica's face. "To you?"

"Well, he used the word *pure*, but yes, he was worried he'd ruined you. He seems to know you would want to keep yourself pure for a husband. He doesn't see himself ever being one of those." She shook her head. "He would make a wonderful husband and father. It will be tragic if that never happens."

Any remaining hope of Clint's love died out in Jessica like the last flicker of a spent candle.

It was close to supper time, so Mary rose and began preparing a meal. When the woman waved off all offers of help, Jessica went in to soak Clint's arm instead.

He was ashen and, while his arm looked less infected, his whole physical state seemed to be deteriorating. Jessica tried to pray for him, but there was a strong interference. She knew she was the cause of it. Her own part in their intimacy had caused an embarrassment toward her Lord. Reminded again at how she must sadden Him, she now understood why Adam and Eve had hidden from God after they had sinned. Her own wanton behavior had caused the same result.

Evening passed while Jessica got to know Mary and intermittently checked on a restless Clint.

Mary rose from the kitchen table, groaning a bit with the effort after sitting so long. And no wonder. She'd told Jessica she'd been alone up here for over ten years since her husband's death. Heaven knew, Montana weather wasn't known for being easy on the bones, especially those of a solitary widow.

Jessica glanced at the darkness framed by the kitchen window and shivered. "Don't you ever go mad with loneliness up here?" Her hand flew to her mouth, but it was already out. Another impulsive, foot-in-mouth question.

"Oh, honey." Mary turned a kind eye to Jessica. "As it happens, a special guest is due to arrive in ten days. Her very first trip to Roy's spread. Can you imagine? All that time gone by . . . but now she's coming, and that's what counts."

There was such delight in Mary's face, Jessica couldn't help but smile back. "Who is it?"

Mary beamed. "My granddaughter."

"All by herself? I mean . . ." Jessica tried to imagine a young girl navigating a road filled with rogue grizzlies and hungry mountain cats. "How old is she?"

Mary looked at her quizzically, then guffawed outright. "Lands, child, you do me a great service thinking me young like that. But no, Rose Marie is one of those liberated women. Educated, sophisticated, as bold and beautiful as they come. Last I saw her, I was at her college graduation, and she was just stunning . . .

Mary prattled on, but Jessica had stopped listening. Maybe because of the ringing in her ears or the dread that seemed to bolt her to the floor. Maybe because this felt like God's devastating answer to prayer. Clint would never be hers, but he would be someone's, at least for a time. It didn't take a genius to figure out who that next someone might be.

Jessica clumsily excused herself from the table, only dimly noticing the shadow of concern between Mary's eyebrows. "It's nothing," she mumbled as she crossed to her cot. "Just tired." So tired of her heart being twisted till it tore in half like dry straw.

CHAPTER 18

Deep in thought, Jessica pulled hay from a bale and hand fed Bonnie the clump.

"Working hard?"

Jessica's pulse went wild at Clint's voice behind her, low and quiet, and rumbling up out of his chest like rolling thunder within the heavens.

"Want a break?"

She inhaled deeply then smiled over one shoulder at him. "You seem to be on the mend, finally. Your ups and downs have been worrisome."

It surprised her how calm her voice sounded when her heart sped more each time he came near. It had been nearly two weeks since the wagon incident, but he'd only been mobile in the last six days. In order to protect her heart, she'd done her level best to dodge him, which meant that lone walks in the woods and visits to the horses had become her norm. She wasn't sure how to slip away now that he'd cornered her.

He lifted a brow. "I know, thank God and all of that, right?"

Yes," she said, happy for the reminder. "That's exactly

right." She looked him up and down, trying to be casual about it. "What are you up to? Your hair's wet."

"Just had an ice cold bath in the stream. One you've probably wanted to give me for a while now. Like with a bucket over the head." He grinned and winked.

That grin could melt a glacier. His eyes were back to their same brightness, twinkling with amusement. He was dressed in jeans and a short leather vest over a green chambray shirt, rolled at the sleeves, flaunting wide shoulders. The shirt was the same one that made his eyes stand out in his tanned and now clean-shaven face.

He had finger-combed his hair straight back. "I've come with a request."

She turned away and resumed her task of giving the horses their hay, not wanting him to see the longing in her eyes that had set up permanent camp there. "And what would that be? I've already prepared your favorite fried chicken meal for tonight." She stopped and glanced back to see his reaction.

"Yeah?" His whole face brightened, squeezing her already pining heart. "I'll certainly look forward to that. But, no. That's not my request." He pulled the hunk of hay out of her hand and fed it to the horses. Taking her by the elbow, he helped her stand, facing him.

Fire shot through her from his touch. She locked her knees and folded her arms across her chest. Maybe that would keep her from collapsing in a puddle at his feet.

He dropped his hand to his side.

With a slightly raised chin, she prepared herself for what he might ask of her. If only it was her heart he wanted. "Okay, I'll give. What is it?"

"Would you give me a haircut?"

She blinked in surprise. He resembled a little boy asking for a piece of candy. She smiled a little, thinking this was a look she hadn't seen on him before. *Could he be more irresistible?*

"What makes you think I'd know how?"

"Because you've cut hair for five of the ranch hands."

Astounded that he had cared to notice, she smiled. "Seven, to be exact." She stared, relishing the hopeful look on his face. "When?"

"Right now. Sun's not down yet, so we've about an hour. I've got everything ready on the porch. Say okay."

She eyed him warily. How could she resist? It crossed her mind that she probably should. Funny thing. He looked as uncertain as she did. "Let me clean up a bit, and I'll meet you there."

* * *

Clint watched her make her way into the cabin, then he ambled to the porch. He sat down on a kitchen chair he'd already drug out and looked up at the cloudless sky, inhaling the piney scent of mountain air. He'd enjoyed his time up here, as hard as it had been health-wise. Contentment like he'd never known before had taken up residence in his soul. It was Jessie. As much as he fought it, he knew it.

She opened the door just then, and it was as if he'd never seen her before. Her gaze drifted to his, and he caught and held it. Those radiant eyes. Pine. No, lime—taking up the color of her blouse. Her cheeks were flushed with color. And, that hair. It was no longer in its usual ponytail. She stepped out onto the porch. The breeze stole the chestnut mane off her shoulders and blew it across her face in riotous waves and curls. She reached up and seized it, pushing it back behind her ears.

Clint's jaw sagged. She'd never looked more beautiful. Funny how he'd never thought of her as beautiful before. But, in that moment, her inner character and outer uniqueness meshed, and he'd never seen a more innately beautiful woman in his whole superficial, wretched life.

The question plagued him. Why was he having her cut his hair? It'd been longer than this plenty of times before. He could easily wait for Mabel to do the task. He straightened his spine as Jessie crossed the porch, picked up the scissors and comb, and continued toward him. His mouth was drying up.

She put one of Mary's small tablecloths around his neck and knotted it at the back. Tense moments passed as he counted his rowdy heartbeats. Jessie sighed from behind him, and he heard it all the way to his toes. Then her fingers were in his hair. She ran them up from his nape to the crown of his head, and he choked on his parched mouth.

Warm breath delighted his ear. "You okay?"

He dragged in a huge breath and managed a nod.

She used the comb next. That's safe. He heard a snip, snip, across the entire length. Good. That was good. He'd neglected his hair for a long while, and it practically sat on his collar. Way too long for ranch work. When he sweated, it hung in clumps and—her fingers were raking through the hair over his ear, once, twice. His eyes nearly crossed with pleasure.

She stopped, skirted to the front and stepped between his thighs. He choked for real this time. She waited while he coughed. He glanced up. She raised her brows in question.

Blasted woman. She looked too darned relaxed while he could barely breathe.

Irritated now, he nodded for her to go on. How was he going to endure the rest of this haircut? He'd thought it had been a good idea. He needed the trim, sure, but something had compelled him to get close to Jessie. She'd been avoiding him for a week, now, and he'd had enough. The hair cut *had* been a good plan. Now, he wasn't so sure.

A sprinkling of perspiration broke out on his forehead. One of the beads slithered down his temple to his jaw. He raised his eyes without moving his head. Her expression was purposeful, and her arms were elevated to allow her hands to do their handiwork. She didn't know he was watching.

Snip. Her fingers slipped through his tangles.

His heart missed a vital beat.

Snip. She sucked in her lower lip in concentration.

His breath lodged somewhere between his lungs and his throat.

Snip. Snip. He drew a hefty breath in through his nose. Bad idea. She smelled like heaven— fresh air, hay, and woman with a dash of lilacs.

He couldn't take much more of this. He squeezed his eyes closed and waited it out.

"There." She untied the tablecloth and tossed it across the railing.

"You done?"

"Yes." Her voice was husky.

His restraint snapped. He grasped Jessie's wrist and tugged her to his lap. She gasped and dropped the scissors and comb. They hit the porch boards with a clink. He wrapped her in a deep embrace. Hungrily he collected her lips in his for a soul-blistering kiss that lasted and lasted.

Breaking free for air, he whispered her name against her lips before he possessed her mouth again. It was an unguarded kiss. Everything was poured into it, as if he'd waited a lifetime for the fierce joining. With her. He felt her heart pound against his side. His matched its pace.

He should stop. Where was his good sense? It had vanished on the wind and he didn't care. He had to possess her. The porch, the pine trees, the breeze all faded out. He noticed nothing but Jessie's sweet smell, her soft lips, her avid response to him.

Suddenly, she broke away, and shoved off his lap. Her limbs trembled as she stood and stared down at him in bewilderment.

Disappointed and dazed, he peered up at her. He was a two-bit heel at what he'd taken, yet his body vibrated with the joy of it. She turned to go. Panic shot through him. He grabbed her hand and towed her back between his legs. "Jessie." His voice was gruff, passion-filled.

Her pupils had dilated, seemed to swallow up the lime green. There was no denying her desire was a mirror of his own. *Relent. Let her go.* But he couldn't. He tried to pull her down to his lap again. She stopped him with a palm to his jaw. Her eyes searched his, as if they were silently imploring him. They seemed to ask: *Is this purely physical? Is that all you want from me?*

He didn't know the answer to that unspoken question.

She must have seen his hesitation, since she backed out of his hold and stripped her hand from his. She turned and swung open the screen door.

"Jessie," he said in a voice hoarse with emotion.

She glanced over her shoulder, opened her mouth as if to speak, then must have thought better of it.

"I don't want you cutting any more wranglers' hair," he said thickly. And he meant it.

She hesitated, looking puzzled, then charged through the door.

Clint raked his fingers through his newly cut hair, feeling a touch of pride for Jessie's abilities. He shook his head. Why was he thinking such things, acting the way he was with her?

Unmoving, he sucked in deep breaths and examined his behavior. He kept flipping her life—and his—on end. He couldn't seem to right them no matter what he did. The only thing he did know, she was all he could think of. He didn't even try to stop himself anymore.

She belonged to him.

No! He needed to slake this all-consuming need to bind her to him.

As he remained fixed to the chair, he watched the western sky. A pale glow from the sinking sun made silhouettes of the tall trees against its fading pink glory. *What a beautiful sky You've painted*— Grunting, he ground the heels of his hands against his eyes. *What am I thinking?* Jessie was rubbing off on him. She was not like the rest. God was the center of her life. She would expect that of him as well.

She wants more than I'm capable of giving.

Clint remained on the porch after the sun had set. The gentle wind tried to sooth him, but pandemonium racked him deep inside. Physically he was frustrated beyond all reason now, which was ferociously clouding his judgment. And, though he wanted to blame the whole mess on his physical needs, he couldn't. It was Jessie. She had a stronghold on his heart strings. It made him feel like a wild stallion on tethers. What was worse, a stallion kept from that which he was born to do.

He dropped his gaze to the fists in his lap. He had to let her go. He had no choice.

The door squeaked open.

Clint bounded to his feet. *Jessie.*

"Clint, I—supper is ready."

He reached up and rubbed the back of his neck. "One of your meals will satisfy, that's for sure."

She seemed to want to retreat to the house, but didn't budge. Before she found her feet, Clint took the two steps to her and wrapped his fingers loosely around her upper arms. "Jessie, I'm sorry I keep . . ." He always knew the right words to say. Where were they now? "It's just that you're, uh—" He let loose of her with one hand and ran it down his face, blowing out a pent up breath.

Those wide eyes of hers were making mush out of his brain. And, he was a loathsome snake. She tried to pull away but he slid his hands down the length of her arms to capture her wrists. "Jessie—"

"Don't. Don't say anymore." Her voice was breathy. She smiled, but it looked pasted on. "Let's go in and eat. Fried chicken, mashed potatoes and gravy, green beans, biscuits, and even my apple pie." The deep breath she took hitched, and he feared the next would loosen a sob.

And just like that the agony on her face made Clint lose direction all over again. *Sweet, sweet Jessie.* He experienced an overpowering urge to sweep her into his arms and carry her deep into the forest; to lose himself in her, away from this life and the past that tormented him. When he could make his voice work again, he said, "You're amazing . . . you know that, don't you?"

Jessie teased her lower lip with her teeth as tears welled up in her eyes.

A pain shot straight through Clint's heart at seeing those banked tears. He wanted to fix this. But he couldn't seem to. Every time he tried, he only made it worse. Why did she have to look at him like that? Didn't she know he was broken? Unfixable?

Clint took another step closer. It forced her to tilt her head back to see his face. He stroked her cheek with his knuckles, planning to explain how it was with him and that there was no recourse for him but to go back to his previous life. It would be altered, but it would be comfortable enough. This tumult he'd been going through up here with Jessie had to stop. The daily flood of emotions had done him in.

And, more importantly, that way she'd be safe from him.

But, when she peered up into his eyes with so much open affection in her own, his gut kinked. Some sort of wall crumbled, along with his resolve to keep her at arm's length. "Aw, Jessie."

Slipping an arm around her waist he molded her to him. He reached up, slid his hand into her hair, and cradled her head. The gaze they shared almost matched the heat of the kiss that came next—the deep, momentous, enduring kiss.

CHAPTER 19

First light sifted through the lemony curtains in the little kitchen, offering an added glow to Jessica's fragile bliss. She stood at the stove and stirred oatmeal, her thoughts on the joy she and Clint had shared last evening. After the cherished kiss, Clint had cupped her cheek with a broad hand and looked at her. Just looked at her. With such deep meaning she'd been sure they'd reached a pinnacle of some kind. After that, both had entered the cabin and enjoyed the meal Jessica had prepared. With Mary none the wiser, she and Clint had communicated with long gazes, knowing smiles, and covert touches. She'd wanted the treasured hours to never end. When finally Jessica had settled on her cot for the night, her happiness had even touched her dreams.

Yet, in the light of day, she wasn't at all sure what had happened. The kiss hadn't been in her imagination. But the rest?

Clint had made a subtle change. He sprawled in the kitchen chair, too small for his large frame, his full attention on the coffee cup he gripped. Lost in thought. Emotionally detached. Dark stubble had already taken shape on his splendid, solemn face, and he seemed to have skipped combing his shorter hair other than with his fingers. She couldn't quite catch a gaze from him, let alone the deeply intimate ones from the night before.

Mary had no idea what had gone on between Jessica and Clint, yet her actions seemed to show apprehension. She was smart and intuitive. Maybe she'd picked up on something Clint wasn't revealing, or maybe it was her own excitement of her granddaughter's planned arrival this afternoon.

As content as Jessica was last night, a premonition that something bad was going to happen clung to her soul like a cold sweat to the skin. Try as she might, she couldn't seem to shake the dark sentiment.

After breakfast the three busied themselves in preparations for Rose Marie's arrival. Clint cleaned his belongings out of the bedroom and set up a cot for himself in the kitchen.

When they sat down for lunch, Clint's aloofness was just as potent as it had been at breakfast. Though she and Clint were cordial to one another, hesitant glances seemed to be their only form of communication today.

Once the food was eaten with little interest, the three continued their tasks.

"I'm taking Jessie's cot to your room," Clint said to Mary.

"Sure, that'll be grand. Are you sure you're up to all this lifting?"

"It's not heavy, Mary. I'm fine, a bit tired is all."

Clint was coming out of Mary's bedroom when there was a quick rap and the front door flew open. Clint sucked in a quick breath. Jessica spun to him to see what was wrong. He was gawking in mesmerized wonder at the front door. His sharp green eyes had widened in a stare of such awe, it multiplied the disquiet she'd withstood all day long.

As if in slow motion, Jessica twisted toward the object of his unquestionable focus. As surely as a curtain drawn open on a stage, her promised foreboding materialized right before her eyes.

In the doorway was the most exquisite woman she'd ever seen in her life—as strikingly beautiful as Clint was overwhelmingly handsome. A tall, willowy, Marilyn Monroe-look-alike. And the minute she started talking she commanded the attention of everyone in the room, including Walt who was now standing behind her, grinning, as if he'd brought them Princess Grace.

"Oh, there you are, Grandma! It's so good to see you again. You look wonderful." Her voice was confident and silky, nothing like the breathy Marilyn's. She floated through the room with the poise of a royal. Her skirt and petticoats—*petticoats?*—flowed as she glided toward Mary and clasped her in a huge hug.

Releasing Mary, the princess swung around. The vivid yellow skirt twirled about her legs like a breeze through daffodils as she offered a hand to Jessica. Her smile was captivating. "Now who might you be?"

Jessica stared at the proffered hand, then took it. Finally, she wrenched her gaze away from their shaking hands to the woman's face. "I'm Jessica, Roy's niece," she said around a throat so dry it felt like the Sahara.

"Well, now, I'm very pleased to meet you, Jessica. Your Uncle Roy was very kind to lend dear Walt to drive me all the way up here." Jessica dropped her hand to her side. In a matter of a few short moments she felt totally inept—outclassed and outmoded.

Rose Marie turned once again as she must have realized there was another person in the room she had yet to meet. When her gaze landed on Clint she gasped and touched her fingers to her lips.

"Oh, my! And who in the world are you? Clint, perhaps?" she said around her fingertips. By the look of appreciation, it was clear Rose Marie was as captivated by Clint as he was of her. Withdrawing her hand from her mouth, she offered it to him.

In a flash Clint became the person Jessica had seen at the dance—charm extraordinaire. Even though he was not wearing his Stetson in the house, he brought a hand up to pull on its imaginary bill, and with casual charm said, "Hello, beautiful. A real pleasure to finally meet you." He gave her one of his famous smiles, and took her hand in a gentle shake.

Jessica froze. *Hello, beautiful.* It was all she could do to force her lungs to take the next full breath. What she wanted to do was run out of the cabin in screaming hysterics.

Clint and Rose Marie gazed over each other's faces in full perusal, still clutching hands. Jessica looked on in a torturous, endless, out-of-body sort of moment. So awkward were the next few seconds that Jessica thought she would faint dead away from lack of oxygen.

"Jessica, let's go get your cot fixed up, shall we?" Mary said, recognizing her distress. "Clint can explain to Walt why the Big-H's foreman has been up and missing for so long."

Mary shifted her gaze to Rose Marie. "I'm sure you'll want to put your things in your room and freshen up. We'll be back in a minute."

Mary's orders broke the spell between Clint and Rose Marie. They released each other's hand and did as Mary suggested. Mary grabbed Jessica by the arm and pushed her through the bedroom door. She closed it and wrapped Jessica in a huge bear hug. Jessica struggled to control her ragged breathing, and then slowly pulled out of Mary's embrace, unwilling to appear so weak.

"I'm fine, Mary. Really."

Mary studied her face. She knew it must be fuchsia by now since blood had filled her head, making it pound with unbearable pressure. Mary pushed her to sit on the bed and sat down next to her. She put a finger under her chin and pulled it up, forcing her to look straight at her. Mary wiped at tears on Jessica's cheeks she hadn't even known she'd shed.

"Jessica, I have to admit there was a time I'd hoped Rose Marie and Clint would meet and fall in love. It was a selfish dream. Since then I've realized they'd be no good for each other. They're too much alike. Now, after meeting you, I have no doubt God has a different plan. If Clint hadn't had his mishap, you would have long since been back at the ranch when she arrived here today. I would have preferred that for your sake, but truth is, we have to trust God in this since you *are* here. Only God knows the plan."

Jessica's heart floundered. After her elation last night, there seemed no graceful way to retreat from this cold reality. Quite suddenly she felt trapped. *Why did I have to witness this monumental meeting?*

"Clint is fighting with all of his might against God and good sense," Mary went on. "But because of you I can see that he has come closer to God. He is drawn by your goodness and purity, Jessica. That's why you must cling to God, continue to do what's right, and wait."

That last comment woke Jessica out of her stupor, opened her ears, and stung her conscience. When it came to Clint she *hadn't* done what was right. She hadn't pleased God at all. She hadn't even asked God if Clint was who He wanted for her. So, why should God help her in this?

"Jessica, are you okay?"

She looked over at Mary, shook her head, hesitated, and then nodded. "I'm going . . . I'm going outside. Maybe you c-could give my apologies if anyone asks?" She groaned at the arrival of the dreaded hiccups.

Mary gave Jessica's arm one last squeeze and cracked the door open. Jessica could see Walt and Clint sitting at the table, visiting. Rose Marie hadn't come back into the kitchen yet. Mary opened the door wider. Jessica slipped out and rushed toward the front door, not stopping to talk to or even look at either man.

As she crossed the room a huge hiccup escaped her. Grimacing, she hurried to open the door and sped out.

* * *

Clint spotted Jessica scuttle across the kitchen toward the front door, heard a hiccup, and immediately came to his feet to follow. Mary put a hand to his shoulder, pushing him gently back to his seat. She came around the table, caught his gaze and shook her head, then turned to the stove.

Clint was torn. He wanted to follow Mary's lead. Plus, he should stay to visit with her granddaughter. But his heart was aching, familiar enough with Jessie's hiccups to know she was upset. He thought back over his fixated reaction to Rose Marie and knew he'd been the cause of Jessie's pain. Hurting her shattered him. Over and over.

For now, he needed to go to her, but he didn't know what he'd say and he was tired of doing it all wrong. Rising annoyance was churning his blood. Okay, so it was true. He couldn't deny he'd had an initial reaction to Rose Marie, and Jessie had witnessed it. Rose Marie was the most beautiful woman he'd ever laid eyes on, and he'd seen plenty. But, this was his way. This *was* who he was, and Jessie had better get a hold of that. Hadn't he already proven he couldn't fix this thing between the two of them?

So, why was not fixing it grating against his soul?

He sat with Walt, not hearing a word the little man said, when Rose Marie made her re-entrance. She had freshened up and was now in a dress the color of wild violets. Low cut. Definitely not appropriate for Montana, but what an image. Clint couldn't hold his tongue. "You look remarkable, Rose Marie." He rose to pull out a chair for her.

But concern for Jessie tugged on his tattered conscience, so after pushing Rose Marie's chair into place he turned to head outside.

Mary gave him a chastising stare. At the same time, Rose Marie fastened a hand to his arm. "Clint, I had hoped we'd have supper together and get to know each other." She gave him a bright smile and coaxed him to sit down with a short tug on his arm. "Grandma spoils me. She's making my favorite tea. Would you like some?"

Clint glanced at the door, then back to Rose Marie and—he was certain it was for Mary's sake—he stayed.

Jessica plodded through the woods and down to the stream. She knew she'd miss supper at the cabin, and was sorry she'd disappoint Mary. But she couldn't go back. She wasn't ready to face the admiration Clint and Rose Marie would lavish on each other.

When trouble hit in Jessica's life, she could usually find peace from somewhere. Today, all she seemed capable of was sorrow.

After wandering aimlessly for some time she found her way back to the horses. Lifting the curry comb from the shelf in the lean-to, she brushed the chestnut's neck and back with long, tender strokes. It was peaceful, caring for the animals, taking her mind off things. At least a little.

A Scripture came to mind. She recited it to Bessie, hoping to find needed peace. Jeremiah 29:11, "For I know the plans I have for you—declares the Lord—plans to prosper you and not to harm you, plans to give you hope and a future." She contemplated her Lord and why His prophet Jeremiah had given those words of encouragement to Israel while they were in exile.

I'm in a place where I don't want to be right now Lord, like they were. I know I have two choices, just like Israel did. Either to see all that's wrong with my situation and feel sorry for myself or to choose to make the best of my situation and live for You. Please help me to do the latter. My heart is aching and my mind is tangled, so I need your help to make sense of it.

She gazed at the western sky. God held all that glory in the palm of His hand. A spectacular shade of ginger lit the treetops up like tapers. She took a deep, admiring breath, and hiccupped.

"You're disturbing the peace with those cute little hiccups of yours," Clint said, in a rumbling voice at her back.

She jumped, then turned to look up in his face. A matching bleakness passed between them. She turned back to the sunset, not wanting his sympathy to bring on tears. "How long have you been standing there?"

"Long enough." He came closer. "Jessie—"She stiffened. "Don't. Please don't try to explain anything to me." Her voice was gruff, but she couldn't help herself.

Jessica wanted to cry or laugh hysterically at the absurdity of it all. Why had she continued to place hope where there had never been any?

He didn't say anything more. Out of the corner of her eye, she saw him studying her profile. Her lids slid closed at the anguish of it, wishing he would go away and let her suffer in peace.

He grasped her shoulders and turned her toward him. She flinched at the wave of heat that coursed down her arms to the tips of her fingers at his touch. His palm cupped her cheek, and with his thumb he raised her chin. His expression was so grief-stricken it pricked the hope she had neatly stored away, giving rise to tears that were too close to the surface.

Though she kept her back ramrod straight, the dam of restraint gave way and a few errant tears spilled onto her cheeks. Clint brushed them away with the pads of his thumbs, and that touched her heart and created more. His own eyes glistened as he lowered his head and gently kissed her lips. Salty tears intermingled with sweet tenderness.

* * *

Agony. So deep it seemed to permeate Clint's soul. His recently resurrected heart, tenuous at best, was fragmenting all over again. Part by painful part. He ended the sweet contact and raised his head. *Where does this leave us, sweet Jessie?* The thought bounced off the walls of his mind as he stared into the depths of her sad eyes. Not able to endure her hopeless look any longer, he gathered her into his embrace, fitting her like putty into the crags of his body. He hugged her as a man about to leave his bride to go off to war. If only they could stay like this and never promise a thing.

It wouldn't take much to pull this sweet thing into an ungodly relationship. She was on the edge, he knew it. But he couldn't do that to her. He had to release her. Allow her to find another. One that would keep her pure and marry her as she deserved.

Johnnie's face swam before his eyes, and an unrivaled surge of jealousy spiked. The thought of her with another man clawed at him—especially a man he knew. How could he stomach it if she married someone and lived on the ranch? To see her every day and know she belonged to someone else—offering the man private smiles, and a shared bed . . .

No! He couldn't—wouldn't. Yet his past prevented him from going where his heart so desperately tried to lead. Never before had he allowed a woman to wind her way around his heart like this. When he let her go—and he *would* let her go—that part of her, hopelessly entangled in his heart, would eventually wither and die, and take a big chunk of him right along with it.

Jessie leaned away, looked up, and searched his face. The evidence of sorrow was there in her beautiful, glistening eyes. "That felt a lot like a good-bye kiss, Clint." Tears streaked her flawless skin. "Is that what it was?"

He still didn't have the answer. The silence between them became unbearable, forcing him to find his voice. "Jessie," was all that emerged. The lump that was cutting off his air supply kept him from saying more. He roped her to his chest again and rested his cheek on her head.

Finally, when he thought he could withstand the absence of her touch, he loosened his hold. But, the need for one last touch brought his callused fingertips to her soft face. He slid them down her cheek, gathering up the gut-wrenching tears he'd evoked. Ducking down, he gave her a lingering, open-mouthed kiss on her forehead. Her soft flesh beneath his lips tore the last trace of resolve out of him. He'd fall apart right at her feet if he didn't leave her. Now.

He turned away, and a deadly fog of loss settled over him.

Clint entered the cabin, burdened with hopelessness. He was glad the ladies had gone off to their bedrooms, and Walt had taken to the stream with his bedding. He stripped off his shirt and boots and lay on the rigid cot wanting for sleep, hoping tomorrow would carry with it some answers and a suitable direction.

Eventually, he heard Jessie open the front door and slip past him, a hiccup escaping as she opened Mary's bedroom door. "Goodnight, little one," he said before the door shut behind her with a soft click. He winced and squeezed his eyes shut in abject misery.

Sick from the ache, he forced his fury to build instead, thinking how Jessie should know better. She knew who he was. How he lived. He was glad she had seen his reaction to Rose Marie. Maybe now she would destroy the pedestal she'd built under him and let him be. Perhaps the longing he saw in her eyes would finally go hollow.

But even as he concentrated on straight forward logic, chaos reigned. He combed his hands through his hair, as if that would control the pain inside his head. He'd only gotten halfway through the motion when he stopped and pulled his hands away from his scalp. He touched his thumb to each fingertip . . . wet. He wiped the back of his hand over his forehead: sweaty. Inside he cringed. The fire and fog were sliding back into his mind and body. As he lay there assessing his life, he finally fell into a fitful sleep.

Clint jolted awake. Heat rolled off him. Delirium had returned in full force. His mind caught fire as sleep and fever dragged him back under.

Nightmares crowded in on him. He saw himself running after two women. Both were laughing and calling to him playfully. One was a beautiful blonde, the other a lovely brunette. As they raced along a path together, with him at their heels, a fork in the road came into view. Somehow he knew a grizzly waited to the right. The blonde took the turn to the left. She stopped to watch and continued to laugh. The brunette looked back as she ran. She reached out an arm to him. The smile she gifted him with was as dazzling as the morning sun.

To his horror, she made the turn to the right.

He opened his mouth to scream, "Grizzly!" but nothing came out. He tried to run after her, but his legs had grown thick and slow. Frantic, he searched for his rifle—nowhere. She didn't see the enormous bear, and he knew when she did the fright alone would kill her. Closer and closer she ran toward it.

Clint struggled but couldn't do a thing. Was his body

bound? He glanced down. No. He concentrated on his feet. Move!

She screamed just then. His head snapped up and he saw she'd lost her footing. Her arms wind-milled, propelling her straight toward the beast.

"No!" He shouted, sure the sound had finally ejected from him.

Someone from behind jerked him away from the carnage.

He whipped around, and there she was, his precious Jessie. Whole. She wore the lacy white nightgown with the ribbons untied at her throat. Somehow he knew he'd been the one to untie them. Frenzied desire for her ignited and shot straight through him. She pulled on his arm, bidding him to follow.

"Jessie," he murmured. He found his footing and stumbled along after her.

She tugged him down next to her on a bed. "My but you're hot. Let's get these clothes off you," the soft voice said.

"No, little one. You don't want to do this." He stilled her hand. Though physical desire was driving his body, his mind was fighting for control.

"It's okay," the voice said as she pressed a kiss to the cleft in his chin. Her hands were traveling to loosen his clothing, unleashing his craving for her. But something was wrong. This wasn't the sweet innocence of an unskilled lover. Even in his delirium, he could sense the mistake. He tried to wake himself out of the stupor, but need and fever took hold and drove him deeper in.

CHAPTER 20

Dawn broke, and slices of light entered Mary's bed-room. Jessica, exhausted from her uncomfortable cot and a long, fitful night of elusive sleep, rose and dressed in all but her boots. She needed to draw comfort from the sunrise the Lord would paint today. Her heart was worn out, as if it had run a marathon on its own. She slipped out of Mary's bedroom, carrying her boots, and tiptoed into the kitchen.

The wood floor felt icy even in her stockinged feet. She would have quietly slipped outside to draw on her boots, but the need to catch a glimpse of Clint forced her around the table to his cot. Empty. He must be outside. He'd be tending the horses, or watching the sunrise.

Jessica made her way out the front door, and slipped it closed behind her. Her gaze roamed about as she caught a glimpse of the horses standing with heads lowered in sleep. There was no sign of Clint anywhere close by.

The air was cool as Jessica breathed it in, trying to revitalize a flagging spirit. Glancing eastward, she noted dark clouds had blocked the sunrise. She shivered with inexplicable apprehension. Jessica lowered herself to the wooden bench by the door. She'd almost finished tugging on her first boot when anxiety over Clint's whereabouts hit again, this time as hard as a brick dropping through her stomach. It was the kind of feeling a person could not ignore. She yanked her boot off, opened the front door, and turned to see the door to Rose Marie's bedroom standing open. Suddenly, overwhelming sorrow shoved her heart straight to her toes.

Please no. Unable to ignore her morbid curiosity, she advanced to the doorway. In the dim morning light, Jessica blinked to clear her eyes. The first thing she saw was a tangle of white sheets. Over one body? She blinked again. No. Two! Her breath squeezed painfully out of her lungs and seized. She struggled to take another life-sustaining gulp of air.

Her eyes adjusted more. There, before her, was the man who owned her heart, sprawled on his back in *Rose Marie's bed*. The princess was pressed to Clint's side with an arm lying possessively across his bare chest, and a leg across his thighs. The sleeve of her nightgown was pushed up to her elbow, and both were fast asleep within that pile of sheets.

For one shock-ridden moment, Jessica stood fastened by despair to the cold hard floor. With wooden motions she caught hold of a curl of hair and twisted it tight around a finger until a welcome throbbing pain began. When her rubbery legs finally heeded her commands, she turned and dashed out the door. She fled to the stream, ignoring the sharp edges of rocks and pine needles on her bootless feet.

Jessica found Walt awake and rolling up his bedding. She stopped a couple of yards away. "Walt," she squeezed out.

Startled, he looked up. He furrowed his gray brows. "What is it, Jess-girl? What's happened?"

She couldn't speak.

He rose and came to her. His face paled as he took her by the shoulders. "Tell Walt here what's wrong."

"It's—" she started, then choked on a sob. "I found them. In b-bed!"

Walt looked stunned. "Who?" He paused and looked toward the cabin.

She squeezed her eyes closed. Tears pushed through her lids and wet her cheeks. "Clint. And Rose Marie. Just now."

She opened her eyes and saw Walt studying her face. He didn't speak for a long moment. "You're in love with him, ain't ya, girl?" He sounded guilt-ridden. "I shoulda knowed." Deep lines etched Walt's leathery skin. "Well, 'ole Walt don't know much, but I sure do know you cain't stay here."

She swiped at tears that wouldn't cease. "But I can't just leave, Walt. I can't leave Mary, or not explain, or something. I don't even know what." Her limbs were shaking now.

"Here." He handed her his bedroll. "Go ta the buckboard. I'll be leavin' Mary a note" —he glanced at her feet—"and grab yer boots, and we'll head back ta the ranch . . ." In all my days I never thought Clint'd ever do such a thing in front of Mary." He shook his head in disbelief.

Jessica watched as Walt went inside. When he came back through the door, his jaw was set and an iron expression shown in his eyes: outrage.

Walt hitched the horse to the buckboard as Jessica numbly climbed in. Not a word was muttered on their ride home.

Clint pried his eyelids open and groaned. His eyeballs stung like he'd been in a desert sandstorm. Had he been on a binge last night?

He glanced around the room to get a fix on where he was. Ah, *Mary's guest bedroom.*

Rose Marie's bedroom.

He bolted upright. The room spun, and he collapsed back to the pillow. Heaving in large

gulps of air, he tried to figure what happened this time. He stared down at the tangle of sheets over him. Slowly, not wanting to—but sure he needed to—he lifted the sheet away from his chest to look underneath. He grimaced and squeezed his eyes shut. *Naked. Now what have I done?*

Clint heard muffled voices coming from the kitchen. He could tell they were angry ones, but couldn't make out what was being said, or who was saying it. Not Walt. No male voice among the dialog.

"You did what?" Mary's voice came through, loud and shrill.

His bedroom door flew open, and a half-angry, half-victorious-looking Rose Marie traipsed through.

Clint tensed. Deep in his bones, he knew this was not going to bode well for him.

Rose Marie grabbed the little chair Jessie had been using to nurse him to health, and scraped it over to him. She plopped down in it, snatched his hand off the bed, and clutched it to her chest. "You remember last night, don't you?"

Clint's tenuous gut spun a mutinous turn. "Last night?"

Some of the high color in her cheeks seeped out. "Yes. Last night."

Clint shot a glare at Mary, who was standing in the doorway. Her stance caught him all wrong. "What's she talking about?" he barked. He wrenched his hand out of Rose Marie's as he narrowed his eyes. "What're you talking about? And how did I get in this bed?"

"Go to the kitchen and prepare a cold, damp cloth for me to put on Clint's head," Mary said to Rose Marie. There was something terribly wrong with Mary's demeanor. "We need to bring his fever down. Also, get the colloidal silver."

Rose Marie looked defeated, but he couldn't worry about her right now. She came to her feet and went to do as she was told.

"Close the door on your way out, and don't come back until I tell you to," Mary said.

When Rose Marie was gone, Mary took in several deep breaths before attempting to speak. "You must have run a high fever again last night, Clint. This time it wasn't Jessica who came to help you, but Rose Marie. She came out to your cot and brought you back to her bed."

Clint dropped his jaw. *How's that possible? It was Jessie. I'm sure of that.* He blinked his grainy eyes in disbelief. He searched his muddled brain for answers, trying to make sense of what he was hearing. *A white nightgown.* He covered his eyes with a palm as memories of the night started to empty into his mind. He gazed up at the ceiling. But, there was no safety in the rafters.

"I was having nightmares about trying to save Jessie. No matter what happened I could never save her." He cringed. "And this blonde . . . pulled me in her direction. I couldn't control it." He stopped talking and gritted his teeth in anger. *No, it can't be.* He remembered only part.

What else happened? He was getting mighty tired of these out-of-his-control kinds of occurrences. One thing he knew for sure, it had *never* been Rose Marie he wanted.

Feeling that *familiar morning* after revulsion, he finally understood he no longer wanted the unlovable, unattached kinds of relationships anymore.

"Mary, where's Jessie?" He swallowed against an unyielding throat. "I have to talk to her."

For a minute, Mary looked like she'd rather be anywhere else. She dipped her head and pinched the bridge of her nose.

Clint felt a great, disastrous black hole open up below him.

Finally, with a huge sigh, she said, "Jessica saw you in Rose Marie's bed. She and Walt have gone."

"Nooo!" Clint bellowed. "Why would she leave? They always leave!"

Mary looked confounded by his statement. Well, frankly, he was too. He didn't know where the thought came from, and he didn't want to dwell on it right now.

"Help me up, Mary. I've got to find her. She has to know." Clint shifted his body to one side and leaned hard on an elbow. Before Mary had a chance to help him, he struggled to sit up, only to have weakness overtake him. Trying one more time he soon yielded and fell back onto the bed.

"Mary . . ." Where did his strength go?

"I'm right here, Clint."

"Go after her."

He slid into unconsciousness.

* * *

Jessica and Walt made it back to the main camp in record time. Jessica sat in paralyzed silence most of the way, with old Walt doing his best to comfort her the only way he knew how, by reminding her that God was in control. She knew who was in control, but her heart was too crushed to listen to reason or to God right now, and it didn't matter that she had no right to feel this way.

Once Walt pulled the buckboard up to the back porch, Jessica jumped down and dashed straight to her room. She closed the door and fell face first on her bed.

Hours later there was a rap at the door. Slowly the door opened. Mabel peeked in. "You awake, dearie? I've brought you somethin' to eat."

"You can come in, Mabel, but I'm not hungry." She just knew Mabel was going to say *I told you so*. And she'd be right.

"Do you feel like talkin', sweet girl?" Mabel asked.

The last thing she wanted to do was talk—to anyone—let alone Mabel. Then again, being addressed as *sweet girl* warmed her, maybe even enough to take a chance. "We can turn on my lamps if you'd like."

As soon as the lamps were on, Jessica realized too late that Mabel would see her ravaged eyes. "Oh, you poor dear," Mabel said, as if on cue. "Do you want to tell me what happened up there?"

Jessica's eyes widened at the motherly compassion she heard. When had that come about?

"I found Rose Marie and Clint in bed together this morning." Blunt words tumbled out. Hearing them again made her choke up, but she refused to blubber in front of Mabel.

"Jessica, let's start from the beginnin'. Tell old Mabel

about your weeks that led up ta this mornin's indiscretion, okay?"

Jessica stared at Mabel, surprised by the large word coming from this back country cook, but quickly forgot it for the explanation of the last sixteen days. Speaking of the sweet times with Clint made her weep, and speaking of the stressful times made her weep. But in the end she had managed to get everything said, right up to the time when she and Walt had left.

Mabel looked strangely contemplative. Jessica awaited the lashing she was sure to get. Then, Mabel said, "Okay. I gotta tell you some stuff about our Clint. He's never been mean-spirited and he's always guarded Mary from his . . . uh . . . ways. He'd have gone outta his way *not* to do what you said he did in Mary's house—*especially* with Mary's granddaughter for Pete's sake!"

Jessica's face flamed. "What are you saying, Mabel? That I didn't see what I saw?"

"Calm down, missy." Mabel looked her in the eye. "All I'm sayin' is there's a good explanation, and you can take that ta the bank! How well do ya know this here Rosemary or Rose Marie, however you say it? I don't trust her. I didn't like how she acted when Walt brung her here."

"I *don't* know her."

"Well, girlie, how do ya know that Clint wasn't in one of his fevers again, and she tricked him?"

A disbelieving snort snuck out before Jessica could stop it. "That's a little far-fetched, isn't it, Mabel? I mean, he had his own cot in the kitchen. How did he end up in the bedroom? With her?" She cringed all over again at the memory.

Mabel patted her hand. "I don't know what happened,

but I do know our Clint. He's a good man, Jessica. Doin' that kind a thing just ain't in him. In fact, more than that, I'd bet when he finds out you saw . . . somethin'—I'm not saying what, mind you—he'll die a thousand deaths."

Jessica heaved a sigh. "I know you love him like a son, Mabel. But I know what I saw. And I know how he reacted when he first met her. And, I know he gave me a good-bye kiss and hug." She blinked and paused for a beat. "He didn't deny it." She tried to catch a good breath. "So what other truth there might be just doesn't matter." All hope drained out of her at her own words. "I need to put this behind me. I'll come help you."

"No sugar, you won't. You rest. You'll be helping me soon enough."

Jessica raised her head and caught Mabel's gaze, stunned by her caring.

"Maybe this isn't the best timing," Mabel said, "but I thought you should know Johnnie is the only cowboy that didn't lose his head over that . . . that . . . *hussy*."

"Mabel!" Jessica began to giggle, the grief of the whole situation making her giddy, then downright slap happy. Mabel joined in until they were both laughing so hard they couldn't catch their breath. The laugh felt good. But the ache in Jessica's heart returned full force, and the laughter died off.

Mabel inched closer, encompassed Jessica in stout arms, and squeezed. Then she rocked to her feet and shuffled to the door.

Jessica stood on shaky legs. "I'll be down to help you clean up, in a bit. The work will take my mind off things."

Mabel turned back with a smile so warm and solemn and heartfelt that Jessica actually hummed inside with gratitude. If she could have spoken over her clogged throat, she would have thanked her.

"Sure ya aren't takin' a shine to Johnnie, dearie? 'Cuz he don't like that Rosemary one bit, and he seems ta be smittin' with you."

Jessica tried to smile, thinking of Johnnie. *Solid Johnnie. Safe Johnnie.*

CHAPTER 21

Clint's eyelids fluttered, but he couldn't open them. He heard a chair scrape, and his heart shot into fourth gear. *Rose Marie?* He jumped slightly at a cold cloth against his eyes.

"Sorry. Trying to loosen the crusties. Hold still a minute."

Ah, Mary. Good. He heaved a breath and his heart settle back into tempo.

Mary pressed the wet cloth against his right eye, then the left, rubbing until the lashes were free of gunk. "Okay. Try that."

Clint slowly forced his lids open to narrow slits and stared at Mary. The light shining through the little bedroom window stung his eyes.

"You lucid?"

"I'm here." His voice was hoarse and weak. "Water?"

"Of course. Here." She raised his head to give him a sip. "Better?"

He nodded.

"Now, tell me how you're feeling."

He cleared his throat and averted his gaze from her.

"Tired. Beat up. Sad about wasting my life on the wrong women." He coughed and swallowed. "Anxious to see Jessie."

Mary laughed. "Well, at least you have your sense of humor intact."

"I meant every word of that." His voice was gaining strength. He looked directly at her. "How long have I been out?"

"Three days."

"*Three days?* Not possible!"

"I wish it weren't true. We thought we were going to lose you." He saw the fear in her eyes and knew the truth. "Your fever got so high we had to douse you with stream water to keep it down. I don't know what *bug* you had in you, but I hope it's finally gone now."

"I've got to get to Jessie. It must be torture for her, thinking I'm up here having my way with Rose Marie." He winced. "She might have gone back to California or done something else rash. I gotta get back to the ranch. Help me up!"

"Wait just a gall-darn minute, young man! The last time you tried to sit up, your eyes rolled back in your head and you didn't come out of it for three days. Now, let's take this a bit easier this time. Can you do that?"

"Fine. But help me, will you?"

Mary tugged at one arm and with his help managed to pull him to the edge of the bed with his feet flat on the floor. He leaned against Mary as she settled in next to him. After he sat for a spell she gave him small sips of water. Tugging the sheet over his hips, she said, "Okay, sit for a bit to get your bearings. I'm going to warm you up some broth. We have to get your strength up."

When Mary left the room, Rose Marie came gliding in, looking every bit the beauty she was. Her day dress was pale blue, the color of her eyes, and her shiny blonde hair hung in waves around her pretty face. She shut the door quietly behind her. Clint pressed his forearms heavily onto his thighs and hung his head, trying to stop the spinning.

"Aren't you an absolute sight? Could they get any more inviting than you?" she whispered on a gush of breath.

Without lifting his head, he brought his gaze to her. Just looking at her made his blood boil. "Turn yourself around and go back out the way you came."

"I know you're not well, but you don't have to be so testy. Listen, Clint . . ." She cleared her throat. "About the other night—I think the best course of action would be to get to know each other better."

"Why?"

He could tell he'd surprised her.

"Are you saying you don't remember what happened?"

"I'm saying I'm not interested."

She looked astounded. Likely no one had ever told her a thing like that before.

"Jessica's sweet, Clint, truly she is. But, you two don't . . . match."

Rage hit him with an extraordinary impact, like the boom of unexpected thunder directly overhead. Part of him wanted the complete annihilation of this puffed-up tart while the other part was trying to analyze why he was so angry. He should be flattered. At the very least he should be in agreement about Jessie. "Truth is, sister, I've never hit a woman before. But if you don't turn your backside right around and go out that door, you'll tempt me to change my good record." "Now, Clint, you don't really mean that. You're worn out and tired and probably hungry."

"Hungry all right. But not for the likes of you!" He felt a flood of relief. No matter how things went with Jessie, he planned to leave the life of endless promiscuity behind, permanently.

"So, that's the thanks I get?"

That comment did it. The last one he wanted to hear from this haughty vamp. He was on his feet then, holding the sheet to his groin, swaying once, then moving toward her. "Get out!"

She backed up, threw open the bedroom door, and dashed out.

Mary staggered out of the way with a bowl of soup in her hands. "What's going on?" Soup sloshed over the sides and soaked into the throw rug on the floor. "Oh, for Pete's sake."

Clint barely made his way back to the bed, hoisted the sheet up to his chin, and flopped backwards. The bed springs bounced under his weight. "Come on in, Mary. Why bother knocking?" With his gaze fixed to the ceiling he ran his hands through his hair in frustration.

"Who put a sticker in your craw?" She sucked the soup off her finger. "You didn't seem to mind when we sat up with you all hours of the day and night fighting for your life, now did you?"

"Sorry, Mary, it's just that your granddaughter seems to be itching for me and—"

"Well, you are very handsome. And don't forget . . . naked."

Clint went on as if she hadn't spoken. "I guess I shouldn't be surprised. My way of life has finally bitten me in the backside. Why couldn't I see that before now?"

Pain etched his face, he knew, since he could see the compassion on Mary's. She set the soup on the nightstand

and parked herself in the chair to have a heart to heart. "I think it took a pure and gentle spirit like Jessica's to show you the way back to God and a righteous life."

"Whoa, now. I'm not talking about God. I'm talking about giving up carousing. That's enough, isn't it?"

"Give up carousing? For what exactly?" She sighed and waved a slender hand at him. "Never mind. Forget I asked that. We'll talk about it another time. Here, have something to eat. We need to get you stronger. We should probably get you dressed, too, so Rose Marie will quit gawking at you."

"Yeah," he breathed out. "Let me do that first, if you don't mind finding my clothes. I'll put them on in layers if need be."

A short time later, Clint shuffled into the kitchen, hands braced on whatever would support his weight as he moved. But at the sight of Mary's bowed head, he made a beeline for the kitchen table. "I heard the door slam. What happened?"

Mary watched him as he came around to sit in front of her. "Rose Marie's upset because I called her on the carpet for what she did to you three nights ago."

Instant heat climbed up his neck.

"I don't think I've ever understood that girl. Sometimes I think she's manipulative and spoiled and full of herself, like now. But the truth is, Clint, other times she is deep and centered and has agendas all her own. One's I don't know anything about. She's a mystery." Mary sighed. "And she's growing farther away from me every year."

"What did she say just now?"

"Right now she seems to want you. I should warn you, she usually gets what she wants. I think it would be prudent if she were to return home. She'll only cause more pain if she stays. I fear she'll stop at nothing to get you interested, or at least muddle things up for you and Jessica—"

"There's no *me and Jessica!*"

Mary waved that off. "Have you seen my granddaughter? As you can imagine, she's not used to losing."

Clint pondered that thought for a long moment. "I guess you'll be praying then."

Mary's face went rigid with surprise.

He saw her pleasure and cringed. "I said *you'd* be praying, Mary. Not that I would."

She smiled sweetly. "Fair enough. I'll do that."

"Now, I need to get back to the main camp."

Rose Marie came back into the cabin in time to hear Clint's statement. "I'll go with you. You mustn't ride all that way alone after being so sick." Sitting down right next to him, she smiled sweetly, almost apologetically, up into his face.

Veronica had been good at this same act. Cocking his head to one side, he studied her intently. She was a ravishing beauty, all right, yet he was surprised at his absolute lack of interest in her. In fact, he felt nothing, except disgust for his own shallowness. He had caught a true glimpse of himself, through his reaction to her, and didn't like what he saw.

"I'll leave at first light. No one is coming with me."

Mary looked troubled. "No, Clint. Rose Marie is right; you can't go on your own. You've been way too sick, and more than once you've fallen into delirium at the drop of a hat. You can't risk it. I won't let you."

"I'll go with him, I said," Rose Marie reiterated.

Mary rounded on her. "Well, I won't let you go with him alone granddaughter. *We'll* leave at first light. All of us."

Jessica missed Clint. Her heart ached with each beat, from the damage done to it, and their permanent parting of ways. The separation only managed to worsen rather than repair her fractured heart. Each day grew more painful, then each hour, and finally each minute until her every thought was consumed by him. In her mind she relived each moment, painful or not. Despite their incredible challenges she loved him so profoundly that the soul-deep love had changed her.

It had been three days. *Three days*. Her mind wouldn't give her relief from the thought of Clint and Rose Marie spending time together. Whenever she thought of them in that bed, it wrenched her heart another twist. Whenever Johnnie saw her anguish, he would gather her into his arms and hold her close. He never once got out of line, only silently held her for as long as she needed. Though she imagined he knew, he never pried as to the reason she was so distraught. Since Johnnie seemed the more deserving, she prayed incessantly for the Lord to replace her love for Clint with one for Johnnie. Yet she waited and none of that came.

On the third evening of her return Jessica stood by the stream, praying the water's journey would soothe her spirit. Johnnie came up next to her and laid an arm across her shoulders. He didn't say a thing—just held her.

A shout coming from the second bunkhouse shredded the peace. Pete was hollering out the door to anyone within hearing distance. "Come quick, it's Walt!"

Jessica burst to her feet and ran toward the building. But her steps slowed when she saw Uncle Roy charging out the bunkhouse door, his face ashen. He caught sight of her and veered her way. "It's Walt's ticker. A bad attack. He won't let us move him, but he keeps asking for you."

"*No!* Can't be." She gulped in a breath. "Can you get the doctor out here?"

"We've already sent for him. Hurry, Jess!"

Tears that seemed permanently close to the surface barraged her eyes. When she came to the door of Walt's bedroom, she slowed before she forged ahead. Two of the men were squatting next to his bed. When they saw her they both stood and moved aside.

"Oh, Walt," she said on a sob. She dropped to her knees to grab his gnarled hand in hers. Paleness invaded his tanned face. "Please, Walt, let us take you to the hospital."

"That you, Jess-girl?" Walt expelled the words in short puffs.

"Yes, Walt, it's me, Jess. I'm here. I'm not leaving. I'll be right here with you." She sputtered her words through the flood of tears that were now flowing across her lips.

"You must listen—" He stared intently into her eyes, and she understood in that instant to stop talking and pay close attention to his words. The strength to speak was fast leaving him. She dragged in a sustaining breath and brought her ear up close to his mouth to hear him better.

"Bring these cowboys . . . ta Jesus. I'm countin' on you."

Jessica's deep sob let loose, and she rubbed her cheek against his.

"Don't be sad . . . sweet girl." Walt stopped a moment to gather his breath. She leaned back to check him, and when she did his weakened eyes pleaded with her.

She put her ear near his lips again. "Bring them ta paradise with you. I'll be waitin'."

When his words stopped again, she looked into his face. The corners of his wrinkled mouth tilted upward. "I love you, Jess-girl. I'll see ya again . . . if ya . . . if ya know . . . . ."

". . . what I mean," Jessica finished for him, then carefully stretched her arms around the little man for one final embrace.

And with that, his body let out a long exaggerated breath, and he was gone.

Without loosening her hold, a huge sob rolled past her lips and was caught in the crook of Walt's neck. Tucked into his now still body, Jessica recognized it as the empty shell it was; it no longer contained the spirit of one of the noblest, most caring men she'd ever known. When she finally could bring herself to release him, she knew with certainty that Jesus had already escorted his soul into Heaven.

She heard sniffing from the men who had filled the room. Johnnie helped her to her feet and enveloped her in a deep hug of comfort. His tears trailed warmly into her hair; her tears streamed down her cheeks onto his shirt. And for one sweet moment of grief, she and Johnnie were one.

CHAPTER 22

Jessica hovered at the edge of Walt's grave and stared down at the plain pine casket. It wasn't what he deserved—he deserved a tomb of gold—but it was what he would want. Walt wholeheartedly believed life on earth was short, to be lived for God and others; and then when life was done, to be laid to rest in a plain box next to others who'd called Harper ranch their home. No frills. No accolades. This was not Walt's home. He was home now.

But, knowing that didn't ease Jessica's hollowed out, crushed soul.

She raised her tear-streaked face, and through glassy eyes, gazed at the people Walt had held dear. Not biological family. No, the ranch had been everything. The ranch hands, her, Uncle Roy.

Jessica opened her fist palm up. A cold rain splattered down from a blustery sky and dotted the dirt in her hand. She dropped the fist-full onto the casket before the rain could turn it to mud. Mud. Exactly what her heart must resemble.

When the service was over and the preacher said a

final 'Amen', Uncle Roy led her back down the path of the small knoll.

All grieved. None knew what to do with themselves—except for Jessica. She had berated herself so much, and wept so much since Walt's death, that her tears had dried up.

She wouldn't waste any more time on her own aspirations for a man who clearly didn't want her. If she'd only faced that sooner, she might have been able to help Walt with his crucial mission while he was still alive.

Now she must go forward, follow her new resolve.

Please forgive me, Lord, and help me to bring Your love to the souls around me. For Your Kingdom . . . and for Walt.

* * *

Clint might not feel like himself, by any stretch, but determination fired his need to get down the mountain and confront Jessie. Four days had passed since Jessie had traveled with Walt to the homestead, and Clint worried that each day broadened the wedge between him and the woman he cared about.

Clint's body ached in new places every hour, but he managed to hitch up the horses while Rose Marie and Mary packed the wagon. He slowly pulled himself onto the bench seat to embark on their half day journey home. Rose Marie insisted on sitting in the middle so she could keep Clint from tumbling off the wagon in the event of a relapse. Somehow he doubted that was her motivation, but he didn't have the strength to argue, so he agreed.

Clint looped the reins through his gloved fingers and gave them a crack. The horses sprang into action, much like Mary and Rose Marie did with their conversation. Clint found himself deep in thought, contemplating what he would say to Jessie.

"You know, I really like it here, Grandma. I could get used to living in Montana in the crisp mountain air. I do love the outdoors—riding everywhere in wagons and on horseback and such."

Tuning in for a moment, Clint frowned, recognizing the usual lie these beauties tended to tell. He didn't believe her any more than he believed the rest. Jessie on the other hand had always told the truth. And she actually did like the outdoors. In fact, she liked most things he liked.

His thoughts scrambled about in his head. How would he explain away what Jessie had seen between him and Rose Marie? Since he hadn't been conscious, he had no idea the view she had been given, though he could well imagine.

When they came to the spot where Clint had killed the bear, his gut tightened. Jessie had thought he was in danger. He smiled to himself over the way she had stripped all restraint and kissed him. That had cost her. She had risked rejection in order to share part of herself with him before he'd gone off to risk his life. The bear had been a feast for the wildlife, and all that was left was gnawed on carcass and a shredded pelt. If he didn't win Jessie's favor back, he knew his heart might end up resembling that bear.

Winning her favor. He rolled the thought around in his head. Would it really matter if he did or didn't? His head said *no*, but his heart said *yes*. Jessie would give any man a lifetime of happiness. He visualized himself as the recipient: Jessie loving him, her sweet sleep-flushed face smiling over at him in their bed each morning; Jessie in her frilly apron cooking for him; Jessie having his babies . . .

Who was he kidding? He'd never *been* respectable enough for her even if he did consider marriage. His breath jammed in his lungs at the hopelessness of it all.

The late afternoon sun dropped near the horizon. The ball of fire would soon vanish, but not before it left behind a colorful remnant of its former glory. A glory Jessie never failed to appreciate, making him miss her all the more.

A plan came to him the moment he set eyes on the grand house—Roy Harper's house. He would straight out tell her the truth of what she saw, and take the risk that she'd believe him. She deserved no less. And since it was Jessie, he knew deep down that she *would* believe him. He ached to see her and make her understand.

As they drew near, the main camp looked deserted. Where was everyone? He made a wide turn to bring the wagon to the back of the main house, and Clint's heart tripped at a sight on the back porch: Jessie with her back to him, and Johnnie in a chair in front of her. He gritted his teeth in instant, seething jealousy when he realized what she was doing. She had a handful of Johnnie's hair in one hand and scissors in the other. Johnnie *of all people!* The impact of the scene hit him so fast and so hard that his foolhardy plan was to jump off the wagon, run straight to Johnnie, and cold-cock him.

Jessie raised her head, swung around, and froze at the sight of them. One hand still held the scissors and comb while the fingers of the other were intertwined in Johnnie's hair. The cozy picture they made sent Clint's fury from a leisurely trot to a full-on stampede.

So busy with his own livid reaction to Jessie's *cutting another wrangler's hair*—after he'd specifically told her not to—Clint hadn't noticed that Rose Marie had moved closer to his side. When the wagon slowed enough, he yanked back on the brake and jumped out. Rose Marie toppled out after him with a startled scream. Clint whirled to find Rose Marie face down in the dirt. He glanced at Jessie, then at Rose Marie. Not wanting to deal with Rose Marie first but knowing he had to, he reached down, grasped her by the waist, and hoisted her to her feet. He lightly dusted off her face, and once satisfied she could make it on her own, he turned to face Jessie, who stood watching, mouth agape.

Clint felt Rose Marie's body squeeze into him. He dropped his gaze to her at the same time she peered up at him. She had successfully snaked her arms about his waist and squeezed, flashing a brilliant smile up into his face. One glance back at Jessie and he knew she had seen more than she wanted, and he'd only just arrived.

Clint watched in torment as Jessie turned her head to lock gazes with Johnnie. He couldn't see Jessie's eyes, but Johnnie's showed pity. A shudder of pure rage swept through Clint.

Jessie opened her fingers stiffly as if they were numb and the comb and scissors dropped into Johnnie's lap. She dashed to the screen door and threw it open with a loud squeak, leaving Johnnie alone in the chair with a neatly trimmed hairdo and the tablecloth still tied to his neck.

"Blast it, woman!" Clint hollered after Jessie. Rose Marie jumped out of his space as if his fury was for her. Weaker by the moment, Clint hobbled over to help Mary out of the wagon, then tromped to the porch.

Rage clogging his throat, and with no energy left, Clint could only pause and glare down at Johnnie. The same glower was being returned to him as both men heaved breaths through flared nostrils. Clint closed his eyes and expelled a final sigh before he turned away and stormed into the house.

Mabel took one look at him and rushed forward. Her stout arms wrapped half way around him and squeezed. She backed out of her own embrace and clutched his forearms in her hands. "Oh my, so thin and drawn. What's happened to my beefy cowboy?"

Clint stared down into her face. "Where's Jessie, Mabel?"

"Not even a hello for your favorite cook? Are you all right? You seem to me like you're gonna faint. You'd best sit right here." She gestured toward the bench.

His eyes narrowed. "If one more woman tells me I'm gonna faint, I will not be responsible for what I do to her!" Swaying, then bracing himself on the edge of the table with his knuckles, he held fast for only a moment before plopping down hard on the bench. "Okay. Afternoon, Mabel. Now will you tell me where Jessie went?"

"What happened? She came through here like a house a' fire and right out that front door. I'm guessin' she went down to the stream. Spends lots of time there these days." Mabel hesitated. Looked him in the eye. "Clint . . . I should tell you—"

Clint held up a hand to stop her words, then rose stiffly to his feet. He made his way to the front door and out to the porch, ambling down the steps and toward the stream.

He saw Johnnie jogging down ahead of him, looking like a fit athlete while he felt like a ninety-year-old man. Jessie was sitting on one of her favorite rocks where she was known to perch while watching sunsets. Time seemed to stop when Johnnie paused in front of her and then drew her into his arms. Clint's chest squeezed so tight it restricted his already laboring breath, but he kept moving forward.

For weeks now, the lasso that was Jessica Harper had been nudging his heart into working order, practically without his knowledge. Since then, Jessie's sweet spirit had settled the snare in place, sunk it deep in the tissue, and secured itself. He knew it was there. What surprised him was he didn't want to remove it anymore. In fact, he'd help tie that tether with an irreversible knot.

The truth was there. In his mind. In his soul. His heart belonged to Jessica Harper and would be there for the remainder of his days.

Yet, now that he'd faced the truth, it was too late. He blinked hard to keep the burning behind his eyes in check. He watched Johnnie with Jessie every step of the way, praying she would reject him.

She didn't.

Clint's temper flared and he sped up, keeping his eyes trained on them. No matter how this played out, she would give him the chance to explain about Rose Marie. But every step stripped a bit of the anger away and left sorrow in its place.

He heard her hiccups—those little noises that had become such an integral part of him. His own eyes grew moist knowing he had once again caused her distress. Would he ever bring her anything but grief? If he could only bring himself to leave her alone she might have a real chance at happiness.

He stopped a few yards from them, too numb to speak.

Johnnie lifted his head. There was pain in his eyes—for himself or for Jessica, Clint wasn't sure. At Johnnie's movement, Jessie leaned out of his embrace and caught sight of Clint. With an anguished cry, she wrenched away from Johnnie and ran downstream.

Clint groaned, then mustered his most commanding voice. "Jessica, stop! The rocks are loose down there." His strength was waning. He could barely walk after her.

Desperate to stop her, he sucked in a frantic breath and tried again. "Jessie. *Little one*. Please stop."

* * *

At Clint's sad, pleading voice, Jessica's legs weakened. She slowed to a halt then fell to her knees, barely noticing the bite of rocks on her skin. Planting her head in her palms, the last shred of fight in her broke. Clint's uneven steps sounded behind her.

Jessica sensed his nearness. He came around to face her, grasped her by the shoulders and lifted her to his embrace, enfolding her into a hold so tight she could hardly breathe. Her ragged breath rippled across his shirt, soon to be joined by fresh tears.

"I'm sorry, little one. I'm so sorry," he kept repeating.

Consumed by his powerful embrace, her heart threatened to beat her to death. She clung to him while his chin rested on the top of her head. This was home, right where she belonged. He was so warm, so strong, his scent—of leather and fresh air—so familiar. This time she wouldn't let go. All doubts of the past few days melted away like lard in a hot skillet.

They stood frozen in time until she sensed him wavering. His body quivered and bobbed. *What's wrong?* The tower of a man began to crumble. She leaned back and was shocked to see a single tear traveling down his cheek. But something else was happening, too. He was losing color, and sweat had dampened his skin. He toppled slowly, like a mighty oak collapsing into the forest. She held him to her, trying to cushion his long fall to his knees.

Once he hit the ground, his whole body buckled and fell to one side. Jessica gasped, rolled him onto his back, and shook him. "Clint! Clint, answer me!"

He didn't answer.

"Lord, help us, please!"

She called back to Johnnie, who stood motionless, watching the whole scene—his own raw emotions revealed on his face. "Johnnie! Get the doctor."

Jessica put her hand to Clint's forehead. Burning. Why hadn't she noticed the heat radiating from his body? Yanking her work worn shirttails out of her pants, she tore at it with her teeth, ripping off a section. At arm's length from the stream, Jessica swirled the cloth in the water then laid it on his brow.

Still not knowing where she stood with this man—only that he was sorry—she was careful with her words. She wanted to address him as *love of her life*, to tell him that she would always be here for him, but she couldn't bring herself to say aloud what lived in her heart. "Clint, it's Jessie. Please wake up."

He didn't open his eyes, but she persisted. Finally, his eyelids fluttered, then rose for a moment. Even though the sun had sunk below the horizon, she could see how dilated his pupils were.

In a barely detectable voice, he said, "Jessie, can you see the sunset God is painting?"

He's giving God the glory for the sunset? She gulped,

hoping to quell the lump in her throat in order to answer him. "Yes, I see it. It's beautiful, as always."

Without moving, his eyes turned toward it. "Will you describe it for me?"

He can't see it? A deep fear knifed through her, so severe she had to cough to free her restricted throat enough to speak. "Swirls of pinks, baby blues, and reds. Glorious reds."

"Red skies at night . . ." He stopped and gazed up, entreating her to finish.

". . . cowboy's delight." *Love of my life.*

She watched helplessly as his eyes rolled back and closed.

Clint's head remained in her lap as Jessica summoned all her strength to beseech her Lord in prayer. "Father-God, I beg of you. This beautiful man needs you. You created his body. You know how to heal it. He doesn't know you yet, Jesus. If he were to die today, he would be condemned to hell. This one doesn't belong in hell. He's a good man. He's just lost his way. Please, give me the chance to tell him about You—"

Clint's eyes cracked open, and his gaze locked to hers. An unexpected sort of peace gushed over her as he found her hand resting on his chest, and placed his over the top of hers.

"Thank you, Lord," Jessica praised without reservation.

He smiled ever so faintly and winked at her, then closed his eyes. His breathing deepened but was steady and solid. This time, in her spirit, she knew he would be all right, body and soul. She praised God in her head, in her heart, and out loud to anyone who happened to be standing by.

The ranch hands who'd been watching and waiting came forward and picked him up. They walked painstakingly toward the main house. When they arrived they laid Clint on Uncle Roy's bed in the downstairs bedroom.

Jessica followed, no longer wrestling with fear, having put Clint in God's capable hands. God's will *would* be done and she would do her part—obey. While caring for Clint's physical body, she planned to read to him from the Scriptures, pray for him, encourage him to join her in God's Kingdom through Christ and Christ alone. As Walt had reminded her, bringing him with her to Paradise, at the end of this life, would be her ultimate goal—above all else.

Johnnie removed Clint's bulky clothing while Jessica waited outside his door. After a short while, Johnnie came out. His compassion-filled eyes rested on her. "You okay, Jess?"

"Yes, I really think I am. What about you?" she asked solemnly, seeing the angst imprinted on his face.

"Now that Clint's back, I won't be seeing much of you, will I?"

She hurt for him, knowing what it was like to love someone who didn't return your love. Still, not seeing what God had in store for each of them, she didn't want to offer too much by way of explanation right now. She only wished she weren't the cause of his current pain.

Carefully she began, "Johnnie, you're an amazing man. Only God knows what's to come. Above all else God wants you and Clint—and the others, for that matter—to know Him. If you would let me tell you about Jesus, I would be honored. Beyond that, I can't say."

He looked surprised but relieved, like she hadn't handed him his *walking papers*. She suspected he would be willing to listen to her about God if for no other reason than to be near her. She would use that opportunity to tell him about Jesus while being careful not to mislead him concerning herself.

"I'll leave you to Clint. Hope he's better soon." Tipping his hat at her, he said, "Evenin', Jess."

Looking weary, he stepped around her and headed for the front door. As he stepped out, Jessica saw Rose Marie greet Johnnie timidly. He shut the door behind him, leaving Jessica to wonder how the beauty could seem so nervous yet self-assured all at the same time.

CHAPTER 23

Jessica squeezed Roy's arm and looked over at Mabel as the three stood nervously in the small bedroom. Dr. Barnes popped his stethoscope out of his ears and looked each one of them in the eye. His expression was solemn. "I'd say he originally had a superficial bacterial infection that weakened his body." His words were measured, sympathetic. "Now, I think he's battling something more serious. What makes me think that is the red and puffy area around the original wound." The doctor uncovered the wound, and a cold dread settled in Jessica's stomach.

"As you can see, it's gone deeper. Sepsis, maybe—that's bacteria in the blood. It's hard for me to know for sure. And we don't have time for tests. He needs antibiotics now, since he's losing ground."

Uncle Roy and Mabel looked thunderstruck, the same way Jessica felt. She had to remind herself that God was in control. She consciously reined in her panic. "What's next?" she squeezed out.

"I'm going to give him a heavy dose of Penicillin by shot right now. I'm hoping he'll wake up intermittently. Fluids are vital. Aspirin to keep the fever down. I'll be back tomorrow to check on him and give him a second shot. If he hasn't regained consciousness, we'll have to consider moving him to a hospital, mostly for intravenous therapy. I'd rather not. He's too weak to move so we'll work from here as long as we can."

Jessica's heart squeezed over that news. The whole time at Mary's, Clint's health had fluctuated. She wasn't sure why he'd made the trip back to the ranch before being fully recovered, but it had been the wrong thing to do. Jessica was sure he hadn't come just to tell her he was sorry.

Sorry about what, exactly, she found herself wondering. That had never been determined. Why *had* he come back while still sick? Her thoughts tumbled backwards to yesterday's arrival. When Clint had stopped the wagon at the back of the house, Rose Marie was clinging to his side. He had looked stricken when she fell out of the wagon, and though he had glanced at Jessica, he'd stayed to help Rose Marie. And the way they had peered into each other's eyes . . .

It was all becoming clearer now.

Her mind warred within—doubts versus logic. *He hugged me hard, and held my hand to his heart. A friendship gesture? No. He came back for me.* But, she had to admit, that didn't seem likely anymore. Her emotions sank right back into the same grief she had struggled to push away. *Haven't I learned anything, Lord?*

Suddenly she needed air.

She jumped up, thanked the doctor, and fled the house. Filling her lungs with the crisp mountain air she soon found herself at the place of solitude and peace—her rock by the stream.

* * *

With his upper back against the bunkhouse, Johnnie raised his knee and braced a boot to the wall. He draped a forearm across his thigh and looked up to appreciate the starry night, his thoughts on Jessica and how his regard for her had deepened. He was drawn to her like eyes to a sunrise. Mostly, he guessed, out of admiration for the deep character she'd so fully developed in her young life. And something else; he was utterly fascinated by her steadfast devotion to God.

Then he thought of Rose Marie. How could two women be so different? When he'd walked Rose Marie to her cabin tonight she'd been obstinate, and highly opinionated. That slip of a woman was a tumultuous, fiery puff of self-absorption. Her exterior was admirable, but she flat rubbed him the wrong way.

And she was grossly manipulative to boot. Not that she'd been successful with him. He couldn't be manipulated. Not anymore.

Thoughts of his past clouded his mind until the sound of muffled footsteps against the dirt road brought him back to the here and now. He pushed off the wall and peered around the corner. In the glow of the moonlight he saw Jessica heading for the stream. It had become a regular event, his being on hand to comfort her. He took off after her, watching to make sure she remained safe. He followed close, not to interrupt but to listen in case she needed him.

At the water, he saw her settle on her favorite rock, then look to the heavens. Once Johnnie drew near, he heard a portion of a prayer she was offering up.

". . . and, Jesus, my heart is broken. Has Clint come to tell me he wants Rose Marie?" Her voice was small and sad. "Johnnie is so sweet and attentive. Is it him you want for me?

If that's the case, turn my heart toward him. Only, please make it clear. And please, *please* heal Clint. Thank you, Lord."

Is it him you want for me? Hope rose up in Johnnie. Maybe now was the time. He came up behind her. "Jess, it's going to be okay."

Startled, she pitched forward and started to slide. Johnnie rushed to catch her by the elbows and lift her off the rock. He pulled her into a hug—this time not merely for her comfort. He reached up and pulled his hat off, dropping it on the rock she had vacated. He raised her chin with his thumb, resting his fingers lightly at her neck. Her eyes went wide, and he wondered if she would resist. She didn't. He urged her chin up more in a confident move he wasn't quite feeling. He tried to read her eyes. They looked tentative, unsure, but they didn't say *no*. Slowly he bent his head to take her lips with his.

* * *

Jessica's heart screamed for her to stop while her confused mind said *go*. She reminded herself that this might be what God wanted. So she let it happen. The kiss was special. But as wonderful as it was, an essential response from her was missing—no racing heart, no drowning desire. No life-sustaining meshing of souls.

The kiss had made something excruciatingly clear. She loved Johnnie, but not in the same way she loved Clint. He must have sensed her hesitation since he drew back. He put a palm tenderly to her cheek while he studied her face. To search for the hope that she returned his affection? All she felt was pain . . . for him.

She knew the moment he read it on her face. "So, that's my answer," he said in a quiet voice.

What could she say? "I'm sorry. I'm so sorry, Johnnie. . ." Even as she said those words, she thought of the very same words Clint had said to her. Instantly she bore the crush of that revelation. So this was how Clint felt. He loved Jessica as a friend and didn't want to cause her more pain. Was that why he'd come back to the ranch?

Johnnie placed a finger across her lips. "Don't say any more. Let me hold you a minute . . . please." He tucked her head into his neck and held her while her heart grieved for him.

They remained this way for a long while, until he finally loosened his hold, and said in a quiet tone, "I'll walk you back. It's getting late. They'll be worrying about you."

Jessica, still reeling from her encounter with Johnnie, entered Clint's room, relieved to see Mabel by his side. "The doctor's gone?"

Mabel nodded. "Try not to exhaust yerself." She rose to her feet and ambled to the door.

Jessica graced her with a weak smile. Truth was, she was already weary to the bone from her own sorrow and the sorrow she'd caused Johnnie. She plopped down in the large leather chair Mabel had been sitting in and observed Clint. She watched as he labored in each breath, finding herself trying to breathe for him. She had come to love this man so deeply. Even in his sleep, he tugged at her heart strings.

Leaning over she touched his forehead. Still ablaze. Her stomach dropped. On wobbly legs she went to the porcelain bowl by the bed and retrieved a damp wash cloth. She placed it on his head. He jerked in his sleep from the cold.

"It's okay. It's Jessie. I'll be with you all night." Knowing he was asleep, and with no one else around, Jessica felt emboldened. "I'll be with you for as long as you need me, *love of my life*." It felt so good to say those words to him, even as they made her chest tighten in the knowledge it would never be.

"Love . . . of my . . . life . . ." he said on gusts of breath, shocking her. Did he really say those words, or had her own longing made her imagine it? She snatched the cloth up. Forlorned, she sighed. He was still fast asleep, talking in his sleep. Still, it sounded so good coming from his lips.

Scooting the big chair forward to be closer, she settled in for the night.

* * *

Jessica cared for Clint in the days to come. She read to him from the Bible, prayed aloud for him, nurtured him, sat with him. She never left his side, other than to clean up and eat, or while Mary bathed him. She made sure someone was with him at all times. The care for Clint from everyone was immense; the love for him ran deeper yet. All the people at Harper ranch wanted this normally great pillar of strength back in their midst.

All the while, Jessica's love for him intensified, growing deeper with each passing day. Johnnie kept Rose Marie from coming near him. Jessica was grateful for that. Her energy was flagging, so she knew a confrontation with Rose Marie would put her over the edge.

On one occasion, when Clint awakened for a short time on Mabel's shift, Mabel told him of Walt's passing.

He'd been so stricken, she wished she'd waited. It had broken her heart to see

tears squeeze out of the corners of his eyes and slide past his temples until grief threw him into another round of sleep.

While Jessica continued her daily reading of the Bible, God's peace took root in her spirit again. First she read all of the verses about God's healing power, then those on hope, and relationships. But her favorite Scriptures were the gospels: Matthew, Mark, Luke, and John, where she read the account of what Christ has done for all His children—to be scourged almost to death; to be humiliated and suffer unbearable pain as he was nailed to the cross; to take mankind's sins on His blameless, sinless body, to save those He loved from eternal damnation and separation from God.

After reading these verses, she talked to a sleeping Clint about how they had touched her heart. Many of the cowboys, including Johnnie and Uncle Roy, had come and gone to listen as Jessica talked, read, and prayed incessantly. She was never silent. They seemed amazed and moved.

The Lord used this time to bring many to Him. As Jessica's love for God poured over them, several of them came to a saving faith in Christ. At the point of their readiness Jessica prayed with each individual, never forgetting that Walt had been the one to sow the soul-redeeming seeds, and she'd been blessed to witness the harvest.

Nearly three weeks into Clint's horrific illness, he took a turn for the worse. Jessica was frantic with worry. Thankfully, Johnnie had been spending a great deal of time with her and was here now. He pulled up a chair to within a couple feet of hers.

"He's going to be all right, Jess."

Moisture filled her eyes as they met Johnnie's. "I pray you're right. He has to be."

Johnnie grasped her hand and turned her toward him to take hold of the other as well. "Why don't you pray for him? Right now. It'll make you feel better."

She nodded. Her voice cracked as she began. "Father, only you know what your plans are for Clint. But my prayer is for You to heal him. I promise to do my best to introduce him to You and to make sure he knows You love him unconditionally."

Johnnie seemed particularly roused by Jessica's faith and Christ's offer of eternity. She could see it in his eyes when she lifted her head after her prayer.

"Jess, I know you're worried about Clint, but can I ask you something . . .?"

Jessica pulled her hands from Johnnie's to re-apply a cool cloth to Clint's forehead, then turned back to him. "Of course you can. Anything."

"I believe I've learned about Jesus from you. And I also believe I have committed my life to Him, in my own way. But, I know it's important to be assured of this . . . so . . . I mean . . . will you pray with me?"

Tension drained off and the lines from fatigue and stress smoothed out as she smiled with her whole face. "Johnnie, that's wonderful. Absolutely!"

Jessica shifted back around and recaptured Johnnie's hands in hers. She looked into his startling blue eyes that had grown larger and more alive in anticipation of the most life-altering step he would ever take.

Jessica dropped her chin to her chest and closed her eyes. "Lord we come to You on this special day. Johnnie wants to give his heart to You and receive Your gift of eternal life. I pray he will have a repentant heart and faith in You."

When she had explained the gospel message in detail and he prayed to receive Christ, Johnnie brought his head back up and met her gaze. They smiled as emotion gripped them both.

Johnnie struggled with speech. Jessica watched as his Adam's apple bobbed in the effort to swallow, and he finally hurled out a laugh. "I've never been so choked by emotion in my entire life!"

Jessica's heart beat against her breast bone as she grinned and nodded in agreement. Clint let out a moan and began thrashing about the bed. Jessica spun to him. She laid a hand on his face, then to his chest. "He's burning up!" The fever had sky rocketed. She had never felt him this hot before. "Johnnie, we have to bring his fever down, now!"

"Tell me what to do."

She leaped up, grabbed the alcohol bottle from the dresser, and returned to pour a great deal of it in the porcelain bowl that was already half filled with water. Dipping a hand towel in it, she then wrung it out, and handed it to Johnnie. "Here, uncover his legs and run this down each one, over and over again. I'm going to crush up some aspirin, add water, and try to dribble it down his throat. The fever *has* to come down."

Clint mumbled, "No! No, don't . . ."

"What is he saying?" Johnnie asked.

Jessica shook her head. Worry flooded her.

"No! Stay away. Please John . . . sir!" Clint whimpered and his voice was an octave higher, making him sound unusually young. His body thrashed about but his arms were stretched oddly tight across the bed, as if secured there.

"Clint, can you wake up? It's me, Jessie. You're here with me. You're safe—"

"What is that he's saying?" Johnnie asked as he worked at cooling Clint's legs.

Jessica was working frantically at cooling his head and chest. "I don't know. He's having nightmares, Johnnie. It sounds awful. He actually sounds young. Tortured."

She prayed fervently for him, wet another towel, laid it across Clint's torso, then crushed aspirin into a tablespoon of water. Using an eyedropper she sucked up some of the liquid and placed it through Clint's lips, squeezing slowly. Clint's throat convulsed. He gagged and coughed, but didn't wake up. She tried again with the same results. Finally, when all of the solution was gone, with most of it making its way where it belonged, Jessica turned her attention back to the dampened towels on his fiery skin.

Clint's fever finally broke near midnight, and sweat gushed from him, pooling in the grooves along the hard planes of his body. His breathing quieted, his writhing ceased. Jessica used the damp washcloth to clean his sticky skin, dried him, and then pulled the sheet up to his chin. She sat back in the cushy chair, and inhaled a ragged breath.

Johnnie waited another hour, then finally rose and took himself off to bed with a pat to her shoulder and a kiss to the top of her head.

CHAPTER 24

Clint watched with interest as a sunbeam crept across his bedspread. Eventually the light landed on Jessie's face, and he was shocked to see how tired she looked, even in sleep, with pale skin and purplish half-circles hemming her lower lashes. She stirred under the sun's warmth, tucked in a ball as she was, dwarfed by Roy's brown leather chair. Her thin blanket had fallen to the floor, and he wondered if she'd gotten cold in the night.

Jessie raised her lids to slits. Her eyes squinted in discomfort and soon skittered about the room as she oriented herself. When sleep had finally given way to wakefulness, she struggled upright and gaped at Clint.

"Good morning, sunshine," he said in a hoarse voice. He tried a smile.

Her eyes widened in delight. He could see her pulse hammering a fast tattoo in her neck. "How long have you been awake?" she asked, stretching now. She probably had little sleep in that overstuffed chair.

"Long enough," he said, smiling a little bigger now.

Her relaxed pose vanished as she stiffened. "Long enough for what, exactly?" Her voice showed her concern as she threw herself to the edge of the chair and bent to check him. Dizziness seemed to overtake her but she caught herself with a hand to his chest, then dropped her head and shook it.

He put his hand over hers. "Easy does it, little one." He paused for a moment to study her. "Long enough to watch you sleep all curled up in that chair." Though her shorts outfit was twisted and wrinkled and the hair that had pulled out of her ponytail fell in strings along her soft cheeks, it touched him that she had wrapped herself up in that chair, all the way to the light of day.

"I'll bet that was an appealing sight, huh, drool falling out of my face and all?" She groaned, and swiped a hand across her mouth.

He chuckled.

She paused as she gave him a once over. "You really had me worried last night with what I'm sure was the highest fever you've had yet." Her whole body quivered. "It finally broke around midnight, thank God."

"Sorry for the trouble." He hated that he'd given her nothing but grief practically every day since he'd met her. "Jessie, I need to talk to you—"

A knock interrupted him. "Well, good morning, sunshine," Mary said, peeking around the door.

He tried another smile. "Good morning to you, too."

"How are we feeling this morning?" Mary asked, coming into the room, looking delighted.

"Well, I'm pretty good, but our nurse here is a little worse for the wear. Didn't have the most comfortable of beds." He smiled tenderly at Jessie. She was busily straightening her clothing and pushing her hair out of her face.

"She should look worse for the wear. She's been sleeping in that thing for nearly three weeks now, taking care of you!"

Shocked, he tried to rise up but lost the battle and sank back into his pillows, weak as a kitten. "I've been in this bed for *three weeks?*"

"More like two and a half. The doctor said as sick as you were most men would have died. So you see you're tougher than you give yourself credit for. We're all grateful that God allowed you to stay with us. Here." Mary came toward him with a tall glass of water. "We've been pushing liquids into you each time you woke up."

"Yeah." He snorted. "I remember. With glasses, eye droppers, even a bowl, if I remember correctly. I seem to remember a canteen, too."

"That was Pete. Said you'd be more used to that form of hydrating," Mary said, then laughed.

"The doctor was in at dawn this morning," Jessie reported, bringing Clint's attention back to her. "He thought he'd check on you before he headed in to West Yellowstone. He thinks last night's fever going so high, then breaking like it did, means you should improve daily now. But you must rest." She wagged a finger at him, smiling, then turned to Mary.

"Mary, will you keep an eye on our patient here, please? I need to clean up and change my clothes."

"Sure thing, sweetie. You go right ahead. I'll get this cowboy washed and help him with seeing men about horses and the likes of that."

Jessie came to her feet. Clint caught her by the wrist. She took a sharp intake of breath. He needed to talk to her alone. At least try to explain about Rose Marie. For now he said, "Thank you, Jessie, for taking care of me."

She stared at him. Love radiated from her. She tried to mask it, but he could see it, sense it. Normally, those looks of want would send off warning bells and cause him to cut off a relationship. Not this time. In fact, he found himself wanting to be near her and bask in the sensation.

"Let me go clean up. I'm sure I look a sight."

He gave her a lopsided grin and a wink, letting her hand slide slowly out of his.

* * *

Once in her room, Jessica shed her clothes, exhaustion seeping in and robbing her of strength. She would ponder that episode at Clint's bedside later, when her mind could function correctly. After freshening up and putting on a change of clothes, she decided to stretch out on her bed for just five minutes. That's all she needed.

Startled by a sound, Jessica blinked awake. *How long have I been asleep? Clint!* She jumped to her feet, stopping only long enough to glimpse herself in the mirror, then smoothed out her sleep-mussed hair and flew down the stairs. Opening the bedroom door, she rushed in and instantly froze. Rose Marie was perched by a sleeping Clint. The sheet was pulled down, leaving his chest and abdomen bare.

Hearing her, Rose Marie turned to face Jessica. "Oh, look who's here," she said as if Clint could hear her. "It's Johnnie's girlfriend." She grimaced at her own comment, then snapped out of it and placed a hand on Clint's chest. Her apprehensive expression and her brazen action were at odds with each other as well.

"You don't know what you're talking about," Jessica

said, irritated her own voice sounded so puny. Her stomach started to churn.

"Oh, but I do," she said in almost a whisper. "You see, I watched your little episode with Johnnie, down by the stream." Again what she was saying belied her expression, which was one of empathy, or was it confusion? "It looked pretty intimate to me."

Jessica was stunned. What could she say to this? And why was Rose Marie delivering

such a blow with compassion on her face? But, Jessica couldn't very well deny what she was saying, since it had happened just as she'd said. What would she do now? She didn't want Clint to find out, but she knew Rose Marie would happily tell him. And why shouldn't she? The way her hand lay possessively on Clint's chest forced Jessica to face the facts. They wanted each other. Rose Marie wouldn't be this bold otherwise, would she, right here in Uncle Roy's bedroom where anyone could walk in?

Had she misread Clint's tender look, his thankfulness? Was it only because she was his caregiver, his nurse? That *is* what he'd called her, wasn't it? His *nurse*.

You fool! You've done it to yourself again.

Hiccups erupted from her. Trying to stifle them, she turned to escape, but Rose Marie caught her hand and stared into her distressed face. "Jessica." Her voice was low and compassionate. "I'll take good care of him."

Appalled by Rose Marie's apparent takeover, she tugged against her hold and dashed for the door. In her zeal she over-twisted the door knob, causing it to screech with the strain—like her heart.

* * *

Clint awakened with a start. He heard a loud hiccup and turned his head in time to see Jessie exiting the room. He drew his gaze back to Rose Marie's profile. Her manner was subdued, but somehow he knew she'd caused Jessica's harrowing escape.

Clint glanced down at Rose Marie's hand on his bare chest. Rage fired through his lethargic body with such force his blood raced through his veins. With the energy of a man in the height of good health, he wrenched her hand away to bring her gaze back to his. "What the devil's going on here?"

Panic seized her expression as she gaped at his grip. "You're hurting me, Clint. Let go!"

"Why did she leave me? Why can't *you* leave me alone? Can't you see that I want *nothing* to do with you?" He released her hand and tried to sit up. "What did you say to Jessie to upset her?" He panted, losing more breath from his effort of sitting up too quickly.

"How do you know she's upset?"

"Hiccups!"

She looked confused but inhaled a tremulous breath. "Y-you should know that she and Johnnie are together now."

"You wicked woman! What foolishness are you talking about now?"

She flinched at his words. "I saw them, down by the stream in each other's embrace, kissing." She sat up straighter now and raised her chin, though he could have sworn he'd heard a warble in her voice.

Heat climbed up his neck and filled his face. Finally, having wrestled himself to a sitting position, he lashed out and grabbed her by the throat, loosely, but enough to hold her in place. His head spun, and bile scalded the back of his tongue. Through clenched teeth, he said, "What possesses you to meddle in other people's lives?"

By this time several cowboys had gathered around the bedroom door, peering in, gaping, unsure what to do. He knew they hesitated because he was their boss. If he hadn't been, they would have trampled each other to come to Rose Marie's rescue.

Clint saw Mabel peek through gaps between the hard, lanky bodies and gasp. She squeezed through them to Clint's side. He unhooked his fingers from around Rose Marie's throat when he saw Mabel's glare, appalled at his own actions.

Sputtering, looking genuinely flayed by his words and frightened by his assault, Rose Marie raced out the door.

"What's goin' on here, Clint? You'd better say you're delirious," Mabel demanded.

Hauling in deep breaths, he tried to calm down. He stared furiously into Mabel's eyes. "That woman has given Jessie the wrong impression of us for the last time! Jessie's run off again, Mabel. Help me up. I've got to find her."

Mabel put a hand to his chest and easily pushed him back to the bed. "Yer goin' nowhere, big man. What good're you gonna do her if yer dead? Doc says yer to finish that medicine before yer to move outta that bed."

His lips curled. "No. She can't take another blow like this. Someone needs to find her!"

"Okay, okay, settle down. Someone'll find her." She turned and nodded toward the other men. Two of them scurried off as she turned back. "But *you* have ta rest. You won't survive this thing if you have another relapse."

Clint twisted to his stomach. He stuffed his face into

the pillow and slammed a fist into the mattress. He knew Mabel was right. He'd barely had the strength to raise his arm to that wench's neck.

But as he lay there waiting for his heart to slow, he finally figured out the truth. His true fury wasn't with Rose Marie. It was with Jessie.

Why do the ones who should care always leave?

CHAPTER 25

Jessica barely found her way to the barn through the blur of scalding tears. Body and soul, she suffered the slam of this latest incident with a finality that dazed her. A spigot had opened to her spirit, and joy was swiftly draining out. This time she hadn't the reserve of strength to twist that spigot shut.

She gathered up a blanket, saddle, and bridle, and went into the gray mare's stall. The horse eyed her warily, picking up on her distress. "It's okay, girl. We'll get through this." She patted the mare's neck, then saddled, mounted, and galloped her way up the road toward Mary's cabin.

Only God could give her peace now. Hours clicked by as she prayed. Her rational side gave her all the reasons she needed to let go of Clint, while her heart futilely clung to him. By the world's standards, Rose Marie would make a more suitable mate for a man like Clint, yet Jessica thought he deserved a more selfless, godly woman. And that didn't describe Rose Marie.

She chirped a laugh, startling birds out of a nearby fir to take to the air. What a laugh. It didn't describe her either.

She let that troubling thought go while she pictured Clint in her mind, remembering with solitary warmth his touches and even his telling gazes. A ceaseless ache radiated from deep in her core and spread. How would she ever stop loving him?

God, do You want Rose Marie for Clint? Is that why these incidents keep happening; to give me the hint? Wasn't it time she wanted what God wanted? Still, she found herself wanting to fight for Clint, whether God agreed or not. She shuddered with guilt and hopelessness.

Rounding a bend in the rode, she spied Mary's cabin. Had she really come this far already? But in every other sense, she still had a long way to go.

* * *

A grueling day passed. Clint was beside himself with worry. He lay in his bed as the doctor had demanded but could only toss and turn, desperate for someone to find Jessie, sickened it couldn't be him. The ranch hands and Mabel reported to him frequently. None of them had found her anywhere.

"What good does it do me to wait in bed when I can't rest anyway? Where would she go?" he spouted to the empty room.

Unwilling to wait any longer, Clint heaved out of bed and got to his feet. Weakness prevailed in his limbs, but in determination he found his clothes to dress. Just as he finished buttoning his pants, Mary came into the room.

"What're you doing, son? You may be well of the infection, but you're not strong enough to go looking for Jessica."

His body was heavy, unyielding as lead, but he was sure it was from despair. He sat on the edge of the bed, his hands shaking as he worked to pull on his socks. "I can't wait any longer. No one's found her." He halted and blinked at Mary. "I never got a chance to tell her what happened with Rose Marie . . ." He swallowed convulsively. "And then she catches us together again. I can't imagine what she must be thinking." He raked his hands through his hair. "*I love you*, Mary, but I'm very close to hating your granddaughter!"

Mary squeezed her eyes closed for a moment. "I know, Clint. I'm so sorry. I wish we could go back and leave Rose Marie in San Francisco. All I can say is God is in control. We have to trust Him."

Clint stopped buttoning his shirt for a moment to consider his next words. He looked Mary in the eye. "In the last two weeks I spent a lot of time listening to Jessie read aloud from the Bible while she thought I slept—"

"*What?*" Mary interrupted. "You didn't let her know you were awake? How could you do that? She was so worried."

"I know, Mary," he said. "Most of the time I didn't have the strength to speak. The rest of the time I was curious as to how she could bring these rough cowboys to faith in something they couldn't see. So, I didn't let on I was listening."

Mary looked disapproving.

"Okay, so I was wrong." He finished buttoning his shirt then rose to stick a foot into a boot. "She was so amazing, Mary. So in love with her God." He stomped until his foot slid in, then looked over at her. "But that's the problem, see? I even began to wonder, maybe it's time He was my God, too. And now this! How do I trust God when He allows so much pain to hit someone who loves Him like she does, someone who only wants to please Him? How cruel can He be?"

"Clint, you know how Jessica misinterpreted seeing you in bed with Rose Marie."

He groaned and stuffed his shirt in his pants, then headed for the door.

She stepped in his path to stop him. "I have a point, Clint. Stay with me on this."

He stopped, impatient.

"Jessica didn't see that for what it was, right?" She didn't wait for an answer. "You see the situation that happened with Rose Marie, and you think God is being cruel. But I see it and believe He must have a plan. He always does." She eyed him carefully but still blocked his path. He didn't like this one bit, feeling trapped like a cornered animal, waiting to be pounced on.

Mary lifted her chin. "I've prayed for and wanted you and Jessica to be together."

He didn't want to hear this. He'd worked hard stuffing feelings for Jessie down deep, not wanting to look too closely at *what* exactly his need was for her. He sure as heck didn't need Mary dredging up and dissecting those feelings. But he'd listen. Because it was Mary. Hands went to his hips as he forced himself to focus on her.

"I've seen the way you look at that sweet girl, Clint. You may not have faced it yet, but it's obvious you're in love with her."

Clint ground his teeth. He bent closer. "Wait a gall darn minute, Mary," he said, wagging a finger in her face. "I never said I loved—"

She clapped a hand across his mouth, shocking him. His eyebrows shot upward.

"Let me finish." She released her hand and raised a questioning brow.

He wanted to put a fist through something. Instead he nodded in acquiescence.

"Even though I believe it to be a great match and that God wants this, I've often wondered how our sweet girl would do with the best-looking, most desired cowboy in Montana territory."

Clint rolled his eyes. He was sick to death of that assessment. "Mary—"

"You've been in the limelight with beautiful women your whole adult life. Your looks alone bring attention from the women, but when they get to know you, the package becomes sweeter. What's not to love?" She smiled tenderly, then hurried to finish. "Now, you have to ask yourself, how will our simple and plain little Jessica manage the ever so handsome Clint Wilkins?"

"Enough! You're exaggerating about me. And Jessica isn't simple and plain, she's—"

"Clint!" She grasped Clint's biceps and squeezed. "Be realistic. Don't ignore the truth here. You will need to convince her you will love her and only her for the rest of your life."

Her eyes searched the depths of his. What was she looking for? He was in a bad way and woefully unsettled. Didn't she realize he didn't know which direction to go? Now he knew what a stray experienced, hemmed in on all sides by the cowboys that only wanted the best for it, when in fact it felt like a fatal trap.

"Mary, I don't have time for this."

"Come here . . . sit down." She tugged on a sleeve. "You're wavering a bit."

"I'm not staying. I may not know how I feel about her—Stop it! Stop looking at me like you know my mind better than I do. I'm going to find her. Then talk to her. That's it!"

"Sit down for a minute. You only have one boot on."

He looked down. Imparting a huge sigh he grabbed his other boot and strode to the bed. The springs groaned as he sat too hard.

"You see? You're still weak."

Clint glowered at her.

"I won't keep you, but I will have my say first."

Fine, he'd let her say her piece. He shifted to put on his boot.

"It might be wonderful for a while, maybe even for years. But she's going to worry about you, Clint, whenever you even look toward another woman, especially the pretty ones."

He dropped his chin to his chest in defeat and exhaustion. Mary may have thought her little speech would ensure he could make Jessie happy, but all she'd accomplished was talking him straight out of any future with her.

Mary patted his arm in comfort. "Now, don't lose heart, dear. There's a lesson in all this. Let me tell you a little about my love life."

His head snapped back up. That got his attention. Mary had always been so closed about her marriage. Plus, Roy worked in there somewhere. He just didn't know where. Still he said, "Make it fast, Mary. I need to go." He yanked harder on his second boot while she jumped in to finish.

"There's a long, sad story about my past I'll let Jessica tell you about someday." Mary saw his surprise. "Yeah, she knows all about it. There wasn't much to do but talk while we tended you, dear." She smiled. "Anyway, back to my point. When I married Bill, he had a lot of insecurities about us. We were young and Roy had been in the picture. And I was pretty popular." When Clint raised an eyebrow, she said, "Let's just say Rose Marie got her grandmother's good looks." Clint raised both brows.

"Bill worked hard to get my attention and married me as soon as I agreed. We were great for a time, I'd say the first two years. After that Bill became jealous and possessive. He had to be gone a lot as a logger, which nearly killed him thinking of me at home alone. He worried incessantly that I would draw the attention of the men in the area and then didn't trust me to resist them. He never could just believe that I loved him and was committed to him for life."

Mary waited a moment for that to sink in. It seemed like she could always tell when his wheels were turning.

"Consequently our time together became strained and unhappy. We stayed married, but something that could have been glorious had been eaten away by needless jealousy and strife—so very sad. And now he's gone." Tears filled her eyes as she stared across the room at a picture of Bill and Roy with arms slung around each other and a large brown trout held by the gills between them. Huge smiles spread across both handsome faces.

Mary sniffed, and then faced Clint, determination on her face. "Now this thing with Rose Marie can help you with Jessica, if you play your cards right." Mary searched Clint's face.

He mulled over her words, but he saw nothing beyond

telling Jess the truth and letting the chips fall where they may.

She went on. "Of course, you will have to work on your reactions to women in the future, you know, especially beautiful ones."

He cringed over how he had lived his whole egocentric life. His senses, like live wires, were all firing at the same time. He couldn't take much more of this new-found current of feelings awakening his insides. He closed his eyes and with profound effort found the door to the familiar wall of resistance—raised it and slammed it shut. Instant relief flooded him as he sensed his emotions shutting off one by one like bright candle flames beneath the snuffer.

No Mary. Not this time.

Mary noticed his sudden change.

"Thanks, Mary, for caring. But you got your cinch too tight." He stood to leave and looked down into her upturned face. "I can't love Jessie—or anyone else for that matter. Not now, not ever."

His anger toward his mother had never left him—never would. He wouldn't take a chance on loving a woman. He couldn't trust them. If he opened his heart to love one, when things got tough, she'd leave him to face life alone. To face pain alone. Hadn't Jessie done that very thing? Not just once, but twice?

He reached for the doorknob. Mary stopped him again with a hand to his arm. "Clint. Don't be a fool. I don't know what happened to you in your past. But don't let what happened back then dictate how you live your life now. Take it from me. Don't lose the *love of your life*."

When Mary said those words, Jessie's same words to him flashed back in his mind. And he *had* said them back to her. She'd thought he was talking in his sleep, but he'd said them all right.

He cursed. He had no more time for talk. He had to find Jessie.

"Clint, I have an idea. I should get Rose Marie out of the way anyway, so why don't I have Johnnie take her and I back to my cabin. You can take the Packard into town to see if Jessica caught a train back to California."

Blood started pounding in his ears. "She can't have gone back to California." All at once the thought of facing life without her seemed empty, pointless.

"Let's hope not."

"I'll look wherever I have to, to find her."

"Yes. I know." Mary walked out the door.

Clint pushed his hat on. With renewed resolve, he left his room of convalescence to f'ind the woman who hadn't left his thoughts since the first day he'd met her.

Though weak, Clint managed to get himself to town and the train station. He parked the Packard at the entrance and entered through the large double doors. After letting his eyes adjust to the dimness inside, he made a beeline for the ticket booth—and the attractive young redhead behind its counter. As he sauntered toward her, he recognized the all too familiar ogling.

"You must be the most handsome man I've ever seen in my whole life," she blurted out, then flushed the color of her fiery hair.

Clint was too weary to deal with this young lady properly. He frowned in hopes of deterring her, ignoring her forwardness. "Can you tell me if a particular person has purchased a ticket from you?"

"I'm not supposed to, but for you I'd probably do

anything." Again she blushed, but was getting noticeably bolder.

Okay, he thought, *I'll play your game, if that gets me what I want.* "Well, beautiful, if you'd tell me if a certain Jessica Harper has purchased a ticket in the last two days, I'd really appreciate it." He gave her his hundred-watt smile. The one he usually reaped gasps from.

She almost swooned at the sight of it. "Oh, oh, sure, okay," she said. She fumbled through her records. At length she gave him an apologetic look. "No one by that name has purchased a ticket on August 16th *or* 17th. I'm sorry."

Clint squeezed his weary eyes shut and blew a breath out through puffed cheeks. So, Jessica wasn't running back to California, at least not by train. Then where was she? Now, more worried than ever, he pivoted to leave. Over his shoulder, he burbled, "Thanks for checking."

"Sure. Hey, wait a minute."

He stopped in place but didn't look back.

"I thought you said you'd be *very* appreciative. How about you buy me a drink in town when I get off?"

He thought back on Mary's words, wondering how he could have handled this without using his looks or his charm. Groaning inwardly, and trying to get his agitation in check, he twisted his head to speak over his shoulder. "Sorry, young lady, but I'm otherwise engaged." Stunned at the irony of his own words, he remained frozen to the floorboards.

The girl misinterpreted his hesitation. "Are you sure?"

When he continued to stand with his back to her, she heaved a loud sigh and said, "Wow, she's a really lucky girl."

Her comment snapped him out of his thoughts. He twisted so she could hear him well. "No, actually it's me that's blessed to have her." He only said that to be done with the girl's attention, he told himself. He turned back and sidestepped the line that had begun to form. Gawks from the ladies in line only managed to twist his already raw guts. The rustic floor boards vibrated beneath the heavy tread of his boots. The sound echoed off the walls of the massive room, hollow like the hopelessness inside him.

He wondered how things would turn out when he found Jessie. But first he had to find her, and that's exactly what he intended to do.

Back at the camp, Clint saddled the black and pushed through his weakened state to search every building, every path, even her special rocks by the stream. No Jessie.

Disheartened and exhausted, Clint slid from his horse and guided him to a stall in the barn, rattled by a deep sense of loss and panic he'd never before experienced. He tugged his watch out of his pants pocket and saw it clearly in the moonlight. Just after 11:30 pm. *She's been gone for a day and a half now. Where could she be, Lord?* Instead of rebuking himself for offering up the small prayer, this time he hoped God would answer it.

Just then the ranch's short, stocky maintenance man came from around the corner to enter the barn. "Oh! It's you, boss. I was coming in to turn off the lights."

"Sam."

"You're up awful late after being so sick. You look plumb wore out. Here, let me take the black." He grabbed the reins out of Clint's hand. "Why *are* you up this late?"

"I'm looking for Jessie. Have you seen her?" He knew he sounded a bit desperate, but didn't care. He glanced around the barn, not really looking for anything and not really seeing anything, but hoping something would give him a clue.

"Sure. She went up to Mary's yesterday," Sam said, offhandedly, while pulling the saddle from Clint's horse.

Clint's gaze shot to him. "She—How do you know?"

Sam was busy sliding the bridle off the horse's muzzle, so he didn't bother to look up. "She took that dapple gray you let her ride. When I asked where she was going, she seemed upset. Barely heard her say *Mary's*."

Clint scraped all ten fingers through his hair, pulling his head back to stare at the ceiling. "Thank you, God."

Sam turned and gaped. Clint offered no explanation. He ambled out of the barn and toward his bunkhouse to get some sleep before his ride to Mary's at sunrise. He would finally see Jessie again. This time he didn't try to talk himself out of what he truly wanted—her—and he didn't dare reflect beyond that.

As Clint slogged down the road toward the bunkhouse, a thunderous clap split the noiseless night, followed by a shudder, then a steady rumble. *A freight train?* Clint spun in a circle, searching for the source of the sound. He saw nothing but deep night. A gust of air blew past his ears, speeding his pulse. A deep vibration rumbled under foot.

What. Is. That? Earthquake?

The ground shook, and every one of Clint's organs seemed to shift. He tried to take a step, but faltered, unsteady. He needed to plant himself on solid ground. But where?

His only experience with an earthquake was in Wyoming when he was only eight. He remembered his dad explaining it to him. He'd learned then that he just had to wait it out. That was all. It *would* stop.

CHAPTER 26

Clint's muscles were tiring as he fought against the juddering earth. Rooted to the road between the main house and barn, he began to doubt the quake would quit. The fury of this force of nature seemed more like earthquake *and* cyclone. And the noise was unbelievably deafening.

He tried to reason through a jumbled brain. *Jessie. Was she safe? Sam. He might be hurt.* The barn was breaking up. He needed to get to Sam. Shuffling along the vibrating earth he labored toward the barn.

Just then, a powerful wind whipped hard against his back, throwing him off his feet. He caught himself with one hand against the road. Wind was spiraling around him. Dirt and debris stung his face like buckshot and filled his mouth. He sputtered and spit, and took another breath. *What is happening?*

He squinted over at the house, the heart and soul of Harper ranch. Mabel would be in there. And Roy. Pushing to his feet, he held an arm across his eyes and fought to make it to the house. He stooped into the hurricane-like gusts, forcing his legs to move in that direction. A violent swirl of wind smacked Clint broadside. He lost his footing and fell hard, landing face first on the trembling earth. Circular airstreams seemed to ride his back, like a tornado finding its mark. He couldn't move against the pounding force of it. Would he be carried off? Out of desperation, he gripped the ground with his fingertips.

Brief flashes of moonlight slipped through the gale, giving Clint a chance to finally see his surroundings. Closer to the house now, he scrabbled toward it, but only managed two pushes along the ground when he caught sight of something coming at him from the north. He strained to see. It drew closer. *What on earth?* The road was undulating, like a daunting wave rising against him. Helpless to do anything, he bent his arms around his head and waited for impact. It reached him, elevated under him, and then snapped. Like an amateur bronc buster, he was bucked airborne and flipped once, his big body landing in a heap as the buckling road continued on a southward course.

Clint pressed his nose against his shirt sleeve and sucked in a breath of debris-free air, then another. Unnatural winds continued to circle him, but he had to get up. With all his might he shoved off the ground. He stuck his hands out in front of him like a blind man, pushing against flying bits of soil and gravel and wreckage as he went.

He heard a splintering sound—from the house. He caught a glimpse of intact porch, moonlit eaves, sturdy walls holding the wind at bay . . . and portions of roof lifting, twisting, shredding . . *No!*

A new gale wrenched the top beam free of its trusses. Like dominoes, one truss slammed against the other until they trounced the second floor, cracking the house in two. Clint stared, unblinking, uncaring that grit sandblasted his eyes. Even his breath had stoppered itself, blocked by an unvoiced scream in his head. *Who is trapped inside?*

He tried to wedge his feet under him and run for the porch, but the ground toppled him to his backside. He cracked his head on hardpan and popped around like corn in a hot skillet, useless to do anything but endure the riot underneath. The taste of this evening's jerked beef came up his throat. He gagged. His head pounded, his muscles throbbed, and his limbs were scratched and bruised . . .

God, please make this stop!

The prayer left him dumbfounded. Because for the first time in his life, he believed wholeheartedly that God was real, and He controlled this storm. And Clint wanted to live . . . to see Jessie again. The truth vibrated through his bones with more force than the earthquake and wind combined. And the only one who could make that happen was *The* one Clint had run from his whole life. A Scripture shot through Clint's mind from the days of his youth, and he shouted it into the wind. "If God is for me, who can be against me?"

Another loud crack hit him like a wall of sound breaking over his back. He wrenched toward it. His gelding bolted out of the barn, stumbling about in need of escape. In the brief slices of moonlight Clint caught its wild-eyed look of fright. The barn's roof ripped off in pieces. Surging fragments joined the darkened sky and were caught in a gale of debris, up and up and out of view.

The quake gave another sharp jolt and then it stopped dead, like a supernatural switch had been flipped. Stunned, Clint lay in a heap, his whole body vibrating. A Bible story he had read as a child filled his mind and quieted his soul. The story was of a turbulent boat ride the disciples had taken with Jesus. Jesus had calmed the seas, as He had just done the quake. An inner peace warmed him from within.

With great effort he thrust himself up from the fractured ground. His body hummed. He sat up, waited for all the tumblers to fall back into place. Once his equilibrium seemed to adjust, he raised his head heavenward. "Thank you. I promise. I won't forget this." It was all the words he could manage through the emotion electrifying his system.

Clint tried to stand, but his legs were rubbery. Determined to find out who might be hurt, he willed energy into his limbs. He pushed forward, thinking of Jessie. Was she hurt, or worse? The agony of not knowing turned his stomach.

Concentrate! People here need you. With a near impossible effort he pushed all thoughts of Jessie aside and staggered toward the house, stunned by the collapse of the second story into the first. The front steps had separated from the foundation. Mabel's potted flowers, and the swing-hammock, were no longer visible.

He stepped over the fractured door frame, taking a moment to assess the ruin. Heavy ceiling beams had flattened furniture. The deer head rested askew on the splintered timber. He stooped, searched through the rubble for the flashlight that usually hung on a peg by the front door, and clicked it on. He skipped the ray across the room: particles of wood and dust swirled within its glow. The staircase had shifted and fallen away from the second floor and was now slanting to one side.

Clint noticed a light in the kitchen. Clicking off his flashlight to conserve the batteries, he kicked his way into the great room and toward the light. He heard a faint moan and froze in place, listening. It was a woman somewhere in the kitchen, whimpering.

The kitchen was in shambles, the stove the only thing still in its place. The refrigerator had been dislodged and was now lying on top of someone. Hurrying through the debris, he saw Mabel's face pinched in pain, her breaths reduced to tiny puffs that seemed to require all of her attention.

"Mabel! Hold on. Let me get this thing off you." He squatted, lifted, and shoved the refrigerator away with one hefty push.

His eyes flew over her small, round body, looking for wounds. "Are you hurt?"

She gulped a full breath of air. Then her hands went up to cover her face, and she began to sob. Clint grasped her wrists to carefully peel them away. "Mabel, look at me," he demanded. "You a'right?"

She shook her head and continued to sob hysterically.

"Hurt or just scared?"

She stopped crying for a moment and with frantic eyes searched his face. "Are we in Heaven?"

"Mabel, listen to me. It was just an earthquake."

"*Just* an earthquake," she screeched. "God's destroying the earth. We're goners!"

"Mabel," he said with his foreman voice. "Calm down. I need to get you out of here. There'll be aftershocks. Come on." He grasped her upper arms and began pulling slowly, testing her ability to sit. "Now, can you tell me if you're hurt?"

"Other than my dignity?" she asked, flushing with embarrassment. She pulled her robe tighter around her stout body.

"Let's try to stand you up if you think nothing's broken."

"Sure," she grunted. He rose with her to a standing position. Once stable, she wiped her tears away with a shaky hand.

"How's that? Feeling okay?"

Mabel stared up into his face. "I think I feel better than you. You look like a bronc-snapper what lost the battle. We both need to sit our backsides down somewhere."

"We're going outside to the middle of the road. Need to get out of this house before the rest of it comes down around our ears. Do you know if anyone else is in here?"

"Just me. I was getting a late snack." She flushed. "Roy's out of town on business."

"Good, let's get out so I can go check the bunkhouses for others. Can you make it?"

"Yep, give me a hand."

Clint guided Mabel carefully over the wreckage in the two rooms and out the broken door. Once he deposited her in the middle of the road, he put a calming palm to her cheek. "Got to go get Sam. Stay put. I'll be right back."

The interior of the barn looked to have experienced its own personal twister, yet the small light still shone inside. One glance at the dirt floor, and Clint found Sam sprawled out, not moving.

"Sam!" Clint ran to his side. Nothing had fallen on him, amazingly. Clint leaned down to check his neck. The pulse was there, though weak. And he was breathing, though shallowly. Clint carefully turned him over, checking for injuries. Taking the chance that his back wasn't broken, he squatted and lifted him. His legs burned from the effort, but he forced them forward. Once he placed Sam in the open area of the road where he'd be safer, he worked at trying to rouse him. Soon Sam groaned and opened his eyes.

"Thank you, Lord," Clint said.

Sam gawked at Clint.

"Yeah. I know. I finally figured out who's in charge, is all," Clint said. "Now, tell me, where're you hurt?"

"That horse of yours decided to dance on my face and chest before he took off," Sam rasped. "Think I have some broken ribs, for sure."

"I'm thankful you're alive, Sam. Had me worried. Will you be all right here if I go check on the others?"

"Sure. Breathing okay, so don't think I punctured a lung. You go. I'll be fine right here. You okay, Mabel?"

"Just shaken. Never experienced nothin' like that. Couldn't have been *just* an earthquake, could it?"

"Don't know. Never been in an earthquake before," Sam replied.

"God must be mad at us," Mabel said.

Satisfied that Mabel and Sam would watch over each other, Clint slogged down the road toward the bunkhouses. Shining the flashlight over the destruction of the two structures, he groaned aloud. One barely stood, while the other was destroyed with beams, roofing, and splintered two-by-fours in a heap like a giant pile of pick-up-sticks.

Several wranglers were already digging through the rubble, calling out to those who had been trapped inside. Clint hobbled toward the first bunkhouse. Two bodies lay to the far left of it, with Pete's brother, Max, hunched down beside them.

By the way they lay, Clint feared the worst. "Are they gone?" Clint asked as he approached, recognizing them.

"'Fraid so," Max answered in a strained voice.

Clint drank in a deep breath. He and Max joined the men knee deep in rubble. "Who else are we looking for?"

"Many of the guys are out with the herd, but we had about twelve men here, so we have six that are unaccounted for," Max said as he hauled another board off the wreckage. "By the way, Pete's gone a little crazy.

Clint straightened from his task. "What do you mean?"

"He's hysterical. Over yonder." Max nodded toward him. Pete lay in a fetal position near one of the trees. "Thinks the end of time has hit."

"You gotta admit. It did seem that way," Clint said. "He'll snap out of it. He always does."

They searched and uncovered the lost men. Two more were found dead, and three were alive but injured. With Sam already found, all six were accounted for. The men carried the wounded to the makeshift treatment area in the middle of the road. Clint staggered the last few steps. Max came alongside to ease his load.

"Max, we need to get into the main house for bandages, alcohol, blankets, anything we can find," Clint said. "We'll go in together, but if we hear any rumblings of aftershocks, you get out of there pronto. Don't even hesitate."

He'd barely gotten the words out when another rumble came from deep below. "Aw shoot, here it comes." Clint shouted over the noise. "Try to relax your bodies and roll with it."

CHAPTER 27

Once again the quake began with a mighty jolt, rattling Clint's teeth. It increased until he thought the earth would split into pieces. Even over the horrendous noise, Pete could be heard wailing in the background. Mabel sobbed. Clint saw Sam place a hand on her head to calm her.

A loud crack of splintering wood caused everyone to shift their gazes to the barn. It leaned hard toward the corral, groaning with the strain, then abruptly cut back the other way, toppling into a mass on the ground. Lumber ruptured and exploded with the momentum.

A strange sound crept up from below. At once a massive crack in the earth crawled out from under the rubble of the barn, heading for the bunkhouses. It opened wider, devouring pieces of the structures on its way toward the stream, like a ravenous prehistoric creature unearthed.

Soon the quaking stopped.

Clint clicked on his flashlight. "Is everyone all right? Mabel, Sam, Max, everyone? Are you still with me?" He shined the flashlight into each set of stricken eyes.

Mabel spoke first, her voice croaking from the dust

and her tears. "I think we've lost Gary. He's not breathin' no more."

Clint shined his flashlight into the ranch hand's bearded face. He leaned down to listen for breath and to take his pulse, but blood bubbled up through the stiff hairs surrounding Gary's lips. As the facts sunk in, Clint crammed a fist to his brow, trying hard to keep it together. They would all need him to. He slipped a blanket up over Gary's face.

"We've gotta go now, Max, since we don't know how long the house will stand, and we need those provisions. We'll be racing the clock to the next quake." His voice was hoarse, a scrape of noise in an emotion-ridden throat.

They jogged as quickly as the glow of their flashlights would allow. Once they reached the doorway, Clint put a hand to Max's arm. "We'll pick our way through the house to find anything useful. But like I said before, listen for anything that doesn't sound right. If you hear anything shift or collapse, get the heck out of here—every man for himself. Got it?"

"Only if you take your own advice," Max countered.

He nodded his agreement. "Let's go."

Clint and Max stepped over the bare threshold and navigated a path around splintered boards, broken beams, and shattered furniture. Each sifted through the remains of the kitchen and pantry to gather all they could hold of medical supplies, food, blankets, flashlights, jugs of water, anything they thought beneficial. When their arms were full, Clint followed as Max quickly but carefully threaded his way back through the rubble to the front door.

They were halfway there when Max stopped and froze. Not realizing he'd stopped, Clint rammed headlong into his back. They both scrambled from the impact to keep their footing. "What the heck are you doing, Max?"

"Hear that?"

Clint stopped to listen intently. "No."

"From Roy's bedroom. Don't you hear that?" Max headed toward the room.

They squeezed past the misplaced staircase and ducked under dislodged beams until they came to Roy's room. Max tried the door. It was stuck. Clint came up next to him and with shoulders to the door they gave a weighted shove. It gave way. Max forced it in, kicking away pieces of the fallen ceiling as he went.

There, under a broken beam across his bed, lay Roy moaning in distress.

"Roy! I thought you were out of town." Clint shuffled around Max and to the bed. He dumped the supplies in the corner and looked over the situation. "His body's pinned. Let's get this beam off him!" Both men clutched the beam, lifted, and shouldered it off Roy. It crashed to the floor. Clint came back to his side. "Roy. Can you hear me? Roy!"

"Yeah," he said, barely discernible.

"Okay, before we move you, we need to know what shape you're in." Clint looked over his body. "Do you feel pain anywhere?"

"Pretty sure my legs are broke," Roy rasped.

"Max, grab some loose boards for splints. We're running out of time. " Clint ran his hands carefully down Roy's legs. No compound fractures.

Roy hollered out in pain as they strapped boards on the sides of each leg.

"You feel pain anywhere else? Back or neck?" Clint asked.

Perspiration oozed from Roy's pores, dampening his face and hairline. He panted an answer, "Nothin' hit me . . . anywheres else."

"Okay, Max, get these supplies outside, then come back with some of the guys and we'll take him out. Hurry."

Max scooped up the goods and left the room. Clint heard him kicking away garbage as he hustled out the front door opening. Soon he returned with Pete and two other men.

Clint shined his light in Pete's face. "You got it under control now?"

Pete looked ragged, but calm. "Who me? I'm fine, fine, fine—don't know what you're talkin' about."

It would have to do. The five of them jostled into position and carried Roy out of the house.

Once in the road with the others, Mabel gasped. "Roy! I thought you were away! When did you get back?"

"Tonight. Was wore out. Saw my bed empty and collapsed on it."

"I'm so glad the fellas went back in the house for supplies, or they may never have found you! I told Clint no one else was in there," Mabel said in a sob of anguish.

"You couldn't have known," Clint said. "He's here now. We've God to thank for that."

All heads whipped his direction, astonished.

"Yeah, I know. You're all wondering when I 'got religion', aren't you?"

They all nodded in unison, still silent, waiting for his explanation.

When Clint didn't speak, as he was considering the words to use, Mabel jumped in, "Does this mean you're gonna stop prowling around with those pretty, snotty girls who think they don't need God?"

Pete snorted, then erupted into laughter. Though it seemed they tried not to, the rest soon joined him one by one. Laughing, at Clint's expense, for several long minutes allowed the stress of the last couple of hours to drain away some. So he let it go on.

"Okay, I guess I deserved that one," Clint said, though not particularly amused. "It has been a long time since I spent time with anyone who believed in God, except Jessie that is. Now, let's keep in mind we have injured people here. I'm sure they don't appreciate all the laughter." "I liked it," Roy said quietly, surprising everyone. "You usually . . . get all the fun. About time you're made fun *of*."

Slap happy from lack of sleep and the horrors of the earthquake, Pete started chuckling again and soon the others burst into laughter. This time Clint joined them.

CHAPTER 28

Clint lay on his back inspecting the colors of sunrise as they appeared one by one. Swirling and intermingling reds, pinks, and orange pushed the dimness of the early hour back across the sky.

He was gravely worried about Jessie, and missed her more than ever while experiencing the sunrise she loved so much. When his eyes lowered from the beauty, tightness seized his chest at the devastation he saw surrounding them.

He felt furrows gather between his brows. "How can you create such a beautiful sunrise, Lord, when you've allowed your creation to take such a beating?"

The aftershocks in the night had been hard to get through. Those who were injured had been shaken up pretty badly. Clint was anxious for the group to head off to the clinic, hoping it was still in one piece. He suspected Doc Barnes would ultimately cart the injured off to the nearest hospital.

Stretching to relieve the painful kinks, he sat up. The others were sprawled out next to him. He inspected each one for evidence of their breathing. *Thank you for that,*

Lord, he thought, and warmed at having talks with God again. Before his dad had died, they were a *pray without ceasing* family. Conversations with God had been the norm from the tender age of three. He wondered if he'd ever trust God enough to have them regularly again.

Gathering his strength, with every muscle stiff and complaining, he walked around to test his legs, then woke up the group. He covered the dead for a later burial before dealing with more pressing issues.

After the small troop was on its way to Doc's clinic, Clint found and saddled his gelding. He filled his saddle bags with food, ammo, and medical supplies, then threw his rifle into its saddle scabbard. Once his bedroll and canteen were in place, he mounted, offered up a small prayer, then hit the road toward Mary's place, dodging broken ground along the way.

Clint found it increasingly difficult to ride the gelding while negotiating large boulders and cracks. The horse had become agitated at his frequent commands to shift his walking patterns. Clint knew he would soon have to dismount and pull him behind. His plan was to wait as long as possible, knowing that he wasn't at full strength himself to take on the strenuous trip. It was already midday, and he hadn't even made it a third of the way.

Just then his horse balked and reared. Clint leaned into the action, clamping his thighs tight against the saddle. The black came down hard and danced backward.

"Whoa, boy. Easy now. What is it?" Clint asked, wishing the horse could answer. Clint's eyes shifted from one pine tree to the next, then shot up to the rocks above. Scanning fast, he saw nothing. But soon he heard what the horse had sensed. The unmistakable scream of a mountain cat resonated in his ears. His heart thundered against his ribs. The "Rrrrraaaow," sounded again, close. Too close.

This one sounded angry. Distressed, from the quake no doubt. Stripping his rifle from its sheath, Clint slid quietly from the saddle and pulled the reins over the horse's massive head to ground tie him. He thought of tethering him but disregarded it. The black would destroy the bridle if he wrenched free.

Stealthily, he followed the sound, the rifle in place against his shoulder. He stalked over the rubble in the road, glancing down from time to time so as not to trip over any of it.

Then he saw it: the sleek, lithe cat, a good eight feet in length. It stood very still and looked straight into Clint's eyes as if deciding whether to attack or escape. As they struck a mutual fixed pose, Clint noticed the cat was missing an ear—*The one I shot*—the one who had been doubly dangerous even before the quake.

With supple, muscular moves the cougar bounded twenty feet up to the large boulders above and dashed out of sight. In another place and time Clint might have been awestruck by the grace of this creature. Today he worried it would likely return when he least expected it. Now his night activity would be that of watchman instead of getting the rest he so desperately needed.

Clint propped the rifle backwards on a shoulder, a hand to the stock. His skittish horse followed behind as they trekked higher in altitude. Large boulders from the bluffs above had tumbled down to the center of the road. Clint was amazed at how many trees had been dislodged, as if an avalanche rather than an earthquake had displaced them. God's creation had been disassembled like a complex puzzle gone wrong.

As he trudged uphill, every step draining his strength, he looked for a place to bed down for the night. The sunset was nearing, and he craved the closeness it would give him to Jessie.

Clint halted. Johnnie was with her now. Something burned deep inside Clint, like a hot coal sizzling through his chest. He yanked on the reins, too hard, and started walking again. He liked Johnnie, even trusted him. So what was the problem? He could leave her to Johnnie . . . to his care . . . to his protection. *To his kisses?*

"Come on," he growled at the horse, and worked to settle in for the night. He had to focus. The mountain lion was going to be a problem, if not tonight then tomorrow night or the next. When they got this close to humans they were after something. He looked for a place he could be safe from the cougar and the aftershocks. He spotted a large boulder that had been sliced in half by the impact of its fall. The flat half was stuffed deep into the earth. Undisturbed pine trees stood majestically around him, like they had triumphed in a contest of strengths.

Once he'd decided his best location for the night he settled against his saddle with his meager dinner of fruit and jerked beef, weary to the core. His body needed the nourishment, but his stomach was on fire. Everything he ate wanted to come back up again. For someone who'd always had control over his body and his emotions, neither seemed to be within his grasp anymore. It wasn't the cat that made him unsettled, or even the earthquake. It was how he'd find Jessie. And, the idea of Johnnie and Jessie together was eating a hole in his heart—and his stomach.

He crossed his legs at his ankles and gazed at the sunset. A hundred shades of rose blazed across the backdrop to the pines' silhouettes. Another one of God's masterpieces displayed. Clint's gaze crept over the trunks of the pines, fiery red in the glow of the setting sun. Erect as sentinels standing at attention toward their sustainer of life.

"It's a beauty, Jessie," he said wistfully, wishing they could see it together. "There are red skies tonight . . ." He heard sadness in his own voice. "I'll find you. I'll bring you home, and you'll be safe."

Seeing the first star peak its bright face against the blackening sky, Clint began to sing. "O Holy night . . ." Thoughts of that night when they shared this song hung heavily in his memory.

He raked his fingers through his hair, feeling warm in spite of the nippy breeze whispering through the pines. "Jessie! What is it about you? You heat my blood, tamp down my good sense, scramble my thoughts . . ."

This kind of preoccupation was dangerous for someone avoiding marriage at all costs. Roy had teased him for some time now about being a misogamist. It wasn't true, of course. He didn't hate marriage. Just didn't think anyone in his family should attempt it. After all, though his mother had been happily married to his dad, she had failed miserably at picking a second mate. It had been an important lesson for Clint to learn, since his mother must not have known the man's true nature until it was too late.

Face the facts, saddle bum. Marriage is the only feasible outcome for Jessie. And, just thinking of it made his lungs feel like they'd shrunk. Made him want to slide back to his former way of life—to Veronica and the others before her.

It figured he'd want to hide there, in that eddy of bad behavior. But he couldn't do that anymore.

CHAPTER 29

Clint awoke abruptly, sure he'd only just dozed off. He scanned the area for what had awakened him. When nothing became obvious he sighed in relief.

Dawn was breaking, revealing a gray mist that covered the earth. He inhaled a deep breath of the clean, moist air and sat up, working stiff muscles. Despite the coolness of the morning, a coating of sweat covered his body. His clothing stuck to his skin, his hair was matted. With the pace he'd kept it was no wonder his body hadn't gotten a chance to fully recover. But he didn't have time to worry about himself.

He stumbled to his feet and retrieved his saddle bags, rummaging around in them until he found a piece of jerky. Popping it in his mouth, he chewed while saddling his horse.

The road was annihilated. Forcing his weary body forward, he tugged the gelding along behind. Thankfully his horse had stayed put throughout the night. He knew the mountain lion was lurking about, no doubt waiting for the perfect time to strike. The gelding would alert him to dangers, though he didn't know how long he'd be able to take the horse along. Already he'd found it difficult to squeeze him through the larger boulders that cluttered the road. The black had always been a spirited horse—ran like the wind, excelled in working cattle—but he'd never done well in tight spaces.

Shouldering his rifle, Clint zigzagged through the rubble. Hours passed slowly, each mile demanding physical strength he lacked. He walked in a daze until his horse balked at a boulder and about tore his arm out of the socket.

"Easy, boy," Clint said, trying to pat the black's shoulder. The horse spooked to the side and trampled a pile of splintered pines, then bolted forward and knocked its knees against a boulder. "Whoa. Whoa, boy." Clint tried to keep his voice as soothing as possible, but this was downright dangerous. He glanced around for the cat, but deep down he knew the culprit was no predator, but outright skittishness itself. Clint coaxed the horse forward. They'd only made it ten steps when the black reared and almost twisted a leg on a boulder.

That was when Clint knew it was time to leave the horse behind.

Clint searched and found a clearing with tall mountain grasses and a brook passing through it. He stripped off the saddle bags, rifle, and saddle, stuffing the saddle behind a large pole pine. The bags went over one shoulder, the rifle on the other. He slid a palm tenderly down the horse's muzzle and rubbed. "It'd be good if you were here when I got back, fella."

The ascent up the hill was grueling. The midday sun bore down, burning the back of his neck. He stopped to take a drink from the canteen. He wiped his mouth with the back of his hand then screwed the cap back on. Uneasy all of the sudden, he straightened to full height and listened. All he heard was dead quiet. *Where's the noise?* Absence of forest sounds wasn't a good sign.

With the movements of a barn cat on the prowl, he slid his saddle bags and canteen to the ground. Raising the rifle, he planted the butt deep into his right shoulder, cocked the hammer, and waited—his ears tuned in to any change in the atmosphere. Twisting lightly on his heels, rifle in place, he scanned the area. A trickle of sweat from below his hat inched over the stubble on his jaw before dropping onto his shirt. Still he waited. Time seemed endless while the weight of the rifle weakened his muscles. Finally, he spotted his adversary moving across boulders overhead.

Without forewarning the cat gave one giant leap toward Clint, his outstretched body blocking the sun. Clint shot. The report of the rifle rang out across the dale, and the cat jerked in midair. Clint dodged the falling carcass, the shot still ringing through his bones. With the smoking barrel, he gave the cat a nudge. *Dead on! Thank you, Lord!*

Wasting no time over his kill, he re-shouldered the saddle bags and rifle and continued up the mountainside.

After hours of exhaustive climbing over splintered rock and fallen trees, he pulled out his pocket watch. Past two. The heat, unbearable now, forced him to give his lagging body yet another break—the third one in the last hour. He was getting closer though, and slowing wasn't an option. Jessie was just ahead, and the farther he went, the more convinced he was that she was hurt. Giving his worn-out body a much needed reprieve wasn't going to happen. Not today. Not tomorrow.

Catching a glimpse of movement, he stopped short. Other than the lowering of his shoulder imperceptibly, allowing the strap of his rifle to glide down his arm, he remained still.

There it was again. A glimpse of gray racing between trees. Rifle in hand now, he shifted his gaze to the right in time to see a pack of wolves advancing through the copse of trees. Incredibly close, the alpha male led the pack toward him, his yellow eyes fixed to Clint's. Confusion muddied Clint's brain for a minute. Wolves never came close to humans, despite the stories the old timers liked to tell. *Of course, unless there was a very good reason.* The earthquake alone was reason enough, but right behind him came the *true* reason—the alpha female with the same gray coat and penetrating yellow eyes. Following her were four blue-eyed pups. When she came to a halt they began scampering about her feet. The wolves were disoriented and probably hungry. The female looked thin, almost gaunt, and her coat resembled an eagle's nest, unkempt and matted. Each time a pup tried to latch on for a meal she turned on it, bumping it from her with a growl and a snap.

Clint felt the last of his blood leave his face. Sweat trickled from his hairline and drop-by-drop slipped into his eyes. Stinging with a fury, he didn't dare move to wipe the sweat away. Instead, he squinted in order to blink without much notice. *Look away. Show submission.*

The wolf raised his nose to the air and sniffed. Clint knew the animal could detect food in his saddle bags. Except for a bear's, he knew a wolf's sense of smell far surpassed all of God's land creatures.

He didn't want to shoot any of them. Besides, the odds were against him. Which one would he shoot first? The protective alpha male or the overprotective alpha mother? Either way, if they decided to attack, things looked grim for him. While he worked at devising a strategy, the male stepped closer and raised his nose to sniff again. Then, his whole demeanor changed. No doubt about it, he'd caught a whiff of food. Muscles taut, the wolf lumbered forward but stopped again and perked his ears.

At only thirty feet away, Clint had to make a decision and make it soon. Before he had that chance he heard a boulder give way from the cliff above, smashing against others as it came skidding down the craggy wall toward him. He afforded a quick glimpse to make sure he wouldn't be crushed and immediately glanced back toward the wolves. They were gone. Vanished. *Thank you, God.* He leaped over some rubble and ran all out uphill. He looked back the instant the boulder skipped off the road and slammed into the very place the animals had deserted.

He staggered to a stop, heaving a sigh of relief mingled with fatigue. He removed his hat to swipe a forearm across his face, then stuffed it back on. Putting his weary legs back in motion, he plodded up the rock-littered road and prayed exhaustion wouldn't take him.

As he rounded the last familiar bend to behold Mary's place, he gasped in horror. "My God. Please, no!" The cabin was totally demolished, flat as a hotcake. He ditched his gear and ran. "Jessie? Mary? Johnnie?" he hollered. "*Jessica!*"

No! They can't be under this thing. With strength born of an adrenaline rush, Clint tore into the rubble, flinging lumber in all directions. He loved Mary and cared about Johnnie, but if he lost Jessie . . . The admission sent his thoughts into a tail spin he didn't have time for.

"Jessie, you can't be in here. You can't!" His hands and

arms worked tirelessly for untold minutes. His strength waning, he fell to his knees on the now cleared pathway into the cabin. He bent to look under the rubble for any sign of life or bodies.

He couldn't see a thing. It was dusk, light was limited. He raced back to his saddle bags and found his flashlight. Another scramble brought him to the cabin. He flashed the light under the debris. "Jessie, Mary! Are you in there? Anyone?"

Sick to his stomach, his body rebelled from the two days of travel when it was still recuperating. He ignored its needs and began to tear into more fractured lumber. Stepping in now, he shouldered a big portion of roofing and gave it a shove. Encouraged that he'd uncovered a good portion of the kitchen to his view, he dug some more. Laying the flashlight on the rubble, he began again—lifting, straining, pushing, and tossing.

"Jessie?" he called out one final time, hearing the weariness in his own voice.

Defeated, yet somewhat encouraged that he hadn't found any bodies yet, he trudged up the road a ways to retrieve his gear. He turned and flashed the light on the tree in front of Mary's cabin, thinking it would be a good place to bed down for the night.

He would begin again in the morning, though the longer he waited the less likely he'd find anyone alive. He snatched his hat off the ground, gave it a slap across his thigh and positioned it on his head. He needed to be honest with himself. If they were in there, they couldn't have survived. Yet, he had to know. He wouldn't leave until he found them.

As he came closer to the tree, something white in the greenery at its base caught his attention. He bent down to pick it up. A piece of gauze for bandaging! Exhilarated, he looked for more evidence that someone had been out here. Yes, a ways from the tree, he found an empty roll of surgical tape. The kind Mary kept on hand for injuries. *So someone's injured.* It's Jessie. Instinctively, he knew it. His many dreams had pointed to it, hadn't they? His stomach surged.

He had to find Jessie. She needed him. They must have started down the mountain. But why had he missed them? Suddenly, a terrible thought struck him, so intense it blurred his vision for a moment. Flashing his light around the area he looked for a grave of any kind. He strayed from the cabin for the next hour but found nothing to indicate someone had been buried.

Somewhat mollified, he made his way back to the tree and proceeded to lay out his bedroll. He found another chunk of jerky in his saddlebags, propped himself against the tree, and chewed on the meat and a plan. At first light he'd venture on in search of the group he now figured had to be headed home.

Morning arrived as a streak of light through the tall pines. Clint squinted against its brilliance, forcing his muddled brain into wakefulness. *Where am I?* Then he remembered and shot to his feet, nearly blacking out. Placing a hand against the tree, he shook his head. He glanced at the treetops. Direct sunlight peeking through the bows meant only one thing—it was late morning. Disgusted and impatient with his perpetually weakened state, he hustled through preparations to get back on the road to find Jessie.

Jessie. Oh, how he missed her. Admitting that much to himself seemed to offer the needed fortitude.

Loading up his arms and shoulders with saddle bags

and rifle, Clint took one last look at Mary's cabin, grieving over memories they'd never again have in that special place. Then he turned and strode down the road. Though worried, a strange contentment filled his soul. A small smile curved his mouth as he journeyed ahead to find her, until the gravity of the situation re-registered and the smile slid from his face.

The day had stretched on endlessly, with more aftershocks and no sign of the group moving down the mountain. Clint took few breaks and pushed himself to the limit of endurance. His entire world became very simple very quick: he would keep putting one foot in front of the other until he found Jessie or died trying.

A flash of white caught his eye, and he jerked toward it. It was only a harmless rabbit, running in circles like a child's wind-up toy. Feeling the effects of little food for several days now, Clint decided it was time for a longer break and some fresh meat. Sliding the rifle off his shoulder, cocking, and aiming, the simple shot hit the rabbit right between its ears. Retrieving it, he remembered that past this quarter mile deluge of boulders a pretty little meadow stretched out along the road for a spell. It would be perfect for building a fire and roasting his game. He opened his saddle bag, pulled out a red handkerchief, and wrapped the bloodied end of the rabbit in it, carefully positioning it back in his bag.

Back on the road he began the tedious task of negotiating the mass of obstructions. *I should have gone around the long way,* he thought, his legs weakening with every ascent over a boulder.

A peculiar sound made him stop to listen. The sound imitated his own—grunting and skidding across tops of boulders, a scraping of boots sliding down the other side. Human.

"Who's out there?" he hollered.

No answer.

He tensed. "Who's there?" he tried again.

"It's Johnnie," he heard off in the distance. "Is that you, Clint?" came the muffled reply.

For a split second Clint experienced a stab of jealousy, thinking of Johnnie with Jessie. Directly behind that emotion came disgust—at himself. Then fear for Jessie.

"Yeah, it's me." Ignoring his fatigue, he sped forward.

When they drew closer together, both broke into huge grins. Once they took the last few steps, they grabbed each other into a quick hug with slaps on the back.

"Is Jessie with you? And Mary?" Clint asked.

Johnnie's smile dropped away. "Yes. All three women."

Clint's relief was so profound, he barely registered Johnnie's frown. Clint gave out a loud sigh of relief. "Thank God."

Johnnie's eyebrows shot up in surprise. "Come again?"

Clint gave a weak smile. "It's a long story. More on that later. I just came from the collapsed cabin. Scared me to death, Johnnie! I thought you guys were in it." He swallowed hard, waited a beat, then asked, "Where're the girls?"

Johnnie turned. "Come on. Left them back a short ways. I didn't dare go too far since I have the rifle. What'd you shoot? It's what got my attention."

Now that was a quick shift. An instant dread washed over him. "Rabbit. Tired of beef jerky. Johnnie—"

"I'm glad, or likely you'd have missed us," Johnnie said as he hastened his steps. "We had to take the long way around this batch of rubble."

"Why?" Clint lunged the next two steps and grabbed Johnnie's sleeve to stop him. He turned the man toward him. "I've had a bad feeling about this. Jessie's hurt, isn't she?"

Johnnie's face looked ashen.

Clint's heart flipped over. A small gust of wind ruffled the hair under his hat, and though it was a warm breeze, it chilled him to the bone.

"During the initial earthquake," Johnnie finally said. "She took a hit to the head. She's been unconscious ever since."

Clint scrubbed a hand down his face and the breath he was holding burst out of him. "She's been out for *what*? Three days now?"

Johnnie nodded. "She's not feverish, and she's breathing normally. Can't seem to wake her. Rose Marie and I've been carrying her on a cot that we made into a stretcher—"

"Aw, son-of-a—!"

Johnnie's face reddened. "She's plenty capable."

Johnnie had misunderstood the reason for his near expletive. But fine. The way he felt now, he'd gladly take him to task over Rose Marie. "Oh, she's capable, all right." An instant rage seized his gut. Setting his jaw, he turned sharply and walked on. *But* for Rose Marie, he'd have been with Jessie.

Johnnie stopped him with a hand to his arm. "Listen, Clint, no matter what she's done, she's been through a lot up here. Go easy on her."

Clint furrowed his brows as he stared. Well, now, that was an interesting shift in attitude. He yanked his arm away from Johnnie's hold. He didn't give a plugged nickel how Johnnie felt about Rose Marie. He was angry as Hades at her for complicating his life. But mostly for causing Jessie to run away in the first place.

Jessie's unconsciousness scared the living cockcrows out of him and made him burn with fury all at the same time. If she'd stayed put, he could have explained himself. Yet she'd run from this trouble instead of standing up to him and facing it. It was just like a woman. Just like his mother! Never having the back bone to face a man when it was called for. Now look what happened to her.

"Jessie would've been fine now if she'd been with me," Clint hissed, taking his full wrath out on Johnnie.

Johnnie narrowed his eyes as he snarled back, "You could have kept her from harm and I didn't, is that it?"

"Take it how you want. Let's go! I need to see her."

Johnnie seethed in angry silence. Clint didn't care. He let Johnnie lead the way toward the women. Now that he'd faced his feelings for Jessie, jealousy toward Johnnie raged like a wild animal trapped in his chest. At least it fueled his depleted body, helping him navigate the maze to their destination.

When Clint finally spotted the women off to the side of the road, he pushed past Johnnie to jog the rest of the way. Seeing Jessica lying there unconscious nearly crumpled his legs before he reached her. He threw off his hat, dumped his belongings on the ground, and fell to his knees at her side. "Jessie, it's Clint. Jessie, can you hear me?" He cradled her face in his hands, stroking her pale, motionless cheeks with his thumbs. His heart raced with a terror he'd never felt in his life. "Wake up, little one."

An emotive upheaval whipped through him like the undulating road he'd endured during the quake. Dazed and stunned, nothing could have prepared him for the anguish of this moment.

And just like that, between one breath and the next,

between one heartbeat and the next, he fell hard. Awakened to a love so strong and so powerful it jarred his very soul.

He never dreamed he'd fall in love. Nonetheless, against his obstinate will, it had happened. But how, when he'd fought against it so? An array of memories tracked through his mind just then: Jessie's cold hand in his the day they met, her compassion for critters and people alike, the gentle warmth of her lush body as they rode double on his gelding, uncontrollable hiccups, her tendency to blurt out everything on her mind, her cheek against his chest at the dance, her display of wills across the fence from him at the round-up, the be-safe kiss before he downed the grizzly, his thumbs sliding across damp cheeks from her tears of anguish, of love.

Memories continued to spill into his mind, but one in particular came and stuck—Jessie looking up at him with wide-eyed innocence before *his* delirium had cleared a bit, in bed. In his bed. Suddenly, he wanted to be the one—the *only* one—to take her there. Every. Single. Night.

Jessie.

He needed her to live! Releasing her face, he leaned over to scoop her into his arms. He sank back on his heels and rocked, pulling one hand out to stroke her cheeks and hair.

"Jessie." His voice cracked. "Wake up. *Please!*"

The rest of the group circled around and one by one plowed their knees into the ground by Jessie, gaping at him.

But she remained motionless, breathing in and out in a steady rhythm.

Clint looked up and eyed each one of them. His

despairing glare searched deep before moving to the next person. "What've you been doing for her, *exactly?*"

Mary planted on a small smile. "She's been fine, other than her unconsciousness—"

"*Not* fine then," Clint snapped.

Mary took a deep breath and tried again. "No. But it's all we have, Clint." Mary studied his face like was her norm. "You're exhausted. Where've you been?"

Clint clasped Jessica tightly to his chest and rocked back to sit. He looked at Mary. "I've seen the cabin. I'm sorry, Mary."

Mary's gaze landed on his damaged hands as they held Jessica. "Your hands. You tried to dig through that rubble, didn't you?"

"When I saw it, I thought the worst. I'm thankful you're all alive."

"I'll doctor those hands for you."

"They're fine." Looking to Johnnie, he said, "What's the plan?"

"Carry her back home, then to the clinic."

Clint nodded, drained of all energy. "I'll help you carry her the rest of the way."

"I figured."

Clint stared into the baby blue eyes of an uncharacteristically quiet Rose Marie. He had so much to say to her, but knowing it would take strength to do it, he frowned at her for a few heartbeats, then sighed and closed his eyes.

"Are you hungry?" Mary asked.

"Famished. Have a fresh rabbit in my saddle bags you can use."

"Fresh meat!" Rose Marie exclaimed, speaking for the first time.

Clint ignored her and looked down at Jessie. He brushed her hair away from her forehead with light strokes. "Sweetheart, can you hear me? Jessie?"

It was eerie how still and pasty she was. Something unfamiliar gripped him and swelled. His throat tightened and his eyes burned. He swallowed hard, tried to push the sensation back to the smallest corners of his heart, where it belonged. But, before he knew it, scalding tears streaked down his lean cheeks. Not a few, but a flood.

As the minutes ticked on, Clint hadn't released Jessie in spite of the rest coaxing him to do so. *For his own sake*, they'd said. *He needed rest*, they'd said. Well, though his body screamed in protest, he would rest soon enough. He'd even had words with Johnnie to leave off and let him tend to her now that he was here.

His gaze rarely left Jessie's face, in hopes he would see her open her eyes. A flutter of her eyelashes a couple of times sent his heart into his throat. He'd coaxed, pleaded, prayed. Nothing he tried had worked, and he grew grim as the sun slid behind the great pines and a light evening breeze brushed against his sticky skin.

"Clint. Son. Please, put her back on the cot. Laying her down would be better for her recovery," Mary said.

He raised his head enough to see open sympathy in Mary's eyes. He blinked. A fire flickered between them in full blaze. He hadn't even noticed it being built. Mary's eyebrows drew together in concern, and Clint relented with a nod. Maybe laying her flat would be better.

Mary shuffled around the fire. "Here, let me help you. Your body must be stiff as a board by now."

"Mary." His voice was so weak and scratchy, he hardly recognized it as his own. "She has to wake up soon. Has to!"

He and Mary lifted Jessie to the cot. He kissed her on the forehead, then stretched his arms over his head and groaned. Mary covered Jessie with a blanket, felt her forehead, and looked back at Clint.

"You have to trust God in this, my dear. He loves her more than we do," Mary said in a soothing tone.

"I know," was what squeezed past his throat.

She handed him a portion of rabbit and some water and sat back down to study him. "You're in love with her."

Clint stared into Mary's eyes for several long moments, considering how to respond. But this was Mary and why would it matter? "It shows, does it?"

"Yes."

"I don't care if the whole blasted world knows. In fact, I'll shout it to anyone and everyone if she'll just wake up. Drat, Mary! I can't take this!" He reached up and shoved both hands through his hair, then stood. He started to pace back and forth in front of the fire. "I should have told her before now. What if I never get the chance?"

"If God wants you to, you'll have the chance. Now, get some rest. Maybe tomorrow's the day."

Clint stopped in front of Mary and gave her an imploring look. "Will you pray for that?"

"Of course."

"Now. Please."

He knelt on a knee before Mary and grasped one hand. With her other, she stroked his hair, then bowed her head, giving his hand a squeeze. "Father God, we pray for Jessica. Please heal her body and mind. And wake her up. Help Clint, and the rest of us, to wait on You. Thank you, Lord, for Your many blessings. In Your name we pray. Amen"

"Amen." That prayer was simple enough. He could

probably handle those in the future. A measure of relief flowed through him, quieting his mind and relaxing his dog-tired body. After spreading his bedroll, he lay next to Jessie and positioned a hand on her arm so he'd be alerted if she awoke in the night. "Night, Mary."

"Good night, son. Rest well."

* * *

Clint jolted awake. His hand, still resting on Jessie's arm, had shifted. Had he moved it, or had she? The pre-dawn light was almost enough to see by. He rose up on an elbow and peered into Jessie's face.

"Jessie? Little one?" He whispered so near she'd be able to feel the warmth of his breath on her face.

He shook her arm a fraction. "Jessie?"

As he watched her face, miraculously she stirred.

Clint sat up and twisted around so that both bent arms straddled her head. His face was within inches of hers.

"Jessie, wake up, sweet girl, please." Clint kept talking, hoping to coax her up from the depths.

Mary, Johnnie, and Rose Marie stirred out of sleep and came to join him.

He pleaded and cajoled until dawn broke and streaks of light stretched across the sky, but still, nothing. He clamped his eyes shut, wondering how he would survive another day with her so close and so far away. But his eyes only burned with unshed tears, so he went back to looking at her sweet face again.

And then it happened. Jessica's lips parted, and the muscles around her eyes fluttered like she was trying to see but her lids wouldn't cooperate.

Clint about choked on his own breath. "Mary, get a cloth and wet it like you did for me."

Handkerchief in hand, he dabbed at Jessie's eyes. She flinched, maybe from the cold, maybe from surprise.

"It's okay, little one. It's me. I'm here."

He continued to dab and wipe until finally her eyes opened.

"Thank you, God!" Clint said. Johnnie and Rose Marie gawked at him. He ignored them. "Jessie, can you hear me?"

She nodded so slightly it was almost undetectable. He stroked her hair back from her face, a lump swelling at the back of his throat. "Her lips are dry," he said with a croaky sound.

Mary remoistened the cloth from the canteen and squeezed some onto Jessie's lips. Her tongue instinctively flicked out to capture the moisture.

"More," Clint said. Mary continued until Jessica stopped collecting it into her mouth. "Can you speak?" Clint asked.

As he stared into her eyes, all he saw was fear. "Are you able to speak?"

Her eyes grew larger, the fear greater.

"What is it?"

She formed words on her lips.

"Need more water?" he asked. She shook her head.

She looked directly into Clint's eyes, a pleading sort of look. Beneath his frustration helplessness churned. Her fingertips brushed the front of his shirt. He grabbed her hand and brought it lovingly to his lips, kissing her fingertips. Her look was of surprise. *Those beautiful hazel eyes.* He drank in the sight of her, his wild pulse thrumming at his temples. *She's disoriented. Soon she'll grace me with one of her incredible smiles.* He smiled tenderly and stroked her cheek with a long finger.

She was trying to speak again.

His eyes urged her on.

"Who are you?" she whispered.

CHAPTER 30

Clint's stomach climbed into his throat. "*What?*" He refused to believe what he'd just heard.

A little louder now, she asked, "Who are you? Where am I?"

Clint's jaw unhinged, and he stared at her for long breath-constricting moments. The heart that was finally alive may as well have been wrenched from his chest. The pain would have been less.

"You don't know who I am?" he asked, hardly able to speak.

When she shook her head, his blood all but dropped to his boots.

Mary scooted closer. "Do you know who I am?"

Jessie studied her face for a moment, then shook her head again, eyes widening.

"How about me, do you know who I am?" Rose Marie.

She looked carefully, shook her head.

"And me?" Johnnie.

And again, she shook her head.

Clint's eyes squeezed shut. "Oh, God, what are you

doing?" he mumbled. He leaned in closer and pressed his forehead into hers, startling her. His angst was so great he barely registered her reaction. *Lord, let her know us. Please.* When he leaned back to look into her eyes, all he saw was confusion there—and fear. "Little one, do you know your name?"

"Yes, of course. My name is . . . That is, I'm . . ."

Horror swept across her face. And, in that moment, Clint would have traded all his memories, past and future, to give hers back.

She sucked in a choppy breath. "What happened?" Her voice grew a tad stronger. "Why am I here? I don't understand."

Clint pulled away, realizing he was adding to her discomfort with his intimate contact. He struggled to string words together. "Your name is Jessica, sweet thing. Jessica Harper." He waited while she absorbed that, disappointed the revelation hadn't seem to ring a bell. "There was an earthquake, and you were hurt. Do you remember any of that?"

Concern showed on Jessie's face as she studied his. "I should know you, shouldn't I? I'm sorry."

He blinked several times, then gave a sad smile. "It's just like you to worry about *me*." He hesitated, trying to get hold of his rampaging emotions. "What exactly *do* you remember?"

She pondered his question. "I remember . . . I remember . . . that 'God so loved the world that He gave His only begotten Son that whosoever believeth in Him should not perish but have Everlasting Life." Her eyebrows raised in surprise.

Clint grinned at her. "That *would* be what you'd remember."

Her gaze floated over his face. "You're very handsome, you know. Especially when you smile." Her eyes went wide, and she blushed all over.

He laughed as warmth spread through him. At least her not-thinking-before-speaking disorder was still intact.

She looked at him apologetically, and he felt a flicker of hope.

Trying not to think of the unfairness of it all, Clint vowed to care for her, to make her whole again. *Lord, she's yours. I have absolutely no control. Help me to trust you and take one step at a time.* "Do you think you can sit up?"

She nodded.

He propped her against a nearby rock and eased to the ground beside her, his arm around her shoulders.

She dropped her chin to her chest, shaking her head as if to clear the fog.

"Dizzy?" he asked.

"A little woozy, and my vision is a bit blurred."

"You should only sit up for a minute, then. Mary, let's give her more water. Maybe her dizziness will stop once she rehydrates."

Johnnie strode up next to him and lifted the canteen to check if it needed refilling.

Clint glanced up at him. Jealousy shoved in, wanting control of his mind. It certainly had his emotions. But, what right did he have to feel jealous? Concern, yes. Jealousy, no. Yet, a vision of Johnnie marrying Jessie flashed in his mind's eye, setting his blood to boiling.

"Thanks for taking care of her," he managed blandly.

Johnnie's jaw ticked. "Of course we'd take care of her.

What did you think we'd do?" With that Johnnie flung the canteen to the ground by Clint and stalked off, disappearing into a thicket of trees.

Clint stared at his back as he strode away, then shared a glare with Rose Marie before looking back at Jessie. "Enough sitting for now," he said, lifting her to the stretcher.

Once she was settled, she began to drift off to sleep. Fear gripped Clint. What if she didn't wake up again?

Mary touched his arm, breaking into his thoughts. "Clint, let's take a walk, shall we? Rose Marie, will you keep an eye on Jessica? Please." Mary eyed him carefully. "Come with me, dear boy."

Clint hesitated, not wanting to leave Jessie—especially with Rose Marie—but Mary wasn't asking.

They both rose and headed in the opposite direction of Johnnie. After strolling far enough away so as not to be overheard, Mary said, "Clint, you know I love you like a son, don't you?"

Clint pressed his back against a pole pine, set the sole of his boot against the bark, and an arm draped across his thigh. "Uh oh. This can't be good."

"I know you've had a big shock here. So have we. I know how you feel about Jessica—"

"Listen, Mary—"

"You have to tread lightly here," she went on. "We've been through a lot as well. You wouldn't believe the change to our Rose Marie for one—"

"She's not *our* Rose Marie."

Mary kept right on talking. "I know you blame her for a lot of the heartache you've had with Jessica, but since I see that you've begun to change your mind about God, it means you must also do what God would have you do. And that's forgive her."

He groaned. Stuffing hands in his front pockets, he pushed off the tree and started to pace. "I'm not ready for that. I'm still so angry with that girl I don't even know how to act around her."

Mary put a hand out to stop him. "Okay, I understand that, Clint, but promise me you'll work on it. She's changing. Since the earthquake. I know you don't want to believe it, but watch, please, and try to hold your tongue. The same goes for Johnnie. That boy's got strong feelings for Jessica. Though I must admit, there seems to be a spark between him and Rose Marie lately." A tenuous laugh spilled out. "I just hope it doesn't start a forest fire! Anyway, try to remember that others care about Jessica as well."

Clint started pacing again, then stopped, head bent under a weight he couldn't possibly

bear. Sunlight speckled the thick cushion of pine needles beneath his feet. He cleared a spot in the needles with his boot, half-aware his heart was about ready to drop right through the leather sole. "She doesn't look at me the same . . ."

"What are you talking about?"

He looked up at Mary. "Jessie. The way she used to look at me." He waited a beat. Two. "It's not there, Mary. In her eyes . . ." He shook his head.

"Relax, sweetie." She patted his arm. "Everything will get back to normal."

"What is normal for Jessie and me? I've botched that so badly! And what . . . what if she never remembers me?" His throat tightened. "What then?"

She considered him for a moment. "Well, if she never remembers you, what will you do?"

What would he do? Confound this woman and her questions. Fear turned to fury in a heartbeat. "Will I forget about Jessie and go back to my old ways, you mean? To my former"—what could he call them to Mary?—"*paramours*? Is that what you're asking?"

"Yes, Clint. I guess that's what I'm asking."

Shame flooded him. He'd never tell Mary the stupid thought *had* actually crossed his mind. Not because he cared about Veronica or any of the others—in fact just the opposite. Veronica and he were two of a kind. Both tainted and undeserving of decent people. And, with her he hadn't had to involve his heart. Guilt free—pain free.

But, he'd buried that possibility on his trip up here and had no intention of exhuming it now. "Just because a person has amnesia doesn't mean they change who they are. I'll make sure she's safe and I'll make sure she understands about the two times she saw Rose Marie and me . . . and . . ." His mind drifted. Truth was, if she didn't remember him, he'd be sick at heart. So what *would* he do about her? Maybe the bigger question was what would he do if she *did* remember him?

"Shoot, Mary. I don't know beyond that. What do you want me to say?"

"Say you'll marry her. Say you love her. You admitted you do."

His jaw clenched, and he pressed his lips together. "I can't marry her."

Mary looked cross. "Then why not let it go? I mean, what's the point of explaining about you and Rose Marie if it doesn't matter anyway?" Her eyes penetrated his, like if she stared long enough she could extract his real reason.

Clint glanced away and rubbed his temples. Inhaling a deep, calming breath of mountain air, he swung his gaze back to her and stared. Moments clicked by. This was Mary. He could tell her. "You want the truth?"

Mary looked at him like his nose had just slid off his face. "What *do you* think?"

"Okay, fine." He plowed a hand through his hair, hoping she'd forget all about this conversation and walk away, but that wouldn't happen. "I'm not good enough for her."

Her jaw dropped. "Why ever would you say such a thing?" She scrutinized his expression, and a new awareness seemed to cloud hers as her eyes narrowed. "Are you saying this because you're thinking of running scared? You've done that before when someone got too close."

He glowered. The impulse to run was great. Mary was right. But the reasons were complicated. He *wasn't* good enough for Jessie. But he also didn't trust her. He didn't trust any of them. He'd been fooling himself. He'd been toying with thoughts of a future, when the truth was, he couldn't have a future with her.

But, if I don't marry her, someone else will.

He wanted to tear his hair out. Forcing his fluxing mind back, he had to get first things first. Jessie had to remember him. Then he would decide the next step.

Mary sighed. "God's in control. Of even this, dear boy."

He stared into her kind eyes—eyes that had watched his ungodly way of life for years without hating him for it, as she could have—as she should have. If anyone was the epitome of godliness, it was Mary. He fell so short of all she stood for. Unworthiness, guilt, and shame had all crowded into his decaying soul. And he was helpless to do anything about it. "I don't deserve God's help," he said in a constricted voice. "Why should He give it to me?"

"Oh, sweetheart." Mary's eyes filled with sympathy. "You don't think He will."

"No."

"How sad. And how very wrong you are." Mary came forward and swung her arms around his ribcage. Speaking into his chest, she said, "He loves you, Clint. Believe me."

He pulled Mary into the deep hug and squeezed hard. "I love *you*, you know." He was about to make a fool of himself and break down like the child he'd never been allowed to be. He sought levity. "Thanks for always looking out for me . . . *Granny*."

"Granny! Ugh. Never liked that nickname. Should be mom rather than granny anyways." She smiled up into his face. "I love you, too."

"And yes, I promise I'll *work* on treading lightly around Johnnie and Rose Marie—and sit back and watch," he said, tongue-in-cheek. He grinned down at her.

On the way back to the campsite, Clint sensed his tattered emotions were on the rise again. He guessed he needed to apologize to Johnnie, but for what exactly? All Clint had done was thank him for taking care of Jessie, though admittedly it *was* less than heart-felt. By the time he planted his first step into the circle of firelight, he was ready to bite someone's head off again.

He huffed out a breath. Turning on his heel to find Johnnie, he halted when Rose Marie jumped to her feet and barked at him.

"Clint, you insensitive—" She started, then stopped when she saw she'd startled him. But her eyes still blazed. "Johnnie's been taking good care of Jessica, doing all he knew to do. You unfeeling, big old . . . lout!"

He stared at her, dumbfounded. At that, she up and tromped off to find Johnnie first. That was fine by him. Forcing calm he didn't feel, he sat down by Jessie, picked up her hand, and threaded his fingers through hers.

Jessie struggled to open her eyes.

"Well, hello, sweet girl. How do you feel?"

She looked scared again. "May I have some water, please?"

Still polite. She may not be remembering it, but she had the same gentle spirit.

"Of course." He looked to Mary, who already had it ready.

"Here, let's sit you up and see how that goes." Once sitting, Clint leaned her back against him and Mary helped her drink from the canteen.

"Do you think you could eat something?" Mary asked.

"I can try." She looked pensive.

"What is it?" Clint asked.

"Would you tell me your names, please?"

Clint's gut rolled with the same turbulence he experienced with every quake. He squeezed his eyes closed, tried to settle his stomach and quiet his mind. He thought he'd finally gotten used to the constant upheaval of emotions regularly afflicting him since meeting Jessie. But this uncertainty was killing him.

He raised his eyelids, smiled meekly, and hoped his voice would not sound as strained as he felt. "Of course." He turned her to the side a little so she could see his face. "I'm Clint. This is Mary. The other man is Johnnie, and the other woman is Rose Marie."

"And who are all of you to me?"

Clint's heart gave another dull thud. "Mary here is a

friend. You and I stayed at her cabin for a couple of weeks while I was recovering from an injury." He couldn't believe this was happening. "Johnnie works on the ranch with me. We work for your Uncle Roy. Rose Marie is Mary's grand-daughter. Remember any of that?"

Her face fell, and sadness loomed in her eyes. "I only remember that I have family in California. Where are we, exactly?"

"That's great you remember your family." A burst of relief railed through him. He smiled. "Montana."

"Montana. Why'd I come to Montana?"

She looked so lost that pain shot through his temples, and ricocheted straight to his heart. Would they make it through this? "To help Mabel, Uncle Roy's cook. You're helping cook for two dozen employees on his ten thou-sand-acre cattle ranch, for the summer."

"And you, Clint, who are you to me?"

The way she asked gave Clint hope. "I . . . I'm a friend."

CHAPTER 31

Clint lounged against a sheered boulder and stretched his legs toward the fire. Anyone looking on would see the confident, relaxed leader he wore so well in public. Known throughout the state as the self-assured man who had the world—at least its womenfolk—by the tail made him want to laugh. No one had ever suspected that, instead, self-destruction had been his constant companion since age twelve.

Mindlessly he watched the fire dance, but tonight its familiar crackle didn't soothe him. It reminded him of the night he and Jessie had enjoyed a similar setting—one of only a handful of times in his life he'd felt whole. He glanced over at her dozing profile and wished he could turn back time.

But now, all that was gone.

His stomach hadn't stopped objecting since the moment he'd seen Jessie as white as death on that make-shift stretcher. They weren't far from the place he'd killed the grizzly, and he'd hoped familiar surroundings would trigger a memory in her. It hadn't.

Hearing a rustling in the nearby bushes, Clint

snatched up his rifle. Before he could rise to his feet, he caught Johnnie's approaching silhouette in the firelight. The muscles in Clint's back relaxed as he set the rifle back down at arm's length.

Johnnie entered the campsite and glanced at a sleeping Jessica. "I saw tracks," he said, quietly. "We have wolf in the area. We should get settled in for the night and stoke up that fire."

Shoot. One more thing. Clint rolled to his feet, caught Johnnie's eye, and nodded toward a tree a couple feet away. The night was still but for the evening breeze ruffling through the trees. "I've already made their acquaintance— at least the alphas and their pups." He glanced back at the women, satisfied they were okay.

Johnnie's eyes went wide. "When?"

"On my way to Mary's, looking for Jessie—couple days ago. Thought I'd have to shoot them, but a boulder gave way above me and scared them off. They're hungry, confused."

Johnnie lifted his hat and wiped his face with his sleeve, then settled it back before he gave a nod of agreement. "You shot something else before."

"Cougar. At the ridge. Same one I nicked two months ago."

"Settled the score for your gelding, then."

Clint nodded while scanning the area—the meadow, the pines, the splits in the earth. "The quake sure rattled the animals. They've been out of character—before and after. Shot that rogue grizzly on our first trip up."

"Thought so." "We'll need to take shifts."

When they returned to camp, Clint sat down by Jessie. He glanced around the fire at the others, and caught

Johnnie watching their sleeping angel. Clint bristled at the yearning he saw in Johnnie's eyes. He glanced Mary's way. He'd schooled his features, but she knew him too well. She was staring at him with heat in her eyes. Well, that was just too bad. Johnnie shouldn't be having thoughts about his girl. Jessie belonged to him. He didn't know how he'd convince her of that now, but it didn't change the facts. Clint leaned back against the boulder, and openly glared at Johnnie.

The silent group stared into the blazing fire, each held by their own private thoughts.

A piercing cry from Jessie rent the air. Clint all but jumped out of his skin. By the time he realized what he was doing, he was squatting face-to-face with Jessie, grasping her arms. "Jessie. It was only a nightmare."

She looked bewildered.

With a knuckle he tilted her chin up to look at him. "Jessie?"

The firelight danced about her terrified face. Her gaze locked onto Clint's chest and she shivered. He gave her arms a squeeze to get her attention. "Jessie!" She brought her eyes up to his. "There you go. It's okay, little one."

Bleakness dominated her face. He wanted to take her in his arms and crush out the confusion, to make her remember him and what they'd shared. Instead he draped her blanket about her shoulders, then brushed the hair back from her face.

He sat back on his heels and watched her. The strength and spunk that had so captured his attention from the start were gone. And this fragile, scared girl tore at his heart. He felt her trembling hand touch his arm. The pleading in her eyes made him forget all propriety, and the others looking on. He pulled her onto his lap. Her breath stirred at the hollow of his neck.

When finally her shuddering stopped, he loosened his hold and pulled back to search her face. "Better?" She was a frightened little rabbit. He scrambled for a way to distract her. "Do you want something to eat?"

She let out a shaky breath. He watched while she pulled herself together, a semblance of her gumption returning, and breathed a sigh of relief.

"Okay," Jessie said.

Though she had agreed, he sensed her trepidation, and knew he should release her from his lap. But, he couldn't seem to obey his good sense. Instead he handed her a piece of jerky. "It's not like your suppers, but it's all we have right now."

She tilted her head up to him, her eyes huge. "I cook?"

For a lengthy moment he allowed his gaze to roam over her face—along her hairline, cheeks, chin, up to her supple lips. He fought the overwhelming urge to lean in and kiss that delightful mouth. The urge nearly won over, so before he did anything stupid he nodded and gave her a grin.

Her smile dropped, and her eyes grew distant.

He tensed. "What is it? Are you remembering something?"

"Your smile . . ." She shook her head. "I don't know . . ."

He grinned bigger. "Thank God!"

"Oh . . . do you know Him?"

"Who?"

"God."

"I—well . . . I'd like to think I do." What he did know was that God likely didn't want him. Not after the way he'd lived. Not when God had people like Jessie and Mary and Roy to choose from.

"I may not remember much, but . . . you'd know if you were a Christian."

He nodded. "I believe in God. I may have run from Him for most of my life, but during the earthquake, He and I came to a sort of . . . well, an understanding."

A quick glance told him Mary, Johnnie, and Rose Marie watched him intently. Uncomfortable with their scrutiny, he settled Jessica onto the blanket and rested his back against the boulder.

This time it was Jessica who leaned toward *him*. She planted her forearms on her crossed legs and bit her lip with a smile. "Do you know who Jesus is?"

He chuckled, remembering her innocent expressions and questions—the way she would blurt out everything on her mind. Oh, how he'd missed that.

Rose Marie bounded to her feet just then. All eyes turned toward her. The evening breeze caught up her blonde locks in an otherworldly swirl about her as she glowered. She turned on her heels and dashed out of the campsite. As he watched *the beauty's* retreating back, Clint was reminded matters were not going to be easy to settle between him and Jessie concerning Rose Marie. What was she going to think of him when her memories returned?

He looked back at Jessie. "Yes, little one, I know who Jesus is. I had the privilege of hearing all about Him when you nursed me back to health."

"Oh. I'm a nurse."

"No." His heart sank. "No, you're not. But you helped *me* get better." He didn't want to talk about that, afraid the conversation would lead to the confusion with Rose Marie. And now was not the time for that particular discussion.

The night was black as soot without a moon of any

kind. Clint scanned what he could see of the area, wondering where Rose Marie might have wandered off to. She'd have known better than to go far. At least he hoped so. She wasn't his problem. Yet, he had a sudden irrational need to watch out for her.

Jessie had fallen silent. One glance told him she was deep in thought. It must be horrible for her to wrestle with her own mind, forcing it to divulge secrets.

He laid his hand on her back. She turned her head and gave him a smile that warmed him all the way to his toes.

A loud snap brought Clint's attention to the man across the fire. Frowning, Johnnie had a dry stick in his hands, and with a vengeance, cracked it across his thigh. He picked up another and did it again, dropping the broken pieces into a pile by the fire. He swung his gaze out to where Rose Marie had disappeared into the night, then back to Clint. "I've been meaning to ask, did you walk the whole way up here?"

Well, that was sure a change of direction. Was Johnnie worried about Rose Marie, or jealous of the smile he'd just gotten from Jessie? Clint shook his head. "Rode the black halfway. Had to leave him before he hurt himself, or me. You know how he hates tight spaces."

"The black?" Jessie asked. "Is that his name?"

Clint turned at the sound of concern in her voice. "How about you name him?"

She flashed him a smile. "I'd love to."

There went the tightness in his chest again. Her genuine enthusiasm so captured him. One of the reasons he'd fallen so hard for her was how much she enjoyed simple things he'd never taken the time to appreciate.

"I'll have to see him first, though. Then I'll know what we should call him."

Clint smiled at the *we* in that statement. "Sounds like a plan. You'll need to pray that he's still ground tied where I left him."

Thinking of his gelding brought him back to Harper ranch. His gut twisted at the devastation he'd left there. "Listen, Johnnie, Mary, I should warn you what to expect when we get back home." What he'd give to not have to face this. But it was real. "The ranch is pretty broken up. Many were injured, and we lost several good men."

They both spoke at once, so Clint raised a hand. "Hold on. I'll tell you everything."

He spent the rest of the evening telling the gruesome details of the ravaged homestead. He found it difficult beyond words to tell of those who were lost to them. "I still don't know how the others weathered this thing out on the open range. Hopefully there'll be better news from them."

Rose Marie took that moment to re-enter the camp, looking grim. She sat a little ways from them like a child who'd been shunned. He knew that feeling and was irritated with himself for the pang of sympathy he felt for her. "We should call it a night. We have some distance to cover yet, and we'll be carrying Jessie."

Jessie's head snapped up. "Carry me? No. I can walk."

"Oh no you won't." Clint gave her his most intimidating look. But her opposition secretly pleased him.

"No. I couldn't. How embarrassing."

"So, you remember embarrassing, do you?" he teased. "Here's the thing, Jessie. You were hit hard enough to cause unconsciousness for two days. That means we don't risk your exerting yourself at this point, and that's final."

She sighed heavily. "If you insist."

Clint shook his head and smiled. Trust came so easily for her. She hadn't lost that quality, thank goodness. He might give the illusion of such strength of character. But Jessie? She actually lived it.

CHAPTER 32

Dawn broke, and though the eastern horizon was hidden by the lofty mountaintop behind them, it couldn't conceal another awe-inspiring illustration of God's splendor. After Clint had refreshed the fire and pressed the makeshift coffee pot into the heat, he reclined against the boulder, humbly studying the brilliance that pushed the darkness away and brought a golden light in its wake. Admiring sunrises had always been a favorite past-time of his. Now, in light of his new relationship with God, the beauty seemed magnified.

"What's the smile for?" Jessie asked.

Thrilled and relieved she was awake, he grinned down at her. She had turned over sometime during the night to face him. Her slender hands rested under her head in a prayer-like manner, her eyes half lidded. Admitting his love, if only to himself, had calmed the sea of emotions. Now all he wanted was to love her, protect her, and spend every possible moment with her.

"Good morning, sunshine," he said.

"Good morning, sunshine."

Hearing her say those words momentarily gripped

him. He stared into her eyes, astounded she had burrowed more deeply under his skin just since awakening from unconsciousness. And how had she accepted her circumstances so well? She didn't remember herself, or any of them, yet she still had that unwavering positive outlook.

"How are you today? How's the head?" Clint asked.

"Let me sit up and see."

He leaned over to help her.

She smiled up into his face. "I think I'm pretty good, other than stiff from sleeping on the ground."

"Good. What can I get you? Water, coffee?"

Worrying her bottom lip, she didn't speak for a moment, then, "I need to use the little girl's tree."

He chuckled, delighted she'd called it the same thing as before. Memories might still be in tack, if somewhat displaced. "Sure, let's get you up and go handle that."

"*You're* going to help me? Shouldn't we get one of the ladies up?"

"I can handle it. You'll have your privacy, I promise."

She eyed him warily, but nodded.

* * *

Jessica loved how this kind man was taking care of her, causing her to wonder more each minute what he'd been to her. Constantly, she prayed for her memories to return. It must be how a woman feels, waiting for the man she loves to ask her to marry him—excited and nervous all at the same time. And yet, chances were her memories wouldn't return at all. She wasn't sure how she knew that, but she did. The thought made her empty stomach queasy.

Clint put a strong arm around her shoulders and

guided her over uneven ground. His target seemed to be a dense grove of trees. He had everything with them for this private moment, including the rifle she hoped he wouldn't need.

She hurried through her task. Upon their return Jessica saw the others stoking the fire and filling tin coffee cups—that is, except for a slumbering Johnnie.

"Let him sleep," she heard Rose Marie say to Mary. "He was awake most of the night guarding us."

Rose Marie stared at Clint's arm around Jessica's shoulders and said, "Where've you two been?"

Jessica glanced up at Clint. He ran a hand slowly through his hair, and looked . . .angry? "Why do you need to know?" he barked.

"I was just asking. You don't have to bite my head off."

"Let's be clear here, Rose Marie. Stay out of our business."

From his prone position on the ground, Johnnie reached over and clamped a hand across Clint's boot. Clint looked down as Johnnie glared up. "She just asked a simple question."

"What're you, her guardian angel now? I'm sure you already know she's fully capable of taking care of herself."

"I heard her tone and it was fine. You need to get that chip off your shoulder."

Clint dropped his arm from Jessica and turned to square off with Johnnie. In one fluid movement, Johnnie pushed off the ground to face Clint nose-to-nose.

Clint pushed Jessica behind him. It was clear the action infuriated a rumpled Johnnie.

Jessica was amazed at these two beefy cowboys. Clint was a couple inches taller and bulkier, but that didn't keep them from a formidable confrontation. They were quite spectacular to watch, silhouetted in the bright morning light like two powerful stallions battling over their brood of mares. Her eyes centered on Clint—shirt sleeves rolled up to his elbows, jaw muscles set, sunkissed brown hair ruffling in the gentle breeze. Just watching him shortened her breaths.

As she stood observing, she couldn't help but wonder what had happened with Rose Marie to make Clint act this way toward her. It was obvious his blood boiled whenever she came near.

Mary stomped forward. "Okay, enough! You two strapping men need to stop acting like pint-sized banty roosters. Rose Marie meant nothing by what she said, Clint."

Clint pivoted, effectively cutting Rose Marie off from his sight, and ticked his head down a few degrees to trap Mary in his glare. "How 'bout you tell her to stay away from us, and we'll call it good."

Rose Marie blinked as if she'd been smacked, and then fell to studying the dirt.

"It's been a rough end-of-summer." Mary patted Clint on the arm as she moved past him and took Rose Marie's hand to lead her away. "Let's go home."

Clint and Johnnie were outwardly calm as they turned to pack camp, but their eyes raged at each other. Clint marched Jessica to the far side of the campfire and started flinging their gear into a pile. Johnnie busied himself rolling the blankets so tight it would take some doing to unravel them later.

Clint took a gentle hold of Jessica's elbow and guided her to the stretcher. She looked down at the contraption and took a step back. Raising her eyes to Clint, she hoped she'd see he really didn't mean for her to be coddled like this. He gave an uncompromising nod, and she wondered if he was always this domineering. She sighed and reluctantly moved forward. Once Clint eased Jessica onto the stretcher, she folded her arms across her chest and furrowed her brows. That triggered a smile from him she was too irritated to enjoy.

Once the men had groused over who'd carry her feet and who the head, they draped themselves with gear, and to her consternation, toted her out of there. Who were these remarkable men who were so willing to safeguard her to the point of her embarrassment?

Jessica sensed the war hanging heavily between them, though she had no idea what it was about. They grunted, tugged at the cot, navigated boulders and broken ground, and all around pitted brute strength against one another. Never did one appeal to the other over the pace, and their pace was far too relentless considering the hazards in their path.

It seemed hours had passed with both men drenched in sweat. Their hats, Clint's black suede and Johnnie's beige straw, had darkened considerably above the bands. Peeking out from under her bent arm, Jessica caught furtive glimpses of Clint. Regular trickles of sweat traveled down his tanned cheeks and off his jaw line. He blinked periodically, wincing, no doubt from salt stinging his eyes. They had long since left Rose Marie and Mary behind to follow as best they could.

Johnnie stumbled. Before she could grasp the slats of the cot, Jessica slid headfirst into Johnnie's backside. "Oh!" Once she caught a good hand-hold she struggled to sit upright.

"Whoa. Easy now," Clint barked. He straightened the

cot while Johnnie steadied his end. Clint peered at her, breathless. "You all right?"

"Stop and let me out of this thing."

Clint's face showed the surprise of her curt words, but she was beyond caring. The men found a clearing, and veered off in that direction. Jessica bailed out of the cot before they could lower it.

"Okay, here's what I've decided," she said with hands on her hips. "I'm not going to ride anymore."

Seeing Clint start to speak she held up a palm. "I've had it. You two bucks need to work out whatever it is you're having problems with, and I'm going to walk. That's the end of it!" With that she proceeded down the road. Glancing once over her shoulder, she saw Mary and Rose Marie arrive, eye the two men, then make a slight shift to follow after her.

* * *

Clint stood there, dumbfounded, holding his end of the cot. Johnnie seemed to have the same reaction. Feeling foolish, Clint finally dropped his end, and walked off after the women.

Johnnie's boots crunched broken ground behind him. "What the heck's up with you?"

"*Me?*" Clint swiveled to a stop and glared at Johnnie. "What's wrong with *you?*"

"What were you trying to prove? That you're stronger? Tougher?"

"Like you were slowing down any," Clint snarled.

"You were showing off for Jessica!"

Furious, Clint planted a forearm to Johnnie's neck.

Johnnie wrenched it away and twisted Clint's arm behind his back. Clint bent and flipped Johnnie over his head. But rather than let go of Clint's arm, Johnnie hung on. This time, Clint flipped head over heels and crashed down beside Johnnie. His shoulder burned something fierce, and he just knew Johnnie had torn something in there. "How the devil'd you learn to do that?" Clint panted.

Johnnie sat up slowly, looking much like Clint felt. Johnnie bent his knees and planted his heels in the dirt. Drying his face with a sleeve, he took a few more breaths before he looked over at Clint. Between breaths, he said, "Since the girls are out of ear-shot, we need to talk."

Clint hadn't budged yet, since his body was still screaming at him. "I agree. So what's going on with you and Rose Marie anyway?"

Raking his fingers through his hair, Johnnie said, "That's *not* what I wanted to talk to you about, but okay, let's start there. There's nothing between Rose Marie and me. I've seen a different side of her, that's all. Something you're not willing to see."

Clint sat up much the same way Johnnie had to face him. "I don't want to see *any* side of her. Do you know the grief that girl's given me? I mean, you're judging me and you don't even know anything about what she's done."

"Fine, tell me what she's done."

Surprised by Johnnie's words, Clint took a moment to consider how to answer, and then realized it wasn't something he'd ever share with another man.

Johnnie's fury seemed to be rising. "Well, I'm waiting. What horrific thing did that little wisp of a girl do to the almighty Clint Wilkins that you can't even be civil to her?"

Clint winced. He was right. What harm had she done to him that he hadn't allowed? A new conviction tore through him, getting a stronghold on his heart. *What is this new feeling? From You God?*

"Well?"

Clint cleared his throat. Hands dangling between his knees, he spoke with resignation. "You're right." Though he'd had no control over what she'd done, somehow he knew it was payback for his own bad choices in life. "If I can accept Christ's forgiveness, I guess it's time I try to forgive, huh?" Clint said, surprised at his own admission. He glanced sideways at Johnnie and saw the man's perplexed look.

"Where'd that come from?" Johnnie asked.

"From here." Clint tapped his chest. "Trying to condemn Rose Marie and I'm suddenly reminded of my own faults."

Johnnie's eyebrows shot up.

"Don't look at me like that. I'm amazed too." He choked out a laugh. "Besides, don't expect miracles. It's just a start."

Clint struggled to his feet, grabbed his hat out of the dirt, and dusted off his pants with it. He offered a hand to Johnnie.

Slapping his hand in Clint's, Johnnie stood. "There's something else I need to talk to you about."

Clint braced himself. "What now?"

"Do you remember when I came to the ranch a year ago?"

"You were quite the greenhorn back then."

Johnnie bit the side of his lip.

They didn't have time for this. "We've got to catch up to the girls." Clint turned his back on Johnnie and headed downhill.

Johnnie trudged along behind him. "Did you ever wonder where I came from and why I came here?"

What was this all about? A headache started to grab hold at Clint's temples. He slowed up, waited until Johnnie was beside him. "No. Lots of men come here looking for work. Not my business to ask about their lives. Work hard, stay honest, that's all I ask." He ventured a glance in Johnnie's direction. "You're not thinking of confessing anything, are you?"

"No. Well, yeah, sort of, but it pertains to you."

"What're you talking about? You're starting to get on my nerves."

"What the heck are you getting so riled up about?"

"Spit it out, Williams, or shut the heck up."

Johnnie stopped so short Clint felt the rubble he'd freed sting the backs of his legs. Clint whipped around. Johnnie met him with silence.

"What is wrong with you? Just tell me what's on your mind."

Johnnie scrubbed a hand up and down his chest. He looked away, convincing Clint he was guilty of some diddly-dang thing.

Clint swiped at the sweat dripping off his face and held his tongue. Fine. He could out-wait this cowpoke till the cows came home.

Johnnie took a deep breath. "I'm not a true cattleman. Oh, I have a background in it from way back. But not in the last ten years."

Clint went rigid, torn between what Johnnie was trying to say and how far away the girls were getting.

"Clint . . ." Johnnie looked glum, like he was about to confess he'd ruined Clint's best boots. "I was hired by your mother to find you."

It took a minute and still the words didn't fully register. "You—What did you just say?"

Johnnie curled in his lower lip and bit down. "I'm a Pinkerton Detective. I work in the missing persons department. Your mother hired our agency to find you. She was desperate to know if you were alive and well. Wyoming didn't have a missing persons department, so our agency in San Francisco got the job."

Sensing his knees growing weak, Clint did a quick scan of the area and plunked down hard on a boulder before they could buckle. He couldn't speak. He had tried to forget his mother, yet all these years she had been a dark influence on his life.

Johnnie found a spot next to him and sat, waited.

Clint's heart pounded painfully. A flurry of memories twisted together in his mind. Johnnie put a hand on Clint's shoulder. "Your stepfather passed away two years ago. It took some time before your mother could afford to hire us. Her request was for me to find you, to stay nearby for a time. She never explained your past to me, but was pleased to find out you were safe and had turned out fine."

Clint focused on a flat rock in the road while trying to wrap his mind around each new shock. "You could bowl me over with a feather right now. I know I don't ask about the men's pasts . . ."

"Sorry I had to deceive you, but I was doing my job. Well, actually, I started out doing my job. Once I found you, I took a leave of absence to observe you for a time. It was what your mom wanted, but couldn't afford. I liked being at the ranch so much I decided to stay on as a favor to her. We stayed in close touch. Recently, I talked her into letting me tell you, since it's past time I return to San Francisco."

Clint blinked in disbelief. "Where is my mother? My sisters?"

"Your mom is still in Cheyenne. Your sisters live close by. Both are married with families. You have two nieces and four nephews."

"No kidding." Clint shook his head again. He found himself surprised that numbness had moved in where anger used to be. "Well, I'm happy my sisters are okay." He lifted his hat, scrubbed a hand through his hair, then replaced it. "And Mom—did she survive that sham of a marriage?" He swung his head back to watch Johnnie's reaction.

Johnnie's expression remained impassive. "She's well."

"So, you're a Pinkerton. Always knew you were a mystery, Johnnie, but this . . ." A humorless laugh escaped him.

Out of the corner of his eye, Clint could see Johnnie eyeing him warily.

Clint stood. Johnnie did as well. "What are you going to do now?" Clint asked.

"Believe it or not, I had planned to stay on at the ranch and continue to work for you. That was before Jessica."

Clint instantly saw red. "What do you mean before Jessica?"

Johnnie stared off in the distance. "She's an amazing—"

"You don't have to tell me how amazing she is!" Clint cut in. Blatant jealousy seared a path right through him. His hands made fists but he managed to control the urge to slam them into Johnnie.

Johnnie's jaw muscles knotted. "It's about time you figure out what you've got your hands on."

Clint swallowed hard. He had two choices. Beat the heck out of Johnnie and kick him off the ranch, or confess his feelings—ones he hadn't even told Jessie—and see if Johnnie would back off. His heart started to pound as he looked Johnnie right in the eye. "I'm in love with her."

Johnnie's shoulders slumped. "Yeah. I figured. Question is: What're you going to do about it?"

And therein lay the problem. What *was* he planning to do? Johnnie wouldn't hesitate. He'd marry her. The thought made Clint violent. He growled. "That's none of your business."

Johnnie gave him a sobering look. "Guess you still have a lot to think about. Just don't take too long." With that Johnnie strode down the road after the women.

Clint was livid. He wanted to pummel the man and leave him for the animals to clean up. Instead, he clamped his jaw and followed in silence.

When he'd successfully squelched his desire to punch Johnnie, he asked, "You've been at the ranch quite a while. Why'd you delay telling my mom and me for so long?"

"I didn't want to tell your mom you've never married and were going through women like our bulls go through the herd."

Clint cringed.

Johnnie caught the look and shrugged. "Anyway, I did tell her that you were the foreman of a prosperous cattle ranch, so she knows you're successful in your work."

Clint's gaze drifted off where the girls had gone around a curve in the road. He still heard their voices. No matter what turbulence had just ripped through his insides, the dangers of the outside world were doubly real and at least partially under his control. He picked up his pace to close the gap.

"Let's just keep this bit of information between us," Clint said.

Johnnie eyed him with a mixture of cynicism and respect. He nodded his agreement.

* * *

Jessica heard the footsteps of the men behind them and slowed so she could talk to them, but just then Rose Marie edged up next to her. "I know you're not remembering stuff, Jessica, but there's something I want to apologize to you about."

Jessica glanced to the side at her, but kept walking. "You do?"

"I've done some things that I'm not proud of—some things I did to you . . . and Clint."

Jessica stopped short. So did Rose Marie. Facing her, Jessica couldn't help but feel her heart sag. Rose Marie had a creamy complexion, sun-streaked blonde hair pulled back in a ponytail, sky blue eyes. Snug jeans and a simple sleeveless blouse emphasized a tall, shapely body. Any man's dream. *Not Clint's*, came the unbidden hope.

Out of the corner of her eye Jessica saw the men come into view around the bend. "*Me* and Clint? You do know I don't remember."

"I know, but that's why I want to apologize to you before you remember everything. Just know that I'm sorry for the problems I've caused you in the past, and I'll never be a problem again, okay?"

Jessica kicked at a piece of crushed rock and turned to walk on, skirting around broken pieces of boulder. She shot Rose Marie another glance and saw true misery on her face. She let out a long sigh. "Listen, if I can receive full forgiveness of my past, present, and future sins from Jesus, how can I not forgive you—even when I don't know what you did?"

Rose Marie looked taken aback. "How can someone forgive when they don't even know what they're forgiving? When you get your memories back, you'll change your mind."

Jessica shook her head. "Because of what Christ did for me, I have already forgiven you, and I won't change my mind."

"How're we doing, ladies?" A deep voice called from several yards away.

Jessica swung around to see Clint walking toward them. His Stetson was pulled low, so his eyes were hidden from view, but her gaze traced the length and breadth of the man. She'd been attracted to him the instant she'd open her eyes. Now, the attraction was escalating. His relaxed gait was pure grace as he strode toward her.

"We'll stop here for a rest. We're only a few hours from home," he said to Jessica. "I was expecting to have come across my horse by now so you could have ridden in. So, Jessie, if you're too tired to make it we can carry you again."

Jessica felt her irritation rise until she spotted the amused twinkle in his eyes. With a long sigh, the tension drained a little. She grinned. "Oh, no you won't. I'm fine to walk."

He chuckled and whisked her into his arms to swing her around. Startled and a little unnerved, she looked straight into his eyes and with mock harshness said, "I don't even know you, mister. You'd better put me down."

He froze in place. Still holding her, he studied her face a few inches from his own. His smile vanished and he looked unsure and . . . hurt. So different from the imposing figure she had witnessed thus far.

His vulnerability knocked down whatever walls she'd built to protect herself. "Just teasing," she whispered hoarsely. She snaked her arms around his neck and nuzzled his rough cheek.

He let out a long, hissing breath past her ear. When his clasp tightened, she felt his heart pound in his solid chest. He whispered, "Sorry if I scared you. You don't think you know me, but . . ."

She whispered back, "Well, I *don't* know you . . ."

His head shot back, giving her a full view of the most amazing eyes. Apprehension seemed to spring from their jewel-green depths.

She leaned to his ear again. "But I want to."

CHAPTER 33

*W*ant. Carried on Jessica's warm breath, the word stirred something not so innocent in Clint. He plunked her down and stepped back so quickly he nearly knocked her over.

She looked puzzled.

He worked at quieting new thoughts that had been tossed into his mind. It was his responsibility now to keep her pure. That would take re-training. He didn't know how to go about that and love her as well—without the bonds of marriage, at least.

He'd never felt so inept. All at once his flight mode kicked in. Mary's words came back. *Are you thinking of running scared like you usually do when someone gets too close?* Was that true now?

After a rest and a snack they continued their trek. In order to keep his distance from Jessie—in spite of her bewildered look—Clint had busied himself securing their supplies and then followed at the rear of their group. The day had grown warm, and as they continued to descend the mountain, the change in altitude brought more heat and a western sun blazing straight into their eyes. They had all grown weary, and Clint was anxious for the familiar place where the main camp came into view.

At the next switch in the road, a large shadow crossed in front of the group. Clint watched as it grew larger and stretched farther. Jessie gasped, and jumped backward, hitting the wall that was Clint.

Clint caught her in his arms. "Steady, now," he said next to her ear, then spun her behind him. "Hold up, ladies."

With his rifle tucked into his shoulder, Clint stole around the bend with Johnnie close on his heels.

Seeing what had caused the shadow, both men broke into hearty laughter. Jessie rounded the corner. Her face split into a delighted grin when she saw them patting his horse. The gelding casually lipped meadow grasses, as the afternoon sun cast his shadow across the road.

"So, you decided to stick around, huh boy?" Clint said as he stepped closer to run a hand down the gelding's neck.

The others crowded around, stroking the horse like he was some sort of homecoming all his own. All but Jessie, that was. Clint glanced over his shoulder and caught sight of Jessie standing off from the group under the shade of a pine, her brows furrowed. A tingle of trepidation skittered down Clint's spine at her expression. Grasping the reins, he handed them to Johnnie and strode over to her, careful not to block her view of his horse. "What is it, Jessie?"

"I remember him. I remember riding on him . . ." She turned to face him. "With you," she said, blinking in surprise.

Relief spread over him like a warm blanket on a wintry day. "That's great."

"Shadow," she said.

"Yeah, he did cast a big shadow, didn't he." He chuckled.

"No. I mean, I think we should call him Shadow."

He paused, and then threw his head back and gave in to a long overdue belly laugh, so reassured and down-right happy, he could bust.

Jessie watched and listened, smiling up at him. The first unguarded smile he'd seen from her since she'd awoken. It took him aback.

"I remember that laugh," she whispered. "I know I've always loved it."

Laughter drained away. His eyes blurred with tears. *Thank you, Lord. She's remembering.*

Jessie looked back at his horse. He watched as her brows knit together and the smile slid away, and just like that a river of dread coursed straight through his soul.

Without a trace of doubt he knew she was straining for a memory—one that was going to bring pain.

Still watching the gelding, she said, "When we were on your horse, another woman was there." Bringing her fingers to her temple, she rubbed, as if doing so would make her remember. "She was mad." Jessie turned her face up to him. "At you. Because of me." She swallowed hard, then on a whisper said, "She's your girl . . ."

"No, Jessie—"

"Please stop. Don't explain."

He didn't know what to say. Her hurt expression staggered him as much as it seemed to have surprised her. He tried to swallow the growing lump. Would all her memories come back this partially? If he wasn't with her to explain each one, would she misinterpret what she was remembering? Considering his unsteady feelings and their tumultuous past, he was already unsure of their future. As prospects of that future dimmed, fear set in again, and with it a new understanding. He cared deeply about having a future with this woman—however he could have it.

The nagging question remained. Would she love him or hate him when she finally remembered it all?

She looked ready to flee so Clint grasped her elbows and brought her close. Her eyes glittered. "Jessie, listen to me carefully. I don't know how your memories will return, but I'm asking you to please come to *me* if they're not making any sense. Will you promise me that?"

She seemed conflicted, still locked in thought about her latest revelation. His anxiety rose when she didn't answer.

"Little one?"

Still no answer.

He took hold of her shoulder and gave it a slight shake. "Jessie!"

The fog seemed to lift out of her eyes as she focused on him. "Yes?" she said weakly.

She was tired. To press her now would only create more doubts. Not able to help himself, he pulled her to him for a deep hug and was reminded how she fit so perfectly, locked in his arms with his face nuzzling the top of her head.

He forced himself to release her and took her by the hand to the gelding's side. While Johnnie saddled the animal, Shadow lifted his muzzle and snuffled Jessie's hair. If a horse could sigh, Shadow did, and then he leaned his forehead against her chest. His hide rippled in pleasure as he nudged her.

Clint chuckled. "He remembers you."

Jessie smiled up at Clint, making his hide react the same way. Wrapping her arms around the gelding's head, she kissed him between the eyes then scratched behind his ears. "Yeah, I guess he does."

"Come on. It's getting late." He helped her into the saddle that Johnnie had just cinched up, threw the saddle bags into place, then looked at Rose Marie and Mary. "Which one of you wants to ride with Jessie?"

Rose Marie looked surprised at his offer to them both. "Grandma should ride. I'm fine."

Jessica relaxed once she and Mary were aboard, secretly glad for the reprieve to her recovering body. Clint took the reins in hand and headed on down the road, pulling his newly named horse behind him.

Jessica fell into the sway of Shadow's gait and glanced about the countryside, sighing at the assault of its beauty, until her gaze landed on the mystery man in front of her. Who was he? He treated her like she meant something to him, but that was impossible. She may not remember *who* she was, but she seemed to know the type of men she would attract, and none would be like him. He was charming. Of course he was. Just look at him. So, the only answer was, he was being attentive because of her amnesia. That had to be it.

Jessica knew she should be tied in knots over her loss of memory. But all of that took second place behind the cowboy in front of her. She studied him. Thick, saddle brown hair curled beneath his cowboy hat. His shoulders seemed to go on forever, which made his waist that much leaner and his hips that much narrower. Well-constructed legs. She was mesmerized by his loose-hipped strides, his brawny backside flexing . . . with each . . . and every . . . generous . . . step.

Heat powered up Jessica's neck, all the way to the top of her head. A thought came to her, as potent as the warmth filling her cheeks. Was appreciation of a male body the same as lust?

She cleared her throat with gusto.

Clint whirled around. His hand caught the bridle to keep the gelding from tossing his head. He raised his face to her, revealing concerned emerald-colored eyes beneath that worn black hat. "You all right?"

Her *appreciation* was running rampant now. She cleared her throat a second time, smiled, and waved him on.

* * *

As they arrived at the homestead, Clint was once again shaken by the complete devastation surrounding them. Men were at work rebuilding the main house, the barn, and the bunkhouses, but the lives that were lost could never be restored.

Three men rushed to greet them. Pete helped the gals down from the gelding. "Hey, ladies, good to see you. Glad you're okay, Jessica. Everyone was worried, you having gone off like that by yourself."

She stood on the ground now, studying his face, no doubt trying to remember who he was. Clint came to her side. "Pete, will you let the rest know that Jessie had an injury to her head during the quake. She won't be remembering any of you right now. Amnesia." His chest tightened again. He could have lost her. He put an arm around her shoulders, giving them a squeeze.

"Is Max around?" Clint asked. "He's had experience with head injuries. I think he should take a look at Jessie."

Pete stood rigid. He finally nodded. "He's in charge of the barn project. I'll get him."

"Wait. How're the rest of the men you took to the clinic, and the ones on the range?" Clint asked.

"Roy had two broke legs," Pete began on a sigh. "Sam, a few broke ribs with some facial injuries. Nothin' permanent. Steve needed surgery for internal injuries so we took him to Ashton Hospital. But Doc says they're gonna be fine. They're still there. Mabel's fine, but she stayed with them. We've . . ." The timbre of his voice changed. ". . . already buried seven of 'em. Smittie, Ralph, Jimmy, Robbie, Charlie, Ted, and young Jack." Clint sucked in a breath, and it burned as though he'd inhaled the campfire. "Got caught on the southwest pasture near Lake Hebgen when that tsunami rearranged the countryside."

Clint cocked his head, wondering if he'd heard right. "*Tsunami?*"

"Yeah. The quake caused a tsunami; shifted all its water up the mountainside. Created us a new lake up there. Flooded everything else. The cattle, the horses, the wranglers . . . all got caught in it."

Clint couldn't speak. Pete looked empathetic as he went on. "Laid 'em all to rest in the little cemetery on the hill, next to Walt. The ones we found anyways." Pete swallowed hard then. Tears shimmered in his eyes.

Clint was frozen to the broken ground, as was Johnnie, like if they even stirred, their composure would splinter. None of them spoke.

Pete tried to go on but his voice cracked. He waited as he hung his head and dragged in deep breaths. Finally, he said, "Found two of 'em just south of here. Trampled to death by the herd. The rest in that pasture were fine. Only minor injuries." His body shuddered. "I'm . . . I'm real glad you guys are okay though." His last statement was so quiet Clint barely heard him.

Clint ran a hand down his face, collecting stray tears that had reached his jawline. He coughed. "Gather the hands." He glanced away, cleared his throat again, then managed to meet Pete's eyes. "I'll . . . um . . . I'll come over and talk to everyone in a minute. Looks like you have the rebuilding under control." Some of his control returned at the change of subject. "Who's in charge of that?"

"Nick, 'a course. He's better at this than blacksmithin'. Things are going well here, boss. We . . . uh . . . got a lot done since the funerals." Pete turned away.

Clint turned his attention to Jessie and the others. "Will you be okay? I need to talk to my men."

They all nodded solemnly.

"Johnnie, maybe you could set up camp for us down by the stream. Or, maybe one of the small cottages is still in one piece. Would you handle that?"

Johnnie nodded.

Clint felt one weight slide off as another slid on. Johnnie would take good care of Jessie. There was no room for jealousy in him now. For that Clint was grateful. "I'll send Max down to check out Jessie." And with that, he turned and walked away.

* * *

During the days to follow, Jessica was completely lost. She observed Clint from a distance as he took charge. Though obviously saddened by the loss of the men, leadership came naturally to him. She almost wished she could experience the loss with all of them. Watching them grieve people she should have remembered left her feeling bereft and brittle, sad and empty.

The cowboys worked on the reconstruction of the homestead, and each day, they said, it looked more like it had before. Mary and Rose Marie stayed with her in one of the small cottages that had withstood the quakes, yet she didn't feel she belonged with them. Life had settled into a routine of caring for the crew's needs—cooking, washing clothes, treating minor injuries—and yet she seemed more alone than ever.

Clint stayed with the men most of the time. She knew they needed him for guidance during this tough time of rebuilding through their grief, but still she found herself missing him in spite of what little she knew about him.

Each day the struggle to remember the past brought her to a point of exhaustion. A dark hole of depression loomed before her. She was sure she'd never allowed herself the trap of that state of mind, so what she needed was something constructive to do. Mary had asked her to retrieve a few household items from the main house. She'd start there.

It was a hot day—not unusual for late August. Perspiration already dripped from her neck and skittered down her chest. Jessica fanned herself with her collar, glanced down to dodge broken ground, and looked up in time to see a striking blonde sashaying toward the barn from the other direction. Her fancy western outfit peaked Jessica's curiosity. Shorts, *very* short, revealed sleek, tanned legs. Her beaded cowgirl hat and boots matched. Long, fuchsia nails couldn't be missed, since every finger was graced with a ring of some sort. Her hair was pulled behind her ears, but otherwise floated in the light breeze at her back. *Impressive*, was the only thought that crossed Jessica's mind.

Jessica slowed her pace. What in the world was this beauty queen doing on a cattle ranch amid shattered earth and splintered buildings? Jessica swung her gaze toward the woman's destination and saw Clint standing in front of the barn with those big hands spread at his hips. His Stetson was tilted back on his head while he conversed with a man on the roof. Jessica shifted back to the female.

Wonder what she's doing here? The moment the question had fully formed, she found the answer. From behind, the *beauty* snaked her arms around an unsuspecting Clint and pressed her petite, though well-endowed, body into his back.

Jessica's heart shot to her throat. Jealousy seized her like a fire-breathing dragon. All she wanted was to wreak havoc on the woman and fight for her man. *Her man?* What a laugh. Ever since she'd arrived at the cottage by the stream, she'd spent hours in front of a mirror trying to evoke memories, or at least trying to remember her own image. She knew, without a doubt, she wasn't in the same league as this stunning woman. Clint belonged with someone like her. Though it didn't surprise Jessica to see him with someone like that, it didn't relieve the feral jealousy or lessen the knife of pain.

Not able to tear her gaze away, she watched Clint's reaction. At the initial contact he dropped his head to study the hands, then casually turned his head to one side to speak over his shoulder, as if he'd done it a hundred times before. Without letting loose, the woman slid under his arm to the front of him. This time she tilted her face up to his and smiled—a sparkling white smile.

Lightheaded, Jessica realized she'd been holding her breath. *I can't watch this.* Gasping for air, she twisted about and ran full on toward the stream. Her eyes burned with tears even as she tried to convince herself that Clint wasn't hers to moon over. She had no rights to him. *But, none of this makes sense. What of the way he held me and cared for me?*

She sifted through current memories for evidence of feelings he might have for her. Her heart sank. He'd been attentive on the trip here, yes. Concern only, then. That must have been all, given he'd left her in Johnnie's care and she'd barely seen him since.

As she walked along the edge of the stream, her thoughts shifted. This path seemed familiar. The stream gurgled—almost melodically. The tension in her shoulders eased as she breathed deeply of clean, crisp air—cooled from its sweep over icy mountain water. The crystalline flow burbled over boulders and eddied into the banks. Jessica scanned the area for a place to sit and enjoy the serenity. A slightly angled boulder a few feet from the water's edge caught her eye.

She continued forward and sat on the rough surface of the rock, pulled her knees up within her arms, and prayed for the umpteenth time that the Lord would return her memories. As she prayed, her attention drifted to a large rock in the center of the stream. It looked like a large hippopotamus's head just under the surface. The water flowed up its back, rushed to either side of its peak, and eddied back together beyond it. Her memories were like that; now precariously disrupted, needing to come together so she could move on with her life.

She turned her gaze to the western horizon, wondering how the consummate artist would color it, when she heard a voice from behind her.

"Hullo, pretty lady. Out here watching a Montana sunset, eh?" the deep voice drawled.

She glanced over her shoulder and saw a cowpoke. "Oh, hello."

He gave her a suspicious look.

Seeing his reaction she added, "Do I know you?"

His head tilted to one side. With a scowl of disbelief, he said, "You saying you don't know me?"

Warmth rose in her cheeks. "I'm sorry. I was injured in the earthquake and lost a good bit of my memory. Where do I know you from? Are we friends?"

A smirk drew his lips up in an odd angle. He leaned against the rock and struck a match across it. They both watched the bright flare come to life as he lifted it to his face to light a cigarette held by tobacco-stained lips. He spoke around it. "Oh yes, we're *very* good friends," He dragged in a puff of smoke and came closer.

"Maybe you could tell me how I know you. What's your name?"

"Name's Brad. I'm really disappointed you don't remember me, pretty lady. We're quite close. As a matter of fact, we're pinned, you and me."

He sat down on the rock next to her and reached for her hand. With his other hand he took a deep drag and flicked his cigarette out into the stream. He turned and blew the smoke into her face, causing her to sputter and cough.

She drew her hand out of his, dread coming over her like a black cloud. "I don't think we were all that close."

His lips curved into a sinister grin. "Now, how would you know that?"

"Listen, I need to get back to the cottage. It was . . . interesting seeing you again."

She started to slide from the rock, but he encircled her waist and tugged her back to him. Reaching up, he captured her chin in a crushing grip. She shuddered in revulsion when his gaze centered on her lips. Knowing what he intended to do, she wrenched away. He grabbed a handful of her hair, and yanked back. She yelped and writhed, trying again to dislodge herself. Restraining her, he leaned in and slid his mouth down her neck, then back up to the soft skin beneath her ear.

"You owe me a dance, pretty lady." His hot breath tickled her ear, and the rancid smell of it reached her nose, making her stomach turn. "I think I'll be taking more than that, if you don't mind." His whisper burrowed into her like a hideous tick.

No, this can't happen! "Let go of me!" She screamed, scrambling to get off the rock. His hands pawed at her, ripping her blouse before he got another hold. His eyes scanned what he'd revealed and a lusty grin unfurled his mouth. He dragged her beneath him and held her down with his rangy body. She curled her fists and pummeled anything she could reach, even with the rock tearing at her back with every move.

"Hold still! You're mine now." He trapped her lips with his.

She bit down hard, bringing his blood to the surface.

Rearing back, he raised a hand to strike her. "You stupid—" Someone caught his hand in midair.

Jessica sensed the weight of his body being lifted off her as two men threw him to the ground with a thud. They were landing hard punches to the beast's gut and face while curses flew on the air. Before they could get a strong hold on him, he ran off into the woods. The two men gave chase close on his heels.

* * *

Clint stood with fingers spread at his hips and head tilted back. "You about done up there, Pete?"

"Sure, boss. I've spread the shingles out over here"— he circled a palm, showing the side of the roof he spoke of— "but not so much over here." Again he circled a hand on the other side. Repeating the same action, he said, "Here. But not so much over here. Course, I'll put some more here where there's a hole, but won't need so much over here where the hole isn't as big. Course there coulda been a bigger hole, but—"

"What hole, Pete?" Clint interrupted. "The whole roof is one big hole."

"Yeah, but this side has a bigger hole, so I put extra shingles here, but won't need so much over here—"

"Okay Pete, I get it," Clint said around a chuckle. "It's time for you get down before you hurt yourself."

Clint was still laughing at Pete's craziness when arms encircled him from behind. Feminine palms glided up and stroked the washboard of his belly.

"Mmm, you feel good. I've missed you," came the seductive voice.

He recognized the voice, but dropped his head to check the familiar, caressing hands. Twisting his head, he spoke over his shoulder. "Hello, Veronica."

She slid under his arm and squeezed him again from

the front. She was looking into his face with one of her most seductive smiles. "*Veronica?* What happened to Ronnie?"

"You don't like Ronnie."

Clint's normal behavior should have kicked in, with his body responding to this carnal beauty. Especially when he knew first-hand what she so patently offered. A lustful stare flashed in those coffee-colored eyes that had once so intrigued him. Now, all he could imagine was the chance to drown in innocent hazel ones.

He was no saint. So, why did Veronica's advance make him feel so disgusted? What right did he have to be so repulsed by Veronica and what she offered—what he'd so ravenously taken in the past?

Clint wanted to send her on her way. He hated to do it to her again, but he knew firsthand the only form of persuasion Veronica would respond to. So, he reached behind his back, grasped her roaming hands and stripped them from him. Still gripping her wrists, he pushed her back. "Go home, Veronica. I've already told you we're through."

Her beautiful face distorted into a grimace of such magnitude that outrage, at himself, climbed up from his chest and burned into his face. Only pain could produce the behavior she displayed. Overwhelming guilt rode right along with his fury as he finally faced the facts. He'd hurt this woman. Really hurt her. And, not just her, but a plethora of others before her.

Just then, a scream punched the air. Clint's head snapped in the direction of the heart-rending sound. "Jessie!" Without another thought for Veronica he lit out toward the stream.

His long strides made short order of the distance between the barn and the water. Taking the little path, he wound his way toward one of Jessie's favorite rocks and saw her perched on top. She was alone, her back to him, but her arms were wrapped tightly about her. Tiny dots of red sprinkled the white cloth of her blouse. His eye caught, and recognized, three figures disappearing into the grove of pines that bordered the stream.

As he drew near he noticed her body trembling and heard her small whimpers. In that instant, the woeful sound slashed through the last remaining safeguards to his heart.

"Jessie?" Clint called from a short distance, not wanting to scare her more. He advanced. "Jessie. Honey, it's me, Clint." Still no reaction.

* * *

Jessica felt large hands clasp her shoulders. Startled, she screeched and flailed her arms. The hands slid to her upper arms and restrained her. "Whoa, sweetheart. It's Clint."

She stopped thrashing and whipped about to face him. Relief washed over her in waves as she threw herself into his arms. He held her tightly for a few heartbeats, then carefully shifted to lift her into his arms.

"Oh, Clint . . ." She wrapped shaking arms around him and pressed her face into his neck.

"It's okay now, honey. I've got you." Pulling her closer, he pressed a kiss to her temple. Her body shook as he carried her back to the cottage.

Once inside he took her to the bedroom, situated her on the edge of her bed, and crouched on his haunches before her. He reached up to cradle her face in strong, callused hands and stared into her eyes. His were distressed.

"I'm sorry, Jessie. I had no idea Turner would still be lurking about after I fired him, or I would have warned you about him. Can't imagine what it must have been like to be attacked, not knowing who he was or that you should stay clear of him."

She was still trembling, but managed, "I somehow knew he was up to no good." Her voice shook. "I did try to get away from him pretty early on. It's just—he was so strong—"

"Aw, little one." He stood, scooped her up, and turned to sit on the bed, bringing her to his lap. He held her in his embrace and tucked her head under his chin. Did he . . .?" He swallowed. With her ear pressed to his chest, she heard the depth of that gulp.

"No! No. He never got the chance." She leaned back and fixed her gaze to his. "I'm fine, really. He didn't get very far before he was yanked off me by two men. I think it was Max and Pete."

"I heard your scream." He sighed heavily. "Can't tell you what that did to me."

As he gazed down into her face, she couldn't restrain the silent tears that slid down it. His hands cupped her cheeks, and with the pads of his thumbs, he wiped the tears away.

She felt her eyes glaze over as a memory came to her.

"What is it, Jessie?"

"I remember you doing that before."

"You mean this?" His thumbs passed over her cheeks again.

She nodded.

"Yeah. I did. Right before I did this . . ." He leaned in and brushed a sweet, tender kiss to her lips. Her head spun with sensation and elusive memories.

"Clint?" A man's voice drifted in through the open front door.

He lifted her from his lap and onto the bed. "That's Max. Stay, here."

She watched as he left the room. In minutes he was back.

He sat on the bed next to her and captured her in a side hug. Loosening his hold, he looked her in the eye. She felt pulled in by the longing she saw there. But, his captivating eyes, one minute full of warmth, in the next went cold. "Jessie. I have to go."

Surprised, she frowned. "You do?"

Muscles bunched up in his jaw. Delicately she touched them.

"Brad got away, but they know which direction he ran off to. We're going after him.""Clint, no! I don't want you hurt. Please, just let him go."

He brought her to her feet with him and towered over her. "Sorry, Jessie, can't do that. He attacked you. He will *not* get that chance again, I can promise you that." Clint pulled the edges of her torn blouse together. Her hands went up to hold it in place. "We'll leave right away, and I'll be back once we've jailed him. You'll be safe here."

Worry deluged her. "Can't the sheriff track him?"

"No time to get the Sheriff or we may lose his trail. Don't worry. There'll be three of us."

With that he leaned down, kissed the top of her head, and walked away.

CHAPTER 34

Clint yanked his hat off his head, slapped it against his thigh twice, then stuffed it back on. "That's the fourth time we've followed tracks that went nowhere. Where'd that slime-sucker go?"

Max peered around him at the tracks. "I don't understand how he could have evaded us again. He was never that cunning."

"There's a box canyon over the next rise. We should look there," Pete said.

Clint led the men to the top of the ridge, but when he summited, he reined in hard at what he saw.

Max stood in his stirrups beside him. "What in the world—"

Clint let out a string of curses. "That scoundrel's been stealing from us!"

"I count about two dozen head of our best Herefords," Pete said.

"He must've been gleaning a little at a time, since we haven't missed them," Clint said. "And, it's a good guess he didn't do it alone." His temples throbbed in beat with his drumming heart.

"Darrell and Randy?" Pete asked.

Clint gave a curt nod. He reined his gelding onto a narrow trail. "You two set up camp in that clearing we saw back a piece. I'll go take a look." He suspected the three men, but couldn't take the chance there may be more. "Max, give me your revolver."

"Clint . . ." Max rode up where they were knee to knee as he handed Clint the gun.

Clint checked the cylinder for bullets, snapped it shut, then looked up.

Max leaned over, squeezed his shoulder. "Don't be a hero."

* * *

Once Jessica settled into the main house, she was back to helping Mabel fix larger meals for the cowboys, giving each one of them a greater sense of sameness. Names still eluded her, but she was beginning to recognize some of the men's faces. And she could rejoice in simple recollections, such as when she remembered where the bulky egg beater was kept.

But it was the unbidden recollections of Clint springing loose that unsettled her. Memories that didn't come all at once in their entirety, but more like having a steel rake grating through her mind, loosening fragments that didn't make much sense. She couldn't seem to string all the pieces together. And, what she *could* piece together was troubling. No. More than troubling. The memories were always tainted in some way and were always of Clint with a different woman.

Clint's kiss had been so sweet before he left to find

Brad that she knew there had to have been other heart-warming moments like it. Times where he had shown his love for her, and where she had fallen for him. Times where his true character showed through, since she couldn't quite wrap her mind around him as the scalawag the new memories painted him to be. So, she begged God for those particular memories to be the next to return. The ones that filled in the gaps.

Jessica's mind continued to chew on her recollections as she rummaged in the potholder drawer for the lemon sticks she'd only just recalled when Mabel tapped her on the shoulder.

Jessica's head whipped up, and she smiled sheepishly, as if she were an unruly eight-year-old with her hand in the cookie jar.

"We need to hurry, girlie. Supper shoulda been on the table by now. Where's our helpful Johnnie-boy? And where's Rosemary or whatever her name is?" Mabel slapped a hand onto the counter. "That girl always seems to dodge work."

Mary waltzed into the kitchen just then, and answered each question in turn. "Johnnie's in town finding Clint some new ranch hands to break in. Rose Marie stayed at the cottage to change into a dress. She says she's tired of looking like a man. She'll be here any minute."

Mabel snorted. "We'll see."

"Back to work with you, Mabel. There's no time to be missing what we don't have," Jessica said.

Mabel cocked an eyebrow. "Well, my girl, you may not think you're rememberin' much, but you're startin' to sound like me, so I know your mind *is* rememberin' plenty." She chortled. Jessica grinned. "Hope so." She breezed to the far table with a platter of roast beef in her hands.

The back door flew open, and cowboys flooded in. Johnnie followed them with a half dozen men she figured must be the new recruits. Each one tipped his hat at her then came to rest at whatever open bench he could find. Apparently, Johnnie had already enlightened them on the routine around here.

Trailing a ways behind the last cowboy was a solemn man with features that might be considered good looking if they weren't covered by a thick, black beard. His height and stature resembled Clint's, but his eyes and hair were as black as night. He seemed to carry the weight of the world on his broad shoulders, and when he stepped closer, Jessica shivered at the chill of enmity that seemed to sheathe the man.

He tipped his scruffy hat as he came near. "Name's Jake. Jacob Cooper, ma'am." She almost jumped at the low timbre of his voice, and the offer of introduction that was so unexpected. His eyes pierced hers for a moment, and she saw emptiness in their depths before he strolled past her to follow the others.

She cleared her throat. "Perfect timing. Supper's on," Jessica said to their backs.

Just as Johnnie started to address the crowd for introductions, the front door opened, and in walked Rose Marie. She was wearing a bright yellow dress with ivory trim. Her long yellow hair waved freely about her face and shoulders. There was a huge intake of breath, in unison, by every male in the room. Except Johnnie. And the new man, Jake. Johnnie's only reaction was a deep scowl. And Jake's was even more disconcerting. No reaction at all.

Rose Marie's gaze caught with Johnnie's, and Jessica noticed a slight pinch of her facial features as if Johnnie's well-aimed glare was causing her pain.

And then time seemed to slow. Her own gaze dove back to Rose Marie, and slid from the top of the beauty's flaxen head to the tips of her slipper-like shoes. Jessica tilted her head to one side, as if by doing that she would dislodge the stuck memory and it would slide into full view.

And it did.

Jessica sucked in a burning breath of awareness. Fastened to the floor by shock, she grasped the edge of the door. The grim memory of that day—that sickening day—when she'd first met Rose Marie, unfolded itself into her unprepared mind. Caught in the force of recollection she tried to grasp onto the good, but she felt as though she'd just awakened from a long sleep to find half her heart had been amputated.

Clint and Rose Marie.

Jessica's stomach twisted into one big aching knot. Her mind shuffled through each awful memory. Soon, the only thing left was a million pieces of shattered emotions.

If she remained here one minute longer, everyone in the room would witness her break apart, and she knew sympathy was *not* something she could endure right now. Willing her legs to move, she slipped out.

A dry, hot sensation in her throat and eyes halted the tears that should have come as she ran toward one place she knew she always loved. The stream. Once there she sank down and stared into the water, waiting for her breathing to return to normal and the peace to come.

It didn't happen. She needed to escape her inner self, close it off until it calmed and brightened again. Instead, she forced herself to pick through the memories. *Clint hurt me . . . time and time again.* The longer she lingered over the distressing remembrances, the more each crushed her anew.

"Why didn't you answer *no* to my prayers for memories about him, Lord?" she wailed into the night. She wrapped her arms around her knees and rocked. Feeling betrayed by Clint *and* her Lord, hot tears finally came in torrents, spilling down her cheeks and blouse, followed by gut-wrenching sobs.

Memories continued to tumble into her mind. She wanted to reach in and stop them, organize them, have them make sense to her, to somehow catch at least one that proved Clint's

love, or caring, or at least not pain. "Has he ever not caused me pain?" she cried out into the approaching darkness.

It was little wonder Rose Marie had asked for her forgiveness. She had *been* with Clint. Why couldn't God have permanently buried that particular memory in the dark, bleak recesses of her mind?

After what seemed to her an eternity, she glanced at the setting sun. Usually God's beautiful sky gave her comfort when nothing else could. But, now she wondered if anything would ever give her comfort again.

She took her thoughts back to her past with Clint, trying to force the good times to the forefront. Every special moment she had with him had ended at another woman—at his side, in his arms, in his bed . . .

How could a man such as this be faithful to just one woman—especially a woman as unremarkable as herself? Clint's past dictated how he would run his life, and his looks dictated how much attention he would draw.

What was I thinking? How could I have been this naïve? This shallow?

The darkness crawled across the sky from the east. The

beautiful colors of the sunset began to turn gray, leaving lifeless streaks of clouds and finally a jet black mantle. She had never noticed that before—how darkness overtakes God's beautifully crafted horizon. It seemed fitting somehow. Like she alone held the memory of a sun that would never shine again.

A hand touched her shoulder.

She nearly jumped out of her skin.

"Easy, Jess. It's Johnnie."

He came to the front of her, opening his arms in the now familiar invitation. She hesitated, and then slid off the rock and into his embrace. "Oh, Johnnie, I'm such a fool," she cried. "I wondered at Clint's interest in me. Somehow I knew I was imagining something that wasn't there. And then, I caught him and Rose Marie in bed together at Mary's—"

"Wait. *What?*" Johnnie pushed her shoulders back to see her face. He paused as he studied her. "Your memories are back."

She nodded. "Why would I have loved such a man?" She leaned into Johnnie. "I remember being in your arms a lot. Is that all I've done? Come to you to cry over Clint?"

Jessica pushed away from Johnnie's embrace. The moonless night had blanketed them in darkness, just like her withering heart. "I'm fine, Johnnie." She swiped away errant tears.

"Jess . . . I'm happy to be here for you."

"That's just it. It seems you've been here for me while I've been falling apart over another man. Over and over again." She threw her hands up in disgust and started pacing. "Why am I doing that? I really don't remember my love for Clint, but I sure do remember what he's put me through." She stopped and looked up at Johnnie. "And I'm putting you through the same thing. How could I do such a thing?" Guilt flooded her face with heat. "Shame on me!"

"Stop worrying about me, Jess."

She looked away.

He took a step closer. She felt the heat of his body. "I didn't have any idea about Clint and Rose Marie. I would have treated her differently had I known." His voice sounded stilted and angry.

Jessica swung her gaze back to him. "Well, it's best you didn't know then. You've treated Rose Marie with kindness. It's how we *should* treat people." Her throat tightened. "What I don't get is why Clint has been so angry with her. My memories aren't totally clear yet, but wasn't it as much his fault as it was hers?"

* * *

Helplessness and no small degree of anger burrowed into Johnnie's core. "You're not asking the right person, Jess. I wasn't there, remember?"

Johnnie gathered Jess in his arms. Her hot breath seeped through his shirt, warming his chest. His blood was on a slow boil. He marveled at Jess's capacity for compassion after all Rose Marie had put her through.

In truth, after the earthquake he himself had begun to see Rose Marie differently. Like, there was more to her than harsh first impressions told. But, he was a Pinkerton, for crying out loud. He had experience in reading people's intentions, their motivations. How had he missed this? Rose Marie had a way of inducing male attention. Considering his past, and his training, he thought he'd long since been immune to such women. How wrong he'd been.

And then there was Clint. He had worked for him for over a year. Had watched him lead his men with honor and respectability. Had considered him a true friend. When Clint had told him of his love for Jess, out of regard for their friendship, he'd decided to back off. Well, no more. His protective instincts had now spurred into full gallop. Clint thought he could have Jess and continue this immoral lifestyle? Not happening. Not if he had anything to say about it.

Clint and Rose Marie could have each other. Jessica was too special to keep going on like this.

Maybe now she'd let Clint go.

He inhaled the scent of pine on the warm breeze, lifted his eyes to the million stars above, and knew . . . if Jessica let go, he could be a happy man here, with her by his side.

CHAPTER 35

Once he had the fire blazing, Max eased back against the trunk of a pine, trying to relax the overused muscles from Clint's relentless pace. Pete snored next to him, his chin resting on his chest, while evening breezes swirled through his hair and the branches overhead.

Max repositioned his rear-end for the third time. Night would soon be upon them and still no sign of Clint.

Something rustled in the trees. *Clint?* Max squinted, trying to get a fix on what he'd heard. But, it was pitch black beyond the firelight. Pete had heard the sound too, since the snoring had stopped and his eyes were now locked on the same section of pines.

"An animal?" Pete whispered.

Max saw a glint of firelight off metal and grabbed for his rifle.

"Hold it right there, Maximillian."

Max knew that voice. Stomach acid burned up his throat. "So, we were right about you, huh, Brad? You've been stealing from us."

"From *you?*" Brad barked a laugh. "A lowly cowhand? No." He stepped into the campfire's light. His hat was pulled so low Max could only see a shadowed portion of his face. "From that lout Harper, and his high-handed foreman. Get their weapons, Darrell."

Darrell trod into the circle. His pockmarked skin glistened in the firelight. He spewed a stream of tobacco at Max's feet and then wrenched the rifle out of his hands. He plodded around Pete and snatched his rifle, too.

"You won't get away with this, Brad. Everybody knows we're after you," Pete said.

"Who's got the gun, huh, Mr. jokester? Tie 'em up, Randy, back-to-back. Seems to me they could have sent a little better team than you two." Brad's laughter rang out into the night.

* * *

Clint rode Shadow down the steep slope to the canyon floor below, on the alert for the three he felt sure were responsible for stealing the cattle. He weaved his way through the cover of Limber pines and junipers.

His anger flared as his thoughts shifted from Turner's thievery to his attack on Jessie. Not only profoundly murderous toward Turner, he was furious with himself for not having protected her. He felt guilt, too, at pushing Max and Pete beyond exhaustion on their week-long chase. But, the skunk needed to be found and justice served.

Shadow slid on his hocks the last few yards down the crumbling slope to the base of the canyon. The foliage was sparse here, so Clint dismounted, tied the horse in a grouping of Rocky Mountain Maples and pulled his rifle from his scabbard. He stalked the rest of the way on foot. Quietly, he forged ahead to the edge of a makeshift camp.

He scanned the area. What he saw made his pulse race. Rumpled bed rolls, a smoldering fire, clothes hanging over low branches . . . they'd definitely made camp here while plundering Harper ranch.

A shout brought his head up to scan the ridge. The boys were in trouble. He sped back to Shadow, mounted, and spurred him up the steep grade. When he drew near the spiral of campfire smoke, he reined in and slid off his horse. Before he could tie him and sneak into camp, Shadow blew out a hefty breath of uneasiness. Clint stroked the horse's muzzle. "No nickering now, boy," he whispered, effectively calming the horse.

Rifle in hand, and pistol in his waistband, he inched forward through pine branches, toward voices. Too many voices, just as he figured. He paused behind a massive lodge-pole and listened hard. One voice was definitely Turner's. Clint crept to the next pine to get a better view. Dropping his hat on the ground, he peeked around the tree. Turner. Next to him, Randy and Darrell. No surprise there. From what he could see, Randy was the only one palming a gun. He shifted his gaze. Aw, hellfire! Max and Pete. Tied back-to-back, sitting next to the fire.

Sending up a quick prayer, Clint sucked in a breath and shouted from the tree line, "Stay right where you are!"

Randy whipped his revolver up and trained it on Clint. Clint fired off a shot. The gun flew out of Randy's hand and spun into the dirt. Randy scrambled after it, got it in his grip, then turned back. *No, Randy. I don't want to kill you!* Clint shifted the rifle to his left hand and yanked the revolver out of his pants for a better aim. He cocked, and fired a shot through Randy's leg a split second before he'd have shot Clint. The swine yelped, chucked the pistol, and grabbed his thigh.

Shoving the gun into his pants, Clint darted toward a now armed Darrell. He slammed the rifle butt down, and Darrell landed hard, out cold.

Randy rose again. Bouncing on one leg, he hopped toward his rifle. Clint swiped a leg around. Randy landed at Pete's feet, and Pete rammed a boot to his jaw.

With two down for the count, Clint started to turn toward Turner, but the man beat him to it with a driving punch to the kidney. Pain shot through Clint's side straight into his lungs. Gasping for breath, he barely turned in time to dodge the knuckles that flew past his face. He stumbled back, tripped over Pete's boots, and smashed his tailbone into the dirt.

"Sorry," Pete hollered. "Watch out!"

Clint had only managed to gain his feet when Turner leaped toward him. His head rammed into Clint's chest. Clint went down like a tree, the breath driven straight out of him. He tried to suck in air. Couldn't. Agony and the fear of suffocation paralyzed him.

Turner rolled off him. He seemed to be as stunned as Clint. Clint needed a breath before the other man could gain his wits about him. He rolled from side to side on his back, trying to force his lungs to work. Clint heard Turner stumble to his feet and knew he had to get off the ground. Turner stood over him now. Dread seized him as visions of a boot to his face flashed in his mind.

He caught a glimpse of Pete and Max. They'd managed to move as one to get closer. Pete raised a foot and jammed it into the backs of Turner's knees, sending him sprawling over Clint. Sucking in small drafts of air, Clint got a stranglehold on Turner's neck and shoved his thumbs into the hollow of his throat. Turner tore free of a still gasping Clint, and crawled toward Randy.

"He's going for the rifle!" Max yelled.

Clint drank in a deep, ragged breath, then another. He jumped to his feet and faltered. Gaining his footing, he roared, and charged the man. A crack sounded as Clint's head connected to Turner's nose. Dark red blood spurt in all directions. Turner cursed, stumbled back a step, then lunged again, right into Clint's cocked fist. The impact to Turner's jaw sent a shockwave up Clint's arm as the man twisted to the ground.

"Get up, you *wretch*. You'll never hurt Jessie again!"

Turner didn't move, just stared up at Clint with defiance and pain in his eyes.

"Get up I said!"

Clint's pulse throbbed at his temples. Turner still didn't move. Breathing hard, Clint snatched a handful of the man's shirt and jerked him to his feet. The rascal took a swing. Clint ducked then slammed a fist into Turner's cheekbone. The man catapulted backward, barely missing the fire. Pain radiated from Clint's knuckles clear up to his elbow.

The good-for-nothing lay on the ground, writhing in pain.

Clint stood over him and snarled, "Get up."

"He's had enough," Max bellowed from his place on the ground. His look spoke volumes. Clint knew Max had never seen him this angry before. "Get us out of these ropes and we can help you, boss," he coaxed. "Come on, get us out of these."

Clint couldn't even hear him right, the blood pulsed so hard in his head. Shaking with fury, he hovered over the degenerate—every muscle fueled with adrenaline—and stretched down to drag Turner to his feet. The man wobbled as Clint stared into his pulverized face. Turner's nose still gushed blood, and his eyelids had swollen to slits. But all Clint could see was Jessie—shaking, torn blouse dotted with blood, eyes reflecting a loss of innocence that should never have been stolen.

Crazed with rage now, Clint pulled his arm back to finish the man when he heard—as clear as if it were audibly spoken—Clint, my son, you must stop.

Like he'd touched a white-hot branding iron, Clint dropped Turner. His arms fell to his sides like anvils.

Turner crumpled to the ground in a heap.

Clint stood as a marble statue, staring down at the disfigured man.

"What is it?" Max called out.

No answer.

"Clint, what happened? Did you kill him?" Pete demanded.

Clint rotated to face them. His astonishment was mirrored on the faces of Max and Pete. Mute, he dropped to his knees to untie his friend's bonds.

Once freed, they clambered to their feet. As they rubbed sore wrists, both waited for Clint's explanation. When none came, Max asked quietly, "What happened to you?"

Clint watched Pete go to Turner, surprised at his own relief that the reprobate was still breathing. When Pete finished tying Turner's hands behind him, he wrested him to his feet and sat him hard on a nearby rock—then did the same with his partners.

When the three captives were secured tightly together, and Randy's leg bound, Pete joined Clint and Max.

"I thought you were going to kill him, then you stopped, like you'd seen a ghost," Max said. "Clint?"

Clint shook his head. "God spoke to me. I heard Him."

Max and Pete's gazes met.

Max turned back to Clint, "What did God say?"

"He told me to stop. That I needed to stop," Clint said in a near whisper.

Clint swung his eyes from one man to the other. Max and Pete looked flabbergasted.

"Well, what do you make of that?" Pete asked Max.

Max shrugged. "I'd say, he heard God speak."

CHAPTER 36

Jessica stepped through the back door ahead of Johnnie, straight into cowboy chaos. Rose Marie stood in the center of it all, besieged by men jawing over the top of each other, fighting like young bucks for a spot next to her. Jessica had never even seen some of them smile before. Typical. Yet, as she looked closer, she realized this was different. This time Rose Marie actually seemed agitated by it all.

With a scowl on his face, Johnnie sidled up to Rose Marie and said something in her ear. Her face paled as she stood absorbing what he was saying. When he strode off with the present scowl still knitting his brow, Rose Marie smiled weakly at the cowboys, then tread into the kitchen and straight for Jessica.

"I need to talk to you," Rose Marie said in a voice as weak as if it had been bled from her body.

What had Johnnie whispered in her ear? Now Jessica wished she hadn't spilled her heartbreak out to Johnnie. She studied the other woman's face. What could this hussy possibly say that Jessica would want to hear? But, Rose Marie seemed resigned, and a touch contrite, so there was no choice but to do the right thing.

"Okaayy." Jessica swiveled around and headed for the privacy of her bedroom, determined to face Rose Marie with poise. Her heart began thumping like she'd just scaled the side of a mountain before they'd even reached the stairs. She signaled for Rose Marie to go ahead of her, then followed, wishing God would pick now to take her home. "First door on the right," Jessica said.

Rose Marie stopped when she reached the landing. She straightened her spine, a Princess Grace gesture for sure, and then strode to the bedroom door.

Once inside Jessica's room, Rose Marie made her way to the bed and sat on the edge stiffly, her beautiful yellow dress splayed out about her. Her eyes looked blank as if her thoughts were elsewhere. She took a sudden breath, awakening to the present. "Johnnie tells me you have most of your memories back. When did that happen?"

Jessica eyed her, wondering how much to say. Her legs seemed to be losing strength, so she plopped down in the ornate antique chair in the corner. "When you walked in the door in that dress. It was the one you wore when Clint and I first met you at Mary's."

She glanced down at herself. "Oh. That's right."

"Now I understand why you asked my forgiveness ahead of time."

"Yes." Rose Marie lowered her eyes. "And now you've changed your mind."

"About forgiving you?" She sighed. "Of course not."

Rose Marie's head snapped up, and her brows twitched briefly in confusion.

"Jesus never removes His forgiveness from us, so how could I do that to you?" Just speaking of Christ's forgiveness gave Jessica strength to face this.

Rose Marie gave a resigned sigh. "I need to tell you what actually happened between Clint and me."

Blood drained from Jessica's head, making her feel faint. She didn't want to hear this. "No, that's not necessary." She started to rise. "Listen, I should get back—"

"Jessica. I need to tell you, since I know Clint thought it was you and not me."

Her stomach was suddenly queasy. But, hope made her stay. She dropped back into the chair. "All right."

"I'm not proud of it, but it was my doing, not Clint's." Rose Marie seemed to struggle taking her next breath.

The tension in Jessica's jaw eased as she waited for more.

"That day, when I first met Clint, I reacted to his attractiveness and he seemed to do the same with me. I thought, well, Grandma had told me about him. Had thought of him as a son. So I figured maybe we were meant for each other. That she would like that . . ." She raised a shaky hand to push a lock of hair out of her face. "Silly, I know."

She took another breath. "Anyway, that night, Clint became feverish. I didn't know it at the time, or anything about his illness until Grandma told me later." She hesitated for a moment, apparently gathering courage. "I went to his cot and coaxed him back to my bed. I don't think I could explain why, exactly. I'd heard him thrashing on that hard old cot, sounding tormented. When I stood over him, he just seemed so troubled, and needy."

"Needy?" Clint was anything *but* needy, Jessica thought.

"Suddenly, I just wanted to hold him, and for him to hold me, since he seemed so warm and so . . . so docile."

Docile? Clint? Were they talking about the same man here?

Rose Marie sucked in a ragged breath, and closed her eyelids, looking guilty and sick about it. She re-opened her eyes. "He called out a nickname. I didn't even know it was yours, since I didn't know who *little one* was. I do now. "And you should know"—she licked her lips—"he said, *little one, we can't do this.*"

Jessica experienced a funny mixture of relief and torture. "He said that?"

"He was delirious the whole time, Jessica. I didn't know that then, but I did suspect he wasn't in his right mind. And something else—" Humorless laughter broke loose from her. "They say confession is good for the soul, right?"

Jessica's heart already hurt. Even if Clint had confused Rose Marie with her in his delirium, that didn't change a thing. Clint was a serial womanizer. A man living in a fast paced, philandering world. Nothing like the way Jessica had lived—or wanted to live. "No! Please! Don't say anything more. For your sake *and* his. It's not necessary. Really."

Rose Marie didn't seem to hear Jessica's plea. As her lips loosened, Jessica's insides tightened.

"You'll want to hear this, believe me. You see, we didn't . . . I mean, he didn't . . ." Rose Marie sputtered as color dotted her cheeks. Her shoulders slumped as she spoke into her lap. "This is harder than I thought it would be."

She looked up then, straight into Jessica's eyes. "I should have never given him the impression he had gone through with anything intimate that night. He didn't. He was out of his mind so I'm sure he won't remember this.

Thankfully, before anything of consequence could happen he . . . he just fell asleep. Kind of sudden like . . ." Her words trailed off.

The relief on Rose Marie's face was so obvious, you would have thought she'd just vanquished all her demons instead of confessed her deepest shame. But maybe those were one in the same. Jessica released the breath she had held through Rose Marie's confession, letting it escape out her open mouth like the final breath of the dead. "So God intervened again, like that night with Clint and me," she said, mostly to herself, surprised she still didn't feel any better. "Pardon?" Rose Marie asked.

"Oh, nothing," she said with a wave of her hand. She brought her gaze back to Rose Marie's eyes. "Thank you for telling me this." Jessica rose from the chair to see her out the door.

"One more thing," Rose Marie said hurriedly. Jessica grimaced. "When I was with him in Uncle Roy's bedroom, he was sound asleep. I hadn't touched him until you came through the door. And after you left, he woke up and"—Rose Marie massaged her throat—"grabbed me in anger. He was furious I had deceived you, again." Her eyes shimmered. "About him and me, I mean." She gave Jessica a weak smile that didn't reach her eyes. "I should go."

"Wait." Jessica ached like her vitals had been wrung of their lifeblood. "Why did you tell me the truth about this?"

"For Johnnie," Rose Marie blurted then looked shocked she'd said it.

"Johnnie?"

"I don't know why I told you," she barely whispered. She shook her head. "But, when Johnnie doesn't want to talk about something, he says *it's none of your business.*

Otherwise he tells the truth. He never resorts to lies. In fact, he goes out of his way for the truth to be known. I guess he's rubbing off on me."

Rose Marie headed for the door. Before turning the knob she looked back, and opened her mouth as if to say more, but closed it. She seemed so lost that Jessica hastened to her and wrapped her in a hug—non-reciprocated though it was. When she let loose, Rose Marie fled out the door.

Jessica questioned what she was feeling—bruised, confused, sad . . . jealous? Numb—that was all she seemed to feel right now. Couldn't God have left these memories buried forever? Hearing it from Rose Marie had made the memory come alive, and all she could picture was Clint with Rose Marie's limbs draped over him. She wanted to throw up and scream at the same time. She'd believed her girlish pipedream—that Clint could be hers. Well, that dream had been obliterated, as it should be. And, it didn't matter anymore. Clint was not someone she should love.

A suitcase was open on her bed, and she realized she'd started packing while she mulled Rose Marie's confession. She lowered her gaze to the stack of blue jeans in her hands. A tear landed on the pocket of the pair on top and spread into a dark, damp circle. She stared at it till it blurred, then blinked back her tears and laid the pile meticulously beside her blouses.

* * *

The warm morning sun brought Clint a reminder that God controlled the universe. Everything was as it should be. *Or was it?* Even though the natural hum of the woods filled Clint's ears, peace escaped him. God had kept him from killing a man yesterday. That alone should be enough to make any man sing his praises, count his blessings, and move on. All it managed to do was remind him of how short he fell from the man God had intended him to be.

As if that weren't enough, he awoke with doubts about his future with Jessie. Whether or not she ever got her memories back, she loved God and was devoted to Him. How could she harness herself to a man who disappointed God in all things? Who had lived wrong. Had disappointed loved ones. And, had almost killed a man. Could someone as pure of heart as his sweet Jessie consider marrying a man like him? Funny, how it didn't surprise him anymore that he *was* contemplating marriage to her. He was. Probably. Maybe.

But, what did he truly have to offer her?

And then there was his odious past.

The coffee bubbled, sending a fragrance of the heady brew into the crisp morning air. The men stirred. "Come on Max, Pete," Clint said. He filled his tin cup, strode to his friends, and nudged Pete's backside with his boot. "Let's get going."

"Okay, okay. I'm up," Pete said.

"I'm up, too," Max murmured.

"No you're not. I'm standing right over the top of you two and you're both very much asleep. Come on," he barked. "I've got to get this scum to the sheriff and you need to get the cattle back to the ranch."

"Am I hearin' you right?" Pete turned over to gaze up at Clint. "You're gonna take 'em in alone?"

"Yep. We're halfway to West Yellowstone already. So let's go."

The dusty ride back to town took the whole day. Clint only stopped to rest the horses twice, so by the time he arrived at civilization the sun was sinking into the horizon and his captives had lost their arrogance. Clint looked down the street. The *Gallatin County Sheriff's Department* sign swung in the late afternoon breeze at the end of the boardwalk.

After depositing the men with an amateur of a deputy, Clint took Shadow to the local livery and then his tired body off to the hotel. He hoped the lawman was more capable than he looked, but hey, it was outta his hands, at least until the trial. What he wanted now was to bathe, eat, and sleep in an actual bed. Tomorrow would be soon enough to return to the ranch and face Jessie. He still was unsure of his next move. Of course, if her memories had returned, she might have already decided to be rid of him. That would be easier. Easy he was used to, but that wasn't what he wanted anymore.

Sweet thoughts of Jessie filled his mind as he bathed. He closed his eyes and pictured her, smile radiant, eyes the color of autumn grasses. She warmed him in every way, and not just physically, though that topped his list. She'd make a great mate, if she'd have him.

If she'd have him. His heart cramped with doubt. Only two things he knew to be true—he wanted her and his renowned charm would not win her over.

He sank deeper into the water and rested his head against the tub. He closed his eyes and sighed deeply. A vision came to him of Jessie joining him in this tub—

He jerked upright, a wave of tub water sloshing over the

sides. Here he was, trying hard to be pleasing to God, and thinking carnal thoughts would hardly extract him from the sins of his past. Amazing, how God took those who came to Him willingly, right where they were, and changed them from the inside out.

Clint had finally made his way to *willing*, and already he could feel the *changing*.

He hefted himself out of the tub, tired beyond words. Drying with a towel meant for a body half his size, his gaze drifted to the small oval mirror above the sink. Studying his image, he turned his face from one side to the other, contemplating the dark whiskers. He gave strong consideration to growing a full beard until he thought of Jessie's tender skin and immediately threw off the idea. He'd shave in the morning. Finger combing his wet hair straight back, he then donned a clean shirt, the freshest set of jeans he had left, and stuffed his feet into his tired old boots. Leaving his battered Stetson on the bed, he made his way downstairs to the restaurant.

As he filled the archway to the hotel dining room, he caught the I-like-what-I-see looks from numerous women, the same looks he had collected since the moment he'd reached his teens. And not just from the patrons, but from two waitresses who were frozen in place with plates of food crammed up the length of their arms. Such interest used to please him, and cause him to flip the on-switch to his interminable charm. Not tonight. He rubbed his neck. This was giving him a headache. He wished he could bypass the attention and leave for home tonight. But riding horseback during a new moon was too dangerous, so he aimed for a small table in a darkened corner. All he wanted now was to be left alone with a hot meal and his own thoughts.

Hiding behind a menu, he relaxed to study it. Dang if he wasn't hungry enough to eat an entire cow—and tired enough, he'd never be able to choose one cut of beef over the next.

He noticed four petite feet pointing in his direction. Slowly, he lowered the menu back to the table and gave a weary smile he wasn't feeling to the two women. One was tall and thin, the other short and round—both young.

"Hey, big fella. What can I get you?" the tall waitress said.

"This is *my* table, Julie," the short one whined to the first.

He wanted to roll his eyes but instead mustered up what little pleasantness he had left. "Just bring me your special and black coffee."

There was complete silence as both women let their eyes roam over him.

Clint's gaze shifted back and forth from one to the other, waiting to see who would take pity on him and bring him some food.

The two women turned to glare at one another, like they were in their own O.K. Corral with frowns drawn and eyes blazing. A third woman marched between the two and elbowed them apart.

The tall one spun on the newcomer. "What the—" Her eyes went wide.

Both waitresses straightened and drew their pads and pencils up to their chests. Their boss, clearly. Looking back at Clint, they plastered on generic smiles.

"Enough girls, I'll take care of him. Get back to work," the boss-lady said.

One turned and left in a huff. The other studied him a moment longer, then sighed and trailed along behind.

Clint did a quick perusal of the new arrival. Striking, with long, flaxen hair trapped neatly at her nape with an elegant clip. A short black dress clung nicely to her curvy figure, a pearl necklace surrounded her slender neck, and high heels enhanced shapely calves.

Clint grimaced when he realized that without thought he'd just sized her up. Not so long ago he'd have actively planned out his evening with such a woman—probably the owner—and been assured of its success before his dessert even arrived. Tonight, all that the attention managed to do was create in him a deep ache for Jessie, and remind him of his overfed appetite for women.

"Now, what was it you wanted?" the blonde said with a flash of a white smile.

An aspirin. "Whatever your special is and coffee. Black," Clint replied, careful to show no expression.

"Name's Faye. Are you sure food's all you want, cowboy?" She sat down in the extra chair at his table, crossed her arms in front of her, and leaned over them. Her neckline billowed slightly in the front and gave him a direct shot to her ample assets.

Instead of his usual reaction, his stomach rolled with derision. Had they all been this blatant? Even as his stomach churned, making him wonder if food was such a good idea anymore, he recognized he'd been given a gift straight from Heaven. His eyes were opened—truly opened—for the first time. As if God had shined a light on his old life and given him a hardy, lasting view.

His only aim now was to get back to Jessie and beg her to have him. In truth, he'd been missing her his whole adult life. The undeniable joy that seeped through him when he was with her filled a desperate need. One he didn't know he had until she'd walked into his life.

Heartened by thoughts of Jessie, he leaned in a bit. His action brought the same reaction from the woman. Her eyes grew large, and a smile of anticipation crossed her face. With a weary grin he said, "Dinner and *nothing else*." He drew out the last two words with added emphasis.

Her face fell. "You sure?" she tried again, sounding a little desperate.

He had been this bad. He groaned inwardly as he clenched his fists. "I'm sure."

"I'm told you're spending the night here. If you need *anything . . . anything* at all, ask for Faye." She pushed her chair back and stood. Gracing him with a charming smile, she sashayed out of the room.

In ten minutes the tall waitress arrived with his food and coffee, plunked it in front of him, and departed without a word.

Finally, left to have the meal on his own, he lifted his fork to eat. Remembering, he set the utensil back down and lowered his head in thanks.

CHAPTER 37

Jessica stared at herself in the bureau mirror. Her red-rimmed eyes matched her raw, overburdened emotions. Her body was going back to California, but her soul would remain here. Here in Montana where she'd experienced the best as well as the worst days of her life. Her plan was to sneak down to the Packard and drive herself to the train station. A note to Uncle Roy was propped against the mirror. In it, she thanked him for her time here, apologized for being a quitter like all the rest, and promised to mail his second set of keys back to him.

Tears burned her eyes, but this time she wouldn't give in to them. She dressed, packed the last of her things, and tiptoed down the stairs. When she stepped out onto the front porch, she gasped at the beauty she saw there. As beaten as she was, God's offer of the multicolored sunrise soothed her.

Her drive to West Yellowstone was rough going since the earthquake had damaged so much of the road. But she managed to make her way along the broken roadway, thinking that her heart was in the same sort of shambles.

The thought of going back to her cold, unfulfilling

life—and a mother who saw her as nothing more than an old maid—tore at her almost as much as leaving Harper Ranch behind. She had changed. She wouldn't fit in at home anymore; not that she ever had.

As the sun blazed through her window, she wished it could brighten her spirits as well. When she arrived at the outskirts of town, she straightened her spine. She would make a new life for herself, though she fully expected to live it alone. Never again would she feel for anyone as she did for Clint, nor would she even try. Even though her memories were vague concerning any sort of love between them, the reality was she *couldn't* make a life with him; to spend a lifetime worrying when he would tire of unremarkable *her* to go find an attractive and exciting *other*. And there would be plenty of *others* for him to choose from—always.

The streets were surprisingly empty for a resort town. Her gaze drifted briefly toward the hotel, then back to the road. An immediate double-take made her hands grip the steering wheel. She blinked hard. *It couldn't be.*

Before she thought better of it she whipped the car to a parking space in the front of the restaurant, to the right of the old hotel. She threw the car into park and locked her eyes on the two standing at the doorway, a few short yards away. Her breathing constricted a little more with each intake of breath. Squeezing her eyes closed she sent up an arrow prayer and forced a calmness before allowing herself another thorough look. There, before her, was Clint dressed in her favorite green shirt—the one that matched the color of his eyes. His hat was held by one large hand and his saddle bags were draped over the arm of the other, while a blonde woman was pressed against his torso, her arms wrapped neatly around him.

Now, who is this one? And, why was he here? But, she realized, what did it matter? Women naturally flocked to Clint, and this one, whoever she was, had a tenacious hold on him. He took two steps with her clinging like a trap to his waist. Then he stopped and spoke some words down into her face with an exasperated look on his. He tried two more steps with no better results.

Finally, dumping his hat and saddle bags to the walk-way he seized the woman by the shoulders, wrenching her away from him. He shifted her to one side with the action of an incensed man, then bent to pick up his belongings. With his mouth in a grim line, he threw the saddle bags over one shoulder and jammed on his hat. Clint opened his mouth to say something more to her, but before he did he spotted the Packard over the top of her head. Just as Jessica had done, he did a double-take, squinted hard at her, and then barreled past the woman straight for the car.

Jessica panicked. She threw the car in reverse, praying no one was behind her, and skidded out of the parking place. Clint was closing fast. She shoved the gear shift into drive and zoomed down the street. She glanced in the rear-view mirror as Clint took out after her. With the power of a mountain cat, he ran full-on down the middle of the street in pursuit, every muscle alive with motion.

The sight tore her up. She didn't know what to do. She wanted to leave Montana—escape to anywhere. Her grief over him had reached a peak. She knew in that moment, as much as she wanted him, she was not enough for him. Oh, she could handle caring for him, and was perfectly capable of handling matters of the heart—his heart. But, she was certain she could not endure a lifetime of Clint's popularity with women without becoming a bitter, jealous woman herself.

Jessica drove straight out of town with unshed tears clouding her vision. When she could no longer see to drive, she pulled off into a field that had become the parking lot for the local rodeo. The Packard bumped over uneven ground until she brought it to a stop. She slammed her fist on the steering wheel, then dropped her head to it. Sobs rose so brutally from within they nearly choked her on their way out her mouth.

Physically, she was a wreck, spiritually she was fractured, but emotionally she didn't know if she would recover. For sure, she wouldn't look at life the same again. She couldn't remember everything yet, but knowing what a fool she'd been concerning Clint was a hard pill to swallow. Somehow that thought put a halt to her tears, but a knot formed at the back of her throat.

What was she going to do now? Raising her head, bleary eyed, she tried to assemble a plan, but could only focus on the beautiful countryside. Foothills edged the grassland for miles, and wildflowers were scattered everywhere. She would miss this place. Leaving it—leaving Clint—was going to tear her into little unrecognizable bits.

She shook her head, trying to lose the image of the handsome, rough and tumble cowboy running after her down the highway. He was really something. And, like an addict who couldn't be without her addiction, her heart couldn't close the chapter on Clint.

She knew what she had to do. Give herself time to sort through this thing. No California, then. She would buy a train ticket half-way there—Salt Lake City. There she'd spend the night and think—just think, and pray. God would need to give her direction beyond that. She'd bungled things so badly already, she felt compelled to stop overreacting and finally do things God's way.

Bringing the car to life, Jessica backed up, swung around, and pulled out onto the highway to head back to West Yellowstone.

When she pulled up to the West Yellowstone train station, she noticed the empty parking spaces but didn't take the time to wonder about it. Without hesitation, she got out of the car and marched up the path toward the depot's double doors. She had her plan. She'd get her ticket first, retrieve her suitcases, and then be on her way to Utah. Once at the entrance, she reached for the door handle and pulled. Her shoulder yanked almost painfully against the locked door. *Locked?* Frustrated, she glanced up for the first time and noticed a sign posted on the door:

Train travel prohibited due to extensive damage to tracks

Jessica blinked. Confused, she read it a second time. Finally, when the full meaning sank in, she numbly sank down to the stone bench under the depot sign to make another plan.

* * *

Clint ran as far as his tiring legs could take him, to the corner where she'd made a turn. Bracing his hands on his knees, he wheezed in air. He tilted his head up and watched the Packard sail down the street, past the train station, and onto the two lane highway until it was a mere blue dot against Lionhead Mountain west of town.

His heart ached with every stampeding beat, as his lady love fled yet another incident of him with one more woman. He yanked his hat off and threw it hard against the pavement, cursing. "This has to stop!" he shouted to the retreating vehicle. "When are you going to stay and face me?" he yelled after her.

Either he would make her understand she was his one and only love for life, or he would have to live life amputated and bleeding, and somehow survive.

Once he paid the livery keeper, Clint saddled up, threw his saddlebags back in place, and hoisted himself onto Shadow. His plan was to follow the road out of town until he came across Jessie. A fool's errand, but he didn't know what else to do.

He followed the same route Jessie had gone, not caring about the odd looks he received from the townspeople and tourists. His mind was a million miles away, trying to devise a plan where he could tell her he loved her and wanted no other, when he spied the Packard. Heartened, Clint glanced about for Jessie and found her sitting in front of the station. His heart somersaulted. But, as he took in her slumped form with head in hands, a lump grew in his throat. He'd caused her this latest torture—just like always.

He reined in his horse and headed toward her. She had yet to look up. Hadn't she heard him?

Muffled hiccups raised her shoulders every few seconds, though her head remained planted in her hands with her elbows stabbing her thighs. He took a moment to study her, all soft and feminine. Her silky brown hair hung over her hands. A desire flared in him for that same silkiness to run through his fingers as he comforted her. He noticed her little short-shorts and a white ruffled blouse, an obvious outfit for the beaches of California. Yet—he couldn't help but smile—she also wore her western boots. Montana had made its mark on her. He only hoped he had, too.

"You're disturbing the peace with those cute little hiccups of yours," he said, remembering that same phrase he'd once said to her at Mary's—this time praying for a different outcome.

Her head whipped up.

He'd surprised her. "Jessie."

She leaped to her feet and took in a huge breath that caught in her throat. Before he could vault from his horse, she recovered. Barely. "How could I have missed hearing you?" she said in a strangled voice. "How long have you been there?"

"Not long." He swung his leg across the saddle horn and hopped down, tossing Shadow's reins over his head. Jessie was beautiful in her astonishment. Her eyes had gone bigger than ever, and her full lips parted. A deep longing swept through him. Her parted mouth wasn't an invitation, but he contemplated snaring her against him and kissing her anyway. Containing himself for several long beats, good sense finally won out. Tentatively, he reached out and captured her hand, towing her back to the bench seat. He sat, and gave a small tug for her to follow.

If he could keep her distracted with his closeness, remind her she loved him, maybe he could keep her from bolting away. Her scent hit him like a sucker punch to the gut—a sweet, lilac fragrance that went straight from his nostrils to his brain, and triggered a barrage of fresh memories.

She pulled against his hand, but he didn't let her go. "Wait. We need to talk." Still struggling, she tried to rise again. "Jessie stay. Please. Little one."

The minute he said those last two words, Jessie's whole body slumped against his side. She pressed her forehead into his shoulder and took a ragged breath. He knew she was confused and trying to keep from crying. He put an arm around her and tucked her into the crook of his arm, thankful for the moment to just hold her.

When had he fallen so madly in love with this woman? No, not fallen, plunged. His heart craved her, and it ached for the agony he kept putting her through. He prayed, asking God for the right words to say.

Too soon, her body tensed and she wiggled again to be released.

He still restrained her. "I'll only let you go if you'll stay so we can talk about this." With a curved finger he lifted her chin and stared into glittering eyes. "Do you agree?"

The apprehension in her eyes sharpened. His heart swelled with a fierce instinct to protect her, even if it was from himself.

She finally nodded.

He released both arms, and she jumped up. For a moment he thought she would flee and he would have to give chase again. In the end she didn't, but she did start pacing. He remained on the bench while she strode back and forth in front of him—stopped briefly to stare at Shadow grazing—then started again. He smiled to himself at her interest in his horse even when her world was turning upside-down. He crossed his arms over his chest and waited for her to formulate her thoughts. Somehow he knew she would have to start first.

Minutes dragged on, but still he waited.

In time her gaze met his, darted away, and then returned as if the pull to do so was too great to resist. "Clint . . ." At first her eyes were sad and weepy. Then other emotions skittered across her face, one after another. Soon there was no doubt about the one she'd settled on—anger. It was a relief, since her sadness tore him apart. Anger he could handle. Or so he thought, anyway.

"Weren't you out looking for Brad? And who was that woman anyway?" she finally sputtered. Her arms flailed about and her eyes flashed in fury.

This was serious business, he knew, yet a smile tugged at the corners of his mouth at how adorable she was in her obvious indignation. He loved it when she fought back. It gave him hope that they may yet work this thing out. He was anxious to finally tell her he loved her. Biting down on the inside of his cheek, he took a moment to make sure he looked serious enough.

"I did find Turner, brought him here to the Sheriff's office."

Her eyes widened, and she started to speak.

Clint held up a hand to stop her. "Jessica, are you going to believe me when I tell you about the woman?"

Her body seemed to wilt. "You never call me Jessica," she said in a small voice.

She remembered that? Or had she noticed lately that he called her Jessie?

"Yes. I'll believe you." She gazed down into his eyes with such hope in hers it twisted his insides.

But he didn't have time to berate himself again. He delivered his words carefully. "Yesterday, I arrived in town with Turner and his two degenerate friends, and turned them over to the authorities."

Jessie opened her mouth but Clint's hand shot up. "More about that later. The woman, remember?" She nodded and closed her mouth.

"After that, I went to the hotel, tired and reeking, since

we'd been out for over a week. Took a bath, headed for the restaurant. The owner seemed to . . . to take an interest in me." Jessie noticeably stiffened at that. He left out any mention of the first two waitresses. Enough was enough. Even he was sick of the constant attention he received from the opposite sex. There was no doubt about it. He was a changed man.

"She sat down at my table—propositioned me." He winced. "Once I made it clear I wasn't interested, she left. This morning I didn't figure she'd be a problem but she followed me outside. I'm guessing you saw the rest."

Jessie stood in silence as she paled and wobbled a bit. He leaned out and grasped her elbow, drawing her to his lap. To his surprise, she let him. She sat stiffly, though. Her eyes were fixed on a group of people meandering down the other side of the street, but her mind was clearly sorting through what he'd said.

"Do you believe me?" Clint asked.

She turned to face him. Hazel eyes adored every feature on his face with slow deliberation. His hopes lifted. Her expression brimmed with affection, then as quick as that, snapped to disillusionment. His chest tightened. She was wary of more hurt, he could see that. He understood only too well how someone as grounded as Jessie should question loving someone like him.

He tried smiling, but she remained somber. "Talk to me," he said in a strained voice. He swallowed hard and waited for what he hoped wasn't a goodbye.

"Clint, I don't understand any of this. I'm remembering brief interludes between us, but all of them seem to be followed by incidents with you and other women. I realize some of my memories aren't clear yet, but what *were* we to each other? Exactly."

Before he had time to analyze her question, the light suddenly came on. "You have your memories back!"

She started at his sudden exuberance. Her mouth parted again, and he couldn't hold back any longer. He bent to kiss her, but she averted her mouth and his lips landed on her cheek. Sighing heavily, he slid his fingertips into that silky hair he'd wanted to touch. Slowly, he turned her face back to him, and pressed his forehead to hers. "Aw, Jessie," he breathed, saddened that she couldn't bring herself to trust him.

She tensed, and he leaned back to search her eyes. But they looked even more distant than before. He felt like he was losing her before he'd even had a chance to profess his love for her. If he were to tell her now, she wouldn't believe him. She'd only think he was trying to extricate himself from a bad situation.

She put her hands to his biceps and pushed slightly to rise. He loosened his grip and let her stand. A sinking feeling started in his throat and landed hard in his chest.

Jessie looked him square in the eyes. "Why did you bring Veronica to the round-up for me to *baby-sit?*" She bit off the last words with vehemence.

Shocked that she'd picked that particular episode out-of-hand, he rummaged for the correct words. But if he hesitated too long she'd think he was fabricating something, so he jumped in quickly. "I don't know." *Shoot.* That was the last thing he should have said. He watched her lips curl ever so slightly in irritation. He knew why he did it . . . now. "I meant, at the time I didn't know."

Her expression changed slightly, but she still awaited his answer. He let out an audible sigh and ran a hand down his face. "A test, Jessie. At the time I would have sworn to anyone who'd asked that it was a test for Veronica. To see if ranch life agreed with her." He averted his gaze and barked a humorless laugh. "As if I hadn't known the answer to that already."

He stretched out and grasped Jessie's hand before turning his face up to hers. She didn't try to pull away. "It was really a test for you. I didn't know you'd be out there that day and I didn't know why I was testing you. I just knew I had to. In part, I wanted to know how you'd handle the round-up—it really didn't surprise me that you loved it—but more than that . . ." He swallowed hard before letting the truth escape his lips. How would she take it? Would it make things worse? "I was comparing the two of you. I didn't know that's what I was doing, at the time. But that's what happened."

Jessie gave a grunt of disapproval and tried to pull her hand out of his.

"Jessie. Listen. Veronica lost, hands down. Then *and* at the oyster feed. And later." He saw the instant curiosity. "I took her home, broke it off with her, and left."

Somehow he was blowing it. She looked more lost than ever.

"Clint." Her voice sounded heavy with emotion. "I don't know if I can do this."

His heart skipped a beat and his mouth dried up. Their gazes remained locked.

"I . . . I don't trust you." Her words slammed into him with more pain than when the cougar had hit him dead in the chest. No one had ever told him they didn't *trust* him.

His heart tripped at the sadness he saw in her eyes and felt in his soul. "I don't want to be jealous of every woman who'll notice you. And they *all* notice you. But it's worse.

You notice them . . . and more than notice." She tried to swallow and it looked like she couldn't quite get enough moisture to do the job. She searched his eyes, as if she could find answers there. Hers looked tortured. In a small, raspy voice she asked, "What has made you a womanizer?"

He didn't answer that. Even if he could summon up the courage to tell her, somehow he knew it would only make things worse.

Unshed tears made her eyes shimmer. She was trying hard to blink them back, and his heart wrenched all the more. "I don't see how we can build a relationship on such a flimsy foundation, Clint. Trying to do that would be too painful. It already has been."

He gulped, hard. A life without Jessie? He couldn't do that.

His alternative—face his past? He couldn't do that either.

CHAPTER 38

Jessica watched in horror as Clint paled. It filled her with despair, having to tell him they wouldn't make it. She could hardly believe her own words. She almost hadn't told him the truth about how she felt when, as she was formulating her words, his green eyes had warmed with such affection. But, recognizing she would become more resentful each time Clint's admirers clamored over him, then dragged him off somewhere unknown, she knew she wasn't capable of ignoring his notoriety.

Or was she? At the moment she thought not. Marriage was for life, in her book, and commitment forever. So these struggles would be with her for a very long time. And Clint. Well, Clint was used to lovin' em and leavin' em.

This was all so premature. He hadn't told her he loved her. Even if he had, how long before he got bored and moved on? She contemplated a life of distrust and jealousy, and shook her head. As much as she wanted Clint, she was sure her heart couldn't stand a steady routine of splintering.

Her mind hurt against the fog of doubt. Her shoulders slumped. Out of words, and overcome, she turned to walk back to the Packard.

Shadow's bridle jangled when Clint snatched up the reins and was at her side in a few long strides. "Walk with me," he said, catching her by the elbow and steering her toward the street.

Her feet followed his route, though she couldn't look at him, knowing her resolve would evaporate if she peered into those compelling eyes again. "Clint—"

"Don't say anything yet, Jessie. Let me say some things that have been on my mind."

Keeping her eyes focused on the road, she nodded.

They came to where the streets intersected, and Clint guided her down the main boulevard. Their steps were casual, yet Jessica's heartbeat seemed to accelerate with every crunch of their boots. Jessica walked across slashes of sunlight and shadows on the gravel-strewn pavement. What did he want to say? How would she respond? The absolute power of him walking beside her weakened her knees, and her decision that she should leave Montana. She smelled his scent—leather, fresh air, soap—and wanted to tell him she'd stay. She glanced at Clint sidelong, yearning to kiss him full on the mouth. But, she shouldn't . . . wouldn't . . . and that was that.

For a few paces the only sound was the *clop-a-clop-a-clop* of the horse's shod hooves against the pavement.

"Jessie, since your memories are back—"

"Some," she interrupted.

"Pardon me?"

"*Some* memories are back. I'm hoping . . . I'm hoping there are many more I'm not remembering yet."

He released a huge breath. "Thank God for that anyway."

"What do you mean?"

"I'm guessing you're remembering some of our . . . well, our bumpy times."

Her mind jumped to a visual of Rose Marie's arm slung over Clint's torso and a leg across his thighs—both sound asleep in Rose Marie's bed. Tears stung her eyes. That particular image was emblazoned into her memory. How could she ever forget it—even though Rose Marie had claimed his innocence?

They were level with the hotel now. A new image flashed in Jessica's mind. Clint with the beautiful woman's arms wrapped around his middle. *See*, her negative side said. *This will always be the case with him.*

The jail was the next building they would pass. Brad was in there. Clint had found him and brought him in for hurting her. He *had* saved her from Brad. Then, and at the square-dance. *The dance.* Clint had left with the beautiful blonde, from the dance.

Every memory that swam around in her head ended with Clint and a different woman. Perspiration prickled her forehead, her neck, her palms. She couldn't do this. He would be forever surrounded by women. She couldn't keep up with that.

"Jessie," he stopped abruptly, grasped her arm, and swung her around to face him. "Your expression tells me you're remembering one of those times right now." His expression was so dear. Worry for the pain he had caused her contorted his handsome features. He closed his eyes and furrowed his brow. "I want you to know how sorry—"

A loud crack split the silence and Clint's head jerked back violently. A spray of crimson burst into the air. Jessica shrieked. Clint's body lurched backward and smacked against his horse's chest. Before Jessica could even assimilate what had happened, he landed with a sickening thud at the gelding's feet.

Jessica dropped to his side. "*Clint!*"

Shadow balked and danced about, trying hard not to step on him, but the reins were trapped under Clint's body. Jessica could see the fear in the gelding's eyes and leaped to her feet to pull the reins out from under Clint. With a familiarity of horses she didn't remember, she yanked the leather down and back hard, forcing the horse away.

She folded to her knees again. "Clint! Can you hear me?"

"Let's hope not," a sinister voice resonated, only a few yards from her.

She whipped her head up. There towered a man, black and featureless against the midday sun. He hooked a thumb at his belt, rocked back on his heels, and laughed low and deep. "Well, hullo, pretty lady."

Jessica's heart leapt painfully in her chest. *Brad.* A .45 pistol sat in the crook of his right fist. He strode forward and lined up the smoking barrel on Clint's chest. Jessica knew, in that moment, Brad meant to finish off the man who'd brought him to justice.

Without thinking she flung her body over Clint's.

"So you think you can save him?" Brad said, amused. A wicked laugh burst from his throat. Shadow flinched back.

"Your genius cowboy here left me with a halfwit deputy. Ha! Made it easy for me." Brad quieted, and cocked the gun. The sound reverberated in Jessica's head like an echo off a canyon wall.

"Drop your weapon!" a bold, masculine voice hollered from behind Brad.

Gun still cocked, Brad swung around to face the

immediate danger. In the next moment another blast rent the air.

Jessica jerked against Clint in surprise, but didn't release him. Only raised her head enough to look down the street toward the sound. Her heart vaulted to her throat at the horrific scene before her: a truck in the middle of the street, cab door thrown open, engine running; Johnnie advancing with a smoldering shotgun; and Brad's limp body a few yards away, sprawled in a growing circle of blood.

She forced her attention back to Clint—*her* Clint—lying on the ground, shot in the head with *his own* life-blood seeping out. Jessica instinctively pulled her blouse out of her pants and brought the hem to her mouth. She tore at the bottom with her teeth as a new vivid memory struck her with such magnitude it made her gasp. At the stream. A sick—*a dying*—Clint in her lap as she mopped his brow and prayed for God to save him.

Another sob broke out from her throat. "Clint, please speak to me. You can't die!" She raised her head. "Somebody help!" she screamed to bystanders. Blood. So much blood drained out of him.

She pressed the white fabric against a large gash above his right ear. Pressed hard. And prayed. Prayed hard. The reality of the situation, the fact that she could lose him, impaled her soul. How could she have considered running from this man—to lose out on even one moment of loving him. Her mind changed so completely in that moment, she wondered about her prior sanity. She had been so worried about how she would manage life *with* the wonder called Clint Wilkins that she had never considered life *without* him.

And she *never* wanted to find out.

She laid his head carefully in her lap. He was unconscious, his breathing erratic. Jessica forced herself by sheer will to calm down, to think clearly. She was not ready to lose this man—the love of her life. As she kept the pressure on Clint's head, she stared at his shirt. It looked black instead of green, wet and darkened by his own blood.

Forced to be still and silent, with nothing to do but wait for help, Jessica listened for the first time to her Lord. Before now, she realized, she'd allowed her thoughts to scatter about the few memories that had returned—the ones where Clint had disappointed her, or hurt her.

I've never let you have control of this, God. Then she had to face it. *I've never let you have total control of anything in my life. I'm such a fool, Lord.*

As if she had been transported to a different dimension, her mind's eye began viewing memories in a perfectly displayed sequence—one that only God could orchestrate. As vivid as if they were movies flickering against a screen in the solitude of her mind. Memories of Clint saving her: from Brad at the dance and at the stream, from nearly tumbling off the wagon, from the grizzly bear. Memories of Clint holding her: on his horse, in his bed at Mary's, after his haircut, after Brad assaulted her on the rock, today at the train station. Each time they locked gazes, each kind word, each incredible touch, each smoldering kiss . . .

Before now Jessica had only remembered Clint's commanding personality, her own lustful attraction to him, and the painful episodes. But now God was reminding her of the moments where she had lost her heart to him.

Thank you, Lord. Now, please, please *save him. Let him live. With me.*

"Move aside," someone commanded. Jessica looked

up and saw a man with a black bag pushing through the crowd. For the first time since the shooting Jessica noticed the dozens of people encircling them.

"I said move aside!" the man barked again. Finally the crowd shrank back as the man came forward. "Jessica!"

"D-Dr. Barnes," Jessica squeaked out.

"What happened here?" The doc knelt beside Jessica, his eyes wide, face pale. "It's Clint," he whispered. Jessica watched as Doc lifted her makeshift bandage and gave the wound a full perusal. He grabbed a blood pressure cuff from his bag and took a reading.

"He's stable enough for now. Who shot him?" the doctor asked, reaching into his bag for an antiseptic-laden bandage. The gash was oozing pretty steadily.

"Jessica . . .?" he tried again.

"Huh? Oh. It was Brad." Jessica knew her answer must have left many questions in the doctor's mind, but she couldn't seem to manage any more.

The Doc looked over his shoulder to where Brad lay. "That range, and the bullet just grazed Clint. A blessing, for sure."

Did she hear him right? "So, he's just knocked out?"

"Appears so. But, blunt force trauma can cause internal hemorrhage and damage still. We need to get him back to my clinic." The doctor glanced back at Brad. "I'll go check him in a minute."

"No need for that," another voice boomed over the crowd.

Jessica and Doc looked up to see Johnnie walking toward them. "He's dead."

Johnnie's expression was taut. His eyes flashed with a multitude of emotions. She knew he had probably read her note and come after her. He sank to a squatting position next to her and looked over at Doc. "Is he gonna make it?"

Doc just gave him a look. When he finished the bandaging, three other men helped Johnnie hoist Clint onto a stretcher and load him in Doc's car. Jessica rode with him to the clinic.

"Will he live?" Jessica asked.

Doc didn't take his eyes off the road, but managed to pat Jessica's hand. "We'll know more in the next few hours. Try not to fret."

Jessica wrung her hands, knowing that Doc's advice would be impossible for her to heed, especially when her last words to Clint were full of pain. *What if he dies before I can tell him I love him—that I've loved him from the start?*

She didn't realize tears had streamed down her face until the taste of salt hit her lips. "He *has* to live, Doc."

Doc didn't reply. He turned the station wagon into the clinic's parking lot and stopped at the front door. The others were right on their tail and had leapt out of the back of Uncle Roy's truck before it had even come to a complete stop. Both vehicles were left at odd angles, doors open, as the men raced to get Clint into the clinic.

* * *

Johnnie watched from his place in the farthest corner of the sterile room. He found himself rubbing his right thumb and forefinger together, over and over, as if that could erase the memory of recoil that shot up his arm when he'd fired the fatal shot. It was surreal. He'd just killed a man. And he'd do it again. Anything to keep Jessica safe. But he still had to live with it. So be it.

Johnnie shoved his hand in his pocket and watched Doc leave to tend to other patients. The man must've been satisfied Clint was stable. Jessica rubbed her temples with trembling fingertips, staring intently into Clint's face. She grasped his left hand in both of hers, and held it tightly against her chest. Every few minutes she brought his hand up to her lips to kiss his rugged knuckles and mutter another prayer.

Johnnie tried to inhale a steadying breath, but his throat cinched closed on him. He wanted to blame it on claustrophobia from the tiny room, or the acrid bite of rubbing alcohol in the air. But he knew better. The air was thick with grief, desire, regret, and love—such love—all blazing out of Jessica like an aura he had to shield his eyes from. And with each passing minute, his future here grew dimmer.

He'd wait at the ranch for the outcome of Clint's health, and find out for sure where he stood with Jess. But ultimately he knew deep down that he'd be heading back to San Francisco to bury himself in work. His boss had been begging him to return to head up investigations into the latest round of jewel heists going on in the city by the bay. He needed to go. It was time.

Johnnie crossed the room. He leaned down to an oblivious Jessica and kissed her on top of her head. She didn't notice. Or if she had, she didn't respond. He glanced at Clint's pale face, back to Jessica's worried one, then slipped out the door.

* * *

Jessica now remembered praying for Clint the last

time he lay unresponsive. She had begged God to keep him from death. And God had healed him. So that he could come to know Jesus, she figured. But, would He heal him this time?

Her emotions were raw in a way they'd never been before. God might decide to take Clint home and she had to be okay with that—to trust God fully and let Him decide such things. To let God be God.

CHAPTER 39

Clint lifted his head just as his stepfather delivered another blow from a cast-iron fist. His cheekbone crunched, and he spun into the barn's dirt floor. The searing pain penetrated the side of his head with a fire so unbearable it ignited his instinct to run in spite of his fear of the consequences. He twisted to his stomach and scrambled toward the closest stall, but an outstretched hand yanked him to his feet again.

"When are you going to obey me, boy? I told you to clean out these stalls yesterday," his stepfather snarled. "You're not too old for me to take the strap to your backside!" The man loomed over Clint, like Goliath himself. He pulled his arm back to strike Clint down again.

"No!" Clint hollered into the sterile room of the clinic. He flung his arms up, crossing them over his eyes, and bellowed again.

* * *

Jessica, asleep in the only cushioned chair, startled

awake. She bolted to her feet and stood over Clint, instinctively knowing not to touch him yet. "Clint, it's me, Jessie. You're having a nightmare."

The door flew open, and Doc Barnes sped to Clint's side.

"No, Doc! Be careful." Jessica barely got out the words before he grasped Clint's arms and tried to pull them back down to his sides.

Clint swept one arm out and catapulted the doctor like he was a toothpick. Jessica watched helplessly as Doc landed in the rolling chair. It flew backward and slammed into the far wall.

"Doc!" Jessica cried, running after him. She reached him in time to press her hands to his chest before his body could bounce out of the chair from the impact.

Doc shook his head once and glanced back to his patient. "What's going on?"

Jessica's gaze left Doc and landed on Clint. "A nightmare." Seeing that Doc was fine, she hurried back to Clint's side. "He's trying to protect his head. Probably remembering the shot and reliving the pain."

"Clint. Can you hear me?" Jessica pleaded.

"Don't hit me again, old man." He sounded delirious. "You'll never hit me again!" His brawny arms thrashed about as if he were smacking something away, then he crossed them back over his eyes.

Jessica tried again with a softer voice this time. "Clint. It's Jessie. Wake up." She carefully took hold of his wrists. "It's okay now. Just relax. Relax your arms. No one is going to hurt you."

She pulled his arms away from his face, and her heart broke. His eyes were open, huge and wild with fear. He seemed to be looking straight through her. He allowed her to bring his arms down by his sides. Tears flooded his eyes. He bit his lower lip and turned his head, looking like a frightened little boy.

Jessica put a palm to his cheek as her stomach knotted. "Oh Clint . . ." A hiccup broke loose in her throat. He blinked and turned his head back. His brow furrowed as he obviously worked to recognize her. Jessica waited, her heart in her throat. *This is how he must have agonized when he first realized I had amnesia.*

"Do you know who I am?" Jessica wasted no time to ask.

His eyes sharpened and focused on hers. He swallowed, opened his mouth to speak, and only rasped. Instinctively, she knew his need. She started to rise, but the doctor put his hand to her shoulder, already having anticipated Clint's wish. The small cup of water was at Clint's mouth, and Doc lifted his head to receive it. Jessica shifted partially out of the way, but had a grasp on Clint's hand and kept it between both of hers. He sipped, and then guzzled the rest in one breath. Doc left his side to throw the cup away, and Jessie shifted closer.

"Jessie," Clint said in a croaky voice.

Jessica glanced briefly at the ceiling. "Thank you, Lord," she mouthed.

She brought her face to within inches of his and turned her ear toward his lips to hear his words. When she only felt a steady rhythm of warm breath against her temple, she turned back to see he'd fallen back to sleep. He looked younger, less formidable, when he slept, though lines of pain still etched his splendid mouth and a slight frown drew his brows together.

Clint's dreams were sweet at first, filled with pleasurable occasions with Jessie. Some came from memories, others seemed futuristic. All were pleasing, warm and cozy. But in an instant the scene changed. Clint moaned in despair.

The familiar fist pummeled him upside the head and left him reeling. "No!" he shouted at his stepfather. "You won't get away with this. Mom will find out."

"Shut-up boy. What do you think she can do for you?"

The reality of that statement hit its target like a well-aimed bullet. What would his mother do? Nothing. She would do absolutely nothing the old man wouldn't let her do. Even if it meant leaving her only son to suffer, or die, alone. He was left to his own devices to get out of there before his step-father killed him.

"You're going to the shed. I'll teach you to disobey," the man ground out. He unbuckled his belt. Clint could hear the belt slap against each loop of his pants as it slid around his waist. With one last *thwack* it came free, ready to do its damage.

Clint tried to lift his arms up, but didn't have strength enough to defend himself. His head boomed in pain with every beat of his heart. Maybe his stepfather would kill him this time and be done with it. Relief filled him at the thought, especially since there was no power left in him to ward off his attacker.

"Clint," he heard. The woman was beautiful, in a white lacy gown. She had a hold on his hand and was pulling, pulling . . .

As she tugged, Clint looked back. His stepfather stood

in place, a statue frozen to the ground. His belt was still in his grip and the door to the shed was open behind him. The vision grew smaller and smaller and soon darkened, and then disappeared.

". . . Clint, can you hear me?" The woman's voice grew stronger. They were sitting in deep meadow grasses now, with purple, yellow, and white wildflowers all around. The woman was stroking his head and speaking to him in the most soothing of tones. So restful. The fear left him. Only peace remained. Even the ache in his head seemed to subside.

Then lips, warm and moist, were on his.

CHAPTER 40

Jessica withdrew her lips from his and pulled back to see if his eyes had opened. Not yet. He had been dreaming; dark, severe dreams. His face twisted in an anguish that convinced her it was more than physical pain. She didn't want to shake him because of his head injury, so she'd tried to reach him with words and caresses. And, finally a kiss.

"Clint, it's Jessie. I'm here. *Please*, open your eyes." Her hand stroked his arm slowly. She kissed his cheek, his eyelids, his chin, then ever so softly his mouth again.

His eyes opened, scrunched closed, then opened into small slits. A deep frown put a furrow between his brows, and something deeper still distorted his face. Pain. She had come prepared. The wet washcloth was across his eyes before he could even speak. Silence remained for a few more seconds. He groaned, then reached up and pushed the rag from his eyes, leaving it to rest on his forehead.

"Jessie?" His voice was ragged, edged with suffering.

"Clint. You were shot, but you'll be okay. How bad is the pain?" she asked. The washcloth kept slipping so she grabbed it off and waited for his answer.

"Bad."

"Do you think with my help you could raise your head? I want to give you the pain medication Doc left in case he wasn't here to give you a shot."

Clint nodded once. She lifted his head and stuffed several pillows behind him. She gave him water then dropped a pill in his mouth. He swallowed and managed to gaze up into her eyes through lowered lids.

"I'll go find Doc," she said, coming to her feet.

He caught her hand. "Jessie. Give the pill time to work. Sit here. Talk to me."

It was excruciating, staring into eyes that revealed his torture. She sat on the rolling chair and rotated forward. She was thankful at least that he was awake and knew her.

She kept hold of his hand and waited a long while, hoping the pain killer would kick in. "Clint, who—" She didn't know why she'd started to ask him that. She'd intended to sit and hold his hand until the pain had subsided.

He stared into her eyes. "Go on."

"Never mind."

"Jessie . . ."

Shoot. She couldn't keep the question inside any longer, like it had found a crack in her mind and weaved its way out her mouth. "Who beat you, Clint?" she whispered.

The question knocked out the last bit of color from his face, and he grimaced with a noticeable increase in pain. What had she done? She watched as Clint's expression became fluid. Despair then red hot rage. His nostrils flared, his lips flattened. She'd never seen this look of anger on him before. Beyond anger. Hatred.

He yanked his hand out of her grasp and turned his face away.

Jessica sucked her bottom lip in and clamped her teeth down. Somehow she knew this part of his past had molded Clint into the person he had become. And after these vivid nightmares, he needed to get it off his chest. She waited, hoping he would share it with her.

It seemed an eternity before he turned his head back to her. His stare was bleak. She wondered if he would send her away from him, for now—or maybe permanently.

"Jessica." She winced at the formal name. "What makes you think someone beat me?"

So his answer would be avoidance? He didn't trust her with this information? She blinked at the overwhelming disappointment. She stared into his haunted eyes, and the sensation passed. She figured out what he was doing. A ploy. To shock her into dropping the subject. Well, it wouldn't work. Her future with him could depend on his facing what had happened to him. After the crushing nightmares, she knew deep in her heart he needed to do final battle with the demons of his past.

She straightened her spine, then spoke in a quiet, cool tone. "Clint, you were the only cowboy who didn't remove his shirt during the round-up. In fact, not once during any of the hot days have I seen you without one. And then, at Mary's, when you fell off the bed, your back was exposed. I saw the thin scars on it. Only one thing could have done that."

His jaw muscles tightened. She'd never seen so many emotions flicker through a person's eyes. Tears pooled, diluting the sharpness of his green-flecked irises. He blinked fast, his throat pumped. She saw the pain this was causing. His composure was slipping, and it was all she could do not to throw her arms around his neck and tell him to forget it.

She saw when he surrendered. "Okay," he said with way more regret in his voice than she had hoped to hear.

She dropped his hand and stood. "Clint, if you can't trust me with your past—" She halted her words. A flush of guilt and regret rushed over her. Hadn't she just today told him she didn't trust him?

"You're right." He grasped her hand back so she wouldn't leave him. "I need to tell you. I don't want to remember is all. It has nothing to do with you."

She sighed. "Maybe God wants me to know. Your mind is not letting you forget."

He looked skeptical.

He was still locking her out, and that hurt, but she pressed on. "Ever since you were shot, you've been having nightmares. It's like you're a little boy again and fighting off an attacker."

Shock was evident in his expression, and then sadness. He closed his eyes in surrender. Jessica laid a hand to his cheek and stroked it. Covering her hand with his, he opened his eyes to gaze at her. He brought her hand to his lips and gave a warm, tender kiss to her palm. "Come here." He opened up his arm.

Surprised by the invitation, Jessica looked over the bed. Could it hold both of them? He was so large. But when he scooted over, keeping his arm out, she couldn't resist. She slipped in beside him and snuggled close in order to fit. He closed his powerful arm around her, and it felt so right.

Then he told her of his childhood. He didn't look at her. She understood that. The sympathy in her eyes would make it hard to tell his story. She tentatively slid her arm across his ribs, and tried not to move a muscle as she listened.

"My dad died when I was twelve," he spoke into the room, above her head, "and Mom remarried when I was thirteen." His hard swallow reverberated clear through her. "He was a preacher, my stepdad. He liked my sisters, but he hardly tolerated me."

Twilight had begun, and shadows were forming. Jessica stared into the corner where one shadow crept across the room, like a relic of Clint's past trudging along with his spilled memories. She pulled in a little closer, trying hard not to let tears fall against his bare chest.

"I'm sure I was a handful, still angry at God for taking my dad. My stepfather hated it when my mom tried to console me. Thought I should grow up. Be a man. Get over it. One day he found a picture of my dad in my mom's apron pocket. He was so furious she still carried it that he started taking it out on me."

Jessica tilted her head back to look inquisitively into his eyes. He read her thoughts. "I look just like my dad."

"Oh, my gosh, *Clint*." Her resolve broke, and her tears let loose down her cheeks. She whisked them off before they dampened his skin.

They both stared straight ahead then. "He began by giving me tasks—*many* tasks—to do around the place. For a while I was able to keep up. But he kept adding more—or worse yet, he'd say he'd told me to do something when he hadn't. It was his way of finding reasons to—"

He swallowed twice in a row. Jessica waited for him to regain his control.

"He . . . uh . . ."

She heard the lump in his throat.

"He began with hitting me across the face. At first with an open hand. Later with fists."

Jessica covered her mouth with a hand and pressed hard to keep the sobs from escaping. She had to let him get through this. He continued, though his voice had become so pinched she wouldn't have heard him at all if she hadn't been so near.

"Later he decided fists weren't enough, so he used his belt on me. He always made sure he wore the old one where the leather had become hard and brittle. It left deeper gouges. He . . ." Clint stopped, tried to clear his throat. He raised a hand to his head and pressed his fingers into his temple. The pain in his head must have become intolerable since she was sure his blood pressure had risen. Regret seized her. She wanted to stop him, but it was far too late for that.

"He . . . he would beat me and then throw me in our shed. In the summer it became unbearable, and I would pass out. Mom would finally come and get me." He sounded bitter now. "As soon as he allowed her to."

That was all she could take. A huge sob exploded from her mouth, and he stopped while she cried uncontrollably for several minutes. He embraced her and pulled her up so her head rested under his chin. His pulse beat like wildfire in his neck where she rested her cheek. He inhaled a deep breath in her hair, kissed the top of her head. Warm tears hit her scalp and she wept all the more.

For a while neither spoke, just held the other tight. Finally he finished his tale. "When the second June arrived, I knew I couldn't make it through another summer in that shed, so I ran. Ran and never looked back. It took me several weeks to make it to West Yellowstone. Roy found me behind a restaurant unconscious, nearly dead."

Jessica gasped and looked up into his face. His eyes

were red-rimmed. She knew hers were worse. She stretched up, and pressed her lips into his. She wanted to console him, reach to his very soul and soothe the damage that had been done there. Words couldn't begin to say how she felt. She hoped the touch of her mouth could deliver the message. She gave him all she knew how to give, hoping and praying it was enough. The kiss became ferocious, deep and demanding, mingling with their salty tears as if fervor alone could scrub away the pain of the past.

He broke the kiss off and lifted his head to look into her eyes. "Jessie." His voice was thick and his breathing erratic. "So compassionate." He tried to smile, though weakly. "*And* passionate." His big hand covered the side of her face. He ran his thumb lightly over her lips as he gazed into her eyes.

One side of his mouth tilted up in that dreamy, crooked smile of his, making liquid of her insides. "I'm in love with you, sweet girl."

Her heart skipped, then hammered. She couldn't have been more shocked if God had lifted the roof and smiled down at them. *He was in love with her?* She was stunned beyond speech. And it must have shown clearly on her face.

His smile broadened, and he chuckled. "Surprised?"

Her eyes widened, and all she could do was nod.

His face took on a look of contentment, and with each blink his eyes lowered a little more. Soon, he dozed off. She stayed next to him in his secure hold until his arms loosened in deep sleep. She slid out of his bed, covered him with the sheet, and collapsed weak-legged into the old cushioned chair. Her mind reeled. *He's in love with me?* Was she dreaming?

Clint slept through the night and into the next day.

Doc came in and out periodically, bringing Jessica food and checking on his patient. Jessica became worried. When the doctor came in around noon, she delayed him. "Doc. Shouldn't he be awake by now?"

The doctor glanced at Clint, but looked unfazed. He smiled and patted her arm. "Jessica, he's had a major trauma to his head and jolt to his brain. I'm watching him closely. So far he hasn't developed any complications. It seems to me he's sleeping peacefully for a change. No more nightmares?"

She thought about that for a minute and smiled weakly. "No." She wondered if Clint's confession had eased his mind. She hoped it had. She prayed that was all.

But, by three in the afternoon nothing had changed. Jessica decided to go down the hall to freshen up. When she returned, he was still asleep. Worry crawled up her throat. She would not allow worry to unseat her faith, so she decided touch might work on him again. She took his left hand and stroked it. He moaned in his sleep. Encouraged, she squeezed a little harder, and held his knuckles to her lips, planting tiny kisses across them.

Closing her eyes, she prayed. When her lids opened, she saw his eyes on her. A small smile deepened the creases at the corners of his mouth.

Jessica sucked in an audible breath of relief. Without any more thought, and not able to form words anyway, she leaned in and planted a greedy kiss on that appealing mouth.

After many long moments she broke off the kiss and, mimicking his favorite action with her, pressed her brow to his. "Clint. Don't ever scare me like that again."

He laughed, though weakly—a deep, gravelly sound.

It bathed her in its richness, delighting her senses. "I'll do my best, little one."

She leaned back and noticed that the amused expression had left his face to be replaced by a solemn one. She studied him while his gaze seemed to cherish each feature of her face before it returned to her eyes. His look wasn't of pain, but more of worry. Was he thinking about the last thing she'd told him at the train station? By his expression, she thought so. A question lingered there between them, and she had caused it. If she could go back, before their confrontation, before she had given him reason to think she could live without him. If she could just take it all back . . .

He reached up with both hands, pushed her hair back, and held her face. His stare entangled hers. "Marry me."

Oh, my gosh! Yes! But before she could say it, she noticed—really noticed—the apprehension and worry in his eyes. This was a new experience for him. He'd been shot. He'd endured nightmares and confessed the atrocities of his past. And yet, the importance of this moment—to him—unraveled all the fears from around her own heart. She wanted to hold him, to love him, to tell him she would never leave his side. She wanted to remove the fear he'd harbored his whole adult life of having a lifelong relationship with just one woman; the fear that held him back from commitment such as he was offering her now. Somehow a simple *yes* wouldn't do.

Blinking to clear her vision, she cupped her small hands around his face and looked into his magnificent eyes. "Clint. I love you with every fiber of my being. I think I've loved you from the first moment I saw you, and that love deepened with every moment we spent together thereafter, good and bad. I don't want to live this life without you.

And, I trust you. I do. With my very life. And, you can trust me. With your life. With your heart. With your soul. So, the answer is yes. I will share my life with you. I'm yours forever."

His expression showed such vast relief, he looked as if he might break down and shed those tears that were swimming in his eyes. Not wanting even a remote chance he might embarrass himself, she gave him a mock look of annoyance. "But, I must say, this was a pretty dramatic way to convince me."

His laugh was rich and full, and his smile dazzling.

He expelled a sudden *whoop*, then immediately grimaced and squeezed his eyes tight. His breath came on small, ragged gasps.

"Oh no!" Jessica breathed out, then sucked in another breath and held it. When he didn't seem to recover, she turned her face toward the door. "Doc!" she shouted.

Clint flinched at the noise. Tiny streams of tears squeezed out from the corners of his eyes, pooled briefly at his crow's feet, then slid down into his ears.

Doc slammed through the door, saw Clint's face, and went straight to his cabinet. Bringing a shot of pain killer, he administered it while Jessica brushed the backs of her fingers across Clint's cheek and spoke in low, soothing tones.

Clint's jaw muscles bunched, and his cheeks were taut, but he never said a word. He lay with eyes shut tight, trying to breathe deeply. Jessica watched his whole body quiver in painful tension. She prayed and waited for the worst to be over.

It seemed like an eternity before he began to breathe easier. He opened his eyes. She expected to hear how excruciating the onslaught of pain had been. Instead, his eyes locked onto hers with the intensity only Clint could command. He took a deep ragged breath and whispered, "Don't make me wait too long."

She furrowed her brows. *"What?"*

His eyes closed as if that would help him regain the strength to speak again. Opening them, he tried again. "Marry me soon," he said in a wisp of a breath.

Her heart swelled so large it could have completely enveloped them both. Happy tears let loose, tracking her cheeks. He shook off her grip from his hand, reached up, and brushed the wetness away with his thumb. His large hand curled around her nape and brought her mouth to his.

The kiss was tender, and sweet, and filled with the hope of a grand future.

EPILOGUE

Clint swung the screen door open, stomped his feet on the porch mat, and sauntered into the kitchen. He glanced around. "Mabel, where's my bride?"

"Gal's up in your room workin' on thank you notes."

Thinking of their wedding brought a smile to his face. He was amazed at how Jessie had pulled together the blessed event in less than three weeks, complete with her entire family . . . and his. Jessie had known that when Clint saw his mother in this setting, a form of healing would begin. And it had—for the first time in almost two decades.

The ranch house had been decorated with every kind of flower imaginable. Even the deer head above the mantel had worn fancy ribbons draped from its antlers.

He still remembered the joy that sped his heart and stole his breath when Jessie had come into view at the top of the staircase in the extraordinary white dress, affirming her innocence. The breath had squeezed out of his lungs, and his heart had tumbled all over itself. Her dad hesitated only long enough for the crowd below to view the beauty of his daughter—the bride.

His Jessie. *His* bride.

Jessie's eyes had locked to his, and he'd seen the depth of her love mirroring his own. His heart had nearly burst with love for her and the anticipation of a life spent with her by his side.

And now, here he was. Two weeks later. A man wildly in love. And it surprised and pleased him every single day. If anyone had told him, six short months ago, that he'd fall in love and get married, he'd have called them a bald-faced liar. Now he couldn't imagine life any other way.

Clint took the stairs two at a time, heading for the master bedroom. The door was open, exposing the one room that had been closed off to everyone since Roy's father and mother had occupied it decades ago. Roy had been eager to hand it off to Clint and his new bride. *Jessie.* His love. The one God had hand-picked for him.

Still smiling, he peeked in to catch a glimpse before saying hello. Jessie sat cross-legged on their bed reading through the many letters of congratulations that had flooded in from California. His heart swelled at the equal mix of concentration and delight on her face.

He leaned a shoulder against the door casing and crossed his arms to take in the sight of his sweet, remarkable wife. She seemed content, like she belonged here. With her Wranglers, sky blue blouse with silver snaps, and low ponytail, she looked ready for anything a cattle ranch—or he—could demand of her.

A swell of desire enveloped him. He eyed the pile of congratulation notes taking up space on the bedspread and cocked his head. But no. He had other plans for this afternoon.

For the longest time she was too preoccupied to even

notice him. One letter caused her to laugh, and when she did, her head came up and her eyes caught him standing there.

She gasped a quick breath and beamed at him as she inspected him from his weather-worn Stetson to his equally worn boots. "Now there's a sight I'll never tire of."

He chuckled. "Same here, little one. You're delectable sitting there covered in mail. Must have lots of friends. I haven't received anything like that." He pushed off the casing and in two steps he was at her side. He took her by the hands and whisked her up into his arms, delighting in the feel of her.

"That's because all your friends live *here*," she whispered in his ear. "My ears are still ringing from all the whoops and whistles we got the night of our announcement."

He set her down and gave her a lopsided grin. "Do you have a couple hours to spare? I want to show you something."

She stole his breath as she dazzled him with another smile. "You don't have to ask me twice, cowboy. I'll follow you anywhere." She pulled out of his embrace and crossed the room to stuff her stockinged feet into her boots. He swiveled her to face him. Pulling the rubber band out of her ponytail, he loosened her hair with his fingers, clutched her head for a brief, hard kiss, and then tugged her by the hand down the stairs.

He lifted her coat off the hook, helped her on with it, and stuffed on his hat. Only *his* horse waited, tied to the porch railing. Jessie took one look at Shadow, made a display of glancing past him for a second horse, and then gasped in mock horror. Amused, he watched as her feigned gape transformed into one of her adoring smiles. She smiled a lot these days, and he drank in every proffered gift.

Clint mounted, and pulled her up in front of him. They took their time—as only newlyweds could get away with—to meander down to the stream Jessie had grown to love. They proceeded quite a ways until rounding a bend to the sight of green as far as the eye could see. Only a smattering of brightly colored wildflowers was left dotting the countryside.

"Shadow loves the tall grass. Winter's getting a late start, so some of it's still around."

"It's beautiful here, Clint." She snuggled in closer as an October breeze lifted her loose hair and whipped it about. "I've never come this far before."

"Used to come here when I wanted to get away. It's quiet and secluded. Always been a great place to think. Now it's a great place to pray." He tenderly brushed a hand down her hair and kissed the top of her head. Bending an elbow, he waited for her to link her arm through, then gently lowered her to the ground.

* * *

Jessica pulled her collar up and moseyed over to the stream. She listened to its endless melody as it flowed along. Clint came to her side with a small bouquet of the late blooms and handed them to her. "Blossoms for my beautiful bride."

Jessica felt a flush heat her face as she took the flowers from his hand in both of hers.

He turned her by the waist toward him. "Why the blush?"

Their eyes met. "You called me beautiful. You don't have to do that, Clint. I know I'm not beautiful."

He drew her to him as her fingers stroked the flowers between them. "Don't ever say that to me again." With a loose fist, he lifted her chin to look him straight in the eye. "I think I fell in love with you the moment you stepped foot on this ranch."

Jessica wanted to believe that, but could only scoff. "No. There was Veronica, and—" *Stop it!* She dipped her head as if to examine the flowers, and took a sniff. She mustn't bring up his past. That was no way to begin a marriage. But, she didn't want him to lie to her either. There was no need. She knew he loved her. That was enough.

He raised her chin again. "Jessie. You *are* beautiful. In more ways than I can possibly describe."

"Clint—"

"Jessie, listen." He cradled her cheek with his calloused palm. "You jumbled my brain, and woke up emotions I didn't even know I had. When you showed up here, you were sustenance. *My* sustenance. Sunlight to my otherwise murky world. No one—and I mean, no one—holds the flame to my soul but you. You're my everything."

He leaned in, squashing the petals between them, and caught her mouth with his. All Jessica could feel was heat and wetness and depthless love.

"You'll always be enough for me," he murmured against her lips, then took her mouth again.

He was not just good looks, this man. In that moment she vowed to herself—with God's help—that she'd never doubt his love or worry over her own insecurities again. She loved this man with a heart that belonged wholly to him, and she would *not* poison that love.

He released her mouth, but hovered close. "Would you like to live out here?"

"Live out here?" she echoed, in a daze of passion.

"I've taken out a loan so we can build. Right here, next to the stream you love so much."

Jessica laid her fingers on his stubbled cheek. "It's *you* I love so much."

The look of complete, surrendered love on his beloved face emboldened her. She reached up on tiptoes and pressed her lips to his, giving him all that was her, making him groan in pleasure.

When the kiss ended, he pressed his forehead into hers. "I love you, wife, more than this lowly cowboy can put into words. Let's go home."

Clint stepped away then and swung onto Shadow's back. He looked down at her. All at once a long ago memory uncovered itself to her, so intense it brought along a flash flood of sensation.

The dream. On the train. This was *the* man. Tall, broad, rugged—magnificent. Black hat, dusty boots, dark steed . . . , and a smile that touched her soul. Even his eyes were the same shade of green. She shivered at the perfect correlation. In that dream, God had given her a clear vision of her future husband—her soul mate.

She looked up at the familiar picture this splendid man made. Then, thanking God, she smiled up at him.

With the crooked smile that never failed to make her breath catch, he reached out a hand. "Ride with me."

She looked him square in the eyes and poured every ounce of her soul into the only word that existed for her. "Always."

The End

ABOUT THE AUTHOR

My adventure into writing began over six years ago, when I felt the tug from God to put pen to paper, or in today's language, fingers to keyboard. I don't know why God has blessed me with such a wondrous gift—the all-consuming, joyful need to write—but I will be forever grateful.

My writing path is as unique as my name. It started something like this:

"You want me to do *what*, Lord?"

The same challenge repeated in my mind. Had it come from God, truly? Was it even possible to hear God so clearly in the twenty-first century? I don't recall the exact words, but I do remember the exact impression they left in me. I suddenly understood Moses's hesitation. God wanted me to do something I hadn't been educated to do and hadn't even thought of doing before now. Write. Novels.

Now, this hadn't come from out of nowhere. It had come about through a series of specific prayers to God. Prayers like this: "Lord, now that I've finished the one thing I know you put me on this earth to do, what's next?"—The 'one thing' God had long ago requested of me was to raise our four sons as decent, godly men. And, through many long years, with lots of difficulties and equal shares of delight, the task was done. Both my husband and myself can now look upon our handsome, and very tall, sons, with pride. They are wonderful, and they love God. *Done*. Now what?

So you see, my newfound writing career sprouted not in my childhood, or even my adulthood, but in my seniorhood (if there were such a word). Though I must admit, the roots of my passion do reach back to a childhood filled with imagination. I remember creating a constant stream of romances in my head, with the hope that each could one day be mine. Well, I'm happy to say, I am living my own romance story. I have a wonderful husband of forty years, and along the way came the four strapping sons, two daughters-in-law, two granddaughters and one grandson. So far.

Now that our children are grown, my husband and I reside in *Cowboy Capital of the World*—Oakdale, California.

I adore writing and am fully committed to it. I must say, the majority of that commitment is due to the reality that God directed my steps to do it. So, with that being said, I hope you enjoy my stories as much as I have loved creating them.

God Bless, Janith (Jan) Hooper
Visit me at: www.janithhooper.com
janithhooper@gmail.com

ACKNOWLEDGMENTS

This is my first book, my baby. I applaud those who have stuck by me through the long process of learning the craft. It is with love and my absolute honor to thank those who have helped sculpt 'the baby' into the version you can now read. Thank you, my friends and family.

April. You were the very first person to read the original manuscript, and, God bless you, you said you enjoyed it. I was so new to this world of writing, and not at all sure it was what I was supposed to do. As an avid reader, I trusted your opinion, and you have no idea what those first positive words did for me. For sure, they were a confirmation. Thank you, my sweet daughter-in-law.

Mick. You're an amazing editor, and friend. From the moment you read my first draft to the cheerleading you do for me today, you've been the encourager God gave me. You've kept me plodding forward, learning the craft (and by no means have I finished that task), and right on to a completed first novel. Thank you, Mick, more than I can say in mere words.

Doc Holly. You took pity on me, and were the first set of fresh eyes on what I thought was the completed manuscript. You helped turn my vanilla into chocolate ripple with nuts, and for that, and your unfailing way of dishing out the truth, I thank you. Your gift of editing and critiquing, as well as your amazing ability to write, is a true inspiration to me.

Sarah. You were the first to read my book on a kindle, testing that type of read as well as the content. Thank you for raving about the book, and for reading it twice within a week, all while getting ready for Christmas! It was a god-send to know you loved it just the way it was.

Paul. My third son. You have been in this with me since the first, and I thank you for the endless hours of listening, your countless ideas, and great moral support.

Nathan. My second son. Thank you for your genius in creating my website, and for your help in the process of displaying my book to the world.

Hoop. My husband. Love of my life. In spite of the years it took to publish this first book, you have always believed in me. Thank you for your spiritual leadership and your support in my writing process. It is because you are my rock that my mind and spirit are free to write. I do it for you and I do it for God. I love you.

To Matthew, my first born, and Ben my fourth, plus my other sweet daughter-in-law, Marisa, thank you for your part in offering up ideas, support, or endlessly listening about the book. I thank you and love you all.

P.S. Watch for Johnnie's book, coming in 2014

Author's Note

Yes, the earthquake in this book was real. Below you'll see the statistics on it as documented by Wikipedia.

1959 Yellowstone earthquake
From Wikipedia

Date	August 17, 1959
Magnitude	7.3-7.5
Depth	Unknown
Epicenter location	~15 miles North of West Yellowstone, Montana
Countries or regions	Southwestern Montana, Idaho, Wyoming
Casualties	28 plus, dead

The 1959 Yellowstone earthquake also known as the Hebgen Lake earthquake was a powerful earthquake that occurred on August 17, 1959 at 11:37 pm (MST) in southwestern Montana. The earthquake was registered at magnitude 7.3 – 7.5 on the Richter scale. The quake caused a huge landslide that caused over 28 fatalities and left $11 million (1959 USD, $74.1 million 2006 USD) in damage.

The quake-induced landslide also blocked the flow of the Madison River resulting in the creation of Quake Lake. Effects of the earthquake were also felt in Idaho and Wyoming.

The 1959 quake was the strongest and deadliest earthquake to hit Montana since the 1935-36 Helena earthquakes left 4 people dead and caused the worst landslides in the history of the Northwestern United States since 1927.

Made in the USA
Columbia, SC
21 February 2018